LANE TO HEAVEN

To Julie,
a great mom!

May love and hope always fill your life.

Hugs!
Sara Daniel

For my husband David,
for the unwavering support and unending patience.
I love you!

Prologue

The World's Sexiest Viper got religion. Temporarily. As an afterthought, Tanya pocketed her Armani sunglasses. Only someone trying to hide her identity would wear them on a cloudy November day in Chicago. And today she was a nobody preacher lady.

She pushed open the mahogany door. Too bad the person she needed a favor from wasn't male. Men, from age thirteen to one hundred and thirteen, she ruled with sex. But a conservative, upscale woman who had turned her back on Hollywood needed a different approach. Luckily Tanya's looks came with acting skills—not the Oscar to prove it yet, but she had no doubt her role in *Black River* would be nominated in a couple months.

"Welcome to the Vonkall Auction House. May I help you?" The woman at the front desk had a perfectly modulated tone. Her foundation was two shades too dark and left a line along her neck.

"I'm here to see Deborah Vonkall."

The woman looked surprised. "Do you have an appointment?"

"Yes," she lied without a qualm.

"And your name?"

"Reverend Annie Lane." A dead-on imitation of her sister's voice if she did say so herself.

The woman took her sweet time dialing the phone. A minute

later she hung up. "I'm sorry, ma'am. Mrs. Vonkall is not in today. I can schedule an appointment for another day."

"That's impossible. I need to see her today." Tanya silently cursed her worthless husband for putting her in this position. The snooty receptionist with bad makeup and department-store clothes was born to serve at the feet of the World's Sexiest Viper. But she wasn't that icon today. She was a nobody preacher in a horrendous, boxy, black Goodwill blazer.

Although the effort cost her, Tanya maintained a facade of politeness. "Surely there must be someone helpful I can speak with."

"Perhaps you can try me."

A receptionist? No. "Who's taking Deborah's emergencies today?"

"Her son Jason."

"Stop wasting my time and get him out here." Finding good help was beyond impossible.

"Mr. Vonkall is quite busy today."

Nobody was too busy for her. She was too busy for them. Deborah Vonkall was supposed to be at her beck and call. This disguise was backfiring. She'd covered her trademark double Ds and her twenty-six-inch lipoed waist, not to mention donning the ugly black wig, because revealing her true identity was out of the question.

Her marriage had begun solely for the purpose of elevating her career. She wouldn't let everything she'd worked for get flushed away because of her husband's destructive choices, even if that meant she had to turn on him. She picked up the phone receiver. "Dial Jason for me. I'll see how busy he is."

The receptionist glared icicles at her, but the shrew routine didn't faze Tanya. She'd invented it.

Five seconds later she was talking to Jason Vonkall on the phone. A minute later, he was standing in front of her in person, a polished frat boy all of twenty-four years old she was willing to bet. His suit wasn't Armani, but it was custom-tailored. More importantly, he looked like a man she'd eat for breakfast. Unfortunately, her best assets were locked under a chafing beige turtleneck and the frightful blazer. She couldn't reveal her identity, but she could reveal her assets.

Frat boy, it's dinnertime, and you don't stand a chance.

Chapter 1

Nick McAllister was on a mission to heal another family fissure. As soon as he did, he'd boot Reverend Annie down a path to Hell. Old Testament eye-for-an-eye justice. After all, she'd done her best to send his half brother there.

He didn't intend to kill her, of course. Hell for a minister wasn't death. It was life with everyone knowing the depth of her evil and treating her like a pariah. Reverend Annie deserved no better.

For his own sake, Nick hoped he could accomplish both goals without stepping foot inside a church.

With a couple questions around the microscopic town of Maplefield, he learned she'd be walking back to church from the diner after lunch. Nick mapped out the path and settled into a gazebo in the park while he waited for her to walk by.

A teenaged girl sat on a picnic table behind the playground equipment. She noticed him. He could tell by the way she thrust out her chest. Even more obvious, she was freezing and without the sense to cover her thin pink T-shirt in this forty-degree weather. Nick, on the other hand, had far more brain cells and basic decency than to risk his career by contemplating jailbait.

The teenager tossed back her blond hair and turned her back on him.

A woman in a heavy winter coat walked down the sidewalk through the middle of the park. Nick wasn't sure if this was his villain or not. He'd been counting on an ugly blazer to clue him in. She veered away from him and toward the teen. "Heather, are you still out sick, or did school release early today?" Her voice traveled with the breeze back to Nick.

"I'm skipping." The girl's voice held an unmistakable challenge. "Troy's meeting me here and taking me for a drive."

The woman shrugged out of her coat, revealing a boxy, fashionless blazer. Ding! Direct match. Reverend Annie held out her coat to the girl. "Wear this while you wait."

The kid crossed her arms over her chest. "I'll be warm as soon as Troy comes."

Nick decided it was time to make his move. He reached to adjust his tie and then dropped his hand as he encountered the V-neck of his paint-stained T-shirt underneath his scarred leather jacket. He'd been varnishing a bookcase for his office when his mother called about Jason's *accident*. Now the clothes would serve as a disguise so the Reverend wouldn't make the family connection.

"He's not here yet. Don't make your mother worry about you." Annie draped the coat over the girl's shoulders.

She laughed sadly. "Right. Mom only worries when she gets down to her last bag of chips."

Nick ambled toward them. The teen had applied hooker makeup with a masonry trowel. Her bright pink T-shirt proclaimed *So what?* across her well-developed but undeniably braless chest. The shirt cut off before the silver stud poking out from her belly button, surrounded by a band of goose bumps.

Feeling dirty just looking at the kid, he switched his gaze to the preacher. She was dressed in a pale pink turtleneck covered by a brown blazer. Her skin was flawless, and she had high, sculpted cheekbones and full lips. The only thing off from the receptionist's and security camera's grainy description was the hair. Instead of black and pulled back in an austere bun, her light brown hair fluttered around her face in a chin-length bob.

Well, that solved the mystery of what she looked like without the wig she'd left on the storage room floor.

"May I help you?" the preacher asked.

I'm going to land your butt in jail for turning my brother into a suicidal recluse didn't seem like the smoothest way to start his case, and he was nothing if not smooth. At least he was making opening statements in his three-piece suit. But he hadn't slept enough to form a coherent thought since his brother drove his car into Lake Michigan.

"Looks like you're in need of a hot shower and even hotter bed." The teen placed her hands on her hips and thrust out her chest.

Nick kept his gaze locked on the Reverend because there was no chance he could see her nipples through her thick, shapeless clothes.

Annie offered her hand. "I'm Reverend Annie Lane, pastor of Good Shepherd Church." Her gaze held his, blue in its most innocent shade. "This is Heather Fitzsimmons," she continued, nodding at the jailbait. "She hasn't learned she's a beautiful person inside and doesn't need to objectify her body along with the entire male species to prove her worth."

The kid smirked. "You don't have a clue how sex works."

Nick clenched his fists. Reverend Annie knew too well how to make sex work for her and how to turn herself into a shining innocent when it suited her. Hypocrisy 101 was undoubtedly a seminary requirement.

"You've got more to offer the world than your body," Reverend Annie said in a voice anyone with normal hearing would recognize as too nice to be sincere.

Nick uncurled his fingers and took Annie's hand. "People on the inside are never what they appear on the outside. Don't worry. I'm not going to judge your friend." He raked Annie with his eyes, leaving unsaid his judgment of her. Then he turned to Heather and offered a kinder gaze that didn't drop below her nose. "I'm Nick McAllister. Don't you worry about the wrath of God, trying to pick up men twice your age in front of a preacher?"

Heather gave him a cocky once-over. "God won't strike me down with Reverend Annie around. He might hit her, too."

If God had any sense of justice, He'd take His chances on innocent collateral and make a strike at Annie. Aloud, Nick said, "I'm not willing to bet on it. Next time you talk to me, button that coat."

"Your loss." Heather pushed the coat back to Annie. "Troy's coming up the street. Please go away."

"I'd like to meet him if you don't mind." Annie raised her voice to compete with the maroon pickup overdue for a new muffler.

"I do mind." Heather's voice took on a hissing tone.

The truck slowed to a stop and laid on the horn. Annie waited until the blast stopped. "Myra Turnaggle is looking for a volunteer to help her at the food pantry in the afternoons and evenings."

"If you're coming, Heather, get your butt over here now," the teenaged boy in the truck yelled.

"If a guy wanted to be my boyfriend, I'd expect him to escort me to his car and say something sweet in greeting," Annie noted.

"We both know how many boyfriends you've gotten that way," Heather sneered. "If you want someone to hang around food all day, ask my mom. I've got a life." She fluttered her eyes at Nick. "Say the word, and I'll dump Troy for you."

"If you come on to me again," he countered, "I'll haul you to the food pantry myself."

For a moment she looked unsure. Then she laughed and trotted away, swinging her hips.

"Well," Annie said, her gaze still on the retreating form of the teenager as she slammed into the truck. The engine gunned, tires spun, and it drove off. "I don't know whether to thank you for handling the situation so tactfully or give in to resentment. You made headway after two minutes while I've been trying for two years without progress."

Nick refused to feel the camaraderie she was trying to establish. "You lost. She still left with him."

"I can't stop her. I can only plant seeds and pray for rain. Are you a painter, Nick?"

A painter? Where had she pulled that from? Everyone immediately pegged him as a lawyer. He reached for his tie again and encountered the paint stains. Oh, right. "I do a little of everything. Carpentry, plumbing, electric. I guess you could call me an independent contractor." He inwardly winced. He understood the value of spinning and twisting the truth. He made quite a decent living from it, in fact. But he hadn't meant to sound unemployed and desperate for a job.

Annie smiled guilelessly. "You probably believe you stopped in town for some random reason, but I believe you're an answered prayer. The toilet in the men's bathroom at church has been leaking for the past week. Would you mind taking a look at it?"

Nick stared at her in disbelief. She was his father incarnate. No doubt she'd been praying for free labor. "I don't—"

"Twenty bucks an hour. Hundred bucks just to walk in and see if you want to take the job."

He considered going for the bald truth and using the shock factor to his advantage. No. If he blew it, Annie would have the advantage and he'd never get her to agree to make amends to Jason. She was offering him the opportunity to stick close to her and find out what she was up to without her suspecting him. He generally left the undercover work to the PIs, but this time his brother's life hung in the balance.

All he had to do was hang out in God's house. Before this moment he would have said there wasn't enough money in the world to make him agree. And now, for a lousy hundred, "I'll look, but no promises."

He could do it. It was just another building with a roof. He certainly had no intention of communing with the Big Guy.

Annie pushed back her desk chair and stood. Finance committee meeting tonight. Meetings or functions always demanded her time in the evening. They didn't fix people's problems or bring God into anyone's life, just added to the bureaucracy. She sighed and immediately felt guilty. She loved her church. She loved helping people. She loved the Lord and was proud to dedicate her life to His service.

No buts. No exceptions.

She walked to the door and found herself face-to-chest with Nick McAllister. He was tall, and she had to look up to see his face. He had the body of a man who used his muscles for a living. Honed, sleek, and hard. Of course she noticed. Being a woman of God made her, above all, a woman. It certainly didn't render her blind.

His face was chiseled, and he had a thick five o'clock shadow and dark eyebrows. His eyes gave her pause. To fit with the rest of him, they should have been a warm brown. Instead, they were green and very, very cool.

She pasted on her Reverend Annie smile. "How's the toilet?" She hadn't made up the work, although she'd hoped to get a volunteer to fix it, rather than shell out money from the church budget. She didn't expect the finance committee, especially the chairman, to be pleased.

"Still a leak, but I've made progress." When Nick had stepped inside her building, she thought she'd sensed some reluctance. But after locating the tools, he didn't hesitate to plunge in, so to speak. "I'll come back tomorrow and work on it."

She thought of the clothes he was clearly self-conscious about. "Do you have a place to stay in town?"

His mouth curved into a smirk. "Would you invite me to stay with you if I didn't?"

She suppressed the urge to cringe. The gossip from such a move would skewer her closely guarded reputation. "No. But I'd find you a place."

"You're a real saint, aren't you?" His tone conveyed he thought she was anything but, although she'd done nothing but offer Christian charity.

"No, but I try to practice what I preach." She felt the burden of it settle on her shoulders as she walked to the door.

"Do you succeed?" His gaze was downright frosty.

Her failings were between her and her God and not open to public discussion. She changed the subject. "If you're planning to stay in town for a while, Good Shepherd has services Sunday at eleven. Sunday school starts at nine-thirty. We have two adult classes. We'd love to have you join us."

"I'll see how the toilet goes."

She'd expected noncommittal. Most newcomers didn't like being tied to a church obligation. But today was Wednesday. Surely, the leak could be fixed before Sunday. John Patterson thought he could fix it on a Saturday morning when he didn't have any paying jobs.

"Where's your car?" Nick asked as they left the church together. His dirty white pickup sat alone in the parking lot.

"I live two blocks away. Walking helps me work off the potluck dinners and other home-cooked meals people send my way."

He gave her a long look, as if assessing whether the exercise was a success. "I'll walk with you then."

Annie nodded. Her position as a pastor in a small town left her unafraid of being alone with strangers even as dusk rapidly gave way to night. There was a reason Nick McAllister had sought her out, and he hadn't gotten to the point yet. Annie could never turn her back on a lost soul. Unlike everyone else in her life, God had never turned His back on her.

"I do need a place to stay," he said after a block of walking in silence.

"Okay. I'll make a couple calls when we get to my place." Taking this long to admit it must have cost his pride, but he'd feel better wrestling with it in a comfortable bed tonight than sleeping alone in his truck. The carnal image of Nick in bed flashed through her mind, and she quickly banished it. The dimming switch for the sanctuary was acting finicky. Maybe she could have Nick take a look at that, as well.

Accepting the offer of help had been Nick's best decision yet. Annie invited him into her house without him needing to drum up an excuse to come in. He wandered the living room while Annie made her calls, foolishly disappointed not to find the missing jewelry lying on the coffee table. That would have been too easy.

From looking around the room, he couldn't see any sign of Reverend Annie's personality. Only a simple six-inch wooden cross adorned a white wall. Which hardly fit with the one preference he knew she had—a desire for gullible, baby-faced men. "You need a decorator," he said as she returned to the living room. "This place is as impersonal as a hotel room."

"Doesn't offend anyone that way." Annie aimed her sweet preacher's smile at him.

He didn't care for the way his body stirred. He knew what she was about, and he didn't want a piece of it. Apparently, he was going to have to make sure the message was received inside his boxers. "Where am I shacking up tonight?"

Her smile didn't waver. "Tidy Field Apartments has a one-bedroom you can rent. A hundred dollars will cover your first month's rent and security deposit."

The rate was obviously subsidized by the church or the generosity of the apartment owners. Until she made the offer, though, he hadn't realized he'd expected a handout with nothing required from him. He thought she'd place him with a family or in a shelter where he'd be given charity, not pay his own way. Instead, Annie had seen him as a working man down on his luck and was intent on salvaging his pride. He might have liked her for it if she'd left Jason with his pride and self-respect intact.

"The rent sounds pretty low, even for a rural area," he said.

"Some places are higher," she admitted, "but you're not getting top-of-the-line. This one hasn't been repainted from the old tenants, and they left some saggy furniture behind." She was nearly as good at spin as he was.

"I suppose it's too much to hope those tenants left a stocked fridge, too."

The obvious hint got him exactly what he expected, a won't-take-no-for-an-answer invitation to dinner. While she boiled noodles for spaghetti, he excused himself to the bathroom and checked out the medicine cabinet. Advil, Claritin, Neosporin, and Carmex. He hadn't expected the jewelry to be there, but he needed more personality hints to plan his approach.

No birth control or condoms either. He checked under the sink but found only toilet paper and tampons. She wasn't likely to get much action in Maplefield. She probably had to go out of town for that sort of thing—to prey on innocent people like his brother. As a preacher, her primary concern would be her appearance in the eyes of her congregation.

How far would Reverend Annie Lane go to make sure her followers still viewed her in virginal white while she got her kicks on the side? Recovering the jewelry and reclaiming Jason's equilibrium wasn't enough. He needed to expose her to these people, to show them the hypocrite in their midst. The people deserved the truth. The truth wouldn't allow these simple churchgoing people to keep faith in her while she returned to deception and destroying the innocent.

"Got any beer?"

Annie set the pan of meatballs on the table next to the spaghetti and looked up at Nick. He was standing a step closer than her comfort zone allowed. It wasn't a bad vibe, just made her very aware. "Sorry. I've got a half bottle of cooking wine. Otherwise, I can offer you milk, orange juice, or water."

"Don't believe in drinking?" He sneered at her as if purity of lifestyle was something to be ashamed of. She ought to introduce him to her sister.

"I don't have a problem with it. In moderation, of course. Jesus Himself turned water into wine. But alcohol doesn't hold appeal for me. Besides, folks get nervous and disapproving when they open the preacher's fridge and see a six-pack."

"It's important what people think of you?" Again the unmistakable censure.

"Of course. My reputation and my faith are the only things I have to offer my congregation and my community." No one knew better than she how easily a reputation could be damaged beyond repair.

"Worrying about it must keep you up nights," Nick said.

She stared into his cool green eyes, afraid he was going to keep her awake tonight. She couldn't remember the last time a man had invaded her subconscious so completely. On second thought, she could. The memory did nothing to comfort her.

"I'll have milk," Nick said.

She blinked, clueless about what he was referring to. Oh, right. To drink. For supper.

She poured the drinks and said grace over the meal before offering the dishes to Nick. He loaded his plate and ate in silence. His dark hair was tousled in an enticing disarray and curled around his ears. No doubt he was a couple months overdue at the barber. But her fingers didn't itch to drag out the kitchen scissors. Much worse, they fueled a primal need to sift through that glorious hair and explore its texture.

He looked up from his food and caught her staring at him. She dearly hoped he wasn't a mind reader or her reputation would be in danger. She hurried to think of something preacherly to cover her female indulgence. "Do you have any family?"

Something flashed in his eyes. A memory, she decided. A volatile one. "I'm not a stray dog."

She pulled back. "I didn't think you were."

"Then stop treating me like one."

She thought she'd been careful not to. "I apologize." She paused, but he didn't offer any insights into his family. Nor did he pick up the conversation. She tried again. "Do you have a home church?"

"Not anymore." He concentrated on his spaghetti as if he hadn't had a decent meal in a month.

He was reluctant to confide in her, but in Annie's experience most people wanted to tell their story. They just needed the right opening or a little encouragement. "Maplefield's a cozy town but a bit too far off the beaten path for most people to end up here by accident."

"Which makes me wonder how it became home to a young, female minister. Shouldn't you be out clubbing with your friends?"

She had to give him points for so smoothly turning the focus of the conversation. "All my friends are married with babies. The club scene never appealed to me."

He simply raised his brow, demanding more of an explanation.

Usually she didn't mind answering questions when hers were ignored. She listened when others needed an ear and talked when they wanted to listen. But she felt exposed with Nick in a way she didn't feel behind her office desk. She didn't want to open herself up without knowing something about him in return.

No, she was acting overly sensitive. A segment of people needed to hear a minister's faith journey before they felt comfortable confiding their own story. Annie never refused to provide it.

"As a child, I was a voracious reader. My parents had better things to spend their money on than books for me." Like makeup and ribbons for her sister. Her parents had long since died, but Annie's resentment hadn't, no matter how often she prayed about it. "When I was fourteen I was alone in a hotel room for the day, bored out of my mind. The nightstand drawer held a Bible and a phonebook. The Bible, at least, had full sentences. I started reading."

"And just like that, your life took on meaning?" His skepticism was as thick as the olive oil he dipped his French bread into.

"No. But I kept coming back to the Book, thinking about it, talking to people of faith. After college I decided to pursue it further and went to seminary." She gave him her standard short and easy version, which people accepted without question.

"Didn't you want to get married and have those babies?"

She shrugged, ignoring the longtime ache. "So far it hasn't worked out. But I'm a Protestant. Ministry and marriage aren't mutually exclusive."

"Celibacy would cramp your style," Nick said knowingly.

Indignation surged at his casual judgment. Celibacy had been her way of life for over a decade. She'd worked hard to ensure no one had reason to even whisper to the contrary. "You don't know me well enough to know my style."

"Of course not." His tone was flat, no sarcasm, but not a hint of contrition, either, as he forked up his dinner.

Not only did she need to protect her reputation, but she was angry—too angry to let the topic go. "I don't know what happened before you came to Maplefield, Nick, but most ministers give their lives in service to the Lord and His standards. Don't let your bad experience color your opinion of all people of faith." She didn't know the details of his trauma, but she knew he was still suffering.

The corner of his mouth kicked up, mocking her. "Is your dedication too pure to be sidetracked by worldly pleasures?"

"Yes." She believed it completely until she gazed into his piercing green eyes.

Chapter 2

Nick let his duffel bag fall to the kitchen floor with a thud. He set his cell phone on the barren counter, then pulled his wallet from his back pocket and set it next to the phone. A piece of paper stuck awkwardly out of his wallet. Frowning, he picked up the paper. As he unfolded it, a twenty-dollar bill fluttered to the floor. The words *food pantry* and an address were written in loopy handwriting on the paper.

The evidence of Annie Lane slipping her fingers into his back pocket nudged him into a state of semi-arousal. The thought was so erotic he felt almost violated it had happened without his knowledge. A free meal, twenty bucks, and directions to the food pantry—conclusive proof she considered him a charity case. His manhood wilted.

He looked at the fridge. How much of a charity case did she think he was? He opened it. A half gallon of milk with nearly two weeks before it hit the expiration date, a package of turkey deli meat, Kraft cheese singles, a loaf of whole wheat bread, and a carton of eggs. These were not conveniently left by last month's tenants. He slammed the door, not bothering to check if the apartment came with a skillet.

Reverend Annie Lane had a Jekyll-Hyde complex. She could be generous to a fault with strangers and then cold-bloodedly destroy another man's life. He wasn't surprised Jason had been conned. Nick was poised to fall for her pure and generous act, and he'd seen the evidence of her treachery. He punched the numbers on his cell phone to remind himself why he was hanging out in this Podunk town while Jason battled his demons alone.

"Any news?"

"Hello Dominick." His mother was the only one he'd answer to when addressed by his full name. She sounded more weary every time he talked to her. Guilt stabbed him for being across the state instead of by her side. "He's the same."

"Is he answering his phone?"

"No."

"The door?"

"Only for the pizza deliveryman. He told the guy to tell me he was fine."

"Maybe he is." But Nick didn't believe it any more than his mother did. Jason was dangerously suicidal. He'd driven his Mercedes off a pier into Lake Michigan. Nick should be there. If he couldn't break through to Jason and protect him from himself, he could at least offer comfort to their mother.

"Then why won't he talk to me? Why is this Reverend Annie still consuming him?"

"That's what I'm trying to figure out. I'm going to find answers that will make a difference to Jason."

Mom paused. "The jewelry's not important. Vonkall Auction House can weather the storm. The woman's not important either. I'd rather have you here, Dominick."

"But Jason doesn't want either of us around. Don't you think it's more important I do something to change that?"

His mother started crying.

Nick cursed himself. He was an insensitive jerk. No wonder women couldn't love him for who he was. "I'm sorry, Mom. I'll come home tonight."

"No, you're right. What's the point if he walks out of his

apartment only to try to kill himself again? Come home when you can help your brother."

"We have better things to do with our money than waste it on turkeys." Stewart Fitzsimmons puffed up with pompous indignation.

But apparently nothing better to do with their evening than argue about them. Annie stifled a sigh and glanced down at her watch.

"We're investing in the community." Despite her eighty-plus years, Myra Turnaggle didn't give an inch when her precious food pantry was at stake. "Furthermore, it's our duty as Christians to give to those who are less fortunate."

"They should get a job and buy their food like the rest of us," Stewart snapped.

"We understand your concern, Stewart." Annie laid a restraining hand on Myra's arm, knowing the woman would take the comment as a personal affront. "But most of the people who use the food pantry have jobs. And it's still not enough to consistently put food on the table. With Thanksgiving around the corner, we want to ensure no one's sitting around an empty table."

The finance committee chairman didn't relent. "They need better budgeting skills."

"I'm sure many people would benefit from a budgeting seminar by Maplefield's most knowledgeable CPA. Shall I pencil you in for the next community outreach meeting?" Annie asked sweetly.

"I'm not wasting my time talking to idiots."

She'd have been shocked if he agreed. Stewart and his mother, Trudy Fitzsimmons, were the two people in her congregation who jumped to the opposite end of whatever position Annie took. "Speaking of budgets," she said, "our Home

Subsidy Fund for the Needy is going to run over budget again."

"That's impossible. It was on track last week, and we agreed not to subsidize anyone else this year," Stewart said.

"You recommended that course." No way would she have blindly agreed to turn people away because they'd maxed out their budget. "A gentleman came to me today in need of housing. He's already settled in."

"Reverend Annie, I understand your need to support worthy causes." Stewart's tone conveyed his definition of worthy and hers did not mesh. "But I am concerned about our image. We're not growing our congregation or increasing our monthly collection. People can't assume they can turn to the church every time they get into a fix."

"On the contrary, that's exactly where they should turn," Annie argued. "If we can't be of help in time of need, we're useless to our community and have failed God's command to serve."

"We're fostering an image of an organization that can be easily taken advantage of."

"Some can abuse charity. That doesn't mean we should stop giving to those who truly need it. We rely on our faith to do what is right. In this case, offering a home to Nick McAllister was right." She decided to put off announcing that the church was paying Nick for maintenance work, as well. Stewart was in enough of a snit, and she hadn't spoken to him about his daughter yet.

"I move the church provide funds for twenty-five turkeys to supply the needy families in our community," Myra said. The motion was quickly seconded, and Stewart was outvoted by the rest of the committee.

Myra squeezed Annie's shoulder as the meeting broke up. "Thank you, Reverend Annie, for pushing that through. Everyone who uses the pantry appreciates your efforts. Now excuse me while I talk Miles into donating the day-old bread going to waste at the grocery store."

Annie watched Myra walk away, envying the woman her job. She gave to people, listened to them, and offered advice when asked. Nobody would condemn her if her words didn't fit precisely with church doctrine. No one thought less of her because ten years ago she'd had a hot affair. And every night she returned home knowing she'd made a difference in people's lives. Children went to bed with their bellies full instead of crying out with hunger because of her.

As Stewart approached, Annie thought of Heather and wondered what it would take to make a difference with that child. "No hard feelings." She offered her hand to him. "I know we both have the well-being of our church at heart."

"And radically different definitions of the word 'well-being,' apparently," he sniffed, crossing his arms across his wiry chest.

She dropped her hand and would have politely walked away if not for her concern for his daughter. "With her mother's blessing, I suggested to Heather that she volunteer some time each week at the food pantry. Myra is enthusiastic, and frankly, Stewart, Heather needs a healthier social environment."

"Right. Being around lazy, undisciplined people is going make her a better person," he said sarcastically. "Besides, she's not capable of handling that kind of responsibility."

"If she had more responsibility, I think she would rise to the challenge. She needs attention for something positive."

He snorted. "Heather's so wrapped up in herself and her imaginary boyfriends she doesn't care what adults think. She has no aspirations for doing anything worthwhile with her life."

"She cares very much—"

"I know my daughter a lot better than you, Reverend, and am much more qualified to make a judgment of her. I don't need your 'help' with my family, especially when you're taking the example of walking around in the dark with a strange man."

Annie bit back a sigh. She'd known someone would stir up trouble when she and Nick had walked back to the church together after dinner. But she needed to return for the meeting, and his truck was parked here. She wasn't going to make him leave her house at a different time simply so they wouldn't be seen together. She had nothing to hide. "His name is Nick McAllister, and he's doing some maintenance work for the church."

Stewart instantly looked horrified. "That's not in the budget."

So much for holding out that announcement. But when it came to her reputation, she much preferred to be seen as irresponsible with church funds than morally unfit. "He has to eat. We're either going to subsidize him this way or through the food pantry. The most cost-effective solution would be for you to invite him to dinner with your family."

Tanya gulped as she eased the door open. Zeke was on the bed, snorting up another line while a couple groupies stripped for him. The infidelity brought her a measure of relief. She'd be out of here before he could get it up again for her.

Jason had been a big disappointment. Oh, he'd proved to be an easy and willing seduction, falling under her spell so quickly she could almost forget she was living on the other side of thirty. But in the end, it hadn't made a difference. The audiotape she'd recorded wasn't with the tapes of Zeke's song demos and original jam sessions to be auctioned off. It should have been. She'd hidden it there.

Tanya had to find it. It was her get-out-of-jail-free card. Literally. Now she had another chance. Not from any goodness in Officer Hardball's heart, but because he was desperate to nail her husband and choke off the L.A. drug market.

She moved quickly and quietly across the room. Zeke groaned as he reached for one of the naked girls. The closet door squeaked as she opened it. She froze, but no one noticed.

She slipped into the closet. Five more minutes and she'd be out of this house of unimaginable misery. Forever. She pushed aside Zeke's shirts and felt for the edge of the safe where he kept his tapes and lyrics and drugs. She reached inside her bra just as the light flipped on.

"What are you doing here?" Zeke struck out, his hand hitting hers and knocking the key to the floor.

He was looking at her, not the floor. Tanya kept her eyes up, not daring to look down for the key despite her instinctive need to. She was not going to prison over this sorry excuse for a man.

"Hey, Zeke, I was looking for my Manolos. I thought maybe the maid screwed up and put them in your closet again."

"You really think I'm that wasted? You wanted to watch, didn't you?"

Relief flooded her. "That's right, Zeke. I wanted to watch so I can figure out what pleasures you." As if she didn't already know that violence and drugs were his pleasures. And sex. But every man had sex at the top of his list. Except for the one DEA cop who had a balls of stone and only got off on reducing drug traffic. Which was a noble goal. But not exactly arousing.

"As long as you're here, you decided to help yourself to my stash." He grabbed her hand and twisted it behind her back. Searing pain lanced through her arm and popped stars in front of her eyes.

She bit her lip to keep from crying out. Experience taught her she couldn't stop him from hurting her, but she could minimize his enjoyment by not letting him know how much pain she was in. It would be an Oscar-worthy performance, but she was good enough to deserve one. She'd prefer to die than let anyone see her in this role.

"Where's the key, Tanya?"

"What key?" She played dumb.

He cursed her and dropped her hand, bringing her arm a measure of relief. His hands moved to her pants, thrust into her pockets. He pulled out her key ring with other assorted keys attached, glanced at it, and threw it behind him. His hands shoved in her pockets.

"Give it up, Zeke. There's nothing else there. I don't do drugs. Why would I want your stash?"

"A real saint, aren't you?" He grabbed her shirt at the open cleavage and tore.

"You jerk. This is Ralph Lauren."

"Like you don't have others." His breath was foul on her face.

She avoided looking in his eyes. They were crazed enough to unnerve her when he was sober. "I don't. You sold most of my wardrobe."

"Your wardrobe is what put me in debt in the first place."

She didn't argue the drug habit had done it. "I told you I don't have it," she gritted. Her eyes lit on the prize item ten inches to the left of where her ring of keys had landed. Quickly, she averted her gaze and stuck to her excuse. "I came to look for my shoes."

"You're just getting more inventive with your hiding places." He fingered the cups of her bra.

"Get yours hands off me."

He laughed.

Her body was just a means to accomplish her goals. There was nothing sacred about it. She hadn't been untouched since she was fourteen. But having his hands on her made her skin crawl. She raised her knee and plowed it into his groin.

"You're going to pay for that." He shoved her chest as he fell to his knees, clutching himself.

She staggered. Her head hit the wall hard, and she fell. The key was only inches from her knee. Ignoring the pounding in her head, she shifted her leg to cover the metal before he saw it.

"I'm going to make you sorry you ever met me," he groaned.

She already was. She scrambled to her feet, swiping her key ring and the safe key into her fist. She stumbled, catching her chin on the door handle as she ran from the room.

She had no evidence for the police. She was going to jail.

"I'd like to get the youth group involved," Myra explained. "If I can get the shingles donated, John Patterson agreed to supervise the kids and let them use his tools."

"That's an excellent idea," Annie agreed. Getting the church kids together for a service project to fix the leaky roof on the food pantry would help them bond as a group. They'd also feel better about themselves knowing they had made a difference in their community. It was just the thing Heather Fitzsimmons needed to be involved in. "We'll have to watch the weather though. We can't have kids on ladders or going up on a roof if it turns icy."

"I agree. I'd climb up there myself—"

"Let the kids do it," Annie cut in, not wanting Myra anywhere near a ladder at her age. Her mind might be spry, but her bones weren't. "You can't run the pantry if you break your leg."

She sighed. "You're right. I should have paid attention this summer to how bad the roof was getting." But as usual Myra's concentration had been focused on the people using the pantry and on meeting the demand for food.

"We'll get it done, and in the meantime we'll pray for good weather," Annie said.

A short knock sounded on the office door, and since Annie hadn't closed it tightly, her secretary, Kathy Patterson, wife of John, stepped in without waiting for a welcome. Uptight and conservative, she'd been the church secretary for more than forty years. "Nick McAllister is here to see you." Her mouth tightened. "I tried to get him to make an appointment, but he insisted on waiting. He's all sweaty, and his attire's not suitable."

"God doesn't judge the outside, and neither do we," Annie reminded Kathy. "I'll see him as soon as Myra and I wrap up."

Kathy harrumphed and snapped the door closed as she left.

Myra grinned. "A sweaty, unsuitable man. My mouth is watering already. I suppose he's too young for me."

Annie laughed. She couldn't help it. Myra Turnaggle enjoyed life and men, and she refused to believe Annie's sexuality had shriveled when she married Jesus. The congregation loved Myra despite her flirtations, but Annie knew they wouldn't be so forgiving if their young, unmarried preacher began to notice men. Fortunately, her sexuality hadn't just shriveled. It had completely evaporated.

"I did send him your way, Myra, but as a patron of the food pantry."

Myra walked to the door and opened it, shamelessly peeking at the man outside the door. "Nope. He hasn't stopped by. I'd have remembered that body. Let me try to talk Kathy into going out to lunch with me so you can have the office to yourselves." She waggled her eyebrows. Then she walked out, introducing herself to Nick before Annie could stop her.

Kathy wouldn't take Myra up on the offer. Kathy never took lunch away from her desk, and she didn't approve of Myra on several levels. That was fine with Annie. She didn't want to be alone with Nick, even for a church office visit. Speculation was too easy to spark and too difficult to contain. Kathy, as a chaperone, would keep everyone straight on the nature of the visit and her boss's pristine reputation.

"Dinner's in five minutes, Heather. Change your shirt so your father doesn't pop a vein."

She swiped two Snickers from Mom's stash behind the cookie sheets. "I'm skipping tonight. I've got a lot of homework."

Sheesh, that was even lamer than last night's excuse that she had to polish her toenails. She must be losing her touch. Her mom's Salisbury steak made her mouth water. But if she was lucky, Troy Mullins would be waiting in the park like he promised, with a pocket full of condoms.

The sex was lousy, and the front seat of his truck was really uncomfortable. But when he looked at her, she knew he was paying attention—one hundred percent—to her. Okay, so her breasts were really what captured his attention. But that was better than watching her mother shovel down food while her dad criticized every bite.

Mom sighed, kind of like a hippopotamus Heather remembered from the zoo when she was a kid. Her mom wasn't just fat. She was so big Heather couldn't look directly at her. She didn't even have a medical condition to blame it on. She just ate—all the time. Heather pushed the Snickers behind her back. The thought of becoming like her mom—a big, fat wimp—turned her stomach.

"Do you have a test coming up?" Mom asked.

Heather thought of Troy and looked out the window. "An exam or something. I gotta go."

"I made Salisbury steak, your favorite."

Mom was so pathetic Heather felt bad being a jerk to her. "Food's not everything." Appetite gone, she walked to the sink and opened the cabinet below. She dropped the Snickers in the garbage and slammed the door.

"Where are you going?" Mom called as she walked to the front door. "I thought you had homework."

"I'm studying with a friend." She walked out.

"Be home by ten."

She slammed the door, not bothering to respond. All her mom would do if she didn't make curfew was huff and sigh and threaten to ground her. Like that would work. Mom couldn't run after her and catch her. She did as she pleased. It was her one consolation for having lousy parents.

Dad got out of his car as she walked down the sidewalk. She shouldn't have wasted her time with Mom. Now she had to deal with him too, and he was such a jerk. At least Mom tried to understand her.

"My money better not have paid for that shirt," Dad snapped.

She almost told him she earned the money herself in the back of Troy's truck, just to watch him have an aneurysm. But she wanted to get to Troy, so someone would hold her, so she said, "If you let me get a job, I won't have to spend your money."

"Give me a break, Heather. No one in this town would hire you."

Her chest cramped, kind of like her heart was having a period. She wasn't an idiot, she knew that was impossible, so it probably meant she was having a heart attack. Dad would feel bad for all the mean things he said to her if she keeled over. He was probably right about everything, but would it kill him to put a little faith in his only child?

"Reverend Annie wants me to volunteer at the food pantry. She says they'd hire me for that."

"Reverend Annie's trying to keep you away from home and tear our family apart. Now get inside and change your shirt. We're having company for supper."

As if she gave a flying flip about Dad's guest. She needed a hug. If Troy would hold her, she'd let him shove his penis wherever he wanted. Hopefully, she'd distract him into forgetting the condom again. She needed someone who'd love her no matter what, and a baby was her only chance to make that dream come true.

The pickup turning in the drive stopped her. Troy wasn't supposed to come to her. She didn't want any loser guys near her family. No, it wasn't Troy. This truck was white and relatively quiet. And the man getting out was way too handsome and muscled. Nick McAllister.

He nodded politely at her dad and then locked eyes with her. "Nice shirt."

She looked away, for the first time self-conscious and uncertain of her clothing choice. The black fishnet sweater with the three-inch strip of hot pink knit fabric pulled tight across her breasts grabbed attention and was guaranteed to immediately turn Troy on. Not that Troy took much effort. But when Nick looked at her, she felt like he could see straight through to how unworthy she was of anyone's attention.

"You're the company?" she suddenly realized. She expected some fuddy-duddy, like the mayor or the bank president. "How did you manage to wrangle an invitation?"

"No wrangling." His eyes were kind of cute, a twinkling green that reminded her of Tinker Bell. "Your dad offered."

"Heather, stop hitting on him. You look like a fool," Dad said.

For once, she hadn't been flirting, but she didn't expect her dad or even Nick to believe her. She was promiscuous, and she'd done her part to ensure the entire town believed it.

"Nah, she knows better than to waste her time on an old geezer like me." Nick winked at her, not a come-on wink but a friends-sharing-a-secret kind of wink.

She knew it was stupid, but her heart pushed against the wall of her chest—another cramp, only this was kind of a good one—until she was afraid she'd pop through the pink knit. She brushed by her dad into the house to change her shirt. She'd rather stare at Nick's handsome face through dinner with her idiot parents than let Troy sweat all over her. Troy probably wouldn't hug her anyway.

She came back to the dining room in the most conservative shirt she owned, a cream button-down with a preppy collar. Grandma Trudy had given it to her last Christmas without a gift receipt so she couldn't return it. She ripped off the tag and left the shirt unbuttoned to show the pink sports bra—her trademark color—underneath.

Her mother was huffing and puffing as she went to get another plate and silverware from the kitchen. Nick must be totally disgusted. All Heather's friends were grossed out. She never invited anyone over anymore. It was too embarrassing. Lois Fitzsimmons couldn't walk to the next room with getting out of breath. "Nothing that losing a hundred and fifty pounds won't cure," her dad always said when someone would suggest her mom see a doctor. Mom never said a thing about her weight. She just ripped open another bag of Doritos.

Heather ducked into the kitchen and got Nick's drink, so her mom wouldn't wheeze all through dinner. While they ate, Dad yapped about the things the town council was doing wrong since he lost his reelection bid and all the money the church was wasting on the food pantry and everything Reverend Annie did wrong. As if bringing flowers to shut-ins was a capital offense.

"What do you two think of your pastor?" Nick asked, looking from Heather to her mother.

Heather nearly choked on a bite of potato. No one asked what she or Mom thought after Dad gave an opinion. What they thought meant nothing compared to him.

"The flowers are silly. The shut-ins only look forward to Reverend Annie's presence. She doesn't need to bring them a gift," Mom agreed, glancing at Dad as if she needed permission to assert herself.

Dad gave a short nod. "Absolutely. It's a waste of church

money. I don't want my offering money paying for a half-blind person to look at something that's going to die in a week."

"But she's always been very nice to me," Mom whispered, then stuffed the rest of her steak in her mouth, making speech impossible for the next decade.

"She's too nice. She makes me ill," Heather said.

"You don't believe she's genuine?" Nick gave her his complete attention, like he was actually interested in her response.

Reverend Annie was real. Heather had done everything to bring out her bad side, but the niceness never wavered. To Nick she only shrugged. "She wants to be my friend. There has to be something wrong with her."

She meant it as a joke, but Nick looked at her like she was the most pitiful thing he'd ever seen. Dad started laughing. Tears stung her eyes and swelled her throat. There wasn't anything wrong with Heather that a little love from her father wouldn't cure.

Chapter 3

Nick had never been so happy to see a dinner end, so he could make his excuses and escape. Stewart Fitzsimmons had plenty bad to say about Annie. But his grievances were petty, and Nick found himself not wanting to agree with anything the man had to say. Nick's hand ached from clenching his fist and then restraining himself from planting it in Stewart's face. The man was either an idiot or just didn't care how his behavior affected his family.

Nick shook his head. The dysfunctional Fitzsimmons family wasn't his problem. He had his own family crisis to fix. Knowledge was power, and he still knew precious little about Reverend Annie. In his practice he made sure he was always on the right side of the ethical line. But that was business. And this was family. His brother's life, to be exact.

He glanced at the dash clock. Still early. Reverend Annie should be holed up in the church with a meeting or choir practice or something. He drove past her house, which looked dark except for a light on in the living room—the same light she'd purposely kept on when they left her place yesterday. He parked two blocks down and a block over and slipped through the alley, returning to her house.

He tried the back door, but it was locked. Small town living hadn't completely robbed her of common sense where basic security was concerned. Even so, he employed his handyman skills and had the door open in less than five minutes. He avoided the living room with the light on, so no one from the outside would see him snooping. Besides, he'd already scoped out the front of the house.

He gave the laundry room a cursory glance with a flashlight from his truck and then walked into what turned out to be her office. A few devotionals and study Bibles. A computer. College and seminary diplomas hung on the otherwise unadorned walls.

No pictures. It was odd. Annie struck him as the type who'd keep pictures of everyone special in her life on every available space.

On impulse, he switched the computer on. He had the time, at least an hour before he expected her to return. In pure and pious mode, she tended to conform to expectations. He searched the room for a concealed safe but came up empty, so he rifled through the desk while he waited for the computer to boot up. The desk held standard paraphernalia along with a bunch of handwritten cards and notes.

"Thanks for staying at the hospital with us during Ed's surgery."

"Thank you for your prayers for Johnny."

"Thank you for the money for the new business suit. I got the job!"

"Thank you for the happiness on our children's faces when they discovered your gifts under the tree this Christmas."

He set the notes aside. Saint Annie.

Why would this woman sleep with a stranger and steal a few pieces of cheap jewelry? It didn't make sense. She risked her position as a spiritual leader if she were found out. If she wanted a one-night stand, she could have picked someone up in a city bar. Certainly she would have protected her identity enough not to use her real name. If she'd seduced Jason for the jewelry, wouldn't she have taken the six-carat diamond or something with value?

If Annie wasn't the woman who had used Jason so callously, Nick still believed she had a connection to the rocker Zeke Britman. As a lawyer, he didn't believe in coincidences. Neither did juries.

Nick looked through Annie's computer files. Sermons from the past five years were in Word files labeled by date. He skimmed letters to missionaries, e-mails to seminary professors and fellow preachers, details of her savings and checkbook in Microsoft Money. Both were piddling, although well-organized and in the black. Her salary was modest, as was her personal spending, but she gave to everything and everyone who came across her path.

An easy mark. Maybe someone had stolen her identification.

Or maybe not. She was a preacher, a master of hypocrisy. Although it was obvious she practiced what she preached in some areas. He couldn't remember a penny coming from his father's pocket back into the church. Annie's biblical devotion to the less fortunate likely fueled her need to give in to other sinful temptations. She probably thought her good deeds made her immune to the laws and bonds of basic decency others abided by.

He connected to the internet and looked through the history of past hits. A few religious and church sites. He checked a couple, but they were all conservative mainstream. No surprises there. The websites for Vonkall Auction House and Merrill, Thompson, & McAllister were not in the history. He scrolled through, looking for porn or anything odd. She visited eclectic sites, but nothing stood out. He was ready to ditch this effort as wasted time when he came across the site www.World'sSexiestViper.com.

Supermodel Tanya, famous as much for her selfish, demanding personality as for her stunner body, was the kind of woman men had wet dreams about and other women loved to hate.

Zeke Britman had furthered her fame—and his own—by coining the phrase "World's Sexiest Viper" in his chart-topping song about her. Nick figured her image was well-deserved, but as she and Zeke were both celebrities, he took it all with a bowl of salt.

He studied Tanya, posed provocatively on the screen. She and Heather Fitzsimmons appeared to buy their clothes from the same tailor. He shook his head. Annie hadn't visited this site to get fashion pointers. Why then? Curiosity? Perhaps she and Tanya knew each other. Not likely. Maybe Reverend Annie was obsessed with Tanya's man-eating personality, and decided to experiment on Nick's hapless brother.

Annie and Tanya's face shape was similar—oval with a clear complexion. Come to think of it, he could say the same thing about his ex-girlfriend. He was grasping at straws. Their bodies, near as he could tell, held no resemblance. Even under the ugly blazers Annie wore, he was positive she wouldn't be able to disguise breasts like Tanya's.

Though it was only through the internet, the connection to Britman left him uneasy.

He turned off the computer and left everything in the office as he had found it, heading for the bedroom. Books covered the dresser, stacked unevenly on the nightstand, and spilled onto the floor. Not just Bibles, devotionals, and inspirational hogwash he would have expected from a preacher. *Pride and Prejudice* was wedged between a gardening how-to and a *New York Times* best-selling thriller. Civil War history was stacked on top of Chinese culture and a biography of a Fortune 500 business executive.

Annie obviously wasn't kidding about her love of reading. But he couldn't sense a pattern or sinister thread in her reading material to explain her treachery. He turned to her closet. The clothes were conservative and shapeless and, he guessed, a size too big. Like a pervert, he turned to the dresser and her underwear drawer. White cotton, all of it. Nothing to drive Jason—a connoisseur of women in their undergarments—over the edge of desire in an office storeroom.

Nick sank onto the edge of the bed. It didn't make any sense. No condoms or other form of birth control were stashed anywhere. He opened the nightstand drawer and lifted out a solitary picture in a cheap frame. Two elderly people, not smiling but not unfriendly, stared back at him. Nick's mother had worn a similar frilly style blouse when he was young.

He dropped the picture back into the nightstand. He'd made a mistake. It was that simple. Annie didn't have the jewelry, and she obviously didn't have a seductive bone in her body. He'd go back to Chicago, interview the receptionist again, and review the security tapes. He'd climb the fire escape and break into Jason's apartment and make him talk out his problems, not wallow in them. All the things he should have been doing instead of stalking an innocent preacher.

He pushed himself up from the bed and ran his hands through his hair as he headed for the door. Maybe he could fit in a haircut too.

The overhead light flashed on. Something black flew by him and landed with a thump on the bed. Nick turned to identify it. One of Annie's trademark blazers.

A woman screamed.

He swung around and found himself face-to-face with a terrified and unbuttoned-to-the-waist Annie. He glanced around for the cause of alarm, prepared to protect her. But they were alone. He couldn't locate any large insects or spiders.

Then it registered. His presence frightened her.

"I can explain," he said, although he wasn't certain how much of the truth he would tell her. She had every right to call the police on him. That would raise eyebrows at Merrill, Thompson, & McAllister.

"Please do." Her voice was pure frost as she clutched her shirt together in a white-knuckled fist.

Her breasts, despite being high and rounded, were small—nearly insignificant compared to the supermodel he'd inspected online. And Annie's modesty proved she wouldn't know provocative if she tried. His body pointed out she didn't have to try. Her innocence and small, tight body was turning him on more than the overblown sexiness of Hollywood.

He reached behind him and lifted her blazer, handing it to her.

"Thank you." She shrugged into it and wrapped it tightly around her chest. Then she met his gaze. "Is there a problem with your apartment?"

By all rights she should have pegged him as a murdering rapist and run screaming from him. Instead, she gave him the perfect excuse with her charitable naïveté. And because she did, he couldn't use it. So he went with honesty. He was going back home anyway and would never see her again. He might as well lay his cards on the table. "I was looking for some jewelry."

"I've got a couple Avon pieces, but they won't bring you any cash. You picked the wrong house to loot."

Great, now he was a thief, no better than the one who had stolen from Jason. "No, I was looking for some specific jewelry."

"That you think I have?"

"They were old sterling silver pieces. A necklace with a sapphire center. A bracelet with an intricate lace and sapphire design, and matching earrings."

Annie turned stone still during his dissertation. For a moment she didn't speak. "Why are you looking for those things?" Her voice was raspy.

Scratch "innocent." Nick stared at the picture of guilt. The realization sent a shaft of disappointment through him, followed by anger directed more at himself than at her. He knew preachers had two faces, one for their congregation and one for their private life. Annie was so good at keeping hers separate he had lost sight of it. "You could say I have a personal interest in their rightful return."

"Return to whom?"

"My brother." *My baby brother who's locked himself away from the world because of what you did to him.*

"Who is your brother?"

"I think you already know the answer to that, Reverend Annie."

She shook her head, playing the innocent act to the hilt.

"Where's the jewelry?" He was through with the game.

"I don't know what you're talking about," Annie insisted. "I think you should go."

He stepped toward her, pulling the lapels of her blazer from her hands. "I saw this jacket in the security camera footage. The lie is over, Annie. Give me the jewelry or I'll expose you to your congregation as the fraud you are."

"There's nothing to expose." She yanked her jacket back and walked out of the room.

Nick followed her down the hall to the front door. He was so close to accomplishing his mission, to bringing something positive home for Jason. He wasn't going to stop now. "My brother refuses to face the world because of you. You couldn't stop with stealing from him. You had to humiliate him and leave him no choice but to end his life."

Annie stood with the front door open and her shirt and blazer gaping, exposing the white cotton of her brassiere. The underwear didn't look nearly so boring on her chest as it did in the drawer. He tried to keep his attention on her face and on all the reasons he hated this woman.

"I don't know what you're talking about," she said, compassion etched in every line of her lying face. "Please tell me about your brother so I'll understand."

"Jason Vonkall." He spat the name at her. But she was good, not a crease of recognition anywhere. "You seduced him and stole the jewelry from him. When he realized you'd ruined the reputation of the entire Vonkall Auction House, he drove his car into Lake Michigan rather than face the shame. But he was lucky and was rescued with only minor injuries. Now he's locked himself in his apartment and refuses to face the life stretching unbearably before him because of you."

"I don't know who did this to your brother, Nick, and I'm very sorry for him. I've never met him, but if there's any way I can help—"

"Return the jewelry."

"I don't have it. I never stole anything."

"You stole my brother's trust and the life he's accustomed to. Prepare for jail, Annie. I'll bring in the police to prosecute. Someone's going to pay for what happened to Jason." In the meantime, he was leaving hypocrisy behind and driving back to where he belonged, at his brother's and mother's sides.

A car drove by on the street outside Annie's door, then reversed slowly back. A woman gaped out the passenger-side window before the car sped forward again.

"Might want to close your shirt," Nick mentioned, letting his lips curve into a smirk. "You're giving the neighbors a show." And left little doubt she was freezing in the chilly weather. He should be disgusted by her blatant display and forgotten modesty. Instead, he couldn't stop his gaze from straying back for one last look, and he couldn't stop his body from reacting.

Annie yanked her blazer closed. "Come to my office tomorrow morning. We need to talk when we're both thinking clearly."

"Get a lawyer and let him do the clear thinking to get you out of this mess." Nick walked down the front steps to the sidewalk. He didn't know what he was going to do, but calling the police meant the end of Jason's career. The end of Jason's career meant the end of Jason's inheritance. And Jason preferred death if that happened.

"Is your dad home?"

"Who's calling?" Heather asked even though she knew. It was That Woman. She used to only call once a month or so about church stuff. Then it was once a week, and now it was almost every night. Obviously, she was having an affair with Dad.

Heather couldn't imagine Dad or That Woman taking off their clothes or touching someone with their bodies, which pretty much made an affair impossible. Besides, Dad had Mom, and even though he was a jerk to her and they never had sex, he wasn't the super-smooth type who seemed like a cheater. And That Woman was married to the nice and almost normal John Patterson.

"It's Kathy," That Woman said.

"What do you want?"

"It's church stuff."

"Dad's busy." It might not be a lie. She didn't know what Dad was doing. She'd gone out after Nick left two hours ago, but Troy was long gone. All of her usual hangouts were deserted. The girls who used to be her friends whispered behind her back and didn't have anything to say to her face. Besides, the evening was too darn cold to stay outside. So she'd come home and was fixing a temporary tattoo in the center of her cleavage, where everyone would see *Hot* tomorrow at school.

"Don't give me lip, Heather. This is important."

"So is Dad's time. He doesn't need to waste it on you." She hated That Woman. Her parents didn't need anyone to help break up their marriage. The truth was any woman would look better naked than her mom. But Mom was so defenseless it was hardly fair.

"I need to speak to him about Reverend Annie." That Woman hated Heather. The feeling was mutual. But to get to her dad, That Woman had to tolerate Heather. Heather had no intention of making it easy.

"What about Reverend Annie?" She made herself sound bored, which wasn't difficult. The chances of anyone having any real dirt on the perfect preacher were about the same as Heather becoming Daddy's girl again, but she couldn't stop hoping.

"I'm serious, Heather. Let me talk to your father. The church needs to decide how to handle this."

"What'd she do? Give an unbudgeted five bucks to a homeless guy?"

"No. If you must know, she's been doing things in plain view that are better saved for marriage behind a locked bedroom door."

"No way." Hey, maybe miracles could happen to Heather Fitzsimmons. "Tell me, and I'll let you talk to Dad."

Annie checked one more time to make sure her green turtleneck and navy blazer covered every inch of her torso before she opened the front door. It was earlier than she usually left for church, but she wanted to be seated behind her desk long before Kathy arrived. And she hoped God's house would help her feel the Spirit move as she prayed.

She took one step outside and pulled up short. Nick McAllister stood in front of her, his hands in his jacket pockets, his green eyes frozen with contempt. She tugged on her blazer, certain he could see all the way through to her skin. "Are you frisking me for contraband jewelry this morning or looking for some maintenance work around the church?"

"I'm giving you a vacation day today."

She tried not to let her temper kick in at his arrogance. "That's generous of you, but not within your power. Besides, I have appointments this morning."

"My brother's life is on the line, and you've got appointments." His disgust was palpable.

"I'm sorry about your brother, but if you're so concerned about him, why are you hanging around here taking on odd jobs?"

"I came to find the jewelry. That was going to make the difference to Jason."

"I would think having you at his side would mean more to him. I'm sorry I can't help you, Nick. I'll pray for you and your brother." She tried to move around him, but he shifted his weight to block her path.

"Let me put this a different way. You can come to Chicago with me today, or you can convince your congregation I didn't make you come seven times last night."

She froze, the gasp lodged in her throat. "You would deliberately sabotage my reputation?"

"Yes."

The injustice would have appalled her if she weren't so focused on the career-ending disaster. "You're wasting your time. I don't have anything to return to your brother."

"His self-respect, his will to live."

"If I'm responsible for those things, I'll answer to God for them. I'm happy to help anyone overcome their troubles. But you have a plethora of chaplains and psychiatrists in Chicago you can call on."

"Jason needs you," Nick insisted. "You got him into this."

She could turn blue disputing it, so she didn't try. She'd have no better results than trying to counter slanderous rumors. She was a minister. It was her duty to bring comfort and peace to the sick and lost. Perhaps she could find answers and peace for herself as much as for the man who had been wronged. "Not only are you blackmailing me, you're prepared to kidnap me."

The set of Nick's jaw softened. "I would never physically threaten a woman."

"You'd have to be pretty physical to make me come seven times." Oh, no, she couldn't believe those words really came out of her mouth. Just thinking about Nick in such an intimate setting made her cheeks burns. And her face wasn't the only part of her body suffused with heat.

He laughed, and his eyes melted to the color of a tropical sea. "I am threatening you, and I will follow through on those threats. But I won't force you to travel across the state in a car with a guy you've known for two days and have no reason to trust. I mean, what if I plan to chop up your body and dump it in a ditch?"

His concern for her peace of mind over her safety relaxed her into trusting him. She didn't know this mysterious handyman well, but she did know he had a heart of gold where his family was concerned. "So you're proposing?"

"You tell someone where you're going, alert the local police to follow up if you don't make it home, and you take your own car and follow me to Jason's."

She shouldn't abandon her congregation. They needed her. They appreciated her presence. But for one day they could get by while she indulged in a bit of cowardly avoidance. Visiting the sick was more comfortable and less taxing than facing Kathy and explaining last night's debacle. The old prude's thoughts when she'd seen Annie with her shirt undone wouldn't have been charitable. And Kathy had seen her. Annie didn't doubt it. Whatever Kathy had seen, she would believe the worst-case scenario.

Annie focused on Nick. He'd had an up-close view of her uninspiring chest. He certainly hadn't come back for a second peek. Nick was another soul she was sure was lost and crying out for her guidance into the fold. She would use this time to try to reach him as well.

"Okay. Let me make my calls." Annie returned inside the house and left a message for Kathy at church that she was taking a personal day and to call her on her church-provided cell phone for emergencies.

Her church and surrounding herself with God's love was everything she needed. Nick's suggestions were nothing more than temptations. God wasn't lacking. If she considered Nick in anything more than a spiritual realm, the defect was in her faith and devotion. She would use today to realign herself with God's will.

"I'm giving you one more chance."

"Yeah, out of the goodness of your heart." Tanya used her trademark shrewishness to battle back the tears of relief; she'd rather die than shed those tears in front of Officer Hardball. He had another name, but she hadn't caught it and didn't care enough to ask.

"My heart has nothing to do with it. Britman's running a drug cartel. We want him shut down and behind bars."

"So get a search warrant." As an alternative to meeting up with Zeke again, jail was becoming more appealing. If only it wouldn't send her career into an irreversible tailspin.

"Denied."

Figured. Officer Hardball didn't want to put up with her any more than she liked him. But they both needed something from each other. Unfortunately, he was one of the few straight-and-narrow guys who refused to take sex as his compensation.

"Tell me your plan." He folded his arms across his chest, too thinly built to be a bodyguard but sexy in a cocky, pigheaded way. "How are you going to get the evidence without screwing up like last time?"

She lifted her chin, daring him to comment on the bruise

marring her flawless skin. There were other bruises, too. Ones he couldn't see. Ones she wouldn't admit to no matter how severe the interrogation turned. Her gaze slid to Hardball's hands. They were big but not beefy. No rings. Not that a piece of jewelry stopped anyone in this town. Would he be gentle? She thought he might have the depth to see her as more than a sex object.

Which was foolish. She was a sex object. She wasn't ashamed of it. She'd given the guy at Vonkall Auction House an experience to build a lifetime of fantasies on. Sex made her marketable. Without it, she was just another surgically enhanced woman with an abusive husband.

The officer shoved his Listerine-breath, lost-my-razor face in front of hers. "How are you going to get the goods, Tanya?"

The plan. Focus on the plan. Orange jumpsuits didn't flatter her figure.

"Zeke's having a party at the house Saturday night to celebrate his new album. I'll show face at the party. Then I'll sneak back and get the stuff. You'll have it by Sunday morning."

"Make sure of it."

Nick kept Annie in his rearview mirror the entire time he drove, which meant he couldn't go a mile over the speed limit or he'd lose her. He should have yanked her into his truck like he'd planned. But the way she pulled her blazer tight around her when she saw him got to him.

He'd never physically hurt a woman. Annie had treated him well even after he had broken into her house. But if she had hurt his brother and couldn't fix Jason's pain, he would destroy every ounce of her precious reputation.

Annie's car was falling further back in his mirror. She put her blasted turn signal on. What did she think she was doing? He slammed on his brakes and swung in a wide U-turn to backtrack to the fast-food restaurant. "Potty break," Annie mouthed to him as she ran inside the building.

Seeing no other choice, Nick got out of his truck and followed her. They'd made it to Rockford, halfway from Maplefield in Illinois's northwest corner. He hoped she wasn't having second thoughts now. He dug out his cell phone while he waited.

"Nothing new," Mom reported. "I got through the front door with someone going out and spent two hours beating on his door last night. He yelled once that he was fine and said when all his vacation time was used up, he'd come back to work and talk to me then."

"How much vacation time does he have?" Nick's stomach rumbled as he stared at the overhead menu. He should have fried those last four eggs before he left this morning.

"Two weeks, but that's hardly the point. This is the kid who's spent every spring break and vacation on a tropical beach with alcohol and naked women."

Nick flinched. If his mother saw the truth of Jason's vacations, which he'd tried to put a G-rated spin on, she was probably just as wise to the wilds of Nick's past spring breaks too. "Now Mom—"

"We both know it's true. I'm stretched too thin today for sugar-coated versions," Mom said. "Not only do I have your brother's load and have to make excuses for your absence, but—"

"I thought Holly was taking Jason's clients."

"She has to take the baby to the pediatrician today."

Nick rubbed the back of his neck and tried not to think about Holly or her baby. "Anything serious?"

"Just the sniffles. But you know how first-time parents are."

He didn't. "What clients are you meeting with? Britman?" He hadn't realized Annie had approached until he felt her tense beside him.

"No, new business. If they want the contract altered, I'll call you. For the record, I think you should come home, Dominick. I'm worried about that woman corrupting you, too."

"Nothing to worry about." But he couldn't stop himself from thinking about making her come. Seven times. "Tell Holly to stay home with the baby this weekend. I'll be there to take some of the load off." He snapped the phone shut and turned to Annie. "Are you hungry? I believe I owe you a meal."

"Feeling guilty for conning me," she said in a knowing tone.

"One of us has a conscience."

She didn't reply as he ordered and took their food to a vinyl booth. While eating, Annie spoke carefully. "I never heard of the Vonkall Auction House until yesterday, so I'm having trouble figuring out where you all fit in. Your mother and sister run it. You're the maintenance man, and Jason is what?"

Nick choked on his sausage and egg muffin. "Jason runs it. My mother assists. I don't have a sister."

"But I heard you mention someone named Holly."

"My ex-girlfriend." Who could have been his wife with very little effort on his part.

"Oh." He had no idea how to interpret that enigmatic syllable coming from Annie's mouth. "Your baby, too?"

"No." He almost wished he'd married her, so he could make the claim. Almost.

"Do you want to talk about it?" Annie asked.

"No." If he talked about Holly, he'd have to explain he was a lawyer, not a handyman. He'd learned at eighteen that a woman's interest in a man with no prospects waned quickly. He was curious how long Annie would keep up the act. That was all. Mere curiosity.

"Fair enough. Is your brother older or younger?"

"You've seen us both. You tell me."

She didn't tip her hand. "I'm guessing by how protective you are of him that he's younger, but if he's running the company and you have no executive position, I'd expect him to be older."

Nick had no intention of giving her more of the knowledge-is-power cliché so he went for flippant. "You don't believe parents play favorites to that extreme?"

"I know they do." She was serious. "Is that your case?"

"No. Jason and I have different fathers." Why was he telling her this? They should be talking about her if she insisted on conversation with their breakfast. But the words kept falling from his lips. "Mom divorced my dad to marry Jason's dad. Jason took over Vonkall Auction House when his dad died last year. Mom doesn't have a formal title, but I think she knows more and does more than Jason. Cultivating and maintaining celebrity connections are very important to us."

Annie set down her sandwich as if she'd suddenly lost her appetite. "That seems shallow."

"We have something to prove." His mother deserved to get back all that she'd lost by choosing to stick with his dad and give Nick life. If Nick worked hard enough and stayed true to his goal, someday she would stop regretting that choice. Until then, the guilt of his existence weighed on his shoulders.

Annie's hands moved to her lap. "How does Holly fit into this?"

"She's second-in-command under Jason."

Annie looked at him carefully. "You don't look like the type to take orders from an ex-girlfriend."

"You don't know my type," he snapped back.

She lifted her brows.

All right, she pegged him. "Holly's not in charge of maintenance." Deceit was getting tricky. He didn't have as much practice as Annie.

"Normally, I'd say you're very sweet to stick close to your mother and brother. I hope you're not doing it to latch on to their celebrity connections."

"A handyman on an actress's arm at an awards show?" He laughed sourly. "No matter how badly her house is crumbling around her, I don't have much of a chance. Who do you stick close to, Annie?"

"My community, my congregation, my church, and my God." She said it with conviction, but the gap between a preacher's words and reality could put the Grand Canyon to shame. Nick had every intention of exposing that gap.

Chapter 4

"Jason didn't answer." Nick looked stumped, as if he'd really expected evoking the name Reverend Annie would open doors. Obviously he had her confused with her sister.

"Maybe he's not listening as the calls come in to his answering machine."

"Or maybe he is and wants to hear your voice." Nick began dialing again.

A minute ago he wouldn't let her talk in the phone or into the apartment intercom in case she'd say something that would push his brother over the edge. Annie restrained herself from pointing that out as she took the cell phone. Instead of stepping back, Nick hovered next to her ear. She blocked his dark handsome features by closing her eyes, but the smell of his really great cologne penetrated. Jason's generic message played, and she blanked. Nick nudged her with his elbow.

"Jason, this is Reverend Annie. A couple days ago you met someone who went by my name. I'd like to talk about a few things. I'm outside your apartment. Come down and meet me or call me on your brother's phone. I look forward to meeting you." She clicked off the phone and handed it back to Nick. "Now what?"

"We wait." He leaned back against the brick wall of the building.

There had to be a better way to deal with a suicidal man than leaving him alone in a high-rise apartment. "Don't you have a spare key, or can you talk the manager into letting you in for a well-being check?"

"Jason orders in food once a day and always tells the delivery man to tell us he's fine."

Annie still didn't understand why Nick had brought her here. Every time she thought of the importance he put on cultivating celebrity connections her hands started to shake. He didn't know about her yet. He couldn't. "Then why don't you believe him?"

"Because Jason's the most social person I know. He was president of his fraternity. He thrives on human contact."

"Even social people need downtime. That's why all those celebrities pay big money to go to some deserted island for privacy, right?"

Nick's enigmatic gaze held her hostage. "Do they? I wouldn't know."

Annie needed to shut up. If she didn't want him to make a celebrity connection, she shouldn't bring one up. "I need a heavier coat if we're going to hover by the door all day."

"There's a coffee shop across the street. We can watch from there." Nick touched the small of her back as he steered her into the Starbucks and onto a tall wooden chair by the window.

He left her to place an order, and Annie's thoughts immediately swerved to her congregation. She was playing hooky in a coffee shop with a man she'd half-undressed in front of last night. She shuddered at the conclusions they would draw. Trudy Fitzsimmons would link her with Sodom and Gomorrah.

Kathy Patterson might not be so vocal, but she would disapprove, too. Ever since Annie had bestowed her blessing on Kathy's daughter's cross-country career move, Kathy had barely tolerated Annie's presence. It didn't help that the daughter severed all contact with her mother immediately after the move.

Thankfully, Kathy's censure was largely confined to the

pursed-lip variety. But Annie's offenses usually included things like running over the time allotted for counseling sessions and keeping later appointments waiting.

"Hey, you sleeping or praying?"

Annie pried open her eyes and accepted the cup of gourmet coffee Nick offered her. "A little of both."

"Pray while you're sleeping." He sank into the chair next to her and blew at the steam above his Styrofoam cup. "Accomplish two things at once. You should market that. Religion for people too busy for God. Pray in your sleep."

His mocking tone stung. She shouldn't allow it to. She already knew his opinion ranked her below the devil on the morality scale. "You're making fun of me. God does answer prayers, Nick."

"Yeah? What did he answer for you?"

"When Myra Turnaggle's son had a heart attack and we prayed for a full recovery—"

"The doctors delivered," he finished. "What prayers for yourself has God answered?"

She'd handled skeptics before, but the personal nature of Nick's questions made her want to squirm. She refused to give him the satisfaction. She sipped her coffee, scalding her tongue and giving herself something else to focus on. "I asked God for a love that would never fail me, and He gave me Jesus."

Nick snorted. "I bet He keeps you warm at night."

His comment was insulting and blasphemous and not worthy of a response. Unfortunately, it also struck a chord. She placed her hand on Nick's arm. "Please don't disrespect my Lord in front of me."

He glanced down at her hand. "Can you touch me without stepping over the line of propriety?"

Such a prissy word for a man whose picture was next to the words *rugged* and *masculine* in the dictionary. She decided not to mention it. "I doubt anyone in this shop will be scandalized." No one was paying any attention to them. "Even my parishioners approve of me using touch to provide comfort."

"How about this?" He moved his arm, capturing her hand with his and entwining their fingers.

Electricity sizzled up Annie's arm. She struggled to form a coherent sentence. "This feels a bit too intimate to be comforting."

"Intimate? Holding hands?" He looked at her as if she just taken her first step out of the convent. He wasn't that far off. "Are you a virgin, Reverend?"

"What a question!" She tried to pull her hand away, but he held firm. "I believe love between a man and a woman is sacred and is best expressed within the bonds of matrimony."

"You're avoiding the question."

Yes, she was, and not doing a very good job of it. "No, I'm not a virgin, and, no, I've never been married. Unfortunately, I started taking my own advice too late."

"Too late for what?" He scooted his chair closer.

She needed to break away from his touch. If she steeled herself to speak, she wouldn't feel so exposed. "Too late not to get my heart broken and save myself for someone I would be special to."

"He didn't think you were special?" Nick looked outraged. Disgusted a woman of God had such loose morals, no doubt.

"I thought he did at the time. I also thought he loved me, and it would lead to marriage. I was wrong on all counts." She had been so stupid, so naïve, so betrayed.

Nick's thumb stroked the back of her hand with a gentleness that contrasted starkly with the edge in his voice. "So Jesus promised to love you forever, and you went into the nunnery."

"I went to seminary. Nuns are Catholic. Protestant ministers aren't given a celibacy mandate."

"Self-imposed then."

"Not very well, if you think I slept with your brother." She purposely reminded him of the ugliness. Dealing with his disgust over something she knew she was innocent of was preferable to dredging up the pain from her past. She shouldn't have confided in him. He already had more than enough ammunition to ruin her reputation. And her reputation was her life.

His mouth tightened, and he stood facing her. But he still didn't release her. "If you didn't seduce Jason, why aren't you denying it?"

"In my experience, the more you protest your innocence, the less people believe you." A painful lesson she'd learned in her high school years, but not nearly as painful as her college memories. She tugged on her hand again. "Please let me go."

"Why?" His gaze was direct and seared her soul. His thumb skimmed the inside of her wrist.

"Because we've crossed the line of propriety." She needed to wrap her arms around herself. She had to stop the sensual tingle where his skin touched hers. She couldn't afford to indulge in pleasures of the flesh, even for a moment. But for the first time in years, Nick made her want to. Nick made her come alive in ways that were better off dead.

He released her hand but only to touch her cheek with gentle fingers. She gripped the seat of her chair as he leaned down. He dipped his head until his mouth was inches from hers. He was going to kiss her. His body language left no doubt, but she didn't believe it. She dug her knuckles into the chair. She had nothing to offer him. She might not be a nun, but she was only a small step away.

His lips brushed hers and then settled against her mouth. Warm sweetness swept through her body. A heady rush of pleasure combined with a warm lethargy. Her arms fell limply to her sides. She was close-mouthed but far from prim; he drenched her in sensual deliciousness. As he adjusted his slant, she lifted her arms to his neck to hold him in place so he wouldn't pull back.

She couldn't stop herself from kissing him back. Didn't want to stop. She parted her lips and rose from the chair to cling to his shoulders. He slipped through her defenses and exploded her world. She'd never been kissed like this. She wouldn't have given up kissing if she had.

Dimly, she realized he was pulling back. She didn't want to let him, didn't think she could. She curled her fingers around the fabric of his shirt. He brushed his closed lips against hers again, then pressed his forehead to hers. She drank in gulps of mocha-latte-scented air and listened to the sounds of their ragged breathing.

He'd kissed her for herself, not as a consolation prize because he couldn't have her sister. Elation swept through her before she could reason with herself. A chunk of her heart broke off and became irrevocably lost to him.

Nick lifted his head. "Now we've crossed the line of propriety."

Nick spent most of the next three hours on the phone. He conducted business when he was out of Annie's earshot, all the while guessing and second-guessing Jason's actions. But far and away, he spent most of his time trying to ignore the fire in his blood. It had only been a single kiss. With some great tongue action. And complete acceptance.

For a minister she sure could kiss. She thought she was kissing a handyman. She'd kissed him like that knowing him only as himself. He could only imagine how she'd go after Nick the lawyer.

Or Jason the owner of a prestigious auction house.

He snapped his phone shut and focused on the purpose of

having Annie in his company. "It's time to make our move. Jason should be ordering delivery right now." Sure enough, twenty minutes later an Asian delivery man carrying a brown paper bag approached the door and buzzed Jason's apartment. Jason, the little bugger, buzzed him right up.

Nick grabbed Annie's arm to make her keep pace with him and slipped inside the security door before it locked behind the delivery boy. "I'll take that delivery for you."

The man turned in alarm, his stance hostile and inviting a fight. Nick flashed a hundred-dollar bill. The man snatched the money and tossed the bag at him before running out.

Annie's eyes widened at the exchange. He'd allowed her to think he was destitute, and he could feel her hurt over the deception. He didn't have time to deal with it now. He was finally going to see his brother in the flesh. Jason would finally get the help he needed to overcome his ordeal.

Nick knocked on the apartment door and held the bag in front of his face at the peephole. The door opened. Jason looked terrible. He hadn't shaved. His hair was matted. His expression was little more than grim resignation. Nick shoved his way inside, immediately scanning the countertops for knives and other sharp objects. "I brought dinner."

Jason sighed. "I told you I was fine."

"I'm going to get you back to the point where your actions support your words."

"You are such an arrogant jerk. You can't imagine how refreshing it was to have a couple days without you butting into my life."

That stung. Nick slapped their hundred-dollar oriental dinner on the kitchen table. From the moment Jason was born Nick had looked out for his little brother and bailed him out of scrapes. And this was his thanks.

"Your family's worried about you," Annie said from the doorway.

Nick dropped the bag of food and hurriedly turned around so he could gauge Jason's reaction.

"You must be the Reverend Annie who called me today." Jason offered his hand as if she were meeting him for a scheduled appointment at the auction house. "I'm pleased to meet you."

She accepted his hand and stepped inside the apartment. "But not very eager to make my acquaintance, apparently."

He turned on that charming "aw shucks, don't hold it against me" smile that earned him his college diploma. "I was hoping to sort some things out in my mind first. I had a devil of a time making the connection between you and your sister. I don't know why. It seems so obvious now."

"What sister?" Nick demanded.

Annie stood frozen, her face the same sickly shade of green as her turtleneck. "I came to visit you because I was concerned for your life, but I can see I've been conned."

She'd been conned? Nick felt defrauded by both of them, and he still couldn't get a firm handle on the situation.

Jason covered Annie's hand with both of his. "Nick's been unreasonably harsh, hasn't he? All I wanted was a couple days to recover from a minor car mishap without advertising this garish bruise on my cheekbone."

Nick stomped between Jason and Annie, severing Jason's hold on her. "Don't you dare pass this off as a joke. Mom's been worried sick about you."

"I'm sorry about Mom. I had an idea for getting her back the life she lost. I needed to work on it for a couple days before I could present it to anyone."

It was Nick's duty and his dream to give his mother back the life she had before she chose Nick and his father over her Hollywood life. His spoiled little brother's help, although well meaning, was only likely to screw up everyone's dreams. "I went inside a church for you, Jason."

The significance of the sacrifice was lost on the self-absorbed twerp. "Obviously it's going to take a couple more trips for you to work out all that bitterness. Nick, if you'll excuse us, I need to speak with Reverend Annie alone."

"I'm not excusing anybody. If you've got something to say, I can hear it." As Jason's personal attorney and the retained counsel for the auction house, he needed to be included in any conversation. Stolen merchandise was involved, not to mention Jason's unprofessional behavior inside his place of business.

"I'd love to talk to you alone, Jason," Annie volunteered. Her coloring had almost returned to normal.

Nick couldn't believe her gall. "You're here under my direction."

"Exactly. I came here to minister to Jason. With your threats hanging over my head, I can't risk failing my mission."

"Help yourself to dinner before it gets cold." Jason nudged him toward the kitchen. "And try not to be jealous that I'm going for a repeat while you got nothing for your efforts."

Nick watched Annie walk arm-in-arm with Jason to the back of the apartment. Memories of her sweet kiss enveloped him. A repeat was just what his mouth craved, but he wouldn't tangle with a hypocrite minister harboring secrets. He'd learned long ago they used love to control and then destroy.

"Hey Egghead, what's this? Study all day and work all night? No wonder you never get laid." Troy let out an obnoxious laugh.

Heather looked at Egan Dowers—Egghead Egan—standing behind the Subway counter. He had a great big zit on his nose.

"Troy, I thought you spent all your time getting laid and

breaking the law. I had no idea you had time to eat," Egan muttered.

Heather bit her cheek to stop a laugh.

"Huh?" Troy said.

"White or wheat bread?" Egan asked clearly. He started Troy's sandwich and then turned to her. "What about you, Heather?"

He knew her name. That startled her. She wouldn't have known his, except everyone in school knew, thanks to an unfortunate egg incident their freshman year. Troy most likely was one of the guys who pelted him. "I'll have the six-inch turkey sub." She deliberately picked one of the subs advertised with the phrase "under six grams of fat." She looked at their specialty breads. "On whichever of these is the least popular."

He raised an eyebrow. Geez, he had zits there, too. "Least?"

"That's what I said, Egghead."

Something flashed in his eyes, resentment or disappointment maybe, before he ducked his head. He finished making their sandwiches without making eye contact. What a total dweeb. He knew her name but didn't bother to check out her chest. "Total is nine-ninety-three," he said, pushing the buttons on the cash register.

"Hey, lookie here." Troy peered into the Subway cup next to the register. The word *tips* was printed in block letters on the side.

"That's to put money in," Egan said tightly as Troy began pulling out the bills.

Heather shifted, suddenly uncomfortable. It was one thing to make fun of the nerd. It was another to take what he'd earned. At least the dweeb had a job, unlike her and Troy.

"What do you need money for? College?" Troy sneered. "You don't have a date to spend it on."

"It's rent money." Egan reached for the cup, but Troy

dumped it on the counter and covered the money with his hand.

Rent money. Oh, no. "Come on, Troy." Heather cupped his butt with her hand, trying to distract him from acting like a complete jerk. "You told me you had money for dinner."

"Why should I spend mine when I can use his?" He rifled through the bills. "Three, four, five."

"I'm amazed." Egan did a sneer of his own. "I had no idea you could count."

Troy shoved the money at him. "There's enough here to cover it all." He reached for the drink cups and bag of sandwiches.

Egan placed his hand on the bag. Heather hoped he'd tell Troy to get his own money or go to jail. Instead, he said, "You're three cents short."

Troy glanced around and found the give-a-penny-take-a-penny tray with four cents in it. "Here. Your service stinks, but I'll still give you a tip." He shoved three coins toward Egan and flipped the last into the tip cup. He grabbed the sandwiches and turned away.

Egan's gaze met Heather's, and she wished she had some money to pay him back. But her dad hadn't been home for her to hit him up before she left. Now she was sure Egan was looking at her in disappointment. She was the first to glance away.

"Come on, babe." Troy handed her one of the drinks and shoved his hand in her back pocket as he turned her toward the exit.

Troy squeezed her butt, but she couldn't stop herself from looking back at Egan as they walked out the door. He was still standing at the cash register staring at them. Heather felt sick to her stomach.

Even though she'd woken up late and skipped breakfast and then skipped lunch to make out behind the school with Lenny Gibbs, she ended up throwing her sandwich in the garbage in the park. She couldn't even look at it.

Cuddling with Troy didn't help. He wrapped his arms around her, outside his truck, in one of those hugs she usually craved. Tonight she only felt lonelier.

"Come on, babe. I know what'll make you feel better." He sat in the front of the truck and tilted the seat back as far as it would go—a whole two inches.

She stared while he unzipped his jeans. He reached for her waist, and she took a step back. "Where's the condom?"

"Man, do I have to think of everything?" He wiggled his jeans some more and pulled out his wallet. He ripped the snap off her jeans and tried to squeeze his hand inside, but the fabric was too tight without releasing the zipper. "What's the matter with you? You could help a little."

She didn't want to. She didn't want to straddle Troy and have the steering wheel dig into her back and pretend like she was having the best sex of her life when all she wanted was for someone to love her. For all the sex she'd had, she'd never made love. She was a virgin after all. She laughed grimly. Yeah right.

She watched Troy flip through his wallet. No condoms. He slid his hand under her shirt. She pushed his hand away and stepped out of reach. "I'm not getting on you without a condom."

"I didn't have one last week, and you didn't care."

She didn't care because she wanted a baby, but she didn't want a man who stole rent money to be the father of her child. Her stomach turned again. "Well, I care now."

He opened the glove compartment and fished through it. Heather turned to walk away.

"Hey, I got one," Troy shouted.

She glanced over her shoulder at the dirty packet. "No thanks. I changed my mind." Her armpits started sweating. She'd never refused a guy before.

He started swearing and calling her names. Then he got out of the truck and started toward her. Panic hurtled her into a run. She looked over her shoulder once. Troy stood by the truck trying to pull up the zipper on his jeans.

Heather ran all the way home. She ran past her mother, sleeping with her mouth open in front of some dumb TV show, and slammed her bedroom door. She flopped on her bed, hugged her bedraggled teddy bear to her face and sobbed.

Annie stood patiently behind the closed door of Jason's den trying to decide if the face he had shown her in the front of the apartment reflected his feelings or was a mask for them. He fiddled with the knob on the radio, turning the rock music to an earsplitting level. "So Nick can't listen in," he whispered loudly in her ear.

"Why don't you tell me what happened?" Then maybe she could figure out if Nick's concerns had a basis, or if she'd just wasted her time and exposed her Tanya connections for nothing.

"Some woman took me for the most wild ride of my life." Jason grinned without apology. "So I was driving home trying to decide if I was euphoric because hey, I'd just had the best sex of my life. Or if I was bummed because the sex was so good she'd probably ruined me for any other woman. Or if I was really bummed because she'd used me to steal something that was going to cause me a lot of flack and bad press for the auction house. But I couldn't get too worked up about being used because the sex was really good."

"I'm sensing a pattern here," Annie muttered. "I hope I don't have to tell you there's more to life and women than sex."

"I suppose as a minister you're obligated to say that. I suppose Nick told you his dad was a minister."

"Nick's father?" Annie couldn't conceal her surprise. If

someone's second cousin's brother-in-law was a preacher, she usually learned of it in the first five minutes. But Nick hadn't said a word.

"Oh, yeah. He messed Nick up plenty. He carries it around in a bottle, and he sees his father reflected in every person of the cloth."

Ah, now she understood. But the warning came too late. Nick had touched her. The more she learned about him the less she was able to turn away. With this morning's kiss, he'd branded her. She was still reeling, trying to grapple with the ramifications. She might not have looked different, but inside she was changed. Awakened. She'd spent years denying the existence of her own needs, let alone allowing them to be filled. They wouldn't return to obscurity without a battle. "Ministers are human, no matter how much we try to transcend. If you're looking for fault, you'll find it."

"Nick will look, and he will judge. Anyway, I digress. I was driving along trying to figure out why someone would use sex to steal some junk that was buried in with Zeke Britman's music mementos. And suddenly I knew. The only woman other than my mother who knew they were there was Britman's wife. And the only way she knows how to get anything from anyone is to use sex."

"This is the moment of epiphany where you drove your car into a lake?"

"Exactly. As soon as I could, I rushed home and queued up all the internet pictures of her I could find. She might not have used the Tanya name, but I certainly had my hands on the Tanya body."

"And you couldn't have bothered to shoot your family an e-mail that you weren't trying to kill yourself. You were just ogling naked women on the internet." Did this guy realize how spoiled and shallow he sounded?

"I know they were concerned because I was acting out of character, but I don't think they were really worried."

"I am so close to beaning you over the head for your insensitivity."

"Now that's a Christian approach." Jason laughed.

The *what-would-Jesus-do?* mentality was generally second nature to her, but she was having a hard time considering those options. "Your family thought you were going to kill yourself."

"Nah," Jason scoffed. "Nick's just trying to get a leg up on me. Are you sure he hasn't figured you out and that's why he dragged you into this?"

She immediately knew Jason was referring to the sister connection. It was the reason she'd risked Nick's wrath and agreed to speak to Jason alone. "He's still accusing me of seducing you and stealing jewelry. What kind of one-upmanship are you two playing?"

"What do you know about Gloria Glenbard?"

"The name sounds familiar, but—" Annie drew a blank.

"The classic film star of the forties, fifties, and sixties. She died in a car accident thirty years ago."

The name finally clicked, and Annie couldn't help but smile. "I think she's in every one of my favorite movies."

Jason returned her smile, but it didn't jolt heat through her system. No flash of awareness hit her like when she and Nick shared a moment of harmony. "She was my grandmother, my mother's mother. She disowned my mother when she married Nick's father, who was preaching the evils of the Hollywood life. I think it took about five minutes for Mom to regret her decision."

Nick's earlier comment on the importance of Hollywood connections suddenly made sense in the context of his past. "If your grandmother's dead, you're not going to connect with her, no matter how many celebrities you know."

"Mom had friends and her mother's friends are still living. To this day, none of them will acknowledge her existence. She sees herself as a black mark on her mother's legacy, and she wants to change that."

"So she's easing back into that society through the auction house," Annie guessed.

Jason snorted. "We're nothing but hired help to those people. No. I've always wanted to write biographies of the stars. I have a manuscript of my grandmother completely written, but I can't get an agent to take me on because I never met the woman. Tanya's going to be my big break. Let's face it. I've had access to her that not every man gets."

"I think you should tell your mother and Nick everything you just told me." And she would drive back to Maplefield and go on with her life and her church.

"I want to surprise Mom with this big present. I need to show her I'm worthy of all the privileges I've been given. I'm more than an amusing kid to pat on the head. Nick treats me even worse. I'm still his screwed-up kid brother. He's Mr. Perfect. All he thinks about is going after his own celebrity clients."

"No offense to Nick's profession, but what kind of celebrity aspirations does a handyman have?"

"Handyman? Nick?" Jason laughed wildly. "He's not a handyman. He's a lawyer, very successful. He's actively pursuing any prominent clients with celebrity connections that'll make him the lawyer for Hollywood's elite."

Annie groped for the edge of a chair. She was a steppingstone for Nick to get to Tanya. She'd removed herself from Jesus's arms for the crumbs Nick offered. And left her reputation vulnerable and exposed.

Chapter 5

"What's going on?" Nick leaned against the wall on the opposite side of the hall as Annie walked out of her private conference with Jason.

Despite telling herself not to, she glanced at him. Her ears rang in the silence now that the radio was off. Her head still throbbed from the beat of the bass. She thought she'd braced herself to see Nick. Yet, the pain of his betrayal slammed through her. She'd seen what she wanted to see—a handyman kissing her because he liked her. And she fell for it. She blamed herself more than him.

"Jason's doing fine," she said in her professional reassuring voice. "He's a little selfish not to think anyone would worry about him, but he knows what he wants. I suspect he has a good chance of getting it."

Nick pushed himself away from the wall. "Then why has he been holed up in here?"

"That's for him to tell you." She started walking for the front door.

"This is the first time he's met you?" Nick's footsteps shadowed her.

"Yes." She gritted her teeth. He couldn't take her innocence for granted. Not only did she live a calling he despised, she also had a promiscuous, famous sister. She wasn't foolish enough or innocent enough to believe he only wanted Tanya as a client.

"Where are you going?" He caught her arm and spun her

around to face him.

"Back to Maplefield." She couldn't stand another minute with Nick pretending to like her to get to her sister. "I'm glad Jason's situation ended so well."

"Will I see you again?" His eyes burned into her, but she couldn't discern what need of his had prompted the question.

Anyway, it didn't matter. Her heart couldn't handle the emotions and the hurt he torpedoed at her. She cleared her throat. "Actually, if you recover the jewelry, I'd like an opportunity to bid on it. Even if I can't afford the asking price, I'd like to know who buys it. I'll pray for Jason and for your whole family."

"I don't need your prayers."

Against her saner judgment, Annie paused one final time to drink in the sight of Nick. This handsome, magnetic man had stripped away her asexual armor and uncovered a woman's pulse. She wouldn't forget him. "What do you need, Nick?"

"This." He slammed his mouth against hers.

She hadn't expected it. Hadn't prepared herself. Shock came first, stiffening her body. The sensual assault spun her very female pulse into overdrive. Her brain shrieked her sister's name in warning. A very detached practical side of her commanded she relax her body and enjoy what he was doing physically, knowing it wouldn't happen again. But she couldn't respond. The only reason he was touching her was because of her sister. Why, oh why, couldn't he be a simple handyman?

Abruptly, he pulled back.

She tried to collect herself and form a coherent, witty sentence to show how unaffected she was. "Well, then, it appears you're satisfied," came out as her pitiful attempt.

"Not by a long shot." He glared at her.

She walked out the door and hurried to put distance between them before she gave in to the temptation to throw herself at him. Not for his satisfaction but to satisfy her own burning needs, which had been nothing more than cold ash since her one-and-only boyfriend dumped her for the invitation to sleep with her sister.

Tanya wore black Dolce & Gabbana. People sneaking around at night always wore black; at least that's what they wore in the movies she starred in. Unfortunately, her wardrobe wasn't made for sneaking. Her version of the little black dress shimmered, plunged low into her cleavage and even lower in the back. Although it was ankle length, the skirt was mostly sheer except for some strategic beading and slit almost to her waist.

She could move easily in her custom Michelle K. stilettos as long as she didn't have to run. She refused to reminisce about her failure last time. It wouldn't happen again. Not one tabloid had gotten a shot of her torn clothes and bruised chin. Today she'd do her sleuth work the Hollywood way—without breaking a nail or into a sweat.

She made her entrance later than fashionably late, but it didn't stop everyone from assuming she was the party's hostess. She and Zeke might be in the middle of a divorce and no longer living together, but she was the one everyone felt compelled to compliment on the quality of the champagne and canapés. Of course, Zeke was likely stoned out of his mind and in no shape to see to his own needs, let alone those of his guests.

Oliver Gilmer, the director she'd worked with in *Black River*, grabbed her butt and pulled her a lot closer to him than she wanted to stand.

"Well, Oliver, you're certainly feeling friendly tonight." A lot friendlier than when he told her the movie flopped because her acting stunk. As if his lousy direction and the cheesy screenplay had nothing to do with it. The masses bought tickets to ogle her body, not to admire her acting skill. And she'd long since perfected her body as a showcase.

Oliver took advantage of their proximity to look down her top while he chugged his whiskey. "I think we missed this camera angle in the movie."

Body as a showcase, body as a showcase, she mentally chanted. Oliver burped as he continued to leer at her. When had she become so disenchanted with the life she'd made for herself? She knew exactly. When Officer Hardball made his mission in life to make her pay for her crimes in ways far worse than jail time.

"Camera angles are your oversight. Would you like me to get you a little something?" She made herself grind her hips suggestively against his, as if the action could banish the perennially irritated cop whose only good quality was a really tight butt.

"Oh, yeah." Oliver was instantly hard.

She snatched the empty tumbler from his hand. "Then I'll be right back with a refill for you."

"I was referring to—"

"I'm hardly interested in your 'little something,' Oliver." She spoke loud enough for the surrounding couples to overhear and sashayed away amid their snickers. She snagged a glass of white wine from a roving waiter and ordered him to fetch Oliver's refill. Holding her wine, she canvassed the room. She had no intention of drinking a drop. Nothing would jeopardize tonight's mission, but she understood the value of props.

The drink cemented her party image. It could also be used in a number of interesting ways when she was tired of a man making moves on her. The most effective and most subtle was to hand the overeager sop her drink, replacing the empty one in his hand as she worked the room. She did so four times in the next two hours before she decided the guests were sloshed enough that no one would notice her absence.

She set her wine glass on a table littered with empty glasses and overflowing ashtrays. Time for a stroll down the hall to the bathroom. Zeke's drummer was coming out. He didn't notice her immediately, and she was able to sidestep his groping hands as she shut herself in the john.

Back down the hall she hurried to the secondary staircase. Her shoes slowed her progress, but they were vital to her mission. Footsteps sounded as she rounded the top of the stairs. Quickly, she slipped behind the door of the closest bedroom. Too late she realized it was occupied. An A-list actress—rumored to have one of the most solid marriages in town—was going at it with the current male heartthrob of the teen crowd. Apparently, everyone hadn't gotten the Ashton Kutcher thing out of their system.

While the couple worked out on the oversized bed oblivious to her presence, Tanya scoped out her competition. The other woman hadn't just been nominated for an Oscar last year. She'd won. Even from this distance, the cellulite on her thighs was visible. Not that the nineteen-year-old stud-of-the-month was complaining.

Tanya peeked out the door, found the hall empty, and made her move again. Before she'd gone six feet, she heard drunken voices and ducked into a second bedroom that appeared to be empty. Too late she heard someone retching in the adjacent bathroom. She slipped out of the room and ran all the way to Zeke's massive suite.

A quick glance assured her that his room and bed were empty this time. She was going to do it. She was really going to get the tape and get out without being caught. Officer Hardball would be happy. Zeke would be in jail. And Tanya would get her career back on track and finally win that Oscar.

She opened the closet door and closed it behind her. The light flipped on before she reached the switch. "Zeke," she screamed.

"Hey babe, I knew you'd be back."

Drat, she thought she was clever. If her behavior was predictable, why hadn't Hardball warned her? That was easy. Because the cop didn't care what happened to her personally. "My bracelet broke when I was in here before. It was silver, with my initials in embedded in diamonds. Have you seen it?"

"Haven't looked. Why don't you get on your hands and knees and start?"

Not in this lifetime. She needed to look in the safe. The tape had been there before, and it wasn't in Chicago with his music demos. Although Zeke could have noticed—no, it had to be there. She'd listened to all of Zeke's music. He wasn't observant or creative.

His hand smacked across her face, sending her reeling. "That wasn't a request."

She flung her arms out for balance. Cut her losses for sure. She turned for the door. "I'll look for the bracelet another time."

"Oh, no." He slipped his hand inside her dress and squeezed her bare thigh. "You haven't done your wifely duty in months."

She ignored the forming bruise and didn't back away. Showing fear would give Zeke an edge she couldn't afford to lose. "My wifely duty was to boost your album sales, and I've held up my end."

Zeke laughed. "You haven't done anything for my band. It's high time you started."

"I allowed myself to be the subject of your 'viper vendetta' sessions. I worked overtime to promote your albums."

"Really? I thought you were promoting yourself."

"That was the goal of our marriage, to do both at once."

Zeke shoved her back against the wall, knocking her head in the same spot that still throbbed from earlier.

Tanya lifted her foot and slammed it down on his instep. He cursed and pushed her forward. She sprawled on the floor of the closet and immediately tried to scramble to her feet. She made it to her knees before Zeke was there.

"I listened to the tape you made before I burned it. Thinking you would betray my trust and our marriage breaks my heart."

"The thought of losing your drug supply breaks your heart," she shot back. "Hurting me won't help. They'll still find you and stop you."

"The least you can do is offer me a little TLC right now."

Panic truly began to set in. Tender, loving, and caring meant exactly the opposite coming from Zeke. "Let me go."

"Or what? You'll call a press conference. Everyone in the world is going to believe you had it coming."

Tanya, the master at controlling and manipulating men, was at the mercy of a man who had none. Just like when she was fourteen, she had to endure this torture to move her life forward. She hadn't been a good wife, but she didn't deserve this agony. She wished she'd taken the drug possession charges and gone to jail. She wished she'd never left Kansas. She wished she hadn't been her parents' favorite.

She couldn't go back. Her career was all that mattered. Not even Zeke would set her back. She had two modeling gigs next week. *War Liaisons* and *Heart of a Mobster* both wanted her for their female lead for filming in the spring. Smooth-As-Silk skin cream line was begging her to renew her contract as their spokeswoman. As soon as Zeke's debts were resolved, the divorce would be final. Her career would return to the A-list fast track. She would be in control of her body and her future.

But for the moment she was under someone else's mercy for both, and he had no mercy.

"I didn't expect you to actually answer the phone, Nick."

"But that didn't stop you from calling." Nick leaned back in his desk chair. He preferred the solitude of the deserted office.

He'd drafted two contracts and reinforced a wobbly shelf in the last two hours.

"I'm up because the baby's up and Chuck's out of town again." Holly paused, as if what? He was going to invite himself over to play house? "So anyway, I'm getting some work done while I work on my sleep deprivation. What's your excuse? It's Saturday night. Nope, wait, Sunday morning now."

"Wild office party. I'm having too much fun to leave."

"You're sitting there all alone, aren't you? You know, why don't you come over? Just to keep each other company. I'm not coming on to you."

"Forget it." His good humor vanished. She had what she wanted—a lawyer husband. "We're done. Why did you call?"

"Britman wants to move up the auction date to Monday."

"That doesn't give you much time to cultivate buyers."

"There's more. By Monday night he wants the proceeds. He wants us to guarantee him a million in cash that night regardless of how the sale goes."

Contract changes. Unusual ones. The thought of all the revisions made Nick's head throb. "Vonkall Auction House does timely wire transfers. We don't deal in cash. We're not a frigging pawn shop."

"Sure we are," Holly said cheerfully. "Just a high-class one. I told Britman I'd consult with legal, which is why I'm calling you."

In the middle of the night. Nick resisted pointing it out. She'd likely expected him to be here and pick up the phone. And he'd been annoyingly predictable.

"It's not such a bad deal," Holly continued. "After we hit the million mark, he'll split the rest with us even-fifty as long as he gets everything he's owed immediately."

A million dollars. In cash. Pronto.

Something was happening on the wrong side of the law. Nick

considered the possibilities. Loan sharks? Maybe. It was no secret Britman was holding the auction because he was in debt and couldn't touch his wife's earnings. That much cash was usually followed by an out-of-the-country trip, preferably to a place that frowned on extradition.

Nick felt the first tingling of excitement. He would convince Britman to stay put while he worked through the legal channels. He would resolve everything legally, and the spotlight on Britman would once again focus on his award-winning music—and brilliant counsel. This was Nick's break, his opening into the world of celebrities. "I need to speak with Britman directly."

"You're welcome to him," Holly said. The baby started crying in the background. "This is the first time I talked to him directly. The guy gives me the creeps. I gotta go. Bye." She hung up.

Nick took much longer to set down the receiver. He needed to connect with his celebrity ticket. His father, who was so proud when he'd become a lawyer, would hate the turn Nick's career was taking. Thumbing his nose at his dad was just a side benefit to making his mother's dream come true. He owed it to her to sacrifice what he really wanted to give her the chance. It was what she'd done for him.

But Nick couldn't make his fingers dial those crucial eleven digits. He wasn't as selfless as his mother. Or even as Reverend Annie pretended to be. She tasted like a dream and even believed he was a handyman. His pulse pounded, and his hands trembled with the memory. He clenched them into fists. He had worked too hard for his success to turn his back on it over one little kiss. He wouldn't forget where he came from any more than he'd forget who she was.

Tanya returned to awareness through a long, dark tunnel. She kept herself absolutely still, with her eyes closed, and worked on orienting herself. Something was terribly wrong. She thought slowly, trying not to disturb a headache. The party. The closet. Zeke. Not remembering was better, but the terrifying images were imbedded in her brain.

She pried her eyes open. She was still in the closet, her cheek pressed into the white carpet. The light was on. With the carefulness of the elderly, she turned her head and looked over her shoulder. She was alone. Blessedly alone. It was safe for her to sit up. Pain exploded with the attempt, and she kept herself still.

She uncurled her fingers. One nail tip stayed gouged in her palm. So much for not breaking a nail. At least that wound was self-inflicted. Her throat felt raw. She'd give up her entire Gucci collection for a glass of water. Screams echoed in her head until she opened her mouth to let them out. She clamped her hand across her mouth before a sound escaped. She did not want anyone to find her for a repeat performance.

The arm motion from moving her hand resulted in bitter complaints from her elbow and shoulder. Gritting her teeth, Tanya struggled into a sitting position. Every muscle protested.

Her dress was torn down the center. A large bruise bloomed on her left breast. She averted her eyes. A shower, she needed a shower.

Her gaze lit on her right shoe. By some miracle, it was still on her foot, although the heel had broken off. She had not gone through all this for nothing. So Zeke had caught her. She'd still reached the first step, alone in the closet.

A moan of pain escaped her lips as she reached for her shoe, but she remained intent on her goal. After easing it off her foot, she fumbled with the underside of the top leather that covered her toes. The fabric gave way as she tore, and the key fell into her hands. The secret, custom compartment had paid off.

She crawled across the closet, pushed aside Zeke's clothes,

and fit the key in the safe. She turned it and breathed a sigh when it gave way. Life was getting better. *Heart of a Mobster* was a meatier, more emotional role. She'd tell her agent to accept that one.

Now the combination. She held her breath, hoping Zeke had kept the date the same—his birthday. The safe beeped its denial. Her birthday, their anniversary. She discarded them both. He probably didn't remember them. The date his band was formed. The denial beep chided her again, either because he hadn't used it or she'd gotten the month wrong. Now she had only one more chance to get it right before the safe locked her out permanently and set off the security alarm.

Then she knew. The date of his first drug bust. She had been furious, but it had been a source of pride for Zeke. As if he'd finally been initiated into some sort of secret club. She should have bailed on their marriage then. Instead she'd wasted nearly a year and endured—

No, the World's Sexiest Viper was a woman of power and action, not quiet endurance.

She punched in the numbers, and the lock relented. She refused to give in to tears of relief. The door creaked as it opened. The three-foot-cubed space was empty. Now the tears leaked onto her lashes. She pressed the heels of her hands to her eyes to stem the flow. Zeke told her he knew she made the tape and he'd burned it. And yet she expected to find the evidence against him wrapped like a present for her to take to the cops. Or the entire safe filled with cocaine. There wasn't so much as a powdered residue on the floor.

Her shoulders sagged. It didn't matter what she'd gone through to help the cops make their case. Officer Hardball would only see that she'd failed again. She should have listened to her lawyers and paid them to get her off the hook. Instead, she'd fired them to do things Hardball's way, thinking that would help her career. She was paid to look sexy, not to think.

Clutching her tattered dress to her chest, she pushed the closet door open. Zeke was lying face down on the bed, snoring loudly. He kept a gun under the mattress. Just in case, he'd always said. With his penchant for violence, knowledge of the weapon added a hint of danger. She no longer found it the least exciting.

Pure hatred coursed through her, and her fingers itched for the gun. How she longed to put a bullet in his wasted brain. If she was going to jail, she'd go for a reason, not because Zeke had stashed coke in her purse.

She reached under the mattress, wincing as Zeke shifted. She had to knock him off before he woke up. If he wrestled the gun from her and shot her—well, she'd prefer it to the physical assault from last night. But the tabloids would portray her as weak, vulnerable, and a victim. She couldn't imagine a worse legacy for herself.

The gun wasn't there. She pushed her arm in up to her elbow. There was nothing. She moved her hand to the side and touched something. Paper. Sheets of paper were under here. She couldn't imagine what they would contain, but they must have some significance if he'd taken the care to hide them. She yanked the pages out and searched for more.

Zeke's arm flopped over, smacking her face. She jumped back, stifling a scream. His eyes fluttered. This would have to be enough. Clutching the mess of papers in her fists, she tiptoed out of the room and into the hall. Someone had fallen into a drunken stupor at the top of the stairs. The party seemed like a lifetime ago. She stepped over him and hurried down. More people were sprawled out, all as oblivious to her presence now as they were to what had happened to her in the night.

Never before had the celebrity life disgusted her. Had she worked so hard and sacrificed so much for this? Daylight was beginning to brighten the eastern sky as she slipped out a side door. She glanced toward the driveway, but that path to the street was too exposed. She couldn't believe she'd left the house without trying to fix her appearance. Getting away wasn't that critical.

She couldn't make herself go back inside. The bushes behind the house would provide some cover. A flash of light blinded her after she took three steps. She raised her hand to protect her eyes. More flashes. Too late, their significance registered. Paparazzi.

They were snapping pictures of her looking her worst. She turned and ran down the driveway, no longer caring about the potential exposure. It was the quickest escape route. No more bright lights stung her eyes, but she didn't dare look back.

By the time she reached the end of the driveway, her feet were as bruised and bloody as the rest of her. She scanned the street for a cab, a limo, anything to get her home. Traffic was nonexistent this morning. Only a few cars were parked along the curb. She had no skills for starting a car without a key, although she was fairly certain she'd done so in a movie.

A vehicle moved from behind the other parked cars. She prepared herself to run again before she realized it was a cop car. And almost wept with relief.

"Reverend Annie."

Seated behind her church desk, she looked up at the chairman of the church council. Talking to him would get her hormones under control and her concentration in line before this morning's sermon. "John, you're here early this morning. Is there a problem?"

"Quite honestly, I'm a bit disturbed."

She frowned. John Patterson was steady. Usually, she could see a crisis brewing, but she'd missed this one.

"I've heard some rumors. They don't reflect well on our church."

This wasn't about John. This was about her. The kisses. Could he have found out about them? Her guilt was likely tattooed on her forehead. Or her connection to Tanya finally surfaced. She'd always known it was only a matter of time before someone figured it out or Tanya herself made the announcement. "What sort of rumors?"

"My wife tells me you were discovered in a, um, compromising position."

Kathy ought to know. She'd done the "discovering," Annie thought bitterly.

"Apparently, you were partially undressed in the company of a vagrant at your home Thursday night."

Annie took several seconds to process that the so-called vagrant was Nick, a successful lawyer looking to seduce the sister of a celebrity. She folded her hands on the desktop. "I found a man in my house while I was in the process of undressing. The situation was quickly resolved."

John looked alarmed. "Did you call the police?"

"There was no need. He left on his own." Even knowing Nick's intentions, a tiny, carnal part of her wished he'd stayed that night and seduced her. But she'd traveled that road before and was wiser this time.

"What was he doing there? I think we should notify the authorities before he breaks into anyone else's home."

And make everyone aware of Nick's motive for tracking her down. No thank you. "John, it's not necessary. He's not going to break in anywhere else. He left town." Nick didn't love her. Giving him her body wouldn't change the fact. Only God's love was constant. Only God loved her. And taking worldly pleasure in Nick meant turning her back on God, even if only temporarily. God had given purpose to her life. She wouldn't disappoint Him.

"There's no harm in being extra cautious. Do you know this man?"

She resisted the urge to fidget with a pencil. "I've spoken with him several times since the incident. There's no need for alarm and no cause to believe he would harm anyone."

John was silent for a moment. Finally, he said, "This man is the reason you were out of town all day and most of the night on Friday."

The insinuation made Annie cringe. Even without the connection to her sister, her reputation was sliding onto shaky ground. "As a matter of fact, the man—Nick McAllister—was concerned his brother was suicidal. I went to visit him in Chicago and provide comfort to the family." She went for the truth to prove she had nothing to hide—except two kisses that were nothing short of miraculous.

"I told you Reverend Annie had a good reason for taking emergency personal time," Myra said to John as she entered the office. "She understands her duty to reach out to others."

"Yes." John kept his gaze on Annie, and she knew his concerns about her behavior were now greater than when he'd first approached her. "Just be careful what you grab hold of when you do reach out."

"I'm going to have to grab hold of my roof to keep it in place with the rain and snow that's forecasted for next week," Myra said, walking to the middle of the office and mercifully changing the focus of the conversation.

"The youth group is planning to take it up as a service project next Saturday," Annie said. "If the weather cooperates, we'll have it done by Thanksgiving."

"But this week's forecast—"

"I looked at the building yesterday, Myra," John said. "A couple drips may work their way inside, but nothing serious.

The building and food can wait that long for the repairs." He patted her arm. "I'm going to check on the leaky toilet before everyone starts arriving."

Annie took a deep breath, aware she was about to swing back to the topic she wanted to avoid. "No need, John. Nick already fixed it."

"Then I'll look at the light switch in the sanctuary."

"Nick fixed that, too."

He gave her a long look. "Then I'll make sure he did it right." He walked out the door.

Annie took a sip of coffee, long since cold, and looked down at her sermon notes. Putting God first and dedicating your life to His service had seemed like a fitting topic for her five-year anniversary as pastor and a good segue into the potluck lunch commemorating the occasion. But the words were written by a fraud. God had been little more than an afterthought on her ill-advised trip across the state.

"So it's true? You have a love interest?" Myra asked.

Annie choked on her coffee. "Nothing could be further from the truth."

"Now Reverend Annie, it's nothing to be ashamed of. You're a good-looking young woman with blood in your veins. Why shouldn't you have a man in your bed?"

"I'm a woman of God," she whispered through clenched teeth. The office door was open, and her congregation was beginning to gather for the morning service.

"Just because He put the blood in your veins doesn't mean He can make it boil."

Annie nearly nodded in agreement before she caught herself.

"Acknowledging your human needs does not create a crisis of faith. Ignoring their presence can cause you and your faith to shrivel and turn bitter."

"Myra, your experience isn't—"

She jabbed a finger at Annie and kept talking. "I was widowed and celibate for twenty years before I realized the shell of an existence I was living. You've only got one life—"

"Earthly sacrifice is worth the heavenly reward," Annie said stiffly.

"Now you sound like Kathy Patterson, who, by the way, started these rumors. Why can't you have heaven on earth? You tell us every Sunday how generous God is. I'd think He'd be extra generous to those who give their lives in service to Him."

Annie rose from her seat. "There's nothing to the rumors, Myra. Please don't feed the gossip by adding your opinion of my sex life."

Myra harrumphed. "You don't have a sex life."

"I'm glad somebody realizes that fact." She picked up her papers and headed out of the office to find her robe for preaching.

"But I'll pray for God to give you one," Myra called after her.

Chapter 6

"You did good, Tanya. I know this wasn't easy for you." For the first time in all their meetings, the cop looked sympathetic.

Tanya tugged at the blanket around her shoulders and looked away. She wanted him back in Hardball mode. At least then she could meet him on equal footing. "Did I get anything worthwhile?"

"Yes."

She couldn't believe anything had gone right. She expected to be locked in a cell and charged with indecent exposure at the very least. Instead, they offered medical treatment, gave a blanket and a cup of coffee, and treated her like a victim. She hated the last part more than anything. The World's Sexiest Viper was never a victim. She wasn't passive and submissive. This was worse than a misunderstanding of character. The potential to destroy her reputation was enormous.

"I think only one page is missing. Other than that, we have everything we need for warrants and to work toward shutting down his entire operation."

She'd missed a page. She had to go back. She'd kill herself before she allowed a repeat of the past twelve hours. She opened her mouth to plead with Hardball to lock her in a cell instead. The words wouldn't come. Zeke belonged there. She needed to see him put away where he couldn't touch her ever again. She tried to sit straighter without wincing. "What do you want me to do?"

"Nothing."

She blinked. "Nothing?"

"I want you to go to the hospital for medical treatment. They'll do a rape kit so you can press charges against him."

She couldn't meet his eye. "On the case. What do you want me to do?"

He placed his hands on the table and leaned forward. "Nothing. Those papers gave us much more than your tape would have. You're done, off the hook." The former Hardball looked at her with pity dripping from his eyes. "Our sexual assault victim's counselor will be here in a minute to speak with you."

She cringed. She was not a victim. She was Tanya, S-E-X personified. No one would dare assault her.

"She'll help you through filing charges and go with you to the hospital."

"I'm not going to the hospital." People were supposed to ogle her body, but not now, not like this. She hugged the blanket tighter.

Hardball leaned forward but didn't touch her. "I understand this is difficult."

How, Tanya wanted to scream. How could he, how could anyone, understand the stakes and the pressures of her life?

"You need medical attention to help you physically heal," he continued. "You also want to preserve the evidence so we can get the criminal who did this to you."

Although the pain made her want to curl into a ball, Tanya forced herself to stand. "Nothing happened to me. I call the shots when it comes to men. I'm in charge of my sexual encounters."

"This wasn't a sexual encounter," he said gently.

"If you press charges, if this becomes public, I'll say it was consensual. I'll say I instigated it. I'll say I wanted it rough." She wanted gentleness. She wanted a hug.

He stacked his papers without looking at her. His name badge was hidden behind them. If she could have spoken without crying she would have asked his name. He wasn't a Hardball anymore. He was a nice guy who seemed almost capable of giving that hug.

"We won't press charges pertaining to your injuries without your consent. We don't have a case without it." His tone told her that was the only reason he was holding out for her cooperation. "Preserve the evidence now. Then you can make the decision when you're thinking clearly. We can get you into the hospital under a false identity if you're worried about your image."

"I'm not—"

He talked over her lie. "You should also think about blood tests."

"Blood tests?"

"Did your attacker protect you from STDs and pregnancy?"

Tanya dropped back into the chair. Pregnancy wasn't a problem. She'd been on birth control since that first encounter at age fourteen. But sexually transmitted diseases—oh God. There was nothing sexy about a woman with one of those, no matter what she looked like on the outside.

"Miles, did Myra talk you into donating that bread?"

"Oh, uh, Reverend Annie, hi." The man flushed and quickly turned from the group at the table where his family sat. The entire table fell silent.

Annie smiled her polite minister smile. Most people found mingling and making small talk at a potluck dinner nonthreatening, but this was the third time today someone had stammered when she initiated a conversation. "Is everything okay?"

"Yes, of course. Five years. Wow, doesn't seem that long," Miles gushed. "You plan to stick around for five more?"

"I want to, if it's in God's plan."

"Yeah, I guess marriage would change things."

"I don't see why not." She didn't see marriage as part of God's plan for her, but she didn't have to give up her parish if it came her way. "Although I wouldn't expect it in the next five years."

"I thought with that guy, you'd want to—I mean, I didn't think a preacher would just sleep with him and not—"

The entire hall fell silent as Miles stammered and stuttered. The air grew oppressive, choking the optimism and good cheer Annie carried to these events.

"Miles, I don't know what you're talking about." But she did know. The reputation she'd worked so hard to protect was coated in a very bright, permanent stain. "Jesus is the only man in my life. Ministering Good Shepherd Church is my calling."

"I'm getting in line for food before Helen's lasagna is gone," Miles said desperately. "Are you interested?"

Annie glanced around at everyone trying not to look at her. "Food is a great idea." She filled her plate by rote, knowing Miles hadn't set out to damage her relationship with her congregation. Even so, he was obviously uncomfortable with her presence. She made an excuse to eat at a different table, setting her plate down next to Lois Fitzsimmons. "May I?"

Lois blinked in surprise. "Oh, yes, go ahead."

Annie seated herself. "I'm glad you came to church today." Lois used to be the most regular of parishioners. Now she came to church less than once a month. Annie hadn't been able to discern if family problems, loss of faith, or her weight made the outing too difficult. Annie made numerous offers to visit her at home, but Lois had always insisted not to bother. Some people wanted those wishes respected and others secretly craved a visit. Annie always struggled to know when to impose.

Lois glanced around the room. "I wish I could have helped

set this up."

"The ladies miss your help. They'd love for you to come back and join them."

She shook her head and avoided Annie's gaze. "I can't do things like that anymore."

"Why not?"

"That answer's pretty obvious," Heather said snidely as she walked by, taking her plate to another table before Annie could reproach her.

"She's right," Lois said with a sigh. "I'm too fat. I don't have the energy to move around. I just end up embarrassing myself and everyone else."

"As I recall," Annie said gently, "parents are always an embarrassment to teenagers. Don't take Heather's comments personally."

"No, she's right. Stewart feels the same way about me."

Annie covered Lois's hand with her own, pushing down her own feelings about the lacks in Stewart Fitzsimmons. "The important question is how do you feel about yourself?"

Lois pulled her hand free and forked up a large meatball. "You have enough problems of your own without hiding out next to an oversized wallflower."

"If you're unhappy with yourself and your weight, God's not going to change it without your cooperation." And God wasn't going to fix Annie's reputation if she sat back and let people malign it.

Heather hadn't meant to be a jerk to her mom in public. Luckily, Reverend Annie was the only one who heard, so it wasn't a big deal. But Heather still felt bad. Mom was a master at embarrassing herself. She didn't need Heather to make it worse.

She looked around the hall, wishing she hadn't come. She could have had a lunch of chips and cookies at home. Yeah, and put on ten pounds. Her jeans were already too tight to be comfortable. Well, she wasn't going to sit by her mother, herself, or anyone older and geekier than her parents. Which limited her choices to two tables of families with kids. She liked little kids, not that anyone would ever trust her with their kids.

One table was so full the parents were standing and hovering over their children. She headed for the other table, where there were a couple of young families and an empty seat. Just as she arrived, she realized Egan Dowers was seated at the table and he was staring directly at her.

Her steps faltered. Rent money. He'd said the money was for rent, and she let Troy take it. She wasn't just a jerk. She was scum. Again, she was the first one to look away. If she sat here, she'd have to apologize. If she wanted to live with herself, she'd have to apologize.

She squared her shoulders and stepped forward, lowering her plate into the vacant place on the table.

"Seat's taken."

She jerked her gaze back to Egan. "Excuse me?"

His cheeks flushed, but his gaze stayed locked on hers and his voice held authority. "You can't sit there."

"You own the table or something?" In the high school cafeteria only nerds allowed him to sit at their table. He should be grateful she'd chosen his company.

"My sister's sitting there."

She hadn't known he had a sister. Or maybe he was just using it as an excuse. She stood holding her plate and feeling foolish.

"See Egan, I told you I could get my food without spilling," a girl's voice said from behind her.

"Good job." Egan's voice was a lot nicer now. "You can sit there." He pointed to the spot in front of Heather.

The girl studied Heather. She didn't look like Egan, with her curly brown pigtails. But the serious blue eyes were the same. "Are you a friend of my brother's?"

Heather glanced at Egan, but she had no idea what he was thinking. Behind the cash register at Subway he was the nerdy kid who always gave in to bullies. But here, he acted like she was trespassing on his turf. "No, I'm not," she said.

"Why not?"

Heather wished she could be young and innocent like Egan's sister. Life was so much simpler. Her mom was skinny, and she understood Heather. Her dad even had time for her. "Because Egan doesn't like me."

Heather walked away. She was going to dump her plate in the garbage and go outside and then who-knows-where. If no one was hanging out in the town square, maybe she'd go home. Her toenails could use another coat of polish. No one was likely to see them until spring, but at least she'd know they were pretty. She fully intended to have sex before spring, but she never got naked for it. Even if she did, the guys weren't going to notice her feet.

Egan's little sister grabbed her arm and pulled her to the table. "Sit with me."

"There isn't room." Heather didn't look at Egan. She just wanted to get away. Thank God nobody important was witnessing this exchange. She'd be the laughingstock of school tomorrow.

The girl looked around and dragged a chair from a table of old geezers. "Now there is," she announced proudly, sticking Heather at the end of the table between her and Egan.

Heather sat down, peeking at Egan through her lashes. He glared at her, and she wished she'd left when she had the chance. But she couldn't wimp out now, or she'd never be able to look at him again. If people at school found out, they'd make fun of her instead of him.

"I'm Megan," the girl volunteered.

Okay, she liked kids. She could have a conversation with this girl, even if she was Egan's sister. "I'm Heather." She offered her hand in a handshake that she immediately realized was a stupid way to greet a kid.

Megan giggled and shook her hand proudly. "I'm eight. My brother's seventeen."

"Hmm, you're very mature for your age."

She'd meant it as a slam against Egan's maturity, but he muttered, "unlike some people" and turned it on her.

She shoved out her chest to prove just how mature she was. Although the body-hugging aqua sweater was one of her most conservative, Egan's gaze landed on her chest and lifted as far as her neck before dropping back to her boobs. She grinned smugly. "Look all you want. It's as close as you'll ever get."

His gaze snapped to her face and then quickly down to his plate where he concentrated on his food.

"Do you go to school with my brother?" Megan asked.

Oops, she'd forgotten the kid was watching. She didn't mind corrupting high school and college boys. Even the junior high boys could dream, but she wasn't going to corrupt someone's little sister. She'd always wanted a sister. Someone who'd look up to her, imitate her, love her unconditionally. Come to think of it, a sister sounded better than having her own baby. Someone else could change all that poop.

"Good old Maplefield High," Heather wheezed.

"My brother's really smart. He's going to be a doctor."

A doctor, geez. She'd be lucky to graduate from high school, especially since her algebra teacher was a woman with a stick up her butt, not some guy she could flirt with for a free pass. She sent Egan her best sneer. "The only way you'll see a woman naked, huh?"

Reverend Annie's hand settled on her shoulder. "Not around the kids, Heather."

She needed a sassy comeback, but she couldn't think through the hot embarrassment filling her. Embarrassed in front of Egan. She couldn't possibly stoop any lower.

"I'm glad you had some time off work to come by," Annie said to Egan. "Did your mom come, or is she working?"

"She has a big test tomorrow. She's studying really hard," Megan piped up.

Their mother went back to school. Heather couldn't decide if it was cool or just weird. On the other hand, if her mother got off her butt and did anything, it would be an improvement.

"How about you, Egan? Are you finding enough time to study?" Annie asked.

"Yeah." He looked over Heather's head as he spoke. "I should be able to squeeze in a couple hours before I have to work tonight."

A couple hours? She couldn't remember ever concentrating on school for that long outside of class.

"I finished my homework already," Megan chimed in, looking proud. A whole family of goody-two-shoes. "So I'm going to vacuum the living room and wash the dishes."

"What about you, Heather? Afternoon plans?" Annie asked.

"I might paint my toenails."

Egan snorted.

Reverend Annie was silent.

She felt her face growing hot again. Darn it, what was the matter with her? Nothing embarrassed her. But Egan was studying to be a doctor while he worked for—how could she ever forget?—rent money. In one afternoon an eight-year-old did more for her family than Heather helped out in a year.

"Doesn't your family need you for anything?" Megan asked.

Not a thing.

"I assume you'll do the honorable thing and resign."

Annie stared across the parish hall table at the matron Trudy Fitzsimmons, Stewart's austere mother. "Resign because everyone's imagination is working overtime?"

"You are supposed to be a moral beacon to our children and our congregation. Your behavior has been reprehensible."

"Mrs. Fitzsimmons, I don't know what you've heard, but I've done nothing to be ashamed of."

The kisses she shared with Nick seared her brain. No, she wasn't ashamed of them. But she was hardly a moral beacon when her body craved to sample the earthly pleasures he offered.

"Stripping for a man when your union has not been sanctioned by God. With you to offer guidance, it's no wonder my granddaughter has gone astray."

The line between protesting too much and not enough was blurred and subjective. Although she could dismiss Miles's assessment as uninformed, embarrassed ramblings, every word spoken by Trudy was calculated and meant to end her tenure at Good Shepherd. If only Trudy were the softhearted grandmotherly type instead of a sanctimonious prude, Heather might have found the nurturing she so desperately needed.

"I do my best to be an example my congregation can look up to," Annie said stiffly. The oppressive weight pushed on her shoulders, reminding her how many times she'd failed to live up to Jesus's image.

"As I was saying, when your best isn't acceptable, a resignation letter is in order."

"Still got a bug up your butt because you were outvoted on the new carpet for the sanctuary?" Myra asked Trudy, plopping herself down next to her at the table.

Annie stuffed a deviled egg in her mouth to squash the urge to laugh. God bless Myra.

"This has nothing to do with carpet. This pertains to behavior unbecoming of a minister of my church."

Myra patted Trudy's hand. "Well, don't you worry. I have no intention of shepherding this flock, so you're safe from scandal. We already have a pastor with the humble attitude and giving nature of our Savior. Truly God has blessed us with Reverend Annie."

Trudy had no reply to that.

And neither did Annie. Not only did she feel humbled. She also felt like a first-class fraud. She hadn't been a model of Jesus's behavior. Jesus wouldn't have kissed Nick. Jesus would have found a way to help Heather. Jesus wouldn't have turned his back on his own sister. Jesus didn't conform to the church leader's expectations.

She excused herself and moved on to greet other parishioners. No one else was as vocal in their disapproval, but people who normally had no trouble meeting her gaze wouldn't look her in the eye and others who were normally chatty reacted with awkward silences.

Reputations were fragile. Hers was teetering, but she would not allow it to shatter. From now on, she would give her congregation no reason to doubt her purity and dedication to them. She would make sure her lips never touched Nick's again. No, she had to go a step further. She couldn't lay eyes on him again for any reason. God loved her. She would not give Him a reason to turn His back on her.

"Do the words 'common courtesy' mean anything to you?" Nick was so angry at the hoax Jason had perpetrated on him and his mother that he'd stormed out after Annie left Friday evening. But eventually he'd had to return. His mother wanted answers, and Jason had reverted to not answering his phone or the door.

"I told you I was fine. It was your choice to build your own scenario and believe it rather than the truth."

"You drove your Mercedes into Lake Michigan and are alive only because the Coast Guard happened to be in the vicinity and pulled you out before your car filled with water and you drowned."

"It was a simple accident. I didn't have my mind on driving. It could have happened to anyone, at least anyone still in the afterglow of the most amazing sex in the universe."

"Was it Annie?" Nick asked. He didn't believe it, but there was that three percent of doubt he couldn't brush away.

"Dude, I said the most amazing sex in the universe. That woman wouldn't know excitement in the bedroom if she walked in on my fraternity during spring break."

Nick clenched his fists. He pulled back to slug Jason before he caught himself. He was taking the remarks as an insult to Annie when they were the very words he wanted to hear. "Do you know who the woman was?"

"A sex goddess."

"She used you," Nick pointed out.

"Yeah. I hope she comes back and does it again."

"Okay, so you're not concerned about the potential scandal at the auction house?" Nick tread the ground carefully in case Jason was just putting a pretty face on his ordeal. If, on the other hand, his brother was simply being the spoiled son of one of the city's richest families, Nick intended for him to see the consequences of his selfishness.

For the first time Jason looked worried. "I violated the terms of Dad's will, didn't I? Is there any way for me to keep my trust fund?"

With one bad judgment, the first stain marred the Vonkall name and could cost Jason his future in the family business and his hefty inheritance. "There's no scandal," Nick assured him. "Your manager position will wait as long as you need to recover. Your trust fund is secure."

"I hate the auction house. I don't want to run it for another three years just to cash in my inheritance. But I need that money."

Nick thought of Britman's desperation for cash. He'd made numerous calls to the rocker, but none had been returned. "Are you in trouble? I'm a lawyer, remember? I can help you."

"It's not like that. I want to write."

"Okay, then write." Nick had too many important meetings and court filings to prepare for to indulge in his brother's foolish whims. "What does that have to do with running the auction house and needing money?"

Jason closed his eyes. "I knew you wouldn't understand."

"Understand what?" This was why he'd come over here, to understand. But his brother was pushing the bounds of his frustration. "What do you want to write?"

"I want to write biographies—presidents, Hollywood stars, corporate executives. I want it to be my career."

When Jason was six, he thought driving a tow truck was the coolest job in the world. When he was ten, he wanted to be an astronaut. When he discovered women at age thirteen, he wanted to be a gynecologist. "Isn't there a starving artist rite of passage?"

Jason gave him a withering look. "I need to work my way into the parties and levels of society where these people operate. I need to meet them before I can write with their permission and cooperation."

"You don't need five million dollars to get your writing break," Nick said. "And you don't decide hole up and let everyone think you're suicidal when all you're doing is contemplating a career change."

"This isn't just a career change. This is about putting Mom back into the Hollywood circles where she belongs."

That was Nick's goal. Jason couldn't steal it. He didn't have to prove to his mother or anyone that he was worthy of their love. For Jason it was a given. Nick had never been quite good enough.

"Do you have a number where I can reach Reverend Annie?" Jason asked before Nick had recovered from the first bombshell.

"She's not—"

"I know she's not my Reverend Annie. I still want to talk to her."

Nick opened his mouth and then closed it again. She wasn't his Reverend Annie either, but that didn't stop him from wanting to hear her voice. And taste her lips. Unlike two-faced preachers, he was strong enough to resist the temptation.

Tanya pulled the phone away from her ear, ready to push the disconnect button before the answering machine kicked in, when a breathless "hello" sounded.

"Took you long enough." Tanya's greeting came out more caustic than she planned.

"I just came back from a potluck."

A potluck. It sounded so provincial, so innocent. Of all the things she'd done and all the parties she'd attended, she couldn't remember the last time she'd been to a potluck. If she couldn't relate to Annie's life, how could she hope that her sister would relate to hers?

"Who is this?"

Annie didn't even recognize the voice of her own sister. Nobody forgot the World's Sexiest Viper. "It's Tanya."

"Tanya," she repeated, "how are you?" Annie sounded like

she was asking out of obligation than genuine concern. Calling was a bad idea.

"Zeke and I are getting a divorce."

"I heard." Her voice was toneless. "You've been splashed over the tabloid covers for the past nine months."

"You heard your sister was going through a divorce and didn't call to see how she was getting along?" Tanya hugged her arms around her battered chest.

Annie sighed. "It's hardly a secret that your marriage wasn't a love match. It was a union to boost both of your careers. With your success, the marriage outlived its usefulness, or maybe the divorce is another career-boosting stunt. I don't know. I didn't expect you to be broken up about it."

"I'm not." She was counting the days, hours, and minutes until she was no longer legally bound to Zeke.

"So what's the problem?"

"Can't I call just to chat with my sister?"

"I don't know."

Tanya hugged herself tighter. She didn't do girl chats. She had no close female friends. Developing her femme fatale image had alienated her from female friendships. Men didn't exactly see her as friendship material either. "How can you not know?"

"Do you remember the last time we talked?" Annie asked. "And I'm not talking about the monthly calls your assistant makes to keep you updated on my life."

"I don't have time to keep a freaking journal." As a proud first grader, Tanya clutched her sister's hand and walked her to her first day of kindergarten. What would it take to recapture the close sister bond? Probably not the sarcastic comment she'd just made. It shouldn't be so hard to talk to her sister. How long had it been since they'd last spoken?

"If you remembered, it might give you a clue why I'm reluctant to chat."

Her sister was a minister. She was supposed to forgive and forget and recognize when a woman needed a hug and a friend. "You're giving me a headache, and I'm trying to do something nice for you. I bought you a plane ticket and arranged a limo to the airport for you to come visit me."

"Tanya, I have a congregation that needs me. I can't just jet off because my famous sister beckons."

"So I'm not sister-of-the-year. How many times have I asked something of you, Annie? Don't you get any vacation time from God?"

Annie was silent for several moments. Finally, she said, "I'm sorry. I can't leave right now."

Tanya lowered the receiver. She wouldn't cry. She hadn't cried after Zeke's punishment, and she wouldn't start now just because she couldn't forge a bond with the only family she had left on the planet. She dashed away a tear.

Focus on her career. She had a meeting with her agent and P.R. spokesperson in the morning. They were going to announce her acceptance of the female lead in *Heart of a Mobster*. Her career was going to soar. The movie would win her an Oscar. She'd be on the cover of every magazine with positive articles attached. She'd be Tanya, the woman every man lusted after and every woman aspired to be.

And she'd be empty inside.

Chapter 7

Heather was freezing her butt off. Standing behind a building waiting for someone who wouldn't be happy to see her wasn't her idea of fun. But she couldn't walk away. Despite what everyone thought, she occasionally had a conscience. Unfortunately, this was one of those times.

Finally the back door opened. Under the flickering street light, Egan hefted a black garbage bag into the Dumpster three feet away and then closed the door, turning a key in two separate locks. After he pocketed the key, Heather stepped toward him. His head immediately shot up, his gaze crashing into hers. He looked wary and disbelieving as he quickly scanned a full circle.

"There's no one else," she assured him. "Just me."

He looked slightly relieved, but she knew he didn't trust her. And he was even less happy to have her for company. "You should go home."

"I need to talk to you."

He walked away.

She had to jog to catch up. Her boobs bounced when she ran, and her nipples were tight because it was so cold. But his eyes didn't stray to her chest at all. He glanced sideways at her face and then looked straight ahead as he power-walked down the street.

She was impressed and more than a little annoyed. No way was Egan Dowers in the same class as Nick McAllister. Nick was old and pretty cool and had no doubt seen lots of boobs before. Egan ought to look because this was lots better than the potluck show and could be his only chance.

"Could you slow down a minute?" she gasped. She was not going to pant alongside him, like some groupie. He was supposed to be panting over her.

He didn't break stride. "It's late. I'm tired, and I want to go home. That's where you should be, too."

She touched his shoulder and just like that he stopped. In fact, it happened so suddenly, she plowed into him. Yow, that was smooth. His chest was more solid than she expected. In fact, there was a lot more to him physically. His shoulders were wider, his jaw squarer. She didn't knock him over or even cause him to stumble. He just put his hands on her shoulders and plunked her back a step.

"What do you want, Heather?" His jaw was tight, and he immediately took his hands off her.

She felt geeky and awkward. She held out a twenty-dollar-bill she'd held crumpled in her hand for the past hour. "This is for you."

He glanced at it and then back at her. His eyes were two hard blue stones. "I don't know why you're offering it to me, but the answer's 'no.' I don't want your money."

"You don't have to do anything for it. I owe it to you for the sandwiches I ordered yesterday." She opened her hand over his and let the bill float down.

"I don't want your money." He turned and began walking again.

Heather bent and picked up the twenty from the sidewalk and then ran to catch up with him. He was making her grovel. It was no more than she deserved, but she didn't have to like it. "Come on, Egan. We took your rent money. Let me pay you back."

He laughed, but it was a harsh, ugly sound. "Heather Fitzsimmons feels guilty. Am I the first person who's managed to unearth your conscience, or do you just treat me worse than everyone else?"

"I'm trying to treat you better if you'd just take the money."

He turned on her now. "I don't want your money, and I sure don't want your sympathy. Go home and paint your toenails or something. Just stay away from me."

She couldn't believe it. Guys never wanted her to stay away. Having her around guaranteed they could make out or cop a feel or just look at her chest. Egan had plenty of excuses to touch her when she ran into him and when she tried to give him the money. But he hadn't. He'd acted like he couldn't get away soon enough, and he avoided looking at her, especially her bouncy, cold boobs.

Egan was different from all the other guys. She wanted something different from him, too. So of course her old strategies wouldn't work. "I want to hire you," she blurted.

He stopped walking. His eyes were so cold and unfriendly. She pulled up short before she ran into him again. "I was under the impression guys took your favors for free."

She flinched. Knowing she deserved his scorn didn't make taking it any easier. "I need someone to help me understand algebra. I'm flunking, and if I don't pass, I don't graduate."

"Not my problem." He started walking again.

"I'm offering you money."

"I told you I don't want your money." He said it as if his teeth were gritted and he was so mad he could strangle her.

She was the one who should be mad. She was trying to apologize, and he treated her worse than the garbage he'd hauled into the Dumpster. Except maybe she never actually apologized. She tried to remember if the words had come out. She'd meant to say it first thing. She took a deep breath and figured it couldn't be worse than kneeling on the floorboards giving a blowjob. "I'm sorry."

"For what?" Of course, he wouldn't make this easy.

"For letting Troy take your money."

"Did you sleep with him?" Egan asked.

"Not last night." She answered before she remembered that wasn't any of his business.

"You could do better."

She was going to say something flip—*Like who? You?*—except the words stuck in her throat. He'd given her a compliment, and he wasn't trying to get in her pants. She stayed silent until he stopped walking again. "Why'd you stop this time?"

"This is your house, isn't it?"

She pulled her gaze from him to look at the neighborhood. He'd walked her home. A funny lump started growing in her throat. She blinked hard but couldn't be sure her eyes would stay dry, so she looked over his right shoulder instead of directly at him. "If I offer you twenty bucks for walking me home, you'll hate me forever, huh?"

"Probably." She thought maybe he was trying to hide a smile.

"You're a nice guy, Egan Dowers." She couldn't stop herself from brushing her fingers over his shoulder as she walked toward her house. "Stay away from girls like me."

He was silent behind her, and she refused to look back. She walked to the front door and placed her hand on the knob.

"Heather?"

"Yeah." She turned around.

"I can tutor you in algebra. Mondays and Wednesdays after school in the library. It'll cost you twenty bucks a pop."

She laughed. She couldn't stop herself. Her heart felt lighter than it had all year. "I'll see you tomorrow."

Egan nodded once and turned, hunching his shoulders against the cold and rain as he walked away. She watched him until he was out of sight, but he didn't look back.

"The auction's set to start in thirty minutes," Holly said. "Is the contract updated with all the changes?"

"Not exactly." Nick adjusted his tie as he watched the half-dozen buyers peruse the Britman merchandise. "I haven't been able to talk to Britman personally." Too many personal assistants. Of course he knew Britman already had his own team of lawyers, but obviously they were giving him lousy advice or none at all. "We can go ahead with the sale, but payment will be made as specified in the original contract. No cash."

"Our goal is provide to the client's specifications," Holly argued. "He was very specific."

"He signed a contract with contradictory specifications." Part of Nick was thrilled to work through these negotiations with a celebrity. His dream was so close he could taste it. But most of him was bored into a trance by talk of contracts. That part of him dreamed of stripping old floorboards in some rickety house far from the city.

"That contract also included some heirloom jewelry that we let slip through our fingers. He'll let that slide if we do things his way. Do you know what could happen to our reputation if he raises a stink about it? The scandal would ruin us." Holly was becoming frantic. At one time Nick would have felt compelled to plant his lips on hers and calm her down. Now he was unmoved. His lips yearned for a woman whose mouth spewed hypocritical religious babble.

"In that case, Jason will write a book about it," he muttered. His cell phone rang. The caller ID said only *California call*. Finally, his dream was coming to life. He snapped open the phone. "McAllister."

"Officer Jacobs of the DEA speaking." Not Britman. Disappointment was so strong it was difficult to continue holding the phone to his ear. "Am I speaking to the attorney for the Vonkall Auction House?"

"Yes."

"All of Zeke Britman's assets have been frozen. I have a court order not allowing any of his possessions to be sold until it can be reviewed as potential evidence. Once something is sold, the money must be placed in a bank account under the supervision of the court."

"I can't take your word for it." Nick wanted to work for Britman, not against him.

"You don't have to. Within the hour, you'll have the original court order telling you the same thing. I'm warning you so the Vonkall Auction House doesn't make trouble for itself."

This wasn't the way he envisioned getting involved with potential clients. Freezing assets would hardly endear his mother to the Hollywood crowd. "Our building isn't a warehouse for police evidence."

"I shouldn't have to remind a lawyer about the penalties for interfering with an ongoing investigation." The cop sounded supremely irritated. "Is Tanya Britman in attendance for the auction?"

Tanya. Supermodel Tanya here? Goosebumps prickled Nick's arms. "I couldn't say."

"Fine. Have her call me if you see her." The officer hung up.

Nick clicked off his phone and turned to Holly. "Is Britman's wife here?"

Her eyes widened. "Tanya? No. Why?"

"Notify me immediately when she comes." His dream boat was sailing into view. Nick stretched his muscles and prepared to lift his mother with him as he jumped aboard. Jason didn't have a chance of preempting him this time.

Before Heather came into view, Egan knew she was coming. He

couldn't hear her, couldn't even smell her perfume yet. But the air shimmered, radiating her presence. He knew it was foolish. Everyone—including Heather—would laugh if he said it out loud. But he also knew it was true.

He gulped as he thought about her boobs swaying under a tight sweater. He'd fantasize about them later. He gulped again and opened his notebook. He stared blindly at it until he figured she was halfway across the room to him.

When he looked up, she was right on target. He kept his eyes on her face. The last thing she needed was another guy checking out her body. She'd only ridicule him anyway. She'd never let a nerd like him touch her. His fantasies were private, and he'd never use them to hurt or degrade her.

Looking at her face wasn't a hardship. She wore too much makeup, but she had big brown eyes and a high forehead. Her fluffy blond hair floated around her face no matter how much she pushed it away. He gripped the table with his hands, so he couldn't touch the wisps of silk under the guise of pushing her hair behind her ear. Her nose was narrow and maybe a tiny bit too long. Her lips were full. Imagining what they could do to a man made his clenched knuckles ache. Egan wasn't likely to find out in this lifetime.

"Pay first," he said as she stopped in front of the table. He wasn't going to let her think he'd be grateful for an hour of her time, even if it was true.

Her lips curved in one of those amazing sexy smiles designed to bring a man to his knees. "If I do that, how will I be sure to get my money's worth?"

"You'll get it." He uncurled his white knuckles from the table before she noticed his tension. "It'll be up to you whether your grade actually improves."

She wrinkled her nose but tossed a twenty on the table. "I'm counting on you, Egan."

He grabbed the bill and shoved it in his back pocket. If she regained her sanity and spent her afternoon somewhere else, only his ego would suffer. "Counting on me won't do you any good when it's test time. You're going to learn so you can count on yourself during the exam."

She took the chair across the table and pulled it around next to him. He'd set up the arrangement so she'd be as far away as possible. Teacher, student. Lots of distance. He wouldn't accidentally find himself looking down her cleavage or sniffing her neck. And she wouldn't see the sweat beading on his forehead in between his zits or look at his lap and see the boner he couldn't control.

Now she was right next to him and he could hardly breathe, let alone concentrate on algebra. That shimmery thing she did with the air sucked all the oxygen out of it. "Why don't you tell me what you understood?"

She looked at him like he was a moron. "I'm not tutoring you. I want help with what I don't understand."

"Math builds on itself," he tried to explain, though how he made a complete sentence come out of his mouth was beyond him. She smelled incredible. "We need to go back to where you first got lost and work our way up to what Mrs. Handburg is teaching now."

"That would be the first day. I walked in ten minutes late, and Mrs. Handburg had some number and letter thing with pluses and minuses on the chalkboard." She waved her hand. "I have no idea what it was, and I've been lost ever since."

"Okay, that makes it easy. We'll start at the beginning." And if there was a God, she'd stay clueless and need him to help her every day for the next fifty years. By then maybe his zits would be gone and she'd have a few wrinkles and he'd have a chance with her. "Do you ever go to the playground at the grade school?"

"You don't have to go back that far. I held my own on the playground." She smiled, and even though she thought he was a complete geek, he smiled back.

"I take Megan over there sometimes, not as much now because she's getting older and goes by herself." He was rambling. Get to the point, Egghead, before she runs off. "There's a teeter-totter at the playground. If two people who weigh the same sit on each end, they can balance it in the middle."

"Is there a point to this?"

"Yes." *You're beautiful.* No, no, everyone told her that. She had so many others to choose from. He wouldn't make a fool of himself. He scrambled to remember the subject. "Algebra is the balanced teeter-totter. The center is the equal sign. Each side of the equal sign is perfectly in balance."

He waited for her to tell him to go back to making sandwiches at Subway.

"You know, like two plus three equals five." He scribbled the equation in his notebook. "Two plus three means the same thing as five. They both have the same weight on the teeter-totter."

Heather looked at him as if he had more chance of becoming a patient in a mental hospital than a doctor.

"So if you say two plus x equals five, algebra is all about figuring what number x stands for. You subtract two from both sides of the equation. Now you have x equals three." He rushed to finish, scribbling the basic subtraction on his notebook.

Heather stared at the notebook in absolute silence for two whole minutes. Then she said, "Let me try one of those easy ones."

He scribbled "$4 + x = 9$," and she came up with the answer "five" immediately. She lifted her eyes to his, and he couldn't miss the need for approval. "See, you know more than you think you do," he choked out.

She beamed at him, and he was sure that tutoring her in algebra was better than sex. Not that he had a frame of reference. He wasn't likely to ever have sex with her. So yeah, he was certain sitting next to her talking about algebra was better than sex.

Annie pushed her grocery cart with a modest amount of food to the grocery store checkout. Only one of the two registers was open, so she pulled into line behind a young woman with stooped shoulders.

"Oh, go ahead of me. I think I have to put something back." Her shoulders sagged a little more as she counted through the bills in her wallet again. Her cart held two cases of beer, a loaf of bread, a carton of eggs, a half dozen canned goods, a head of lettuce, and a package of lunchmeat.

"Take your time. I'm not in a hurry." Annie smiled and turned her attention to the checkout magazines. One tabloid featured a woman who had given birth to a leopard baby complete with spots. Not wanting to speculate on how that came to be, Annie moved on to *CelebScoop*.

The woman set the lunchmeat and lettuce in a basket underneath the revolving belt.

Tanya's face stared at Annie from the magazine stall, looking nothing like the world-renowned supermodel she'd become. In fact, Annie wouldn't have recognized her, except Tanya had looked the same at age eight when she fell off her bike and tumbled down a muddy hill. Bruised, tear-stained, ratted hair, torn shirt.

Tanya had called, needing her sister, and Annie had brushed her off without trying to find out what was wrong. Years ago Tanya had shattered Annie's dreams and her life. Tanya didn't even remember it. Annie prayed for years to forgive Tanya, but she could not forget.

Supermodel brutalized by husband, the caption blared. Annie had refused to lend her support. What kind of sister was she? What kind of minister was she?

She lifted the magazine off the rack and flipped through to the cover story. Before she could read a word, the woman in front of her spoke again. "Oh, is that Tanya?" She looked at her wallet and then at the canned goods in the basket. "If I could be anyone in the world for a day, I'd be her."

Annie closed the magazine and stared at the picture of her sister. "Why?"

"She stomps all over men. She's got power, and she knows how to use it. She's amazing." She reached for Annie's magazine. Her hand sported a black-and-blue welt the size of a tennis ball. Quickly, she snatched her hand back. She stared at Tanya's headshot, and her shoulders sagged a little more. "Oh, no. It looks like someone stomped all over her."

Annie thought about saying something to the woman about her options to overcome bruises and feelings of powerlessness. She looked at the magazine again. Her own sister was in an abusive relationship going through a divorce. Their private woes were on display for the entire country to see. All Tanya had asked of Annie was to spend a couple days with her. Annie had turned her down because she didn't want to give her parishioners something to talk about.

She'd call Tanya as soon as she got home. Then she'd clear her schedule and go to California. She had no right to offer counsel to strangers when she turned her back on her own flesh and blood.

"Humph. I thought a minister would be above reading that trash." The female voice from behind didn't disguise her disgust.

Annie watched the trampled young woman in front of her set two cans of soup and the beer on the revolving belt. Then Annie turned to the voice. Trudy Fitzsimmons. Her instinct was to shove the gossip rag back into its slot above the register. But she couldn't make herself let go of this link to Tanya. She'd failed her sister horribly. "Hello, Mrs. Fitzsimmons. I expect the people in these pages need God as much as the average person."

"They ought to tell their story to Him instead of selling it to the masses."

"I doubt this person wanted her story public at all." Annie tapped Tanya's face on the magazine cover. She didn't doubt it. She was sure of it. Tanya didn't want people to know her sister was a minister because of the effects on her sexy-tough image.

"That's not stopping you from reading every titillating word," Trudy pointed out. "The Bible admonishes us against gossip."

"You're right." Annie slapped the magazine on the belt with her groceries. Gossip was exactly what Trudy had engaged in yesterday at the potluck.

"Only Tanya could make a black eye front-page news." The young woman in front of them fished at the bottom of her purse and finally resorted to the give-a-penny-take-a-penny dish.

"Then maybe Tanya's doing good by bringing the problem to the attention of the media." Annie added the woman's bread, lunchmeat, and lettuce to her checkout items.

"She's a bad influence on today's impressionable girls," Trudy said. "Look what's she's done to my Heather."

Celebrity influence could surely be counterbalanced by an understanding grandmother. Annie gripped her tongue firmly and said, "Tanya's human. She has good points and faults, just like all of us."

"I'd still like to walk in her shoes for a day," the other woman said, picking up her beer to leave.

Annie paid for her purchases and followed her to the parking lot. "Ma'am, you forgot your soup. I'm Reverend Annie, pastor of Good Shepherd Church."

"Oh." The woman looked flustered to be caught with two cases of beer in front of a minister. She opened her truck and dumped them inside. "I'm Bonnie."

Annie tossed all her grocery bags in the trunk and snapped it closed before Bonnie noticed. "If Tanya can get out of her situation, you can, too."

Bonnie glanced around nervously. "I have to go."

"Come visit me anytime. At church or at home."

"I have to go," she repeated and ducked into her car.

Egan acted like she made brilliant progress. She only did basic math facts his eight-year-old sister could have done. Heather tried not to let his smile and nice words get to her. He was giving her all his attention and saying the things her dad used to tell her back when he had time to notice her.

"I think we've had enough for today." Egan closed his notebook.

She backed away immediately, not wanting him to think she was disappointed. Sitting next to him working algebra problems was better than sex, not that she'd admit it to anyone. "Are you going to work at Subway now?"

"Not until six."

She stood and picked up her algebra book. She should have left it in her locker. Egan hadn't opened it, and he made a lot more sense than the book or Mrs. Handburg ever did. Egan shuffled his books and half-million papers into a pile. A notebook fell out of the stack onto her feet. She bent down to pick it up as he lunged for it.

His head smacked her forehead and knocked her on her butt. For one horrible second, she was afraid he'd cracked her skull. She squeezed her eyes shut as pain zinged through her head. This was it. She was going to die.

"I'm sorry. I'm so sorry." Egan's voice at first seemed far

away. As she realized she was going to live and her head only throbbed, he sounded normal.

She opened her eyes to see him six inches away. His face filled her vision. The zit on his chin was enormous. "Oww," was all she could manage.

"I'm really, really sorry." His hands hovered by her face but never actually touched her. "Can I do anything to help?"

"Do me a favor. Don't ever try to kiss me. I might not survive." She tried to make a joke out of her embarrassment.

"I didn't mean to—"

"Tutoring Egghead in sex, Heather?"

Egan froze, and his face turned as red as his mega-zit. She looked up at Veronica Hastings, the most popular girl in school, with one of her cheerleader friends.

"I know you're the expert," Veronica said, "but some people are beyond hope."

"Yeah," the friend twittered. "When he gave you that bruise on your forehead, was he aiming for your mouth or—"

Heather jumped to her feet. Egan had been so nice to her, and now these two were going to ruin everything. He'd remember he was too good for her, and he wouldn't tutor her anymore. She'd fail algebra. Even worse, he'd never look at her like she had these flashes of brilliance. Then he'd start looking at her boobs and trying to cop a feel. Tears welled behind her eyes.

"He'd never do anything with me." She ran out of the library and as far from the school and her miserable life as she could get. But it wasn't far enough.

Chapter 8

Tanya took a flight to Salt Lake City, rented a car to Des Moines, and bought a piece-of-junk avocado station wagon for four hundred bucks to rattle into Maplefield on Tuesday afternoon. Exhaustion plagued her from driving all night. She nearly wept with relief when she pulled in front of her sister's house and not one camera jumped out of the bushes. Her megawatt smile and saucy, sexy comebacks to their questions would take more energy than she could muster.

She didn't look like herself in a bulky blazer and pants three sizes too big held up by a man's belt. Even so, she continually looked over her shoulder for suspicious movements, through her three-ninety-nine Wal-Mart sunglasses, as she walked to the front door and rang the bell.

Nobody answered. She rang the bell again and tried to peer through the beveled glass along the side of the door. She hadn't considered Annie might not be home. Tanya had driven through town. There wasn't any place to be.

She tried to think. She didn't have the energy to try to break in without a key, and her experience with Zeke soured her on that option anyway. She could sit on the front steps and wait, but that seemed so common. She walked back to her car.

The church. Of course. Annie would be there. She was pretty sure she'd driven past it. If she hadn't, well, it couldn't be that hard to find in a town this size.

The engine coughed and sputtered as she started the ignition and wheezed out of the driveway. Being photographed behind the wheel of this junker would be nearly as bad as those other pictures, the ones she couldn't bear to look at. She couldn't stop for a bottle of water without being accosted by them. This car, at least, she could spin as getting into character for a movie. She found the church too quickly and killed the engine in the parking lot. It was too loud to let idle.

She hadn't hesitated to get out of the car at Annie's house, but here was different. This was a church. She sat and stared at the building. She was parked too close to see the steeple, but she knew it was there. And she couldn't make herself go inside.

God's house. She couldn't imagine a place where she would be less welcome. Before Saturday night she might have flashed her chest and a flagrant finger at Him as she walked through the door. But now she couldn't even leave her car.

God had allowed the devil to give her a private tour of Hell. He knew she deserved it. She shuddered to think of the wrath He'd inflict on her if she insulted Him by stepping into His house.

"Reverend Annie, a rundown station wagon is parked by the front door. A woman's inside. She's been sitting there for over twenty minutes without moving. I don't recognize her. Do you want to take a look, or should I call the police?"

A secretary who wasn't ashamed to press her nose to the glass carried occasional benefits. Annie left her desk, abandoning the letter she was writing to Central American missionaries. "I'll talk to her, Kathy."

She had no fear approaching a stranger's car, knowing her nosy secretary would be watching out the window with one hand on the telephone should the need for police arise.

At first glance, the woman was down to her last dime in a car that needed more than a miracle to keep it running. But there was something familiar about her face, even with the poorly dyed red hair and sunglasses meant for concealing bruises and secrets.

"Tanya."

A small smile tugged at the corner of her sister's mouth. She opened the car door but didn't get out. "Surprise."

"I tried to call you last night," Annie said. "I found some time to visit."

"I was already gone. If Mohammad won't come to the mountain, bring the mountain to Mohammad, right? Or does that only apply to Islam?" Tanya gave a shaky little laugh.

"I'm glad you're here." She didn't let herself dwell on whether she meant the words or only said them out of automatic politeness. "Do you want to come in to my office?"

"No." Tanya's reply was quick and emphatic.

"Oh. Well, how are you?" She couldn't tell Tanya she looked good. That would be an absolute lie. The most positive spin described Tanya as looking like Annie when she'd put off a trip to the dry cleaners too long.

"How do you think I am?" she tossed back bitterly. "You and everyone else on five continents have read every scintillating detail."

"That's how you always wanted it." Annie's resentment broke through.

"Not any more."

"Not any more or just not this time?" Annie asked, genuinely curious.

Tanya said nothing.

Compassion. She had a well of it for other people. She didn't understand why it evaporated around her sister, a sister who had endured unspeakable horrors. "Look, why don't you go to my house. There's a key in the flowerpot. I'll be there as soon as I finish up here, and we can talk. If you go down this street and turn right—"

"I know the way."

"All right then." Annie walked back into the church office, catching a glimpse of Kathy pressed against the window. Kathy's hand on the telephone was hardly a comfort now. That telephone would heat up the wires across town with gossip of the exchange.

"Who was that woman?" Kathy demanded as Annie entered the building.

Annie swallowed. Tanya hadn't said how long she was staying. Any longer than a night, and the truth would come out. "My sister."

"I'd almost forgotten you had one." Kathy squinted at her. "Lives on the west coast, right? What was her name again?"

Annie had never given it out in the first place, redirecting conversations in hopes of avoiding the connection. Now she hoped that a name was just a name. "Tanya. She's going to stay with me for a while." Might as well let Kathy pass along facts to quell the rumors. At least they'd know her houseguest was female. "I'm taking the rest of the afternoon off to help her get settled."

She walked by Kathy, leaving her speechless. It was probably too much to hope the condition would become permanent. Indeed, barely thirty seconds later Kathy stuck her head through the doorway. "You have a phone call. From Nick McAllister. Shall I tell him you're too busy getting your sister settled?"

"No!" She swallowed her instant panic and pulled on her reserves of decorum. "I'll take the call. Thank you, Kathy."

"What do you need, Nick?"

You. He let her voice slide over him and fill him. He'd missed that voice, her conversation that forced him to examine himself and dig deeper than was comfortable. He'd missed looking at her face, covering her lips with his own. "I'm concerned about Jason."

"I thought he was in good spirits when I left. Is something wrong?"

"Yeah, he won't stop bugging me about you. I wondered if maybe something happened in that back room that neither of you are telling me."

"I can't believe it. You're still blaming me."

No, he wasn't. He was . . . jealous, and not just of anyone, of his little brother. "Jason's been bugging me for your phone number and address."

"So give it to him. He's a big boy, Nick. Don't stop him from talking to me. That's part of why he withheld information from you. Because you do the same to him."

"Jason thinks you'll understand him more than me. He's afraid to quit his job, but he wants to write books. About famous people, and he needs—"

"An 'in' with a famous person's sister." Annie cut him off, bitterness clogging her voice.

Huh?

"He's no different than you, Nick. And the sad thing is, I almost fell for it. When you kissed me the first time, I thought you liked me for myself."

He kissed her because he couldn't control himself when he was around her. "Annie, you're not making sense."

"Rent a building in L.A., hang out your shingle there, and see which celebrity takes you up on your offer. I'm tired of being used." The phone banged against his ear.

Nick stared at the receiver in his hand. Reverend Annie hung up on him. He'd called to hear her voice, and she hung up on him. He'd spent two days at the auction house waiting for Tanya to show up. She never did, and he felt like a fool. And now Annie flipped out on him.

Nick marched down the hall to Jason's office. Jason was bent over his computer, typing furiously. Behind him, the television played the entertainment news. They were still replaying the same roughed-up pictures of Tanya. Obviously, she hadn't shown up on the celebrity circuit for the news reporters to run anything more current. Nick was certain she was close by. And she needed him.

"Not now," Jason muttered.

Nick was in no mood to cut anyone any slack, least of all the party boy who couldn't keep his pants zipped. "Who'd you sleep with?"

"Let it go, Nick. If you'd get laid at least once a year, you'd stop being so interested in my sex life."

"Tell me and I'll let you write in peace, without a lecture about your duties to the auction house."

Jason looked up and met his gaze. "I had amazing fantasy sex with the woman on the TV screen."

"Tanya?" He stared at her battered face. Her P.R. person wasn't commenting, and her lawyers claimed she was no longer their client. She was in a mess, and she needed a fabulous lawyer to get her out of it. All he had to do was convince her he was the right one.

Jason turned back to his computer. "I told. Now you leave."

Nick tapped his fingers on the desktop as he continued to watch the face on TV. Tanya had picked the pseudonym Reverend Annie for her hump-and-run session with Jason. Annie thought Nick wanted an "in" with a famous person's sister. Tanya was now in hiding—presumably where no one would look for her. Maybe even in the tiny town where her sister lived.

"I'm taking a couple days of vacation," he told Jason. "You can call me about auction house contracts on my cell while I'm gone."

His brother glanced up again. "Where are you going?"

"To visit Reverend Annie."

Jason jumped up from behind his desk. "Great. I'll come with you."

That Woman had the nerve to ring her doorbell. Heather walked up the driveway, intent on going inside and shutting the door in her face. It was bad enough That Woman talked to her father more often than her mother did. Now she was coming over to the house, too. Next she'd be moving in with them. Wouldn't that be cozy?

"Hello Heather." Her face was pinched like Grandma Fitzsimmons's.

Heather gave her the bird as she opened the door and walked in. Her mother, for once, was off her butt and caught the knob before Heather could slam the door. Heather stopped walking. She would not leave Mom alone with That Woman.

"Kathy." Mom, who could fall all over herself in gushing adoration for a telemarketer, used a voice that could freeze fire. Heather hadn't heard it before. Obviously her mom wasn't as clueless about Dad's other woman as Heather thought.

"Lois." Although she hadn't been given an invitation, Kathy stepped over the threshold. "Is Stewart around?"

"If he was, what would you do?" Mom's face was bright red, and she was clutching the doorknob with white fingers. But for the first time since Heather started junior high, her mom was standing up for herself. Heather bit her cheek to hold back a grin.

"I need to speak to him. It's important."

"I'm not so unimportant you can't share with me, too," Mom said.

"Actually, it's a church matter."

"Heather and I are part of the church."

Kathy spared Heather a glance. Clearly, she didn't consider

herself a member of any group Heather belonged to, and God was on Kathy's side.

Heather studied the chipped nail polish on her middle finger.

"Do you have something important enough to share with my entire family?" Mom demanded. "If not, go share it with your husband."

It took every effort to keep Heather's feet from dancing. She was so proud of her mom.

"Oh, fine," That Woman huffed. "I guess I can tell you. Everyone should know, anyway. Reverend Annie's sister moved into the manse with her and is mooching off church resources." Heather waited for something truly scandalous. Apparently, that was it.

"It's so nice she has family to visit," Mom said. "I don't think she's ever had someone stay with her before."

Kathy deflated like someone had poked her with a pin. "Well, yes, but you didn't see this sister. Her hair was ratted and an awful shade of red. She had an old, noisy car and looked kind of beaten up, like those tabloid pictures in the grocery store of that model."

"It sounds like she needs Annie then," Mom said. "I think I'll bake them some brownies. What's the sister's name?"

Kathy frowned. "Tara. No, that's not right. Tonya . . . or Tanya. Something like that."

"Tanya," Heather repeated. Was it possible? Had excitement really come to boring old Maplefield? "As in the supermodel Tanya—the one in those magazine pictures?"

"No. There was no glamour, no entourage, no expensive clothes." As if Kathy had experience living the life of the rich and famous. "She looked the exact opposite of what you'd expect Tanya to look, although the shape of the face had some resemblance, I suppose."

"What about her eyes?"

"She was wearing sunglasses, like women do when their boyfriend slaps them around."

And Heather knew. She just knew that excitement had, at last, come to Maplefield. And boring, perfect Reverend Annie wasn't so boring anymore. She didn't even seem perfect.

The door was locked. Annie hadn't expected it, and she fumbled for her key. Despite the phone call, she was only twenty minutes behind Tanya. The clouds had pulled together, and the gray day was thickening into a chilly drizzle. Tanya's battered tank was sitting in the driveway. If Tanya had gone for a walk, she'd hurry back soon.

Annie opened the door and closed it behind her. Tanya was lying on the couch, eyes shut. She didn't stir, despite the noise. Annie frowned at the door, wondering why Tanya had locked it. Maybe people in L.A. locked their doors after they came inside. She shook her head and wondered just how her sister was going to react to this small-town community. Half the people in Maplefield still didn't lock their doors at night.

Annie quietly removed her shoes and settled herself for the evening. Then she began preparations for dinner. When Tanya awoke, they could eat. Chatting over a meal would take the pressure off. If they didn't have to concentrate so hard on what they would say, maybe they could make progress in their relationship without hurting each other in the process.

She pulled two chicken breasts out of the freezer and wondered how much of what she'd read in *CelebScoop* was true. Had Zeke's entire band forced themselves on her, as some partygoers claimed, or was the statement of Tanya's P.R. person true? "No one can force Tanya to do anything she doesn't want to do." Even her husband had agreed, "Tanya got what she asked for and more."

There had never been a hint her sister was into pain and

violence. She was the last person Annie would have expected to stick around while a man perpetually smacked her. The image of Bonnie from the grocery store crossed her mind. The woman had never sought her out, but Annie longed to help.

She tossed the frozen chicken in the microwave and punched the defrost option. Hopefully, her sister would share her problems, and they could work through them together. Even if Tanya remained closed-lipped, Annie had a responsibility to help her through her troubles and guide her in discovering the life God meant her to live. Maybe Tanya had finally realized God was missing in her life and how much she needed Him.

Annie glanced at the sofa where Tanya's snores were drowned out by the hum of the microwave. Her sister might have brought their grandmother's jewelry with her. It could be within Annie's reach at this very moment. If Nick decided to track Tanya down, he could end up back in Maplefield. A shiver shimmied up her spine. She shouldn't want to see him. Her professional reputation couldn't overcome another judgment lapse. They'd shared their last kiss. She'd experienced her last kiss until she arrived in heaven.

She slapped a skillet on the stove and gave it a shot of non-stick spray, then transferred the chicken to the pan. Nick. Dark hair, hard jaw, abrasive manner, absurd moments of gentleness. Surely, God planned for their lives to cross again. She wasn't sure she could bear an earthly existence without seeing him. She never experienced such emotions, feelings, and physical longings in her love for God. Nick reminded her that God had created her human.

Of course, what she felt for Nick wasn't love. He was a bad influence on her life. He wasn't good for her relationship with her congregation. God, her church, and her community were much more important than the goofy roller coaster her stomach rode with Nick. God knew best when he'd separated their paths.

Her desire to stay apart was the right decision. Unfortunately, it had nothing to do with her true desire.

Two hours later her dish of chicken and stir-fry vegetables sat cold on the kitchen table with two empty plates on either side. Tanya was still zonked on the couch. Annie sank into one of the chairs at the table and dished herself a scoop. She forked up a bite and forced herself to chew and swallow. She'd been alone more often than not in her life. She'd learned not to let it bother her. After all, she had God, so she was never truly alone. But tonight with her sister sleeping on her couch, she was lonely.

The doorbell rang, saving Annie from forcing down another bite. She hurried to cross the room before the caller disturbed Tanya.

"Heather." Annie couldn't have been more surprised at the person who stood on the other side of the threshold.

"Hi." Heather's smile was slightly sheepish, as if she recognized the irony, too.

"I, uh—" Drat, she couldn't invite Heather in for confidential counseling with Tanya sprawled in the middle of the room. "Would you like to go to the church office with me?"

"No." Her response was emphatic and horrified. "No, I—here, Mom made these for you. They're brownies." She thrust a foil-topped pan at Annie.

"Uh, thank you." Annie took the casserole-size pan. "Any special reason?"

Heather craned her neck and stood on her toes. "We heard you had company—your sister—and wanted her to feel welcome."

"That's sweet of you." And completely out of character. She couldn't imagine the connection that led Kathy Patterson to gossip with a teenager she publicly shunned for loose morals.

"Can I meet your sister?"

"She's sleeping right now." It was the first time Heather had requested anything from her, and Annie hated to deny her.

"Is it true? Is she really the supermodel actress?" Heather's eyes lit up with excitement. She definitely hadn't come to pour her heart out to Annie over brownies.

Tanya had been in town for three hours and already her secret was out. No, that wasn't true. Tanya wouldn't consider her celebrity a secret. Annie's secret was out. The silver lining was that Tanya held the link for Annie to connect with Heather. "Yes, she is."

"Holy cow. Holy flying pigs! I'm at the house of a supermodel. You're her sister so that makes you, like, half supermodel, right?"

Annie nearly laughed at the absurdity. "No. It makes me plain old Reverend Annie."

"Do you have a camera I can borrow?"

"For what?"

"So I can take her picture. This is so cool. I mean Kathy said it was true and I wanted it to be, but I didn't really think it was possible, you know? No one else will believe it either unless I take a picture to prove it."

"She's sleeping," Annie reminded her. She doubted Tanya wanted pictures while she looked like she'd been run over by a truck. "When she wakes up, I'll talk to her about it. We can probably pull an autograph out of her. But there's a condition, Heather."

"I'll do it. Anything. I'll even help with the boring old food pantry."

Don't sleep with any more guys. Respect your mother. Wear decent clothes. Respect yourself. Come to youth group meetings. But Heather wasn't her child or her servant. She couldn't force obedience. Even if she could, Heather needed an attainable goal. They had to start with little battles before she could win the war. "Myra will appreciate your help. I also want you to be nice to Egan Dowers."

Heather rubbed the small knot on her forehead. "Egghead. Sure."

Annie tried to control her irritation. "That means be nice to him around other people, too, not just to his face."

Heather swallowed and avoided her gaze. "Right. So when can I meet Tanya?"

"When she wakes up, I'll ask how soon she'll feel up to introductions to the community."

Heather went home—at least that was the direction she took off in and the assurance she gave Annie. Annie decided to trust her and pray the girl didn't spend the evening with anyone who didn't care about the girl inside the body.

By the time Annie was ready to crawl into bed, Tanya hadn't awakened. When she left for the church office in the morning, Tanya was still sleeping. Sometime during the night Tanya had changed into a blue sweat suit of Annie's. Annie left a note on the kitchen table, wondering when they were going to talk to each other. Perhaps they were destined to remain strangers with simmering resentment for one another.

The Oldsmobile tank had been good camouflage on the highway, but a person would have to be deaf and blind to miss it on the streets of Maplefield. Tanya wanted to blend in today, not have the residents scrutinize her identity. Besides, the paparazzi could be looking for her in a scrap-metal car. They got paid a lot for photos of her. She'd make the pictures worth the trouble to get them.

The rain was coming down steadily. Annie either had a second car or had decided to commune with God in the rain. Her white Chevy Cavalier was parked in the carport. The keys hung on a hook by the back door.

After another detour in front of the mirror, Tanya took the

keys and drove toward the center of town. She didn't have a purpose but figured she'd know what she was looking for when she saw it. She drove twice around the square just because she couldn't believe towns had actual squares anymore. From there, she investigated the small strip of stores by the two-lane highway she had driven into town on. Two doors down from a Subway was a Workout Wonderland.

Tanya might not be acting or modeling this week, but she couldn't let her body go to pot. She'd return to L.A. as soon as she was healed. She wouldn't take every job that came her way. A dozen clones of her couldn't accomplish that, but she planned to pack in as much as a 24/7 schedule could handle.

She parked the car and walked to the desk inside the Workout Wonderland. The woman behind it gave her a distracted half glance and a be-with-you-in-a-minute mutter before turning back to the overweight woman who was filling out forms.

Tanya glanced around, bemused. She wasn't used to being made to wait. Not all of it was selfish conceit. People simply jumped to attention and dropped their other tasks when she entered the room. Tanya Lane Britman was never forced to wait until a clerk finished helping a frumpy, obese patron of limited funds.

The heavy woman seemed to understand her place better than the receptionist. She lumbered around to the side of the desk and pushed her papers clumsily with her. "I'm going to take a while. Don't let me keep people waiting."

The clerk, whose name badge identified her as Peggy Dowers, looked up obediently. "Can I help you?"

She had an urge to remove her sunglasses so this place didn't look so dim and dreary, but she couldn't allow herself that vulnerability. "I want to work out while I'm in town."

"Do you have a membership?"

"No. I'm not going to be in town very long." Thankfully. She couldn't survive this common lifestyle.

"You can come twice as our guest with a nominal day fee, but after that you need to pay a one-time initiation fee of forty-nine dollars, and a monthly gym membership. Are you interested in our weight management program as well?"

Tanya flinched. The insult turned her voice to ice. "Are you implying I need it?"

Peggy flushed but recovered with a surprisingly smooth response. "It's not my place to decide who needs what. We offer the option to all our patrons."

"How do you keep your body in such great shape?" the fat woman asked.

At least someone recognized she wasn't all sag and cellulite, even if it was far from the fawning comments she preferred. Anyway, the question was a standard of magazine interviews, and she answered easily. "Pilates, cardio-intensive workouts, no sugar, no fats, low carbs."

The woman gaped at her. "What can you eat?"

Nothing that she wanted. A brownie hadn't touched her lips in twenty years. "Fruits, vegetables, protein."

The woman groaned and turned to Peggy. "I'm not going to last an hour. I've got three Snickers and a bag of Cheetos burning a hole in the bottom of my purse."

Cheetos. She and Annie used to go through a whole bag together and lick the orange from each other's fingers.

Peggy smiled sympathetically. "Give them to me, Lois. I'll get rid of the temptation for you."

The fat lady's purse was as big as a carry-on suitcase. "Oh, I have a box of Cracker Jacks, too." She laid all the food on the desk top.

Peggy swept it out of sight before Tanya could lunge for the Cheetos. Someone sighed. Tanya hoped it was the other woman.

"Who's going to help me clean the junk food out of my

house?" Fat Lady asked. "If I do it, I'll eat it as I go."

"You don't have to stop cold turkey," Peggy said gently. "Moderation is the key, and don't replace any of the food you do eat."

Tanya cleared her throat. They were supposed to wait on her. Instead, they were ignoring her for their own cozy conversation. "Initiate me and set up my first month's membership." A week of membership should be more than adequate, but she wasn't going to hang out at the desk next time she wanted to exercise. She was Tanya. Her time was meant for greater things than watching a woman take an entire grocery store out of her purse. Her stomach cramped thinking of all the food she couldn't eat without destroying her figure and her career.

Peggy passed her a form and a pen. "Fill this out. We take cash and major credit cards. No out-of-town checks."

Tanya lowered her glasses to look at the insolent woman over the rim. What kind of low-class establishment had she stepped into? She had to fill out their paperwork for them, and they wouldn't accept a celebrity's check. "Where's the next closest gym?"

"Twenty miles away, in Dubuque," the clerk answered cheerfully.

It figured. She snapped her sunglasses back in place.

The fat woman was staring at her now with the same horrified look Tanya probably had on her face when she'd first realized how large the woman was. "You're that woman Heather was talking about."

Tanya didn't have a clue who Heather was, but she suspected she was "that woman." Although Annie spreading the word about her presence was surprising.

"What woman?" the clerk asked.

"That supermodel who's always in the entertainment news. Oh, my, I always forget her name."

Tanya. I'm Tanya. How could anyone forget me?

Peggy shrugged. "I never pay attention to that stuff."

"Heather's fascinated by her. What is her name?"

"Why don't you ask me?" Tanya's irritation bubbled over. She shouldn't be that forgettable when she was standing right next to them.

"Oh, no, I wouldn't want to bother you. You're much too famous."

Tanya didn't know whether to laugh or smack the woman in the head. "My name is Tanya, and all I want is to get some exercise before my muscles atrophy and I look like you. So let's hurry this along."

Nick deliberately wore jeans and a grubby T-shirt, so Annie wouldn't question his handyman ruse. He needed to find out about Tanya, but he wasn't ready to let go of the illusion of Annie liking him for himself. He let himself into the church, wishing she had answered his knock at her home so he didn't have to step into God's house. The first time he'd done it for Jason. This time was for his own dream.

"Here to see Reverend Annie, I presume," the secretary said. "Is this for business or pleasure?"

"I didn't know God allowed anything pleasurable to happen under His roof. Or does the Reverend make that call?"

The prude at the desk sniffed and walked directly to Annie's office. "The handyman's back. I'll leave your door open to ensure nothing unseemly occurs."

Annie gave him a tight smile when he walked in the door. He could see she wasn't pleased with his return. "Nick, welcome back."

He closed the door and walked to the desk. He placed both hands on it and leaned toward her. "Care to accompany those words with a welcoming kiss?"

She flinched, and he backed away. Okay, so his style had been a little slimy. But just seeing her again was like taking a sucker punch to the gut. He wanted her. Bad. And if he guessed right, her flinch was a sign of hurt, not disgust. He hadn't done anything to hurt her, at least not since he was convinced she hadn't hurt his brother. So he'd start there.

"I apologize for accusing you of taking advantage of Jason."

"A phone call or a note would have sufficed. Did your brother fire you, and you've come here for work?"

To her he was a handyman. He wanted to say "yes." But he couldn't. He needed to learn more about Tanya. He needed to speak with Tanya. Right now, Annie was a means to her sister. "No, I'm on a work-related trip." He sat across from her. "I've ascertained the person who usurped your identity in her seduction and destruction of my brother."

"Cut the lawyer jabber, Nick. I liked you better as an unemployed butthead than a pompous—"

"Lawyer? You know I'm a lawyer?" He squeezed his hand into a fist and pressed it against his thigh so he wouldn't slam it through the desk. She was supposed to like him for himself. But she'd known. No wonder she'd kissed him. No wonder she'd acted like he was a man worthy of a woman's attention.

"A lawyer with celebrity aspirations," Annie said. "Which is the only reason you're bothering with me right now."

"Let's cut to the chase. Where is your sister? I need to speak with her."

A light had shown in her eyes when he first arrived. The last of it extinguished now. "You're a resourceful man, Nick. You don't need my help."

He'd been dismissed. Not just from her office but from her life. If she believed he was a nobody, he would have tried to right it. But she knew he was a man of means, of substance. If he salvaged their relationship, she'd fall into his arms because of what he could offer her on a material level. And that left him nothing to salvage.

Chapter 9

After two hours in the gym, ten minutes in the shower, and a makeover of a baseball cap and sunglasses, Tanya looked worse than after Zeke had worked her over. The town didn't have a spa, but it did have a liquor store. If she couldn't work on her appearance, she could at least fix her perception of it. And rum would make a fine dip for those brownies she'd seen on Annie's kitchen counter.

As she stepped out of Annie's car, an ambulance screamed up the street. It sloshed a mud puddle onto the blue sweat suit she'd borrowed from Annie. Gross. And cold. What kind of idiot vacationed in Illinois in November? She walked determinedly to the store. Alcohol. Something to warm her body and numb her brain.

A man held the door for her. A nice specimen. But she looked worse than she ever had in her life. Not to mention, sex had temporarily lost its appeal. She dismissed his presence as nothing but a doorman.

"I'm Nick McAllister." He offered his hand. "Tanya."

Arrgghh. There went her cover. She hadn't asked for confidentiality, but she hadn't expected Annie to broadcast her presence. If she were smart, she'd get in the car and drive all the way to Bermuda. But now more than ever she needed that drink. "I don't respond to pick-up lines before five p.m."

"Strictly business." He dropped a card in her hand. "I heard you fired your lawyers and are searching for representation."

She gave him a chilly appraisal, although his abs were impressive for a paper pusher. "I'm looking for someone established enough to afford a suit."

"Nick McAllister," he repeated. "Ask around."

"Sir," she yelled at the fat man behind the register. "You ever hear of Nick McAllister?"

He barely glanced up from the tabloid with her picture on the cover. "Nope."

She turned back to Nick and shrugged. "Sorry." She let the card flutter to the floor.

Instead of looking crestfallen and begging her to reconsider, he grinned. "Nice performance. You look better on screen than in real life." He hefted a case of beer from the pile on the floor and walked to the register.

She wasn't at her best, she wanted to scream. On screen they could touchup anything. Now she looked so bad no one was supposed to recognize her.

"By the way," Nick called over his shoulder, "Officer Jacobs is looking for you. Are you going to call him or should I do the honors?"

Hardball. He'd promised she was off the hook. He couldn't take it back. Or maybe he could. She'd fired her lawyers when they advised her to put everything into a judge-approved agreement. A little shiver went through her at the thought of talking to him again. She was an idiot. She could have any man she wanted, and she picked the one man who wanted something other than sex. She pulled the biggest bottle of rum off the shelf. Better make it two.

Kathy sniffed righteously as she walked out of the office, which was enough to put Annie on guard that something was up. As of late, nose puffs also signified a degradation of Annie's reputation. She hoped Kathy was only coming down with a cold, but as John and Stewart stepped into her office and shut the door behind them, she had a feeling a case of the sniffles was the least of her problems.

"Gentlemen." She nodded at each of them. "Grim faces today."

"Grim topic," John muttered.

Annie suppressed a shiver. "What's the problem?"

John lowered himself into one of the cushioned chairs opposite her desk and avoided her gaze.

Stewart remained standing, vibrating with disapproval. "Your car was parked in front of the liquor store this morning."

She blinked and said the first thing that popped into her head. "That's odd."

"It's despicable," he corrected. "You are supposed to be in the church tending your flock. Instead, you're buying alcohol before noon to indulge your habit."

"I don't have a habit." Although if a glass was put before her now, she would gulp it down. "Furthermore, I have been inside this room all morning. Your wife can vouch for me," Annie said to John.

"Kathy was out for two hours for a doctor's appointment," John said.

"Coincidently at the same time your car was spotted." If Stewart was trying to conceal his gloating, he wasn't successful.

Annie doubted the timing was a coincidence, but she didn't understand why her secretary would make up lies about her. "I walked to work today just as I do every day."

"In the rain?" John interjected.

"Yes, in the rain." But what if the allegations weren't a lie? Her car could have been parked in front of the liquor store. "My sister came to visit me yesterday. It's possible she borrowed my car for a drive around town."

"Your sister?" John looked dubious. His doubts and quiet

disapproval were harder to face than Stewart's righteous indignation.

"She's going through a rough patch. I invited her to stay with me for a few days until she can work things out." Technically, no invitation had been issued. Tanya had simply shown up and moved in.

"The church won't pay to house your guests," Stewart declared.

"She's staying with me. There's no cost."

"Doesn't she shower? The church pays your water bill. And food?"

"I buy all the food with my salary." Annie's patience snapped. "If I want to buy more, that's my prerogative."

"Not," Stewart said with more than a hint of triumph, "when you start buying liquor."

"Oh, for the love of God." In exasperation, she turned to John. "This is ridiculous. If you want to estimate how long Tanya spends in the shower and whatever else she adds to my utility bills, I'll reimburse the parish. If she wants to borrow my car, I'm not going to refuse her. Although I will ask her to drive her own vehicle on the occasions when she feels the need for alcohol or tobacco."

"She smokes, too?" Stewart asked.

"I don't know."

"You don't know?"

She thought for a moment of what she knew of Tanya's habits. "No, I don't know. Now that your minds are at ease on this topic"—she knew full well the opposite was true—"is there anything else you wish to discuss?"

"You said her name was Tanya," Stewart continued. "My daughter has this ridiculous notion your sister is the same Tanya who bares her body to the world and involves herself in sex scandals."

"You will find," Annie said carefully, "that your daughter's notions are rarely ridiculous. In fact, both you and she would benefit from spending more time together."

John stood up. "I need to get back to my office. Clearly, you've done nothing to cause your parish concern." He took a step toward the door but then turned back. "But be careful, Annie. Who you associate with and what is perceived can be just as damaging if not more so than your actions."

Her reputation. Her reputation was teetering on a ledge. Just a nudge would send it smashing to the ground and beyond repair. She forced a small nod of understanding.

John walked through the doorway. Kathy immediately stuck her head in. The old biddy couldn't even wait a minute for the gossip. Annie's resentment surged. Well, she'd just have to wait. Annie had more to say to Stewart on the subject of his daughter. "Not now, Kathy."

The woman pursed her lips but didn't back away. "Reverend Annie, the hospital just called. Myra Turnaggle was brought in with a broken hip. She's requesting you."

"Myra." Annie shot out of her chair. Myra was more than a parishioner. She was a friend. If Annie's reputation took that final tumble, she had the sickening suspicion Myra would be her only champion.

She gathered her purse and umbrella, leaving Stewart standing in her office with Kathy, and saw no way to avoid disaster.

Egan had felt foolish many times in his nearly eighteen years of life but never more than now. He'd been stood up. For the past forty-six hours and thirteen minutes, he'd counted down the time until he would see her again. Not a passing glimpse in the hall, but her full, undivided attention.

He stared at Heather's algebra book. He'd looked forward to returning it to her. She left it with him. In her haste to run away from him. He shook his head. That should have been his first clue. But no, he'd believed—really believed—that she was as interested in learning algebra from him as he was in teaching it to her.

And he'd hoped that by the time the semester was over he could work his way up to holding her hand. She'd laugh for weeks if she knew his thoughts. Holding hands meant nothing to a girl like her, a girl who knew everything about men and did it all with them. She wasn't a vulnerable, insecure innocent. He'd deluded himself into thinking he caught glimpses of it.

He slammed his notebook shut. He'd waited for over an hour. She wasn't coming, and he had better things to do with his time. Maybe he could fit in a board game with Megan. She'd wanted to play last night, but he had a physics test to study for. Today he'd make time for his sister. He had more important things to worry about than Heather. He was going to get out of this town, and away from girls who used him for his brain and didn't remember he existed the rest of the time.

He shoved Heather's algebra book back in his locker and made his way out of the school. The rain was gushing from the downspout at the corner of the building. He pulled up the hood on his coat and hunched his shoulders as he stepped into the cold, miserable weather.

"Hey Egghead."

His first instinct was to pretend he hadn't heard, but he didn't want to be that wimpy kid anymore. He stopped in the middle of the parking lot and braced himself before turning around. Troy Mullins—bully of the year—lounged against the door of a fifteen-year-old pickup. "Jerk," Egan muttered under his breath and started walking again. He'd choose an easier person to start with.

"Egghead, I'm talking to you."

Egan was a coward. Troy knew it. And worst of all, Heather

Fitzsimmons knew it. He turned around and watched Troy saunter up to him. Troy was soaked from the rain.

"You know, Egghead, that meatball sandwich really hit the spot. What do say you get me another one?" Troy socked him in the shoulder a lot harder than anyone would mistake for playful.

Egan staggered back a step. "I'm not working today."

"What? Got a hot date?" Troy laughed uproariously.

Egan clenched his teeth. It wasn't that inconceivable.

"When are you working so I can stop by and collect?"

Like he was going to answer that. He might be a coward, but he wasn't stupid. "You owe me nine-ninety-three. I'm not making you another sandwich until you pay me for your first meal. I want your money up front before I make you another one." He stared at Troy and waited to get his face bashed in.

"Very funny, Egghead. You owe me. I didn't get laid Friday night because of you."

The fact that Troy hadn't stomped all over him yet gave Egan a burst of courage. "You can't blame me because Heather recognized what a loser you are."

"She felt sorry for you. From now on, you give me the sandwiches free without making big sad eyes at her. Or I'll give you big black eyes to feel sad about. Got it?" Troy plunged his fist into Egan's stomach.

He doubled over and wretched on his own shoes. *Oh, man, that hurt.* The punch sucked the wind right out of his lungs. He hadn't even seen it coming. He watched Troy slosh through the puddles, thankfully leaving him alone.

Egan cradled his stomach and grimaced. Heather felt sorry for him. He wished she'd punched him instead.

"Why haven't you answered your cell phone?"

Tanya's throat clogged, and she clutched Annie's kitchen

receiver tighter. "How'd you find me, Hardball?"

"Hardball?" He laughed. "I don't believe you've had the privilege of checking out my testicles to make that judgment."

She shifted her weight. Once again, he made her feel like a fool. "It's an assessment of your delightful personality. You haven't answered my question."

"A better question would be what do I want?" he pointed out.

"I don't care what you want. I'm done with you and your lousy assignments."

Silence filled the receiver for a moment before his deep baritone rolled through her again. "I'm sorry about how badly things turned out in getting the papers. I underestimated your ability to take care of yourself."

She lowered herself into a chair, hating that she was a recipient of sympathy and hating even more that he was the one doling it out. "Yeah, well, offer your next pawn self-defense classes before you send her to do your job, Hardball."

"Jake. My name's Jake. Jake Jacobs."

She snorted. "Your family was short on creative inspiration by the time they got to naming you. You ought to thank me for calling you Hardball."

"Are you watching the news?" All softness in his voice was gone.

"No."

"Oliver Gilmer mowed down a six-year-old in a hit-and-run, driving on the sidewalk."

She flinched. "I'm sorry."

"Not as sorry as the kid's parents. This happened after he snorted with your husband in the back of Zeke's Hummer. We've got it on tape."

"If you taped it, why didn't you make the arrest before he hurt someone? Or is an innocent kid's life worth you making headlines for bust of the year?" This was not her fault. She wouldn't let him use it to make her feel guilty.

"Is he with you?"

"Zeke? No."

"Does he know about your sister?"

Did he? She tried to remember. "I don't think so."

"Don't hold out, Tanya. This guy needs to be locked up. He's feeding drugs to half the population of L.A. We got Gilmer, but your husband's driving around wasted, too. It's just a matter of time before another innocent person gets knocked off."

The phone clicked.

The doorbell rang.

"Hardball—I mean, Jake." The phone was dead against her ear. He'd already hung up. How could he hang up on her? What if Zeke was on the other side of that door?

"I'm sorry to bother you."

"You are never a bother," Annie said sincerely as she dropped into the chair next to Myra's hospital bed. "Myra Turnaggle, what were you doing on a ladder? You could have called me or any number of people to climb up there for you."

"I knew you were going to give me grief if you found out." Despite the pain in her eyes, Myra retained her spunk. "I imagined you'd say I could have fallen and broken my hip or something."

Amusement, exasperation, and concern warred for dominance of Annie's emotions. "Is it worth saying 'I would have told you so'?"

"Might as well save your breath." Myra reached for Annie's hand, and her voice turned plaintive. "What am I going to do?"

"Don't worry about the roof. We'll fix the leak. If it stops raining, we'll get the youth group up there this weekend as planned. If not"—Annie would crawl up there in the rain and fix it herself, although she didn't know a shingle from a shim—"we'll think of something."

"Oh, Reverend Annie, it's not just the roof." Myra squeezed her hand hard, communicating her fear and helplessness more eloquently than words.

Concern overpowered. "Tell me what else. We'll pray together."

"The people here want to put me in a nursing home for two months for rehabilitation. I can't do that. I've got to be back on my feet tomorrow. Someone has to run the food pantry. Families are counting on me to provide for them. The building needs to be staffed, and someone needs to work the phone and pester businesses for donations."

Annie leaned toward her and cupped her hand. Myra, who had always seemed invincible and tireless, now looked very mortal. Annie's own foundation cracked slightly to see her friend brought this low. "You're not going to be on your feet tomorrow. If you follow the doctor's instructions, you'll get back to where you need to be eventually, but not tomorrow."

"But—"

"I'm not finished," Annie said firmly. "No one's going to starve on your account. You've helped so many people through the years. Now it's time for everyone else to help you. Maplefield will still have a food pantry. It will be properly run, not as efficiently or spectacularly as you do it, but we'll manage."

"Oh, Annie, I couldn't possibly ask you—"

"You didn't ask. I'm telling. I'm not going to run the pantry on my own." Although she would if there was no other way. "But I promise not to let anyone incompetent screw it up for you."

Myra settled back on the pillows, looking more comfortable than when Annie had first arrived. "You're a good girl, Annie. I've always said Maplefield needs more of you."

Annie was going to need more of herself, too, to run the food pantry and tend to her church duties.

The man in the peephole wore a tan golf shirt. Tanya didn't need to look any further to be certain he wasn't Zeke. She unbolted the door and pulled it opened.

"So it is true," he said in greeting, as if he knew her and wasn't surprised to find her here. His voice reminded her he was the guy from the auction house who'd alternately begged and lapped up everything she'd offered him. When she'd still been full of herself. A lifetime ago.

The wind blew, slapping the rain against Tanya. She shivered and stepped back from the door. This was a guy she could handle, as harmless as they came. "Come in."

He stood on the other side, not moving, studying her face. Her makeup, which had been a slap job to begin with, was wearing thin. If he looked at her long enough, he'd see the bruises.

What was his name anyway? The only name she could think of was the man she hadn't slept with yet. Jake. "Did you knock so I could enjoy the draft, or are you going to come in so you can get your chance with me in the flesh?"

He stepped inside. She resisted hugging her arms across her chest as she closed the door. The thought of using her body to get something from anyone made her want to throw up.

He ran his hand over his damp hair, and she noticed a pale greenish-purple lump coloring his cheekbone below his left eye. "That's quite a bruise. How'd you get it?"

"Kinky sex." His tossed her his frat boy smile. She hoped that wasn't an invitation.

"What are you doing here?" she asked.

His shoulders straightened, and his eyes took on a determined gleam. "I came to talk to Annie. You know, the meaning of life and such."

"And here I thought I taught you everything about the meaning of life." She sneered to cover her sudden panic. This man didn't give a flying flip about religion and philosophy. He had an agenda. Annie, who didn't have a clue how to use her arsenal of female weapons, wouldn't be able to handle him.

"I'm looking for a second opinion. Annie's got some good connections." He looked almost cocky now.

And she knew. He'd come to Maplefield looking for her, just like that second-rate attorney. Jake had figured it out, too. Zeke and the paparazzi couldn't be far behind.

She'd proven her dad wrong. Heather danced through the front door. Someone had hired her. Someone had hired *her*.

When she started work tomorrow afternoon at four, she'd actually be paid for her presence. Someone was counting on her to be there. They might even miss her if she didn't show.

"Heather, what's put such a lovely smile on your face?" Mom said from inside the kitchen. "I can't remember the last time I saw you so happy."

She stopped dancing. Her mom was in front of the pantry, throwing bags of candy and chips into a black garbage bag. She should have checked the weather before she planned a picnic. "What are you doing with all that stuff?"

Mom hesitated, her own smile falling off. "I'm throwing it out."

"Throwing it out?"

"I, uh, think it's time I went on a, uh, diet, don't you?"

"Well, yes, of course, but I—" She assumed her mother was going to keep eating until she exploded and died.

"I'm overweight," Mom explained as if it wasn't obvious. "I haven't been taking care of myself. I can't walk across the room without getting out of breath. I'm an embarrassment to you."

"Uh—" Geez, what was she supposed to say to that?

"We both know it."

"I guess," Heather mumbled. "Mom, I got a job."

"A job?"

"I applied at Subway this afternoon. The lady hired me right away and said I could start tomorrow." She held her breath as she waited for Mom to complain about how she was already never home and should spend more time with her and Dad and more time studying.

"I think that's great, honey."

"You do?"

"Yes." Mom smiled at her again, not looking at the bag of corn chips as she tossed it aside.

Heather couldn't believe getting a job was this easy. She hadn't needed to show any cleavage, let alone give anyone a blowjob. "Dad said no one would hire me."

"I'll handle your father." Her mother's voice contained a hard edge. The last time Heather had heard it she'd been thirteen and had backed the family car into the tree across the street.

Her arms twitched to wrap around her mom in a big hug. Instead, she said, "You know, if those chip bags aren't open"—and since her mother ate a bag at a time, they probably weren't—"you could donate them to the food pantry instead of throwing them out."

"You don't have him handcuffed to the bedpost yet. You must be losing your touch." Nick threw his shoulder against the frame of Annie's front door before Tanya could slam it in his face. She definitely wasn't happy to see him.

Behind her, Jason simply looked embarrassed. Which was his own fault. He should have stayed home where he belonged, instead of insisting on tagging along. By approaching Tanya for his own foolish reasons, he risked everything Nick had worked so hard to achieve for himself and for his mother.

"Still haven't bought a suit, Mr. Attorney?" Tanya sneered.

"McAllister. Nick McAllister," he corrected, wincing as he sounded more like a bad James Bond imitation than a serious attorney.

"Bond, at least, could dress himself in style," Tanya noted.

Nick suppressed a sigh. If he wanted celebrity clients, he had to be prepared to suffer through their disagreeable personalities, something that hadn't occurred to him before his first meeting with Tanya. He'd expected clients to give him respect and be grateful for pulling them out of scrapes. Tanya would be pleased to learn she'd smashed her stiletto through his rose-colored glasses.

"Jason, go back to the apartment," he said. "I'll handle this."

"You two know each other?" Tanya asked, turning slowly.

Good. He'd thrown her off balance.

"We're brothers," Jason volunteered. "Nick handles the legal issues for the Vonkall Auction House. He first came to Maplefield trying to intimidate your sister into admitting to your sins."

Tanya laughed as if Nick were monumentally stupid. "That's certainly cozy." She looked him in the eye again. He was convinced she literally tucked her tongue against her cheek as she spoke. "I'm ever so grateful you want to be on my side now, instead of against me."

Tanya might hold the key to his dream, but he wasn't going to beg and let her manipulate him like she had Jason. The first time Nick had come to Annie's front door, she'd let him inside and provided for what she'd assumed were his needs without making him ask. And then she found he was manipulating her and wouldn't lift a finger for him.

As if Annie knew he was thinking about her, her car pulled into the driveway. She stepped out, and he saw her mouth form his name. Her initial reaction seemed to be surprise, but by the time she joined him at the front door she was obviously disgusted. "I didn't know attorneys did door-to-door sales calls looking for clients."

"I'm a little squeamish about leaving my brother alone with your sister." If he didn't know better, he'd think she liked him better as a handyman. Maybe she did. That way he was dependent on her and she could get cheap labor out of him.

"Everyone come in and get out of the rain. Jason"—Annie nodded to him as she walked through the doorway—"nice to see you again."

Liar. She didn't want to see any of them. She'd just have to pray about it while she maintained her Christian facade. "I believe now is a good time to clear up the matter of the stolen jewelry," Nick said.

"I took it." Tanya tossed back her hair. "Sue me if you like. It was mine. Nobody's ever accused me of taking the high road to get what I want."

Well, that cleared up the matter as far as he was concerned. Vonkall Auction House wasn't going to sue their most prominent client to get back an insignificant piece of a collection that she had the right of retraction on.

"It's not your jewelry," Annie said quietly, her fingers hovering around the cloth of her navy turtleneck.

Tanya turned to her. "Mom gave it to me after I got the Prima Bella skin contract."

Prima Bella. Nick wasn't certain, but he thought that was where Tanya launched her career. He shoved his hands in his pockets so he wouldn't give in to the temptation to put his arm around Annie. He didn't know her family dynamics or the background of this jewelry that meant so much to both women, but he did know she wasn't going to shatter, even if she looked like she might.

"It wasn't Mom's to give." Annie bit her lip.

"We'll talk about it later." Tanya's meaningful gaze swept from Nick to Jason. Apparently, this involved some dirty laundry she didn't want aired in his presence. Well, that would change as soon as she realized he was an attorney she could trust.

Annie's throat worked, as if she was having trouble swallowing. "I have more pressing concerns, actually. How long are you planning to stay in town, Jason?" She mustered a smile for him. Even though it wasn't directed at Nick, he still felt the punch of it.

"I'm playing it by ear. How long do you want me?" Jason was flirting, but his continued irrational behavior and this meeting with Tanya proved he needed close monitoring. Nick wasn't going to let Annie exploit his brother as cheap labor, just because she'd scratched Nick off her list of potential candidates.

"At least two months. The lady who operates our local pantry fell and broke her hip today. I promised I'd keep the place running for her."

"Of course you did," Nick muttered. Saint Annie.

"What does this person do?" Jason asked. "Hand out cans of beans and stock the shelves?"

"Something like that," Annie said.

Tanya spoke up. "I'll do it for as long as I'm here."

Annie blinked, looking as surprised as Nick felt. The World's Sexiest Viper running a food pantry? Yeah right. There was an ulterior motive somewhere.

"That's wonderful," Annie said, recovering quickly. "I still need help fixing the leaky roof on the food pantry. You up for it, Jason?"

Nick shifted his weight. He was the handyman. Annie should ask him. Jason didn't know one end of a hammer from the other.

"I'll give it a shot," Jason said.

"Great." Annie looked from Jason to Tanya as if Nick didn't exist. "I'll meet you both at the storefront on Main Street at eight o'clock tomorrow morning."

"If you want favors from me, I guarantee they won't happen at eight in the morning," Tanya said.

Annie frowned but didn't point out, as Nick was itching to, that Tanya had volunteered herself. "How about ten?"

"Sure," Jason said.

Tanya nodded.

"And Nick," Annie finally acknowledged him again. "If your brother's sticking around town, I suppose I'll see you again."

Just like that she dismissed him. Again. He watched her walk across the living room and battled the urge to kiss her until her head spun. Instead, he said, "Aren't you going to ask if there was a reason I stopped to see you?"

She turned slowly. "I assumed you came to see my sister. Did you want something from me?" She looked so tired as she said it, as if she were tired of forever doing things for other people. No doubt keeping up the act of being a perfect, selfless preacher was wearing.

The compulsion to offer a hug of comfort struck again. He'd rather kiss her out of anger. "Yes," he said. "You can keep your sister's hands out of my brother's pants."

Tanya sauntered toward him. With each calculated swing of her hips, Nick felt the slap of blatant sexuality. Even though he wasn't attracted to her, his body wasn't dead. "Jealous my hands aren't in your pants, Mr. Attorney?"

He opened his mouth to deny it but found his throat too dry to speak.

Her eyes locked on his as she pulled the snap on his jeans. "There's enough of me for both of you." She ran her tongue over her lush red lips and lowered his zipper.

She's lethal, his mind screamed. She'll leave you empty and

bitter, his soul warned. But his body gave an unmistakable green flag to her invitation. Before she could act on it, his mind ordered a self-preserving step back. Surprisingly, his feet cooperated.

"Your loss." Tanya didn't pursue him. "I'll be in the bedroom if you change your mind." She swirled her index finger in her mouth and slowly pulled it out.

Here was his chance for sex-of-a-lifetime. No red-blooded unattached man would hesitate.

Tanya swung her world-class derriere around and disappeared down the hall.

"Wow, I'm sweating," Jason said. "If it were me, I'd pull off my clothes and run after her. Come on, Annie. You can stay in the apartment tonight."

Annie. Nick pulled his gaze from where Tanya had retreated. Annie was staring at his open jeans. Horrified. No, her expression was more haunted. Whatever it was, she wasn't staring in rapt awe at his manly glory. Feeling like a first-class jerk, his mind screaming *I told you so,* he turned his back on her and refastened his pants.

"If Nick and Tanya want to get it on," Annie said to Jason, "they can do it somewhere other than church property."

"You don't care?" Jason sounded surprised. "I know it's none of my business, but I thought you and Nick . . ." His voice trailed off.

Nick's fingers fumbled on his snap.

"Oh, come on, me versus my sister. What guy wouldn't dump me overboard?"

"Annie." Nick turned to face her, unable to bear the pain in her voice. "This was just a physical reaction. It's nothing personal."

She laughed humorlessly. "That's a good one. Have you or have you not used me to get to my sister?"

"Yes, but not for sex." His gaze focused on the tear tumbling from her lashes. Hurting her hadn't been his intention.

She swiped the back of her hand across her cheek. "Today's your lucky day. You get it all. You can see yourself out."

"Annie." He couldn't leave with her crying because of his callousness. He crossed the room and wrapped his arm around her. "Tanya's important to my family."

"Because of Gloria Glenbard. Jason told me."

Disappointment curdled in his mouth. "Then you should understand."

"I do." She shrugged out of his embrace. "I'm a minister, worthy only of scorn, but too useful for my celebrity contacts for you to completely discard."

Her words should have completely summed up his feelings, but his heart ached to explain all the reasons he liked her for herself. The admission would free her to point out all the things within him she found lacking. He was looking to create unity and heal old wounds, not slice open new ones. "I'm glad we understand each other. I'll see myself out."

Chapter 10

Annie slumped against the hallway wall outside her bedroom. She couldn't go in there. Tanya would be waiting for Nick in Annie's bed. The thought made her want to throw up.

She clutched her stomach and straightened. She wouldn't let it happen again.

She leaned her head against the cool, beige wall. It wasn't the same this time. She had no claim on Nick. He was free to go to whomever he wanted. He'd only given her two kisses, and those were to get him closer to her sister.

And it had worked. That was the part that truly made her sick. She lifted her head and straightened her shoulders. She was done with Nick. He was behind her. A slight slip in her determination to stay true to God's will.

But Tanya required action. Annie had enough of letting her sister steal everything important from her life.

Annie marched into the bedroom. "Get out of my bed. Get out of my house."

Tanya stood in the far corner of the room. She dropped the framed picture of their paternal grandparents back onto the nightstand, not bothering to right it as it fell face down on the wood surface. "What bug crawled up your butt?"

"I thought I could forgive you for Danny, but I can't." Fury and humiliation swamped her as the memories flooded back. "You're here to ruin my life. This time I'm not going to sit by and watch it happen."

"Danny?" Tanya laughed. It was the sound of the heartless viper Annie had never believed she was until now. "Give me a break. That must have happened fifteen years ago. I can't believe you're still upset about it."

"It was ten and a half years ago." Five days before college graduation. "He was my fiancé." Twenty-six days before their wedding. "And you slept with him in my bed." Three weeks and nineteen hours after Annie gave him her virginity in that same bed. The pain of discovering them ripped through her chest.

"He wanted it." Not an ounce of repentance from her heartless sister. "Even I could see he wasn't good enough for you."

For the second time since she entered the house, Annie found herself close to tears. She blamed Tanya for both. "I was happy with him. You couldn't stand that I might be so happy I'd forget the world revolved around you and your selfish needs."

Tanya walked toward her. "Look, I'm sorry I hurt you." She looked so remorseful Annie had to remind herself Tanya was an actress. "I'm just so—so messed up inside. I walked in, and he was clearly interested in me. I couldn't believe this was your perfect Danny. Letting you find us doing the horizontal mambo was the easiest way—and the way I knew best—to make you see the truth about him."

"And about you," Annie said bitterly.

"Yeah, me, too." Tanya sat down on the bed. "You want to hear how I lost my virginity?"

Definitely not. Her head was crowded with too many images of Tanya seducing men as it was. "Only if you want to tell me." She was a pastor and a counselor before she was a sister and a woman with a grudge. She walked around the bed and picked up the framed picture. She dusted the faces with a corner of her blazer. Loving yet stern, her grandparents had raised her while her biological parents jetted off to tour the country with Tanya.

"I've never told anyone. This isn't something I like to

advertise." Tanya sounded uncharacteristically vulnerable.

"I don't advertise what people tell me in confidence. But I heard the stories at school. You told everyone you lost your virginity to Brian Madison in the janitor's closet during English class." Annie set the photo upright and walked back to sit next to Tanya. She'd taken control of her life after Danny, steering him toward an expensive 900-number psychic line when he'd called and asked for Tanya's phone number. She was still in control now, with God as her copilot, of course.

"True story, except for the virginity," Tanya said. "Two weeks before, I went to the final photo shoot to decide if I got the Prima Bella contract. The pictures were great, but the executive wanted a private interview with me before they made their final decision."

Annie flinched. She didn't like where this was headed. Tanya had only been fourteen years old. "Did Mom have any idea what this guy was up to?"

Tanya drew her knees up to her chest and wrapped her arms around them. "She squeezed my hand and told me to do everything he said, everything he wanted."

"You didn't do it to launch your career. You did it for Grandma's jewelry," Annie guessed.

"I was so jealous she didn't leave me anything personal. Mom promised if I got the contract she'd give the jewelry to me. The executive was very smooth, very practiced at seduction. He made it easy. He taught me my body's only a means to an end. Sex is no place for emotions. He came through with the contract. Mom came through with the jewelry. And I was on my way to fame."

Although their shallow, fame-seeking mother had died before Annie graduated from seminary, Annie had never felt more disgusted and ashamed of her. Annie couldn't resent her sister any longer. "Was the price worth it?"

"No." She hugged her knees. "All I've ever wanted is to be loved, and a necklace can't buy that, especially one that wasn't intended for me."

"You had Mom and Dad. Grandma and Grandpa were the only people in the world who loved me. The jewelry was their way of trying to balance the scales."

"Nobody loves me," Tanya shot back.

"You have thousands of fans who love you, people who drop to their knees in adoration." And it made Annie sick with jealousy to know Nick was among them.

"They don't love me," Tanya insisted. "They can't, because nobody knows me. Not even Mom and Dad did. All everyone loves is the image of me and what they want me to be."

"Do you love the person you are?" Annie asked, her calling as a counselor and her need to help her sister taking over.

"Everything I do is to protect my image. I don't even know who the real Tanya is."

"Maybe she's a girl who's searching for something meaningful in her life." Annie draped her arm around Tanya.

"I don't think I'm searching, but even if I am, I'll never find whatever meaning is out there." Tanya rested her head on Annie's shoulder. "But just knowing my sister doesn't hate me would be a start."

"I don't hate you. I think the real Tanya is a good person who's going to make a positive difference in the world." Annie might even find the love in her heart to forgive Tanya's past wrongs.

"If the World's Sexiest Viper doesn't kill her first."

Tanya was late. The impatient people waiting for her would see her as a lazy and spoiled party girl. She wouldn't correct the assumption. The world was supposed to revolve around Tanya and her selfish needs. Today Tanya needed to help the fat lady—

Lois Fitzsimmons was her name—coordinate her moves on the rowing machine. The hungry people at the food pantry would just have to line up and wait.

Incredibly, she was looking forward to helping someone without any benefit to herself. The feeling wouldn't last. She'd bail when she got bored. Annie wouldn't be surprised.

Annie hadn't even acted surprised when Tanya spilled her guts last night. It was past. It wasn't supposed to matter anymore. But she'd let it matter last night. Somehow having Annie listen with her arm around her, she felt less brittle inside. Annie was good for a battered woman's soul. Tanya was lucky to have her as a sister. She didn't want to spend another decade making her assistant do the monthly calls to check in with her only living relative, the only person who might love her as she was.

Tanya pushed the depressing thought away and opened the storefront door. Annie, Jason, and Mr. Attorney-without-a-suit were already inside the food pantry, staring at the ceiling with the ponderous expressions that incompetent work crews liked to use. She'd seen enough of them on the set to know.

Jason pressed his fingers to his lips and blew her a kiss. Instead of gliding into character to yank his chain and get him all hot and bothered again, she wished she'd never slept with him and let him think he had a chance of going a second round with her.

About Mr. Attorney, on the other hand—she didn't feel an ounce of remorse for coming on to him. She didn't want to sleep with him. The thought of sex still turned her stomach. But he wanted to use her. Worse, he was already using her sister for his selfish goals. Annie knew it, but she was too sweet and too giving to use him back. Tanya wasn't.

"My bed was cold last night." Tanya brushed her breasts against the back of the attorney's T-shirt.

Nick tensed. "That's a shame. Maybe you ought to fly your husband in. Annie, you'll want to rip out the rotting plywood under the shingles first. Once the roof is sealed, you can fix this drop ceiling."

The detestable thug was ignoring her. She slipped a button on her blouse from its straining position across her breasts. Her gaze strayed to Annie. She was staring at her with the same horrified expression as when she walked in on the horizontal mambo. Nick wasn't her fiancé. She couldn't imagine why Annie would like him. He was a bigger jerk than Danny.

If Tanya turned the sexual energy off for Annie's sake, she'd rob herself of her most powerful weapon. On the other hand, she could make Annie see Nick wasn't worthy of her before he hurt her. She might be grateful enough to give Tanya her blessing to keep the jewelry. She slipped another button out of its hole and slithered around Nick until her double Ds were under his nose.

Jason, who had been practically drooling as he watched her, suddenly grinned. "I have to write about you. It's unavoidable."

That stopped her cold. No way did she want another person to make a quick buck by slapping around the garbage of her life. "What do you mean?"

"I'm a writer. I want to write about you."

She stepped back from Nick, her hands shaking as she fastened her cleavage beneath the flimsy fabric. She was at her most vulnerable, brittle from Zeke's working over. And desperate for something real to fill the void inside her. If Jason could see that, he'd expose the details of her sorry life. She could live with him making her look like a monster. Better that than someone to be pitied.

Right now, she craved privacy, a relationship she didn't have to share with the world. Jake. She didn't want anyone to connect them. She suppressed a cringe at how he would laugh at her expense, to find out she was building fantasies around him.

"You manage an auction house," she said to Jason.

"I inherited that job. It's not my passion."

She could handle being his passion, but not like this. "The tabloids are overstaffed with sensationalists blowing up the minute details of my life. You don't have the bloodthirstiness to compete with them."

"I have no intention of competing." There was no trace of a party boy in this earnest, driven man. "I want to write your biography, Tanya, your exclusive life story from your birth to now."

She thought about what she'd told Annie last night and prayed her sister meant what she said about keeping confidences. "Dig out those back issues of the tabloids," she said to Jason. "I'm sure it's all in there." She'd learned years ago she couldn't stop what was written about her. She could only spin it to her advantage.

Tanya turned to Annie. They didn't have a chance of pulling together a real sisterly bond. Their lives were too different. "Tell me what you want me to do for the food pantry. I said I'd help, and I will. But get everything you want out of me today because I'm leaving tonight."

Egan stood next to his locker staring at her. Heather tried to ignore him as she hurried to English class, painfully aware of Veronica Hastings and Troy Mullins walking hand-in-hand behind her. She almost made it past when Egan said her name. She pretended she didn't hear and took another step. If she acknowledged him, one of them would end up being laughed at all over school. She couldn't decide if she was more afraid of it happening to herself or him.

"Heather." His hand shot out and encircled her wrist.

She couldn't ignore him now. She stopped walking and

prayed Veronica and Troy would keep moving. "Egan." His name stuck in her throat. "I'm in a hurry."

His fingers tensed briefly on her arm before he released her. "I just wanted to give you this. You forgot it on Monday."

She stared stupidly at his face. A kiss. He was going to kiss her. Here. Now.

"Here." He pushed something hard between them.

She blinked and looked down. Her algebra book. Her hand shook as she took it from him. Her stomach fluttered, and her heart pounded. What was the matter with her?

"I missed you yesterday." Egan's voice was so low the words barely carried to her.

But she heard them. Her hand opened spasmodically, the book clattering to the floor. For a moment she stared at him, a repeat of last Monday's klutzy head-smack playing in her head.

"Oooh," Veronica cooed. "Is the town slut going to kneel down and give Egghead his first blowjob, or is he going to get on his knees and beg her for one?"

Heather flinched and started to walk away, but Egan bent down. She couldn't bear to hear Veronica ridicule him. He didn't deserve it. She grabbed his shoulder. "I'll get the book. There's no need to embarrass yourself in front of a tramp who settles for the town slut's discards."

Several passing students snickered. Veronica walked off in a huff. Heather slid the book with her toe so she didn't embarrass herself or Egan by pressing her cheek against his fly. Then she picked up the book and saluted him with it, slipping into English class just as the late bell rang.

Her heart still thundered, and her stomach flip-flopped.

Annie's professional side and common sense commanded she say something to make Tanya reconsider. But she couldn't. Tanya wanted Nick. Whether he wanted her physically or not,

Nick certainly wanted Tanya for his career. When Tanya left, Nick would, too. It was best for Annie's well-being. She wouldn't have to watch them getting it on in front of her. She'd shore up her reputation with the folks at Good Shepherd, and they'd see her as boring, dedicated Reverend Annie once again.

"Are you going to let him scare you away?" Nick challenged Tanya. "Jason's never written a word in his life. He's hardly a threat."

Now there was some nice brotherly support. Annie wasn't excited about having her link to Tanya advertised in a splashy book either. But what happened to the Nick who was so concerned about his brother's well-being? "You're both approaching Tanya in the wrong way. Instead of exploiting her, explain the broken family ties you're trying to mend. Gloria Glenbard is their grandmother," she said to Tanya.

"I know. Their mother hates celebrities. That's why I used your name and image as my disguise when I went to see her."

"And ended up with me instead," Jason finished. "My mother doesn't—" The door opened, and he cut himself off.

Lois Fitzsimmons walked in, looking uncertain. "Reverend Annie. I hope I'm not intruding. I'm looking for Myra."

Annie crossed the room to her. "Didn't Stewart tell you?"

Lois's face flushed. "We don't talk as much as—well, you know how it is."

Annie squeezed Lois's hands and filled her in on Myra's accident and Tanya's temporary help. God was still answering prayers. Lois's timely presence proved it. "Would you be willing to manage the pantry for a couple months?"

"Oh, no, I couldn't possibly." Lois yanked her hand free. "I don't know anything about management or running anything. I just came by to drop off a couple bags of food."

"We're happy for the donation, of course, but seriously consider giving your time, too. Myra's really in a bind." Not to mention herself. "I can't conduct my church meetings from here without half the pastoral council threatening mutiny."

"Oh, Reverend Annie, I'd love to help, but I'm not qualified. I haven't worked since Heather was born."

She'd love to help. Annie fixated on that. There was hope. All she had to do was bolster Lois's self-esteem. Tanya and Nick would desert her. But Lois would love to help.

"I work as a manager of an auction house," Jason offered. "I could mentor you on how to be a manager and run a business."

"If you're going to be here, why don't you run the place?" Lois asked.

"Just because I know how to do it, doesn't mean I like to," Jason snapped, but his glare was aimed at his brother.

Lois flushed and stammered, "I didn't mean—I mean I shouldn't have asked. I mean—Oh, see, Annie, I never say the right thing. Myra spent years building this place, and I'll ruin it."

"Don't be silly," Annie soothed. *And please, please, don't back out on me.* "Your question was a reasonable one."

Jason blinked. "You didn't say the wrong thing. I was giving you the truth without polishing it first."

"Practicing for writing your book, no doubt," Tanya interjected.

"Oh, no." Lois looked more upset as she obviously recognized Tanya. "I'll leave. People like me must always bother you. I wasted your time in the gym, and I'm pestering you now."

"If you were a bother, I would have told you," Tanya said, her voice uncharacteristically soothing. "I'm only here for today, so if you want me to do anything for the food pantry, tell me now."

"You're asking the wrong person," Lois said.

Tanya smiled. It was a different smile, softer around the edges than the one she showed to most people. Annie hadn't caught many glimpses of it since Tanya turned fourteen. "No, I'm not," she said. "You're the boss. This is your chance to tell me what to do. I don't give many people that opportunity."

Annie couldn't help admiring her sister's tactics. Tanya was already deferring to Lois as the building manager and offering her services in a way that would clinch Lois's role—at least until Stewart found out and had a conniption.

"I—I think you should hit everyone up for donations," Lois said. "I mean, they could blow me off, but they wouldn't dare for Tanya."

Tanya's flinch was so small Annie doubted anyone else had noticed. "See," Tanya said brightly. "I knew you'd be a great manager."

"Well, that's settled." Annie smiled and silently thanked God for her sister's presence. "You two and Jason can work things out while Nick and I check out the roof."

As soon as she realized what she said, she wished she could take the words back. She didn't want to be on the roof or anywhere alone with Nick. And he'd made it painfully obvious he didn't want to be alone with her when he could be with her sister.

Tanya looked at Jason, and this time her gaze was full of pure loathing. "There's nothing to work out. You're entitled to write your hogwash, just like every other blowhard with a pen."

"If he's only out to smear your name, you have the right to sue him for slander and libel and to do what you can to block publication," Nick said. "You need a lawyer who will help you recognize your power over what's written about you."

Annie shoved her way out the back door, unable to listen to him groveling for crumbs from Tanya. *Jesus, my life is dedicated to the service of You. It's never felt more empty and unsatisfying.*

Nick followed Annie out the door. She didn't glance back, just assumed he would come, which irritated him as much as her taking free handyman labor for granted. He ignored the voice that reminded him he'd been upset last night when she passed over his handyman skills.

She stopped at the ladder propped against the building. "Why do you cut down your brother's attempts at success?"

"Excuse me?" He took two more steps, using his body to block her in against the side of the building. Half of his phone calls in the past two days were attempts to strengthen the Vonkall position in the contracts, things Jason should have pushed for before the terms landed on Nick's desk.

"Jason has just as much right to pursue his dreams as you do, but you treat him like his talent is second-rate."

"What do you know about being second-rate?" Her accusations stung. Jason had been wonder-boy without ever proving himself. Nick had to work over and over again to prove his worth, and he still came up short. Here he was, working his butt off to make his dream come true, but Jason was shadowing his every move and turning the effort into a laughingstock.

"Quite a lot actually. My parents were hoping for a second gorgeous and ambitious Tanya. Instead, they ended up with me."

"They must be very happy."

Her amazing blue eyes didn't waver as she stared at him. "That's the nicest thing anyone's ever said to me."

Nick forgot to be mad over her unfair attack on his treatment of Jason, as he got lost in her gaze. She was beautiful and . . . pure. That was the only word he could think of. Of course it was a mirage. She might not be as evil as he'd first thought. But she wasn't pure. She was a minister.

That knowledge didn't stop her spell from wrapping around him until he wanted to fix her roof just to please her and impress her with his skills and his biceps. He pressed his hips to hers against the wall. An innocent would have run from him or frozen with fear. Instead, he was the one who turned hard but definitely not frozen.

Her smile faded but she didn't squirm away. Her expression was more contemplative than fearful. "Do you salute for every woman, or do I remind you of Tanya?"

Someone pure wouldn't have mentioned it. He stepped back, but it didn't stop the primitive ache. "Tanya's like watching a porn film. No one would mistake you for porn, Annie."

Her gaze dulled. "Don't use your aftereffects from the Tanya show on me."

Now it was Nick's turn to stare. She'd completely misunderstood his meaning. His response to her didn't just come from a physical level. She touched him emotionally, as well. He wasn't prepared to admit it, certainly not to her.

Annie turned away from him and looked up the ladder. "Do you really know anything about roofs, or was that part of your elaborate hoax?"

"I fixed your church toilet, didn't I?" He stepped toward her again, his hands on the ladder rungs on either side of her. No one had ever doubted his skills with a tool belt. They just demeaned them.

She faced him again, but her aversion to him was evident in the way she shift her body to avoid contact with any part of him. "You could have hired someone to do it so you could keep up your ruse."

He'd spent so long denying his handyman skills. He couldn't imagine anyone claiming credit for something no reasonable person would be proud of. "What would have been in it for me?"

"Same thing you're angling for now." She pushed on his shoulders.

What he was angling for was a decent excuse to kiss her. The closeness was making her uncomfortable. All her vibes shouted at him to step back, but he couldn't sever the contact. "Why don't you explain your point? I'm obviously not grasping it."

"Supermodels—they're out of reach for the average guy, right?"

"I never met one before yesterday." He had no problem conceding that point.

"So you'd be happy to settle for the supermodel's sister. Most guys can't claim to have dated one of those. But then the model comes to town. Why settle for the sister? She'll still be here next week or next month, but you may never get another chance with the real thing." She walked up a step on the ladder.

Nick couldn't believe she was serious. He placed his hands on Annie's hips as she took another step up. "I want Tanya for my career."

"At least your spin is original."

He'd never heard her use such a caustic tone before. He pulled her off the ladder rung and turned her so they were face-to-face again. "I don't think you're second-rate. Believe what you will about me, but don't go home thinking I'd rather sleep with your sister than you. Given the choice, I'd be buried to the hilt inside you."

Chapter 11

"Can't you ever keep a low profile?" Jake snarled through the cell phone so loud that Tanya held it away from her ear. She looked through the panel curtains at the large crowd of gawkers who were hoping for a peek at the star in their midst.

Lois was right. Tanya's celebrity power had brought in a record number of donations. Great for starving people in northwest Illinois. Bad for the World's Sex-less Viper. Too many people knew who and where she was.

"Your greetings give me such warm fuzzies, Hardball." Tanya thought of him by his given name now, but somehow calling him Jake crossed a line of familiarity she wasn't ready to forge.

"Every freelance photographer in L.A. is booking a flight to Nowhere-ville."

"Funny, I didn't know there was an airport here. Even funnier, what makes you think you can assign yourself as my personal keeper?"

Silence buzzed through the line for a moment. "Would it be so bad to have someone looking out for you?"

She didn't want him to feel sorry for her again. Even more, she didn't want to relive that awful night, and they were headed for a rehash. "Your idea of looking out for someone is to lock them in a cell for ten to twenty. I'll cover my own butt, thanks."

The front door to the food pantry opened. Lois guided an unfamiliar woman inside and then locked the door behind them.

Tanya covered the mouthpiece on the phone. "You've got

everything you need now. I'm going to bail on you," she whispered.

"You can't." Lois looked stricken. The other woman cowered in her shadow.

"Where are you going, Tanya?" Jake asked.

"None of your business." She flattened her palm harder across the mouthpiece.

"Jason just told the crowd that if they brought a donation, they could have an autograph and get their picture taken with you," Lois said. "If they didn't bring anything and weren't in need of food to feed their families tonight, they have to leave. A dozen people already walked out."

"Probably to go home for their cameras and a can of beans," Tanya muttered, although she did admire Jason's ingenuity. "He's got a lot of nerve to announce it without consulting me."

"It is my business," Jake snarled, "when your husband's on the top of my most-wanted list and the most likely place he's going to show up is where you are."

The lurking woman reached for a can of peaches, revealing a bruise along her forearm culminating in a swollen elbow. Tanya shuddered.

"Since you're still in L.A., I assume you're only paying lip service to your desire to look out for me," she said to Jake and then looked at Lois. "What's Jason's backup plan if I don't agree?"

"You said you'd be here all day, and you'd do what I asked," Lois stammered.

"I didn't agree to do what he asked."

"I'm not asking anymore. I'm telling," Jake said.

"That's why Jason sent me to ask you." Lois smiled nervously.

Tanya laughed. "Your mentor's teaching you well." She spoke pointedly into the phone. "Maybe someone else could get further with me if he found a mentor who taught him how to sweet-talk."

"Should I let people in?" Lois asked.

"No, give me fifteen minutes to fix my hair and makeup." She wasn't going to look like she'd been knocked around, when people were snapping her picture. "First rule of being a celebrity—always keep them waiting. But I'll make an exception for your friend. Introduce me."

"Tanya," Jake said through the phone. "Be careful."

She snapped off the phone without dignifying his phony concern with a reply. Zeke would hide from the law on a tropical island where he had easy access to drugs and señoritas. Jake knew it. If he thought he had a chance of catching Zeke in Maplefield, he'd be here trying to do it. On the other hand, Tanya was already here. Jake could save himself the time and trouble by passing the dirty work to Tanya. Again.

The World's Sexiest Viper was giving autographs and posing for pictures at the Maplefield food pantry. The rumor shot around school faster than the news of the latest person to diddle Heather Fitzsimmons. This rumor wasn't likely to be true, but Tanya *was* in town. Heather knew that for a fact. It was certainly worth ducking out of algebra and skipping the rest of school to find out if there was any truth to the gossip.

A line snaked out of the food pantry and around the block. It had to be true. But the line wasn't moving at all. She was willing to risk flunking algebra and not graduating high school to see Tanya, but she couldn't take the chance of being late for her first day at work. She had a clean slate there. She wasn't a screwup or a lost cause there yet.

Heather walked around the alley to the backside of the buildings. A man was on the roof. She squinted at him, trying to decide if he was Nick McAllister. Kathy had told Dad he'd left town. The man looked over toward where she was standing. He was Nick. She ducked behind a Dumpster in the alley. Amazingly, Kathy's gossip was wrong.

"Scram, kid. This is my stakeout."

Heather jumped. A man was already behind the Dumpster. He was skinny, and his oily hair was slicked back. He reminded her of a snake. He likely used the camera in his hand to weigh him down so a strong wind wouldn't carry him away. The lens on that thing was humongous. "Who are you?"

He held the camera up to his face, pushing her roughly back with his arm. "You're in my line of sight. Scram."

She peeked out and noticed Nick's attention was focused on a woman on a ladder next to the roof. Reverend Annie. Heather made a run for the back door of the food pantry. She pulled it closed behind her and ended up squished. Between the door and a massive rear end.

"To meet Tanya"—the person she was squashed against said—"you have to bring a food or paper goods donation and start at the end of the line like everyone else."

Heather knew that voice. Even with the new ring of authority, a girl could still recognize her mother's voice. "Who put you in charge?"

Mom turned around, her cheeks flushed and her chest heaving. Her voice was hard and certain. "I'm your mother. I'm taking back my authority. You, Heather, better explain why you're not in school right now, and it better be a life-or-death emergency."

Heather blinked. She wanted her mom to get more backbone and stand up for herself, but not now. An emergency. She'd have to think up something. Mom always bought her excuses. "There were these really bad gaseous smells at school. It was horrible. They had to let us out early so we wouldn't die from the fumes. On the way home I saw the line and saw Tanya was here so I had to stop to meet her."

"Then why aren't you in line?"

Heather relaxed. Her mom bought it. She hadn't changed that much. Heather could still work over and around her with a little planning and manipulating. "Because I have to work at four. Remember my new job. It's my first day, and I don't want to be late. I want to make a good impression."

"I'm only going to tell you this once, so listen closely," Mom said, the steel in her tone still strong. "If I ever catch you skipping school again, you won't be allowed to keep your job."

"You can't do that."

Mom folded her arms across her chest. "Watch me. As it is, when you're not at work and not at school, you are to be home studying."

Her mother was grounding her? Heather couldn't believe it. "Why? I haven't done anything."

"You skipped school. That's reason enough. As it happens, your algebra teacher called me this morning. We had a long discussion about your grade, attitude in class, and the fact that if you don't pass, you won't graduate. What class did you ditch to come here?"

"Study hall." She didn't meet her mother's eye. Mom used to believe any pathetic excuse. Nothing should have changed.

"Good. When I talk to your algebra teacher tonight, we'll have a lovely discussion about what you learned in class today."

"I wouldn't waste my time calling."

"Oh, I won't." Mom smirked. Smirked—Heather couldn't believe it. "She's going to call me."

This was bad. Heather would be at work and unable to intercept the call. This was really bad. "I'm going to run and see Tanya so I can get back to school before my next class."

"No, you're not going to see Tanya. You're going back to school, then to work. When you get home, I'll help you with your algebra homework before bed."

"Yeah right." Mom handed all the math homework to Dad when Heather hit fractions. "What do you know about algebra?"

"Not much, but I'm going to find out."

It was time to cut her losses. The meeting with Tanya would have to wait, at least until she could sneak around the front and away from the watchful eyes of her mother. "I'll be home whenever I get home. Don't wait up."

"Your shift's done at eight," Mom said. "I expect you home by eight-twenty."

"You can't—"

"Or would you like me to wait in front of Subway at eight o'clock and drive you home?"

This was unreal. She'd finally gotten a job like an adult, and her mom decided she needed a chaperone like she was a baby. "Why don't you drive me back to school, too, while you're at it?"

"Great idea. I'll get someone else to guard the back door."

Heather grabbed her mom's arm. "Geez, I was being sarcastic. I'm going now."

"No." To her utter mortification, Mom took her hand. "You've chosen to skip class. A couple more minutes won't kill you."

"That's what I've been trying to tell you. Let me see Tanya."

Reverend Annie entered through the back door. The harder Heather tried to pull her hand free, the tighter her mom's grip became. Mom explained the situation to the perfect minister and then walked Heather out to her car. Of course, the car was parked in front of the building. Everyone in town was standing there with nothing better to do than watch Mom stuff her into the car. Word of this was going to get back to the school. Everyone was going to laugh, and Heather was going to die.

"This is all your fault," Heather shouted as soon as her fatso mom had stuffed herself behind the wheel and shut the door.

"What's my fault is letting you get so out of control. Things are changing, Heather, starting right now. Get used to it."

Heather hated this new calm but serious voice that didn't allow for argument. She wanted her mom to stand up for herself, but Mom was supposed to do that to Dad, not to her. Passing algebra no longer mattered. She was going to be laughed out of school long before graduation.

"What are you—a door guard?" Nick growled in Annie's ear.

"Yes." She forced a laugh, hoping it disguised the delicious shiver from his breath on her ear. *Given the choice, I'd be buried to the hilt inside you.* Eleven words were all it took to turn her body into an inferno. "Lois had family business to take care of. What's the diagnosis on the roof?"

"Should have been reshingled three years ago. At least one sheet of plywood is rotted through and will have to be replaced."

"Oh." She'd expected Nick to bluster and defer. She'd been on the roof with him while he'd poked around and made noncommittal noises. She didn't think he'd had the opportunity to consult with anyone since she'd come in five minutes before. "What's the cost estimate for materials?"

"Fifteen hundred to two thousand."

She flinched. She couldn't take that much money from the church outreach budget without the approval of the finance committee, and Stewart Fitzsimmons would fight her all the way. The most she could afford from her personal savings would be five hundred. She still had her living expenses and had to retain a small cushion in case another needy person crossed her path before her next paycheck.

"I'll need to get more tools than what I have on hand in my truck to do the job."

Along with a couple of laborers who know what they're doing? She couldn't help wondering, but, God help her, she was starting to believe whatever he said. "John Patterson agreed to loan his tools if Myra got the shingles. I don't think she was able to convince anyone to donate yet, but I'm sure the offer to borrow the tools is still on."

"What do you need more donors for?" Tanya asked, walking into the room. Her hair was sleek and blond-brown again. Her face was perfectly made up, without a hint of the fear and unrest she wore when she came to Maplefield. "You're going to have enough food to send a barge to China."

"What about shingles? Is anybody standing in line with those?" The roof problem hung over Annie's head. Even if Nick didn't know what he was talking about, his monetary estimate was probably close.

"What's the problem?" Jason followed Tanya into the room. "Why haven't you started signing and posing yet?"

"Because I looked like the inside of a Dumpster," she snapped. "People didn't raid their pantries to see a woman who looks anything less than perfect."

"Then send Annie out to smile for them," Nick said.

Annie froze. It was one thing to tell her in private he liked her better, but he announced it in front of her sister. Literally everyone in the world knew Tanya was prettier than she. Maybe he was being sarcastic. He might want to sleep with her, but he certainly didn't believe she had the corner on perfection.

Tanya gave him a pithy look. "You've got it bad."

Nick clamped his mouth into a grim line and turned away. No doubt he realized he'd made a serious tactical error in wooing Tanya as his client.

"People are getting impatient," Jason said. "A rumor's circulating that you're not really here. It's all a hoax."

"Good," Tanya said, with a toss of her shiny hair. "Half of them will go away, and maybe I won't kill the last person in line when they ask for just one more picture."

"Tanya—" Annie prepared to intervene.

"You want shingles and plywood, you'll get it," Tanya said, "guaranteed."

"How?" Jason asked.

"Celebrity magic."

Nick snorted. "I knew you guys were full of yourselves, but this is ridiculous."

"This coming from a man who dreams of making a career catering to the same ridiculous people," Jason said.

The reminder was another icy smack in Annie's face.

Tanya shot Nick a disgusted look. "Jason's going to announce the building's needs and its estimated cost. Whoever offers to finance the repairs moves to the front of the line—"

"You're not worth nearly as much as you think you are," Nick scoffed.

"And," Tanya continued, "he gets a kiss from me."

"What if a woman comes forward?" Annie asked.

"If she wants a kiss, I'll give her one. But for the women, I'm offering to teach my tricks to make a man beg."

Jason choked.

Nick clenched his jaw.

Annie wished she had more money in her savings account.

Egan's hottest fantasy stood behind the Subway counter in an apron, her hair flattened by her visor. The manager, a twenty-something named Lisa who had never been in his fantasies before, talked Heather through making a club sandwich for the traveler who'd placed the order. Heather lifted her head, blew her hair out of her eyes, and looked directly at him.

Egan stopped breathing. She wasn't a mirage. She was real, and she worked in the place where up until now he'd felt relaxed and in control. He went to the back room, clocked in, and donned his own apron and visor, his hands fumbling with the apron strings. By the time he joined Heather and Lisa behind the counter, the customer was gone and a family of four was eating at one of the booths.

"Egan, this is Heather Fitzsimmons. She's going to work the dinner shift and on weekends," Lisa said.

"Yeah, we've met," he squeezed out before his lungs constricted, making speech impossible. Heather knew he worked here. How far would she go to make his life miserable?

"We'll make a good team." Heather's words were confident, but her smile was tentative.

Impossible as it seemed, her sweet smiles packed more of a punch than her cocky ones. And her cocky I-am-a-goddess smile had knocked him on his butt the first time he'd seen her, which, unfortunately, was in the midst of a nasty freshman initiation.

"Good," Lisa said. "Then I'll leave you two to run the place. Egan will answer any questions you have, Heather. Don't forget to clock out when you leave."

A minute later she was gone, and they had a line of four customers. People always came in spurts. They were either swamped, or there was nobody. And for the next fifteen minutes, they would earn their meager paychecks.

Heather had already stepped up to the counter and was cutting away at a man's white bread. She looked like cool competence until Egan saw her eyes. They were near panic. "What do I do for a Subway melt?"

"Cheese first." He talked her through it. He'd helped train nearly a dozen people who had come and gone during his two years here. And he'd learned about personalities along the way. Some people went through the motions and lived for payday. Others took every instruction to heart as if one misstep would put them out on the street. Heather surprised him by fitting into the second category. She listened to everything he said. He never had to repeat the same sandwich and only had to show her the credit-card machine once.

Officer Michelson was the last to step up to the counter. "The usual."

Heather blinked and turned her troubled blue eyes on Egan. He was sunk. The usual. Officer Michelson came in every evening in the middle of his shift. Egan could make the sandwich in his sleep, but as he stared at Heather he didn't have a clue what it was.

Heather turned back to the officer. "It's my first day. Nothing's usual for me."

"Turkey on wheat, all the fixings, no cheese." He watched her make the sandwich, then paid, leaving a generous tip. "Let's make this our usual meeting, Heather. A lot more enjoyable for all of us, wouldn't you say?"

Her cheeks flushed a dull red. "Uh, yes sir."

Egan scrambled to think of something other than what encounters Heather usually had with the police officer. "You have a good memory," he said, as Officer Michelson left the building swinging his sandwich in its plastic bag.

"Thanks." She ran a rag over the counter, brushing away the crumbs.

His mind repeated what he said, and he wanted to kick himself. He hated when people complimented his smarts. And if the king of geeks didn't want to feel geeky—

"I'm sorry. I didn't mean it the way it sounded."

She looked at him. "You're taking back your compliment?"

He felt his face grow hot. "I didn't think you saw it as one."

"I said 'thanks.' I wouldn't have said it, at least not in that tone, if I didn't mean it. You don't think I have a good memory?"

"I meant what I said."

"Then why are you taking it back?"

"Because I thought you'd want me to tell you how pretty you are."

"Do you think I am?" She stared at him hard.

All he could manage was a nod. He was sure his face was going to shoot into flames and he would incinerate from embarrassment.

She kept looking at him with a serious expression he couldn't begin to decipher in his exposed and inadequate state. Finally, she said, "I like your first compliment better." She went back to scrubbing the counter, giving it way more concentration than it deserved.

Heather Fitzsimmons wanted a man to like her for her mind. Either he'd gotten his signals crossed, or that was the best-kept secret at Maplefield High. "Why did you stand me up yesterday?"

She didn't play dumb and pretend she didn't remember their tutoring session. "Are you going to charge me twenty bucks for not keeping the appointment?"

"No, but I might charge you for making me look like a fool."

"Oh." She dropped the rag and turned to look at him. "I'm sorry. I didn't come because I was trying to avoid making you look like a fool."

"How?" Being seen with Heather could do nothing but help his nerdy reputation.

"You're a nice guy. You deserve a nice girl. Nice girls don't go out with the guys I hang around with."

"You're not hanging around with the right people."

"Exactly. And you don't deserve the things people like Veronica are going to say if you're seen with me."

Heather believed what she was saying. Egan took some comfort in the fact that she wasn't feeding him a line, but even his mega-brain didn't have a clue how to decipher the female mind. All he knew for certain was there wasn't anyone he'd rather be with—or anyone he had less of a chance with.

★ ★ ★ ★ ★

"Oh, thank God, everyone's gone." Nick flopped in the chair Tanya had signed her autographs in.

Annie raised a brow from where she stood stacking jars of peanut butter on a metal shelf. "That's the first acknowledgement I've heard you give to God."

He hadn't let God's name unintentionally slip out in years. "It's a figure of speech. Lots of people say it without a thought to your precious God."

"That's true." As usual, she was unperturbed by his goading, which furthered his aggravation.

"I'm never playing security guard to your sister again."

Annie looked unconvinced. "Seems it'd be part of your coveted territory. If you're going to be a lawyer to the stars, don't you have to protect them, too?"

"They have bodyguards for that. I protect them from themselves."

"I don't know if Tanya needs a lawyer, but she definitely needs better bodyguards." Annie frowned, making him want to kiss her delectable mouth.

In truth, he'd been fixated on it all day, maybe since that day in Chicago when he'd first brushed his lips against hers. "I could help her if she'd let me file a restraining order."

"If Zeke doesn't respect a piece of paper reminding him of sacred marriage vows, why would he take your legal document any more seriously?"

Nick was under the impression Tanya hadn't exactly been a faithful spouse either. "Not much jail time associated with adultery these days."

"Nor for celebrities with expensive lawyers to help them wiggle around their restraining order violations."

"Touché." Restless and unable to pinpoint the cause, Nick leapt to his feet and paced.

"If you're bored, you don't have to hang around here with me."

"I know." He couldn't explain the allure of watching her stash paper towels next to bags of rice, but neither could he look away from the competent motion of her hands and the sway of her hips. Her presence was too compelling for him to grow bored.

Annie, apparently, wasn't convinced. "If you're looking for something to do, Lois said the toilet in the back is clogged."

Looking for a handout from the handyman. Anger surged at the reminder she was just a typical preacher. "Can't you unclog a toilet?"

"Sure, but—"

"Why should you when you've got free labor?" he finished.

She set a box of corn flakes on the shelf and walked toward him. "When I thought you were a destitute homeless man, I would have acted helpless and offered you fifty bucks to unclog the toilet because I understand how both pride and charity work. But you're here with your own agenda and delusions of grandeur."

"Delusions." He sputtered—actually, sputtered—he was so outraged.

"Your ability to fix things is a God-given talent. You shame Him by acting like it's beneath you."

"I'd only make a fraction of the income I make now if I focused on my so-called talent." *But happier, I would be so much happier.*

"Many things that no one will pay us for are worth our time and attention." She framed his face with her hands. "Without your career, without your money, I still care about you, Nick."

Where was she when he was contemplating law school and desperate to hear those words? He stepped into her personal space, his hips nudging hers. "The only people who say money isn't everything are the people who want something for free."

Her expression said he'd failed the test she'd set before him. She dropped her hands. "Go home. I have things to do tonight. If you're not going to help, I don't need to be supervised."

"I can help. Tell me what you want me to do." Desire rose inside him, threatening to drown him.

She leaned into him, thickening his need. "Do I really make you feel this strongly?"

"Yes. You." He pressed his mouth to hers, unable to deny himself the contact a moment longer. He was prepared for pleasure and welcomed it. They'd kissed twice before, after all. He didn't expect his world to be rocked.

With the first touch of lips, Annie knocked out his axis. She didn't hesitate but met each thrust of his tongue with warm tugging, inviting him to stay longer and push deeper. He accepted with a need that consumed him. He needed more. He needed harder. He needed her.

"I want you closer," she gasped. Her hands slid under his T-shirt, scraping his chest with her nails. Pleasure slapped through him.

"Yes." He fumbled with the single button on her blazer and shoved the offensive garment from her shoulders. He'd seen her in her bra once. The memory intensified his need to see her again. To touch, to taste. Oh, yes, he had to taste.

The tiny buttons on her blouse frustrated his suddenly clumsy fingers.

"Rip them," she whispered. "I don't mind."

"No, you deserve more care." The final button gave way, and he pushed back her shirt. He knelt before her, overcome with reverence as he unhooked the front clasp of her bra. He eased back the cups and for a long moment indulged himself in the sight.

She gasped. Her hands clenched against his abs as she

swayed. "Nick, I—"

He'd stolen her ability to stand. Even kneeling he was beginning to shake. He needed to get them both to the nearest bed. Or that chair he'd been sitting in.

"What is going on here?"

Annie pushed back from Nick. Hard. The last of his balance deserted him and he was knocked on his butt. He sat with his shirt bunched in his armpits and his pulse pounding, the unfamiliar male voice replaying in his mind. Someone else was with them in the building. He looked at Annie, and in a split second his hopes of finding fulfillment tonight were smashed.

With a stricken expression on her still-swollen lips, Annie fumbled with her bra. One of the cups slipped behind her back, out of reach. Nick rose to his knees intending to cover her from view. The sixtyish man across the room might have looked distinguished, if he wasn't staring at Annie while working his mouth like a guppy.

As soon as Nick moved, Annie took a step back, her bra still dangling uselessly. She intended to keep a roomful of distance between them before she accepted any help from him. Nick wanted to argue. He wanted to put his fist through a wall. Above all, he wanted to shove her onto the nearest bed and pick up where they left off. Instead, he tossed her the blazer.

She put it on. Backwards. It covered her chest better than a nun's habit. She crossed her arms over the thick wool. "John, what are you doing here?"

"I just came from visiting Myra. She asked me to check on this place." He shook his head. "Never mind what I'm doing. What are you doing here?"

"It's not how it looks," Annie said.

Nick gaped at her. He was positive it looked exactly like they'd being doing exactly what they were doing. Annie didn't glance at him. As if he no longer existed. He was forgotten. At her core, Annie was a preacher. Lust for the woman had obscured the fact. She might be the beacon of morality for everyone else, but she didn't consider herself accountable to her congregation for her own behavior. The signs had been there from the start, but he had ignored them.

For mindless sex, he should have picked up a woman in the bar, not a preacher in a food pantry.

"Why don't you explain how it is," the man said, fixing Annie with a hard look.

Rather than rescue her from the awkward situation, Nick folded his arms across his chest and waited to hear the excuses and hypocritical babble spew from her very kissable mouth.

CHAPTER 12

Heather stepped out the front door of Subway at 8:05 and glanced around. No sight of her mom or her mom's car. She let out a breath. Thank goodness. Another dose of her mom's embarrassment, with Egan watching out the window, would be more than she could take. She started walking toward home. If she let Mom think she was obeying the rules, everything would be normal again—the kind of normal where Heather did whatever she wanted.

An old, noisy station wagon stopped alongside her. She wasn't sure whose it was, but no doubt it belonged to someone she used to date. Either the guy wanted another go-around, or he had another girlfriend and they wanted to laugh in her face. Seeing those losers would make her feel icky after spending the evening with sweet, nerdy, and surprisingly sexy Egan.

"Want a ride home?" The voice and the face looking at her out the open window were female.

Heather blinked. *Holy flying pigs.* Her hero had just offered her a ride. Holy, holy—she pinched herself to be certain this wasn't a dream.

"You want my autograph or not?"

Oh, great, now she'd annoyed the World's Coolest Woman by standing like an idiot with her mouth open. "I want it."

"Get in."

Heather ran around the car and jerked open the passenger door. "How do you know who I am?"

Tanya leveled a razor gaze at her, until Heather squirmed. "How do you know who I am?"

"Everyone knows. You're Tanya." She pulled the door closed behind her.

"And I'm betting everyone in this town knows who you are, too, Heather."

"That's not exactly a good thing." Tanya had elevated herself to goddess status. Heather had turned herself into a tramp. "You must have a million better things to do on a Thursday night than chauffeur me home."

Tanya glanced at her again as she pulled from the parking lot onto the street. "Not that I can think of."

"Did Reverend Annie send you?" Heather stared at the beautiful, exciting actress and couldn't believe she was even from the same planet as Reverend Annie.

"Nope. Your mom did."

"Yeah, right. You wouldn't give my mom the time of day."

"Your mom is one of the nicest people I've ever met."

Heather shivered at the icy tone. "You actually talked to her, even though she's so fat?" Of everyone she knew, Tanya would understand most the consequence of being seen with someone everyone would laugh at.

"I'm talking to you, even though you're a pain in the butt. But don't push your luck and ask for the time of day."

Heather didn't have to pinch herself. Her hero was too rude for this to be a dream. "I didn't ask for a ride. You offered, so don't treat me like sewage."

"This favor's for your mom, not you. I bet you treat her like sewage all the time."

"You can see why. I'm embarrassed to be seen with her."

"Your mom would have picked you up herself, but she's embarrassed at what her friends would say when they see she has a daughter like you."

Heather opened her mouth and then closed it. The more she thought about Tanya's words, the closer to tears she came. "That's the meanest thing anyone's ever said to me."

"Do you want a pity party, or am I supposed to fall all over myself apologizing?" Tanya's tone told her the world would come to an end first.

Heather wished she was back at Subway with Egan, anywhere but taking this abuse from the woman who should have understood her best. The only good thing was no one could spread it around school.

A horrible thought occurred to her. What if the car was bugged? Tanya's nasty words wouldn't just circulate around school. The tabloids would print them, and the whole world would laugh at her. She dashed at the tears on her cheeks. "I used to really like you. I thought you were so cool."

"But I'm just a mean person," Tanya finished for her. "You're not the first person to say it to my face." She stopped the car at a stop sign and faced Heather. "You're free to hate me, but we are alike in one way. We both know how getting mixed up with the wrong guy can mess you up."

"So now I'm messed up?" This wasn't fair. This should be the coolest experience of her life, but she didn't want to remember any of it.

"Maybe you are. Maybe you aren't. Makes no difference to me." Tanya shrugged and sent the car moving again. "But I got messed up because I let loser guys run my life."

Heather didn't believe it. "You run your own life. You're Tanya. No one tells you what to do."

"My agent tells me what scripts and promotions I should accept. My publicist tells me how to act and what parties to accept. I have personal assistants telling me what to wear and how to fix my makeup and hair. I haven't even gotten to the loser-guys part yet."

Heather waited, but the car filled with silence. "You're getting rid of your loser guy. You're divorcing him," Heather prompted.

"That's right." Tanya's smile cracked at the edges, but maybe her makeup lady had caked it on too thick. "And not a moment too soon."

"Have you ever liked someone completely wrong for you? Not a loser, but someone geeky or too good for you?"

"Too good for me? Like a guy I might contaminate with my meanness?"

"Yes." Heather flinched, but she didn't back down. Tanya might be the only person who could understand Heather's perspective. She tried not to think about a tape recorder somewhere in the car.

"My publicist says to do him on the side but keep with the bad boys in public."

"Oh." She couldn't hurt Egan that way. She didn't want to be seen with the scum she'd hung out with before.

"Look, if you want counseling, talk to Annie. That's her thing. I'm nobody's good example. If you follow me, I'll mess you up more."

As if Reverend Annie had anything worthwhile to say. She'd tell Heather to stay away from Egan because he was too nice. She'd probably order Heather to stay away from everyone. Good girls like Annie believed in abstinence-only before marriage. That policy was way too late to save Heather's virginity.

Tanya pulled into Heather's driveway. The gearshift squeaked as she parked the car. "I do have a standard advice line. If you're going to play around with somebody's penis, make sure you cover it with a condom first."

Heather reached for the door handle. She'd heard this lecture before, although it was usually delivered more subtly. Getting pregnant wouldn't be so terrible. A baby would love her. A baby would hug and cuddle all the time.

"A penis can give you worse things than an unplanned pregnancy," Tanya said.

Heather didn't like that she was reading her mind. "Those things only happen in the cities, not in Podunk little Maplefield."

"You're wrong." Tanya reached across Heather's lap for the glove compartment. "I hope you don't find out the hard way." She pulled out a booklet and rummaged for another minute before uncovering a pen. "Here's your autograph."

"Thanks." Heather took the booklet and hurried to her house, glad to get away from the scary things she never let herself think about. Inside, she looked down at the booklet Tanya had signed for her. "Facts and Symptoms of Sexually Transmitted Diseases." She slumped against the door. She had Tanya's autograph, but she couldn't show it to anyone. Her stomach churned until she was sure she was going to throw up. An upset stomach was probably a symptom of something in this book.

Annie's heart raced and her stomach lurched with nausea. Both Nick and John stared at her as if she'd contracted the plague.

Her life as she knew it was over. No, she was kidding herself. Life as she knew it ended the first time Nick stepped into her church.

"I let my emotions get away from me," she admitted. "Both my actions and the place I expressed them in were entirely inappropriate."

"Yes, they were," John agreed. "I'll have to take this matter up with the rest of the pastoral council."

If Trudy, Stewart, or Kathy got wind of this, her career was over. Her marriage to the church would end in an ugly divorce. And she'd be living out of her Chevy, taking donations from the food pantry instead of giving handouts.

"John, I made a mistake. I admit it. Can we keep this between the three of us? It will never happen again." She'd lost Nick. She knew it without glancing at him, had known it as soon as she heard John Patterson's voice.

She had to salvage God's love and His plan for her life. Her moments of pleasure in Nick's arms were over. If she were her sister, she could take what her flesh craved. But she wasn't. She was Reverend Annie. John's next words would determine if her reputation was beyond repair or merely on the line.

"The council has to trust the faith and moral fiber of the person leading our church. I saw your breasts, Annie. I'm never going to look at you without remembering what you look like without your shirt on."

She hugged her arms across her chest and fought the shame and embarrassment burning her cheeks. "I'd like to explain the situation personally to the council. Can you arrange a meeting for me to do that? You'll be present to set the record straight."

John hesitated and then nodded. "I'll organize a meeting for tomorrow. I'll call the church with the time. Is there anything that needs to be done here before I go?"

Neither she nor Nick would consider approaching each other to pick up where they left off, but John's presence also meant Annie couldn't explain herself to Nick. She closed her eyes and tried to pray. Somehow God could make this horrible wrong turn out right. But her prayers weren't likely to sway Him when she'd so utterly betrayed Him. This mess was her own making. He had no reason to help her out of it. "Everything can wait for tomorrow. Will you escort me home, John? I just need to get my purse."

Tomorrow. Her entire life waited for tomorrow's verdict. She risked a glance at Nick. His face was a hard, emotionless mask. She didn't have to wait to know Nick wouldn't be a part of her future. No matter what happened tomorrow she'd already lost.

The continuous tingling of her lips tortured her; the loss of Nick, she realized, was as great as any loss she was facing in her professional life.

"Twenty-one hundred bucks! You spent two thousand, one hundred dollars of my money without consulting me." Dad was on a rampage. For once it wasn't directed at Heather. She pushed herself away from the door and tiptoed toward the living room. Mom was sitting in a recliner with her hands folded while Dad paced.

"You spent thirty-two thousand without consulting me, Stewart."

The vein in his temple bulged. "That was for a car. We needed a new car."

"The food pantry needs a new roof a lot more than we needed a Crown Victoria with leather seating and a moonroof."

"You wasted my money. I can't turn this into a profitable investment."

"The return on my money is well worth the price." Mom sounded uncharacteristically smug. "Tanya's going to teach me her tricks to make a man beg for me."

Holy flying pigs. Heather never thought her mom had it in her to attempt something like that. Mom practically had to beg the man behind the butcher counter of the grocery store to take her order.

Dad wheezed. "Lois, you've missed a lot of Sunday services this year. I think you've forgotten Jesus creates miracles, not Tanya."

I hate you. Heather clutched Tanya's book to remind herself why she didn't want to speak aloud and draw attention to herself. Tanya had been cruel, but Dad's insult was worse. And he said it to his own wife, someone he was supposed to love forever. His daughter wasn't worth loving, but Mom was a good person. Even Tanya thought so. And Heather was going to tell him. She took a step into the room.

Mom struggled to stand and looked straight at Dad. "I want you out of this house."

He laughed. "You can't kick me out, Lois. This is my house."

"It's just as much my home as yours." For the second time today, Mom didn't back down. "I said I want you out and I mean it. I'm tired of letting your way be the way everything has to be done. I'm tired of pretending you're not having an affair. And I'm tired of living in a marriage that's making me miserable. I want you out tonight. You've got fifteen minutes to pack a bag. You can come back tomorrow while I'm at the food pantry and get the rest of your things."

The flesh hanging from Dad's jaw jiggled. "Lois, come on. Be serious."

"I am serious. It's time for you to take me seriously. Go Stewart. You've got fourteen minutes left."

He looked straight at her. "You'll be sorry for this."

"I have a lot of regrets, but this isn't one of them. Thirteen minutes."

Or what? Heather wondered. Dad didn't ask. He stomped back to the bedroom, shouting about their cars and stock investments, all the things he'd worked too hard to let "a crazy woman" take from him.

Heather always thought she had one thing going for her. Her parents weren't divorced. Now that would be snatched from her. There was no point in trying to get her dad to notice her. He wasn't going to live in the same house to remember she existed.

Twelve minutes later as he walked past her and out of the house, he certainly didn't notice. He was too busy shouting to

Mom about the lawyers he'd sic on her if she touched his coin collection.

They were here. So far they'd been happy snapping pictures with their telephoto lenses through the windows of the food pantry, but it wouldn't last. Soon they'd have the flashbulb in front of Tanya's face. She glanced in her rearview mirror. The headlights were still there. She was being followed. Of all the stupid things she'd done, ditching her bodyguard detail for Maplefield suddenly topped the list.

She punched in Jake's number and then tossed the phone aside before she could push the send button. She'd memorized his phone number. As if that wasn't bad enough, she was acting like a helpless wimp who needed a man to tell her what to do. Jake would get a kick out of it. He'd probably tell her to get in the cameraman's car and hold him hostage with sex until Jake could bust him for drugs.

She drove around town for fifteen minutes. The headlights stayed on her bumper. They belonged to a big car—truck-size. She sped down the street in front of the Annie's church, slamming on the breaks and careening into the parking lot. The Oldsmobile jolted as the other vehicle gave it a hard nudge, shattering something—hopefully nothing more serious than a taillight.

The SUV missed the turnoff for the parking lot. She watched it speed away and wished fervently for the overly zealous paparazzi. This red Hummer had her maniac husband behind the wheel.

Tanya jumped out of her car, running behind a grove of trees next to the church. She was less than a block away before Zeke zoomed back, peeling off the side mirror of her car as he parked next to her driver's door. At least, she'd had enough sense to run away.

She reached for her cell phone to call Jake. He was looking for Zeke, after all. She didn't have her phone. She was an idiot. She'd left the phone in the car. She was on her own.

"If I'm going down, I'm taking you with me, Viper," Zeke yelled as he climbed down from his SUV.

Tanya knew better than to fight, but escape was still an option. Tonight the World's Sexiest Viper wasn't going to wait for someone to tell her what to do.

Annie should have called Nick when she got home. He wouldn't accept her apology, but she could have tried. She needed him to believe she truly did care about him even though her actions spoke to the contrary. And she had to explain why she could never see him again.

But she couldn't think about other people right now. The most important meeting of her life was coming up, and she didn't have a clue what she could say to make everyone believe she deserved to continue as their preacher. For the first time she was worried she wasn't worthy.

She slept poorly in between speech drafts for her showdown. When she wasn't worrying about her church, she punished herself for all the other people she failed. Tanya, Nick, Jason, Heather. Every day the list grew, and she couldn't give her full attention to any of them because she was so focused on her own problems.

Her best hour of sleep occurred after she shut off her alarm, turning her morning routine into a mad dash for the shower. She skipped breakfast, scooped up the morning paper, and ran for her car. The car was gone.

She stared at the empty carport. Tanya hadn't returned home all night. Annie assumed she'd left town as she'd promised, but she never expected Tanya to steal her car. In the past forty-eight hours, the chasm between them had narrowed. Completely eradicating it would take hard work and more heartfelt face-to-face sessions. Now it appeared they would never get the chance.

Tanya was in the middle of a divorce and sure to endure more tabloid scrutiny. Annie had to face her own scrutiny and possible divorce from her church. They both needed family, perhaps more than ever, but Annie didn't know how to bridge the gap between their worlds.

With a lightning flash of insight, Annie knew exactly where Tanya was. She'd spent the night with Nick. He would welcome her. As a bonus, Tanya handed him the perfect way to get back at Annie for the way she'd treated him at the food pantry. Although right now, she was sure they were too preoccupied with each other for Nick to consider that.

Annie's first impulse was to run to the apartment to confront them. Finding them together would hurt too much. She still battled memories of Danny. This time Nick had no obligation to her. Besides, Annie was already late for work. Kathy had plenty to sniff about today, as it was.

She saw Tanya's car when she was still a block away. It was parked across three parking spaces in front of the church. Annie approached and noticed the car was unlocked, a cell phone sitting on the passenger seat. Maybe Tanya wasn't with Nick. The relief she felt didn't lift her Christian spirit. "Tanya?" Annie opened the door and picked up the phone.

"You're late," Kathy said from the church doorway.

Annie glanced at her. "Is my sister inside?"

"Your sister's the least of your problems? What do you have to say for yourself?"

If Tanya wasn't inside, she wouldn't have dumped her stuff like this to go sleep with someone. "Have you seen my sister?"

"Not since she was the star of the show yesterday. You're the star today," Kathy said with venom.

Obviously John had told his wife what he'd walked in on. She shouldn't be surprised. Still, Annie was more preoccupied with where her sister had disappeared to and why Tanya had ditched her car for Annie's. "Do I have an appointment waiting?"

"You had three for today," Kathy said stiffly. "They all canceled. Your council meeting is at noon. You can use the rest of the morning to clean out your desk."

Annie couldn't avoid this confrontation any longer. "You work for me, not the other way around. I know you've never liked me, but—"

"Have you read that?" Kathy nodded to the forgotten newspaper stashed under Annie's arm.

"Not yet."

"I suggest you do." Kathy turned on her heel and marched to her desk.

Annie swallowed her trepidation and slowly unfolded the paper. A five-by-seven image of herself locked in Nick's embrace, his lips on her throat, her hands under his shirt taunted her with the memories she wanted badly to suppress. A smaller picture of her backed against a ladder, her hips flush with Nick's, and a picture of Lois smiling with Tanya accompanied the blaring caption.

Supermodel Poses for Charity While Sister Gives Goods for Free.

It was a bad tabloid heading, vastly out of character for the front page of a family paper that usually ran headlines of Little League wins and record attendance for VFW fish fries. Still she had to admit that the people of Maplefield would gobble up this edition.

Yesterday, they had been more interested in Tanya than her local sister. But that was yesterday. Now Tanya was gone. Annie closed her eyes and braced herself to accept the truth. Her God had forsaken her.

Jason looked up from the newspaper next to his morning bowl

of Cheerios. "She could use a friend, you know."

Nick tried to pretend he didn't know what Jason was talking about. He'd seen the papers. Annie was nearly as photogenic as her sister. But Nick didn't need the frozen images to remind him of the heat they'd generated.

"She's not the kind of person who can take this kind of thing in stride," Jason persisted. "It's going to hit her hard."

"She doesn't want me as a friend. She made that clear last night."

Jason looked back down at the newspaper. "Looks like she wanted you as more than a friend."

"That was before." Nick snatched the paper away and flipped it over so he didn't have to see the arousal on her face. Even in black and white, it had the power to stir him.

"Before what?" Jason asked.

"Before she realized saving her own butt was a lot more important than anything we had going on." The back page was full of real estate listings. Nick pretended to study it.

"It probably is," Jason said.

"Excuse me?" He looked up.

"What do you have going on with Annie? You hunted her down and probably treated her rotten because you thought she'd made me suicidal. Then you get cozy with her to get yourself close to her sister. Why would she throw away her career and her calling because of that?" Jason skewered him with his gaze. "Are you in love with her? Planning to marry her?"

"God, no." Nick nearly choked on his tongue. He'd brought God into the conversation again. Twice in as many days. "She's just like my father, hypocrite to the core."

"You're jealous of her. She's got direction. She knows her priorities. And it annoys you that you're not on the top of the list."

His brother was spewing gibberish. Nick stared at the

thumbnail photo of the dilapidated house. Even the camera couldn't give it a good angle. "I don't expect that. After all, Annie doesn't make my priority list."

"Doesn't she?" Jason wouldn't shut up. "Then what are we doing twiddling our thumbs in Maplefield?"

Four bedrooms, hardwood floors, fireplace. "If you don't ruin it, I've got a chance of convincing Tanya she needs me as her lawyer."

"Tanya's gone. She drove off in Annie's car last night, nearly ran me down as I crossed the street."

Needs some TLC, handyman's dream. "If she took Annie's car, she'll be back," Nick said absently, consumed by the forlorn picture in front of him. "We'll wait her out."

"You're deluding yourself. Tanya doesn't want you any more than she wants a second round with me. I'm going to move beyond it and look for some contacts I can develop who want their life story in print. A lot of people would jump at the chance. You should give up on Tanya, too. Go home and do what you're good at—contract law and divorce cases."

Nick stared at the house. Do what he was good at. *A handyman's dream.* Whether he was a lawyer or a handyman, Annie wouldn't make any of his dreams come true. He'd have to make the effort himself. It was time to reach for a new dream.

Annie used her office phone to dial the numbers displayed on Tanya's cell phone. She didn't have time to second-guess her decision before a brisk voice answered. "Officer Jacobs."

Tanya had been about to call a police officer. The knowledge chilled Annie instead of comforting her. Whoever he was, he wasn't from Maplefield's tiny force. "This is Reverend Annie Lane. I'm looking for my sister and was hoping you could help me."

"And your sister's name?"

Annie had a feeling the hard man on the other end already knew. But she was the one who called. She wasn't in a position to question him. What little faith she clung to she put toward trusting she wasn't putting her sister in more trouble. "Tanya Lane. Britman," she added as an afterthought. "Do you know where she is?"

"No."

"Wherever she went, she didn't take her phone. But she had your number dialed like she was planning to call you. I don't know if she needs help or just went her own way and left her stuff behind."

"You did the right thing to call me," the officer said. "Did Tanya leave in that piece of—excuse me, Reverend—Oldsmobile?"

"No. It's in the church parking lot, minus a side mirror and a taillight. She took my car."

Officer Jacobs, whoever he was, took her vehicle information and yesterday's details of Tanya's day. Then he thanked Annie politely without telling her what, if anything, he intended to do with the information.

She replaced the phone receiver slowly. Whether her call had done Tanya good or only served to widen the gap between them remained to be seen, but it certainly didn't provide Annie with any peace of mind.

"You," Trudy Fitzsimmons said, marching into the office and pointing a blood-red fingernail at Annie, "are the source of every problem in this community. Resign. Immediately."

Annie sighed and abandoned all hope for peace. The council would very likely tell her the same thing in just a couple hours and would fire her if she refused. But that didn't give Trudy the authority of a queen. "It's not your place to make that demand."

Mrs. Fitzsimmons sniffed. "Someone needs to preserve the moral fiber of this congregation."

"I understand the pictures in today's paper offended you. I apologize for that. They offended me as well."

"And that's supposed to excuse your actions? My granddaughter wasn't sleeping around until you came to town."

Annie hadn't tried to offer excuses, but she resented her new role as the Fitzsimmons family scapegoat. Heather wasn't the first teen to experience a burst of hormones and sexual awakening in the past five years.

Annie couldn't hold herself completely blameless either. She had failed to steer Heather in a more healthy direction. So had Lois and Stewart. So had the irate woman with the blood-red fingernails. "I'm sorry I haven't done more for Heather. I know she's hurting, and I know she needs help. But I can't help someone who refuses to let me."

"You're blaming an innocent child for your failing."

Annie lifted her coffee mug to stop herself from commenting on the innocence of someone who was *sleeping around*.

"I suppose you blame my son for his wife kicking him out of his own house."

Annie sloshed the coffee, spilling lukewarm liquid across the desktop. "Lois kicked Stewart out?" She believed in the sanctity of marriage, believed the vows should last forever. Yet she could hardly contain her glee. Shaking up the status quo of that relationship was quite possibly the best thing Lois could have done.

"I know you're behind it." Trudy leaned forward and hissed her venom. "You have it in for my son."

"I thought the dynamics ran the other way, actually," Annie said quietly.

Trudy puffed out her indignation. "I've never heard a more heartless, inconsiderate person profess to have God first in her life. The church higher-ups will receive a copy of today's newspaper. I'm going to personally ensure you don't infuse your poison on another unsuspecting parish. You told Lois to get rid of Stewart. She never would have thought of it on her own nor had the nerve to carry it out. You probably encouraged Heather to bring boys into her bedroom as well."

"That's enough, Trudy."

The words so clearly echoed Annie's thoughts, she thought she'd spoken them, but the furious tension didn't come from her. Lois Fitzsimmons stood in the doorway. "If you don't have anything nice to say about Heather, keep it to yourself. You're degrading your own granddaughter behind her back at a time when she's finally trying to straighten herself out."

Trudy didn't look the least bit ashamed. "How could you turn your back on your marriage? Your daughter needs her mother and father together."

"Stewart and I staying together hasn't done her any favors. I finally stopped pretending the problems didn't exist—with my daughter, with myself, and with my marriage."

Confronting the problems hadn't come without a cost. Annie wanted to cheer for Lois, but her position as pastor—although it might only be hers for a few more minutes—called for keeping her expression neutral.

Trudy sniffed. "I always told Stewart he was too good for you."

"We both believed it. I don't anymore. I suggest you reevaluate the worth of everyone around you."

Including Heather, especially Heather. Annie knew she'd never get a chance to be on Trudy's good side, but Heather needed and deserved the opportunity.

"If you've got something to say to me," Trudy said with a regal incline of her head to Lois, "you can say it when you come to my house groveling for your husband."

Lois cleared a path through the doorway. "You must be so pleased your mama's boy is back home and completely under your thumb again. When I think of how much I've failed Heather, I look at you and think, 'I'm not the best mother, but I'm not the worst either.'"

"I hold you responsible for this, too," Trudy sputtered at Annie. She stormed out of the office, slamming her way through the church doors.

The responsibility held the unmistakable threat of payback. Annie checked the minutes left in her countdown to noon.

Chapter 13

"You're supposed to call the realtor to show you the house," Jason said.

Nick shook his head as he slowed his pickup. He hadn't planned to drive by the house in the newspaper, let alone stop, but his tires were already crunching over the gravel driveway. The place was atrocious. Peeling paint, lopsided shutters. "I'm not going to buy it. I just want to look."

"That's a relief. Some schmuck is going to pay three times the asking price just to make it habitable."

"Or spend evenings for the next two years fixing it himself." A shiver trickled down Nick's arm, making his fingers clench for a nonexistent hammer.

"What kind of moron would do that?"

Nick shifted the truck into park. "Manual labor would be a nice change of pace from nights in the office."

Jason snorted. "If you wanted more stimulating evenings, you should have married Holly. She really loved you, you know."

"She wanted me because I was a lawyer." The bitterness churned in his stomach.

"That's part of who you are. She wasn't trying to change you into something you're not."

"No, I had a father for that." Nick slammed out of the truck. No one wanted to change him, because they loved the career he was chained to. Except for one person. Annie saw a worth in him aside from his job and his wealth. He still had trouble believing it. Of course, without her pastor job, she wouldn't have a use for a handyman and her tune could change.

People would lie and manipulate, but buildings laid out all their secrets for anyone to see. This house was begging for a handyman. A lawyer couldn't do anything for it, but a man willing break a sweat could transform it.

"Can I help you?" a timid female voice barely carried from the screen door.

Nick walked up the steps, eager to see more and start negotiations. He steered clear of the railing, knowing it wouldn't hold his weight.

"Be careful. The—"

His foot dropped through the wood plank on the porch. Nick caught himself on his hands and knees as the broken floorboard gouged his shin. He was going to have splinters before he started work on the place.

"—floor's rotted," the woman in the doorway said. "I'm so sorry. Really, really sorry. Do you want me to call an ambulance?"

Nick winced as he pulled his leg up through the woodwork. "No. I'll walk it off—on the grass. Are you the owner?" He hobbled down the steps and paced into the yard to work off the stabs of pain.

"Are you interested in buying?" She skirted the question.

"The fall through the floor cured him of that idiot notion," Jason said, walking over.

Any self-respecting lawyer would be thinking of lawsuits, not juggling bank account funds to lay down cash for the place. But the unexpected fall sealed his fate. The house would be his as soon as a closing date could be set.

"Bonnie," a voice roared from inside. "Who are you talking to?"

Her panicked gaze locked on Nick's, and he noticed the

colorful bruise on her cheekbone. "A couple people came to look at the house. Be on your best behavior, Hank."

"You're entertaining men while I'm sleeping." A plethora of cursing ensued.

"My fault for showing up unannounced." Nick injected cheerfulness in his voice and lifted his hands in a gesture of peace. "I was looking for you, Hank."

The beefy man shoved open the screen door. "Get in here, you good-for-nothing. I'll take care of you." He reached for Bonnie's arm, which was covered in bruises and sported a bandage around her elbow. She jumped out of his reach, stumbling into the hole Nick had just made in the front porch. Jason reached her at the same time as Hank.

"Just go," Bonnie said to Jason. "I'll be okay."

"You've got both of us. You don't have to stay with him if you don't want to," Nick said. Jason was right. He should have called the realtor and saved an innocent woman from the crossfire. His lawyer persona began improvising a restraining order against the abusive Hank.

"Listen to the woman. And get out before I give you trespassers a close-up view of my knife," Hank growled.

"Please go," Bonnie whispered.

All of Nick's instincts told him to stay and protect this woman, but she was insisting they go. The worst thing they could do was cause more trouble that her husband or boyfriend would eventually take out on her. The only protection Nick could offer was as her lawyer. The restraining order would become a reality. He could only hope the hours and minutes until that happened wouldn't be too rough on Bonnie. He backed slowly toward the truck, keeping his gaze on Hank.

"I remember you from the food pantry," Jason said to Bonnie. "Tanya gave you a private autograph session. Do you remember what she wrote with her autograph?"

"'Make your own life.'" Bonnie's voice was so timid she didn't sound capable of making any of life's decisions on her own.

"Do it now," Jason urged.

"I'm your life," Hank shouted. He raised his fist, then met Jason's surprisingly steely gaze. He slammed into the house, shouting about his knife. The moment the screen door snapped shut, Jason and Bonnie ran for Nick's truck.

"Go. Floor the gas. Go!" Jason shouted, pushing Bonnie across the center console of the truck into Nick's shoulder. Nick glanced at her face and saw hope in the place of fear. He threw the vehicle in gear, churning gravel under his tires as Jason fought to close the open door. Hank returned, swearing at them. He tripped on the hole in the porch and fell through.

"Oh, my gosh, I did it." Bonnie laughed. "Tanya's the best thing that ever happened to me."

A dry laugh escaped Nick's throat before he could check himself. He and Jason had once believed the same thing.

Payback tasted sweeter than Stewart had imagined. Driving to the church, he catalogued every instance where Reverend Annie had abused the church finances and went over his head for approval. Even more grating were the times when she undermined his budget cuts and padded her personal expenses with *charity for the less fortunate.*

But professional misconduct paled compared to the personal grievances. Lois stopped going to church after Annie became pastor, and Stewart's marriage unraveled from there. Annie's pathetic attempts at counseling his daughter only succeeded in turning Heather into a girl with an undeserved reputation for being fast and loose with the boys.

He parked in front of the church, armed with a briefcase full of evidence and ledgers. Payback time had arrived. Stewart had every intention of wallowing in the sweetness.

He swung open the outer church door and forgot what he'd come for. His leaden limbs wouldn't allow him to move, as he stared at the love of his life. A woman who was a hundred and fifty pounds heavier than when they married twenty years ago shouldn't have the power to steal his breath away.

He'd thought the spunk of her personality had smothered under layers of fat. Yesterday it reasserted itself in the bizarre and erotic announcement that she was going to learn tricks to make men beg. In the next breath she kicked him out of his own house. He wasn't the man she wanted begging.

"Shouldn't you be home tossing my clothes out the bedroom window?" he asked Lois.

Her shoulders straightened, and some trick of lighting made her look slimmer. "If you want them, you'll have to get them yourself. I have better things to do with my time."

"Like what—eat yourself into a stupor?" He winced at his own cruelty but refused to apologize. He was her life—the only good thing in it, anyway. She couldn't afford to throw him away.

"Actually, I'm running the food pantry for Myra while she recuperates. Who would know more about food than me, right?"

Lois had never joked or referenced her burgeoning weight before. Her self-deprecation made him want to assure her he loved her anyway. Except he wasn't sure he did. He liked her better when he could wrap his arms around her and she asserted her own opinion. The only opinion she'd asserted lately was that she didn't love him anymore.

So he said, "I have an important meeting."

"Don't let me make you late for casting stones."

He couldn't ignore the accusation in her voice. "You would defend Reverend Annie after seeing the pictures in today's paper?"

"I hardly think we have any right to judge. Our daughter

engages in the same compromising positions weekly, if not daily."

"She's not really doing anything with those boys." Stewart knew his little Heather. "She's just trying to make us think she's being promiscuous to get our attention."

"If you really believe that, my years with you were more of a waste than I thought." She pushed by him and out to the Crown Victoria he'd spent thirty-two thousand on.

"It's Annie's fault," Stewart shouted after her. He, his mother, and Kathy could see it so clearly. Why couldn't everyone else? "We're getting rid of her, and we'll get our sweet little girl back." Maybe he'd get back the woman he married, too.

He straightened his shoulders and marched into the church. He'd find a new pastor, one who would remind his wife of the sanctity of marriage and put the fear of God into an out-of-control teenager.

The sweet anticipation had disappeared though, replaced with a dread that no preacher could fix his problems.

"So I'm resigning, effective noon on Sunday." Annie finished her recap for Myra. The guarantee of a sympathetic ear dissolved the tension of the day. The meeting had been predictable, if humbling and awkward. Disappointment, outrage, and remorse had all been expressed by the appropriate parties. She was not granted a second chance, but she couldn't rail against her church for keeping with the best interests of their faith community.

"You let them suck another sermon out you. I would have made them scramble for a substitute preacher," Myra declared. Her arm trembled slightly as she shifted in her nursing home chair.

Annie steadied her and hovered until Myra was settled. "I've been Good Shepherd's minister for five years. I wanted the chance to say goodbye." And she needed the extra day and a half to clear her belongings out of the manse and find a place to live.

"You're leaving town?"

She hadn't thought that far but didn't see another alternative. She sank into a folding chair next to Myra. "I suppose I'll have to. I'm not going to find another congregation in Maplefield."

"I'm glad this debacle hasn't shaken your faith." Myra rubbed her forehead. "This temporary sidelining has shaken mine."

Annie couldn't meet Myra's gaze. Her home was being taken from her, her income cut off with the loss of her job, and her sister had disappeared with her car and family connections. God was all she had. If she stopped trusting He'd come through for her, she'd be left with nothing.

"You don't have to worry about the food pantry, Myra. Lois is handling everything. This opportunity has been a blessing for her. It's given her a purpose and a renewed confidence in herself."

Myra's fingers shook as she pressed them to her temples. "Perhaps the pantry doesn't need me as much as I thought."

"That's ridiculous." Annie couldn't imagine the food pantry without Myra. "You're its life blood."

"Yesterday you probably thought you were the life blood of Good Shepherd. Here's the truth I discovered sitting helpless in this chair. Life moves on, and it does just as well without you."

Myra hadn't meant the comment as a slap in Annie's face. She was a woman nearing the sunset of her life and accepting that fact. But Annie could no longer ignore the truth. She liked being a group's center. She craved it. She needed to know a gathering looked to her for direction. They looked at her. They noticed her. Walking down the aisle to the pulpit was her runway. All eyes were on her. And her sister couldn't upstage her there.

"This is a doozy of a headache." Myra broke through her thoughts. "Could you push the button for the nurse? I can't even get my own aspirin in this place."

Annie quickly did her bidding. "I could run out to the nurse's station. They'll come quicker if I get them personally."

Myra dropped her hand to the arm of the chair. "No, they'll come soon. Bring Lois in, so I can assure myself the food pantry's in good h-h-h . . . ands . . ."

Days ago Annie didn't know how she would handle the extra responsibility of the pantry. Now she was vital to nothing. She understood too well Myra's feelings of uselessness. She squeezed Myra's hand, but the woman didn't squeeze back. Her skin was pale and clammy.

"Myra." Annie squeezed again, but Myra's eyes didn't even focus on her. Annie jumped to her feet. "Nurse, help!" She ran to the doorway. "I need a nurse and an ambulance for Myra Turnaggle. Now."

Myra slumped in her chair, speechless and unresponsive.

Troy Mullins walked into Subway like he owned the franchise. Egan took a deep breath and stiffened his spine.

"You can finish my order," Heather whispered, pushing the sandwich she was working on toward him. "I'll deal with Troy."

"No." He had to stand up to the bully. At first it was because he didn't want Heather thinking he was a wimp, but now the fight was personal. He had to prove to himself he could do it. If he lost this showdown, he would know he was the worst of all cowards.

"Meatball on white, double meat, Egghead," Troy ordered as he sauntered over to the chip rack, taking two bags.

Egan wasn't going to win. Troy would at least walk away with free chips. Only a coward would concede at the first sign of defeat. Egan took a deep breath. "I'm sorry. You still owe me nine-ninety-three from last week. You'll have to pay that first."

"Get over it, crybaby, and make me a sandwich."

The other customer glanced nervously at Troy, paid for her sandwich, and hurried out of the store without waiting for her change. Heather dumped the coins into Egan's tip cup and moved the cup to the shelf under the register, out of sight and out of Troy's reach. If Egan hadn't wanted to kiss her before, her foresight with the tip money would have put him over the edge.

"Taking something from the store without paying for it is called shoplifting," Egan said, locking his gaze on Troy and refusing the distraction of Heather.

"You bought for me last time. You're doing it again."

No way. "Last time you stole money from me. This time I'll call the police." Egan held his breath and waited for Troy to call his bluff.

"You're full of hot air, Egghead. I'm not giving you a penny." Troy grabbed two more bags of chips. "I don't need that sandwich, after all."

Sweat trickled slow and cold down his forehead, but Egan didn't blink as the salty liquid stung his eyes. "Heather, push the red button by the cash register. You know, the silent alarm to alert the police."

From the corner of his eye, he saw her move her hands to the nonexistent alarm. "Done, they should be on their way."

Troy switched his gaze to Heather, but his eyes didn't rise above her chest. "Did you hire her to give you blowjobs on your break?"

Fury whipped through Egan. Fists clenched, he plowed forward to plant them in Troy's smug face and came up hard against the sandwich counter, stopping both his momentum and his courage.

"Maybe you'll get lucky and some guy named Bubba will give you a job in the slammer," Heather shot at Troy.

"They won't lock me up over a bag of chips. I bet you didn't call the police."

"Sure. I'll bet you the next four years of your life." Egan found his voice again. Heather's spunkiness gave him another shot of boldness. He was rewarded with a spark of panic in Troy's eyes and didn't feel the least bit guilty about exploiting it. "Bubba's waiting for you."

Troy swore and squeezed the chip bags to crumbs, throwing them one by one at Egan. He ducked. The first and second ones whizzed by his head, but the third smacked his shoulder, assailing him with memories of that nasty egg pelting.

Once again Heather witnessed his humiliation. He straightened, and the final bag of chips stung his face.

"Leave him alone," Heather shouted at Troy. "You'll go to jail for assault, too."

Oh, man. Egan was such a wimp a girl had to defend him.

The front door chimed and—oh, sweet timing—Officer Michelson stepped in for his daily turkey on wheat, no cheese.

"Nobody named Bubba's gonna touch my privates." Troy fumbled with his wallet and tossed a twenty at Egan. He ran from the store.

"That guy giving you trouble?" Officer Michelson asked.

"Not anymore." Egan grinned as he took the bill. He stood up to the bully and he not only lived to tell about it; he won.

The doctor used devastating words like *massive stroke, brain damage*, and *life support*. Annie could only sit on the sidelines and pray to a God who seemed to have turned His back on her. She waited in the emergency room and then moved to Myra's bedside, continuing her vigil. Myra was stable but much too still.

Annie spent another three hours sitting with Myra's son before the nurse gave him a blanket and a pillow to spread out on the waiting room couch. Myra's daughter was flying in from Arizona and would arrive first thing in the morning. Annie could do nothing for any of them but promise to return in the morning and pray for the best.

She drove Tanya's Oldsmobile back to the manse. The thought of opening a can of soup at home sickened her even as her stomach rumbled. She U-turned and pulled into the parking lot of Al's Bar. Al reportedly had the best sandwiches in town. Afraid of smearing her reputation by entering a bar, Annie had never personally tried one.

Now walking into a bar was the least of her worries. The place bustled with the Friday evening crowd. The jumble of voices and clattering of glasses brought the headache that had been brewing in the back of her head to the forefront. Suddenly the voices and the jukebox fell silent. Annie glanced around to pinpoint the cause before she realized all eyes were focused on her.

Should have satisfied herself with the chicken noodle soup. She started to turn away when Jason stood up and waved from across the room.

Ignoring the stares and loud whispers, she slid into the booth across from him. "Thanks. I didn't think my entrance would be noticed."

"You're the talk of the town." The waitress, who looked slightly familiar, although Annie couldn't immediately place her, plopped a beer in front of Jason.

He handed her a five and held up a hand when she started to peel off change from a roll of bills.

Annie's unwanted notoriety shouldn't have surprised her. She'd lived in this town for five years. A scandal involving a box of missing paperclips in the mayor's office had made front-page news for two weeks last year. A scandal involving sex could feed the busybodies for years. But tonight Annie wanted escape. "I haven't had a beer in seven years."

Jason pushed his new bottle toward her. "Can you bring us two more, Bonnie?"

"Sure." The young woman came close to blushing, then glanced quickly at the door. "Anything else?"

"You have pastrami on rye?" Annie asked. Was this the same Bonnie from the grocery store? Normally, she never had to be introduced to a person twice, but the set of the shoulders was so different. This woman looked energetic and hopeful.

"We do. You want a sandwich, sir?" she asked Jason.

"No sandwich and no sir. Call me Jason. Call me honey. Just call me." He sent Bonnie a blinding smile. "I'll take a double shot of cinnamon schnapps, though."

She did blush this time and scurried off.

"A bar waitress who blushes at a man's flirting?" Annie asked. She took a sip of beer and sputtered, quickly blotting her face with a napkin. She'd forgotten how strong the yeasty bite could be.

"It's her first day. Her husband doesn't know she took the job."

"You're flirting with a married woman?" The pastor in her coated her words with censure.

"She left him this morning. I helped her do it—possibly the most worthwhile thing I've ever done with my life."

"If she's just coming out of a relationship, no matter how unhappy, she's not going to be emotionally ready to jump into something with anyone else. Don't take advantage of her." Annie took another taste of beer, enjoying the chance to savor the alcohol on her tongue.

"I'm hoping she'll take advantage of me." Jason grinned as he reached for her beer bottle.

"Bonnie's not Tanya."

"I know. Honest, Annie, I'm not going to hurt her." He looked surprisingly earnest, but then ruined it by tilting his head and gulping the beer. "Have you heard from Tanya since yesterday?"

Awash with shame over her own selfishness, Annie reached for the beer bottle. For lack of a better vehicle, she'd adopted Tanya's abandoned car. But she'd turned the worry for her sister over to a cop she had no reason to trust. "Tanya doesn't check in with me."

"I can't believe she scared that easily, all because I want to write about her. We have the potential for a great professional relationship, but she only sees her secrets she's afraid I'll betray."

The beer was empty, so Annie pushed the empty bottle aside. "Would you?"

"Leave it to you to ask the tough questions." He spun the bottle around on the tabletop. "I don't have any intentions of betrayal. I want to tell her story. To tell it right, I can't leave out the pieces she's ashamed of. But I'd work with her on presentation, where to drawn the line on things she has a right to keep private. Bottom line, I wouldn't publish anything about anyone without their approval."

Jason might flirt with married women, but on a professional level his morals were on a higher plane. She supposed Tanya would find comfort in that. Annie was more concerned for Bonnie's well-being.

The waitress returned with the drinks. "Your sandwich will be up in a couple minutes." She glanced toward the door, and her face grayed. "I have to go."

"Wait," Jason said.

"You can't run from me," a man yelled above the music. The chatter in the room ceased.

Annie turned in her seat and saw a beefy man headed for

their table. She didn't recognize him, but her heart thudded with fear at the thought his viciousness might be directed at her. She glanced at Bonnie and found the waitress had vanished.

The man's gaze, full of hatred and violence, swept over her and paused on Jason. "She won't get away this time. And she'll pay for the stupid ideas you put in her head."

Jason shrank in his seat, but the man didn't stick around to bully him. He kept plowing toward the back of bar, presumably the direction Bonnie had disappeared to.

"That was Bonnie's husband, Hank," Jason whispered.

Annie picked up her cell phone, and for the second time today she called a police officer. Erring on the side of better-safe-than-sorry, she alerted Officer Michelson to Bonnie's situation. Then she slipped from her seat and hurried in Hank's direction. If she couldn't protect Bonnie, she could at least mediate the situation.

"She told me she quit and walked away without her paycheck. That's all I know," Al insisted, his bobbing bald head reflecting the fluorescent light of the kitchen.

"Which way did she go?" Hank advanced toward him and reached for the little man's windpipe.

"That way." Al pointed to the door next to the grill.

"Hank," Annie called. She didn't know what she planned to say, but she needed to let Bonnie get a couple more steps between them. This man wasn't looking to kiss and make up. Annie didn't want to think about his hand around Bonnie's neck.

He stopped and looked at her.

She scrambled to think of something. "As long as you're here, why don't you pick up Bonnie's paycheck for her? Why not get something for your trouble?"

Al looked at her like she was insane, but Hank paused for a few more precious seconds and then nodded. "Pony up, Al."

The skinny little bartender scurried to do his bidding. Slow down, Annie wanted to yell at him. Think about Bonnie's neck, not your own.

"I'd like to help you and Bonnie sort through your differences when you're both thinking clearly," Annie said to Hank. "Why don't you relax in front of the TV tonight and then come to Good Shepherd Church tomorrow morning? I'll ask Bonnie to do the same."

He clenched his fists. "I'll handle my wife." He took the check from Al and stormed outside.

Annie followed. "If it's the church setting you object to—"

He whirled on her. "No one interferes with me and my wife. Would you like me to show you what I have in mind for her?"

Annie took a step back. Following this man behind a dark building in the middle of the night was not one of her smarter moves. Then again, this wasn't her week for making brilliant decisions.

"Reverend Annie, how are you this evening?" Officer Michelson strode toward them.

Annie had a sudden urge to fling her arms around him and kiss him. Instead, she forced a smile. "I was just discussing the benefits of marital counseling to Hank."

"I'd take her up on it," the officer said congenially. "If there's anything worth saving in your marriage, she'll narrow in on it."

"The heck with both of you. My wife answers to me, and no one tells me what to do with her."

At the officer's faint nod, Annie backed up. She listened for a moment as he talked about respect, especially for one's spouse. When that got the same belligerent reaction, Officer Michelson switched to explaining what constituted assault and battery, along with the maximum prison sentences attached to each. Annie hoped Hank took it to heart.

She didn't immediately return to the bar, but spent the next hour looking for Bonnie. She'd recognized her need when they met in the supermarket but did nothing to follow up. This time she had a responsibility to make sure Bonnie had a safe place to sleep for the night. But the woman was hiding and doing a good job of not allowing herself to be found by anyone. Deciding she was probably safe from her husband as well, Annie's ravenous stomach propelled her back to Al's Bar.

Jason had graduated from the booth to a seat at the counter. His head was propped on his shoulders, heavily supported by his hands. Empty shot glasses littered the table around him. She settled onto the stool next to him, and he lifted his head to look at her. "Where's Bonnie?" he slurred.

"I don't know, but I think she's safe from Hank."

"I gave your sandwich to some hot chick. Forgot her name already. I think I drank the whole bottle." His head fell against his chest. "Good stuff, you should try it."

If the night had turned out differently, she might have. Instead she'd had to satisfy herself with two sips of beer. And she'd missed her chance to discover if Al's sandwiches were worth the hype. She preferred her reputation back. The bar scene was way overrated.

Chapter 14

Subway was empty of customers. Egan was officially on break, but instead of heading to the back he sat on a stool behind the counter to keep Heather company. She tried not to remember what Troy had suggested about their break times. In that regard, Egan was helping. He kept asking questions about her math homework. The words *algebra* and *blowjob* belonged to two different planets, let alone sentences.

"Quit bugging me about it." She finally stomped her foot in frustration.

"The test is Tuesday." The geek in him was relentless. "You have to get a *B* to pull a passing grade by Christmas."

Christmas used to be a time to look forward to. Now it was the dreaded end of the semester. "B minus," she corrected. At work she was supposed to have Egan's company without him watching her struggle with her own stupidity with numbers. When Egan tutored her, her vulnerabilities were exposed to an embarrassing degree.

The door chimed, signaling a temporary reprieve. Except the person walking toward the counter was Dad. Hardly a reprieve, no matter what he wanted.

"Foot-long turkey breast and ham on Italian herb bread," he said.

Heather stared. She could have been a green alien with a pink antenna. He didn't even silently recognize his own daughter. "Is Grandma making you fend for yourself?"

Dad blinked. "Heather." He adjusted his tie. "I forgot you worked here."

Yeah, he also forgot what his daughter looked like. He probably forgot he had a daughter. "You have more important things to remember, I'm sure."

He frowned.

She turned to retrieve a loaf of bread, taking two deep breaths to compose herself before she turned around. Egan stood up. She'd forgotten he was watching her dad treat her like she was a speck of dust. Egan hadn't let Troy get the best of him.

Dad cleared his throat. "Heather."

"You want cheese on this?" she interrupted, as she carved up the bread.

"Yes."

She slapped it on. She'd wanted this job. It was supposed to be empowering. Now she was a servant to her own family.

"Grandma made pot roast tonight," Dad said.

She looked up from peeling meat off waxed paper. When she was little, Dad always made her eat three bites of the roast. Mom never took seconds. Grandma's pot roast was burned and dry and truly the most awful thing Heather had ever eaten. "Serves you right for moving in with her."

"What's that supposed to mean?"

Heather shrugged. If she were smart, she'd keep her mouth shut. "Grandma wants you back for herself. She wants you to do better than Mom and me."

"You and your mom are my family."

"That doesn't mean you give a care about us." She slid the sandwich down the counter. "Everything but tomato, extra olives?"

"I care."

Heather built the sandwich without his confirmation and

rang up the sale. Dad paid with a twenty, and when she gave him his change, he dumped it all into the tip cup. She turned away before he saw her cry. The tip cup was Egan's, but Dad didn't know that. He'd tipped her. As far as signs of approval went, it wasn't much, but it was more than he'd given her in months.

Egan's fingers brushed her elbow. She glanced down and found him offering her a Kleenex. She wadded it into a ball and pressed it to her mouth before she blubbered her sobs aloud.

As she steadied her breathing, she heard Dad fill his drink. Silence followed. He would be eating now. She steeled herself and turned around. He was staring at her. "Thanksgiving's coming up. Can I pick you up and take you to Grandma's? No pot roast."

She looked down at her hands. Things were supposed to get better now that Mom was asserting herself. Instead, Heather was in the middle of the friction. Taking sides against her dad should have been a no-brainer. But she hadn't expected him to turn nice. "I can't leave Mom alone."

He nodded once. "Right. Well, let me know if you change your mind." She waited for him to walk away, but he kept standing there looking at her. "This offer comes a few years late, but I, uh, heard you were having trouble with algebra. I think I could give myself a quick refresher if you want some help."

A sudden image of her twelve-year-old self begging for help with math flashed into her mind. Dad had an important meeting and couldn't be bothered. Three days later, when he remembered she needed him, she'd already bombed the test. "Egan's helping me." She threw a play-along-with-me smile over her shoulder.

"Tomorrow morning," Egan said without hesitating.

Dad gave Egan a long look. "Good." He pinned his gaze back

on Heather. "Tell Mom I'll pick up my things in the morning. I'll check on your progress."

"Is your brother going to be home to look after you?" Annie asked Jason as she helped him out of the passenger seat of Tanya's car.

"Hope not," he slurred. "I'd rather be passed out on your lap than his."

Annie wasn't sure what she hoped. She knew she couldn't leave Jason alone tonight. Her tattered reputation would shred if she spent the night with him after everyone in the bar watched them leave together. The church elders were probably reconsidering their decision to let her wait until Sunday to resign.

The apartment door was unlocked, which was good. In the ten-foot walk from the car to the door, she had to bat Jason's hands away twice for trying to cop a feel. She wasn't in the mood to play search-my-pants for his keys.

She braced herself for the likelihood Nick was on the other side of the door. Then she pushed against it with her shoulder. It propelled open with such force she staggered. With Jason leaning against her, she had no chance to regain her balance. She fell against something hard and unyielding. The breath whooshed from her lungs. She was still upright. She hadn't fallen to the floor.

The massive chest she fell against belonged to Nick. He recovered first and set her on her feet. Disgust radiated from him. "Jason, I know your only requirement for sleeping with someone is they be female, but you can do better than a drunken soon-to-be-ex-preacher."

Annie stood solidly on her feet. Indignation insisted she take control again. She shoved at Nick's chest. "You've gone farther with me than he has, so your standards must be even lower."

Nick looked at her, his expression inscrutable. Annie wished she could take back her words. She'd meant to say something cutting to put him in his place. Instead, she'd reminded him of the attraction between them, which she was doing her best to deny.

"Back off, bro'. She's with me tonight." Jason stumbled into the apartment, bumping into her back.

Annie planted herself before she rammed into Nick again and became a human ping-pong ball. Unfortunately, she was still too close. If she took a deep breath, her breasts would brush his chest. If she shifted, her hips would—

"He's recovering from a head injury, and you got him drunk?" Nick pierced her with a classic if-looks-could-kill.

Annie glanced at the purple bruise on Jason's cheek. "He was already in the bar when I arrived. I neither encouraged nor forbade. But I did want to make sure he got home safely."

"How noble of you."

She winced. Nick was furious, and he had a right to be. "I'll leave now and let you take care of him."

"I can take care of myself," Jason shouted. He started to stomp away, ran into the wall, and fell face-first on the carpet.

"The heck you will," Nick yelled at Annie as if Jason's outburst hadn't occurred. "You got him into this. You can sit up with him and make sure he doesn't slip into unconsciousness or choke on his vomit tonight. And you can start by getting him off the floor and into bed. Undressing a man ought to give you a thrill."

Annie stared at Nick. She'd expected a confrontation, but she'd underestimated how low his opinion of her had sunk.

"Get started. You might not get another chance." Nick walked to the couch and flopped down with the newspaper account of Annie's demise.

He hated her. Not surprising. He'd never really liked her to begin with. Her behavior last night wouldn't inspire a change of heart, especially since she hadn't followed up with an apology. But she couldn't summon one when he looked at her like she was something to be handled with plastic gloves and a pooper-scooper.

So she turned her back on him and walked to Jason. "Hey, let's get you up off the floor. You'll feel better in the morning if you sleep on a mattress tonight." Although not a lot better, considering the well-deserved hangover he had coming.

Jason opened his eyes to send her a crooked smile. "I knew winning the coin toss with Nick for the only bed would pay off. Nothing turns me on like a woman trying to talk me into sleeping with her."

Too much information. "This isn't a college fraternity party. I won't join you in that bed."

"Condoms are in my shaving kit in the bathroom," Jason muttered as he pulled himself to his knees. "I think I'm going to puke."

Her first thought was to drag him to the toilet, but she'd have to enlist Nick's help. He'd made it plenty clear she was on her own. Instead, she pulled the biggest pan from the drawer under the kitchen stove and shoved it under Jason's face.

She located a washcloth next to the fully stocked shaving kit, and ran the cloth under cool water before trading it to him for the pan. After the contents were disposed of, she set the pan in front of him again.

Jason pressed the cloth to his forehead. "I think the moment's passed."

Annie settled next to him, comfortable in the caretaker-counselor role. "We can sit here as long as you like."

"Actually, I'd like to brush my teeth."

She helped him to his feet and down the short hallway. After he closed himself in, she wandered out to the living room to give him privacy. Nick was watching her over a copy of *Remodel-*

ing magazine.

"Sneaking out?"

Every bone in her body felt excruciatingly weary. Yet every muscle felt the pull of Nick's presence. "No." She gathered her composure and her energy. "I should have called you."

"For permission to get my brother drunk?"

She sighed. Nick was going to make this apology as difficult as possible. "For letting things get out of hand at the food pantry last night."

"What sort of things?"

He was mocking her, but she answered anyway. "Desires, physical needs, wants."

He set the magazine aside and folded his arm across his chest. "I personally thought they didn't go far enough."

She felt her cheeks burn. Wrapping herself in celibacy for over a decade meant she was sorely out of practice for these tricky conversations. "I take full responsibility for my actions. I apologize if you felt I mistreated you after we were interrupted."

"By 'mistreating' I assume you mean acting like I was someone you were ashamed of." The hostility radiating from him slammed against her.

She clasped her hands together. "I was not and am not ashamed of you. But my own behavior, especially in light of where I conducted my actions, was deplorable, and I am suffering the consequences."

Nick surged to his feet. "Get off your high horse. You aren't any better than anyone else, so don't put on airs for me."

"Nick." She reached for his arm. His expression was so forbidding she dropped her hand before she touched him. "I'm a minister. My career and my life depend on keeping my reputation clean."

"I thought they would have depended on God."

He might as well have slapped her. Had she put God so far

down her list? Was her reputation more important than her relationship with Him? She knew the right answers dictated by her religion. They weren't the same as her personal truths. "I know you don't think much of me—even less after last night and tonight, I'm sure. But the truth is, I have to live my life to a higher standard than everyone else."

"You don't have to live to a higher standard," Nick jeered. "You just have to make everyone believe you're above the bar."

He knocked the last of her bravado out of her. "Either way, I've failed the community of Maplefield."

Nick swung off the couch and grabbed her shoulders. "Why can't you be yourself? Why do you have to pretend to be something you're not?"

Stung, she pulled back. "You think I'm pretending to be moral, upright, and God-serving?"

"I look at the facts." His voice dripped with derision. "I see a preacher who went after a quickie in a food pantry. What conclusion would you draw?"

Annie closed her eyes. He didn't see her as a woman with a woman's needs. He didn't see a forming bond or relationship. He saw a preacher looking for quick satisfaction for her base desires. Curiosity or perversion convinced him to give her a try. This was far worse than the men who wanted her because she was Tanya's sister. Then again, Nick fit that category, too.

Nick felt like a bully who picked on helpless kids to build his self-esteem. It didn't work for the bully, and verbally bruising Annie didn't make Nick feel better either. Sitting on the couch, knowing Annie was down the hall tending to his brother, he felt worse.

He'd first—stupidly—assumed she was drunk and coming to the apartment to flaunt a fling with his brother.

In truth she'd taken care of Jason without making a single

gesture or comment that any rational person would interpret as more than friendly. Unfortunately, rationality had nothing to do with his feelings toward Reverend Annie.

The bathroom door closed. Ten minutes later he heard it rattle again. After a short movement, silence settled over the apartment. Curiosity—and jealousy, if he was totally honest—got the best of him.

The door to Jason's room was open as Nick walked down the hall. He paused to look inside, telling himself it was just to check on his brother's well-being. Jason was sprawled across the single bed on his stomach, snoring loudly, his lower half covered with a sheet, his upper half in an underwear T-shirt.

Annie sat on the floor below the window, her knees drawn up to her chest and her head down on top of them. He couldn't see her face, and she made no acknowledgment she'd heard him approach. Her position screamed vulnerability and dejection, and it punched him in the gut.

"You can go home. I'll stay with Jason," Nick said.

Her head shot up, and her spine stiffened. "Don't be nice. I hate an act as much as you do."

He supposed he deserved that jab. He walked to her and held out his hand. "Talk with me on the couch."

She glanced at Jason.

"He'll be okay. We'll check on him if he stops snoring."

She nodded and got to her feet, ignoring his hand. Her blazer smelled faintly of bar smoke. He noticed it was still tightly buttoned across her chest as she walked by him to the front of the apartment.

Now that they were alone he had no idea what to say to her. The buttoned blazer and stiffly crossed arms attested to how receptive she would be to picking up where they left off last night. He couldn't convince his libido he'd brought her out here for any other reason.

"What's this?" Annie honed in on his rough sketch of a new porch for the house.

"Just a carpentry job I'm working on." He took it from her hand and gathered all the other papers. He hadn't told anyone he was closing on the house on Monday. Jason hadn't taken his interest seriously. Nick wasn't ready to combat his family's subtle derision when he talked about the labor he intended to put into what most people would see as a dump.

Annie shook her head. "Don't pretend to be something you're not. I know you're a lawyer."

"I'm not—"

"I'll keep your cover if you want me to, but don't lie to me."

She was pleading with him. She couldn't handle the truth behind his identity. A handyman wasn't good enough for her to associate with. She was his father reincarnated, wanting a handyman for his free labor but not as a family member—or in this case, a lover. Disgusted, he turned the conversation around on her. "You're a fine one to talk about lies."

"I haven't lied to you." She hugged her blazer a little tighter. He wanted to burn the hideous thing.

"About the jewelry, your sister, what you and I were doing in the pantry." He ticked off each instance. "Maybe not complete lies. But you know how to twist or avoid the truth to your advantage."

"You asked me to talk so you could harp on your grudges?"

Nick shook his head. He didn't want to argue. He wanted to sit with his arm around her and tell her his plans for the house. But she wouldn't believe him. He'd settle for watching a disgustingly sappy movie. Except he didn't have a TV in the apartment. Making out segueing into mind-blowing sex was a completely agreeable alternative. If only he could stop himself from acting like a jerk.

Annie lowered herself onto the couch. "If you want to kill

time, start by explaining why you hate me. I'm not buying the smokescreen about the Reverend Annie/Jason/Tanya escapade. I've been exonerated, but you're just as contemptuous of me as when you thought I was the culprit."

Nick looked at the tempting couch cushions. He could cuddle with Annie like he'd imagined. But he couldn't do it while talking about his father. And he couldn't answer Annie's question without bringing that man into it. Nick walked to the window and took in the uninspiring view of the dimly lit parking lot. "My dad was a minister."

"Yes, I know." She knew. The revelation was supposed to surprise her. Instead, she caught him off guard.

"He was a jerk." Nick glanced over his shoulder to see if he'd shocked her, but she met his gaze with her nonjudgmental look of compassion. He turned back to the window but saw only the past. "Dad fooled the people of his congregation into thinking he was a true man of God, but he didn't fool the people who lived with him—my mom and me."

"How did he treat you?" Annie asked.

Nick had tried so hard to reach perfection for his father. The only thing he reaped from it was criticisms of what he did wrong. "His treatment of my mother was what was truly awful. He'd go into the city and pick up women for the night and flaunt them in front of her face. Mom eventually found love somewhere else—with Jason's dad. When they had an affair, the scandal rocked the community. The church people blamed it on her Hollywood roots and treated her like a pariah, while Dad was cast as the victim and the suffering saint."

"And you were stuck in the middle," Annie whispered.

"I wasn't good enough to keep their marriage together." He clenched his fists. He was going to be good enough. He was so close now to creating unity and healing old wounds. His mother would finally have peace. And so would he.

"As a child, it's common to blame yourself for your parents' problems, but you know better now." Her voice was soothing and nonjudgmental.

He whirled toward her. "I'm explaining why I hate you, not looking for a therapy session."

"It's a freebie." Annie smiled at him.

He faced her fully, unable to take his eyes off her lovely face and unable to stop talking about what he'd kept bottled inside for too long. "I visited Mom, but I lived with Dad. I guess he was a great minister. Everyone in the congregation loved him."

"But he wasn't father-of-the-year," Annie said, still understanding every nuance of what he said and didn't say. He resented it but not enough to choke off his past resentment.

"A preacher's son has to be perfect. I wasn't a bad kid. I didn't set out to rebel. I was just never good enough." His throat was closing up, remembering all the subtle put-downs. "Compassion was preached from the pulpit. God knows all your faults and still loves you and all that garbage."

"It's the truth, not garbage."

"Yeah, well, at home the message took a different spin. If you can fix your faults, then I'll love you." And he had tried. It hurt to remember. His years in law school had been dedicated to trying to earn his father's love and approval. "But I always needed to improve on something."

Annie rose to her feet. "Do you believe every pastor is like your old man, or just me?"

With one simple question she made him look foolish for carrying his childhood experience around in a suitcase. "I'm a cynic. Being a minister is a strike against you. The rest of my derision you earned yourself."

"By?" Her eyes were clear blue lakes of innocence.

"By asking your church council leader not to hold you to the standard expected of a pastor. You told him our situation wasn't how it looked. We looked like we were on our way to having sex against the wall. If he hadn't come in, I assure you we would have." His loins ached for completion.

"You didn't like me before I let down my congregation and insulted you."

Yes, he did. He was trying not to, but he liked her before. Although he was hurt and frustrated over the way things had ended last night, he still liked her. As much as he tried to block it, he also understood why she'd turned her back on him. "I think I could like you if you weren't a preacher."

"Ministering is part of my identity. You don't get to pick and choose." She stepped toward him.

"What if you could choose? What if I weren't a lawyer? What if I were a homeless handyman looking for odd jobs?" The answer shouldn't matter. He was a lawyer who very shortly would own two homes. Yet he held his breath waiting for Annie's reply.

She skimmed a single finger down his cheek. "If I told you I liked you better as a handyman, you'd say I'm just like your father for thinking you're not good enough now. And that's not true. You're a good man, Nick, just the way you are, no matter how you earn your living."

If she said it one more time, he might believe her. And then what? Years of hard work toward his nearly realized dreams would be null and void. His direction was preordained. He couldn't change it.

Chapter 15

Tanya had no idea where she'd driven. Except whenever she got there, she realized she was running like the World's Wimpiest Coward. She had unfinished business in L.A. and Maplefield. Her west coast life was complicated. There were a million loose ends and contracts to live up to or worm her way out of.

She'd have to deal with the high-profile rat race eventually, but she'd start with Maplefield, where she could, at least, count the dangling ends. Maybe she'd get lucky with a few of them. Zeke could be in Madagascar by now. Jason might have returned to his day job of selling her old cocktail dresses and Zeke's guitars. Hopefully, he took his brother with him.

Hiding behind luck wouldn't work for Annie, though. Tanya was going to have to face her sister and figure out a way to repair their relationship. She had broken it. She had to fix it.

Something—someone—ran across the road. A woman. Tanya slammed on her brakes. The woman changed directions and ran for Tanya's headlights. Her expression was a chilling mix of terror and determination. Blood smeared across her cheek.

Oh, man. She did not want to relive this part of her life. No, no, this wasn't her life. This was a scene from *Bomb Maiden*, where Tanya's character runs toward the car. After all the stunts and special effects, Tom Cruise leans across the seats and pulls her in while driving fifty miles an hour.

Tanya didn't have special effects, but she was going under ten miles per hour. So she leaned across the seat and fumbled with the handle. The latch released, but she had to shift the car into park and crawl across the front seat to push the passenger door open. No one was going to cast her as Tom.

The woman did a great *Bomb Maiden* imitation. She slid into the seat, slammed the door, shoved down the lock, and screamed, "Go. Please. He's coming."

Tanya scrambled to the driver's side and fumbled with the gearshift. She pushed the gas and then looked up to see a man with a knife in the middle of the road. "Cut. I don't star in bad B movies." She slammed on the brakes, but the man kept coming toward them.

"I'm sorry," the woman sobbed.

"Don't you dare apologize for that guy."

"I'm—"

The man reached the hood of the car. All she could see was Zeke's evil face as the closet light flipped on. "Where is the reverse?"

The woman reached over and pulled the lever.

Tanya floored the gas pedal, sending them backwards and dumping the man on his butt in the road. They veered toward the ditch. She whipped the steering wheel, taking out a mailbox on the other side. She drove backwards like a drunken maniac until she was certain she had enough distance to turn the car around without another encounter with a sharp metal object. "Which way to the police station?"

"I'm not going to the police."

"That guy was coming after you with a knife." Tanya reached for her cell phone. She'd call Jake herself. The heck with jurisdiction. He'd help a battered woman.

"That guy is my husband. He already talked to the police once tonight, and it just made him angrier. They can't stop him."

"You married about as well as I did," Tanya muttered. "Which way to the hospital?"

"No hospital." The stubbornness in her voice was eerily reminiscent of Tanya's own resistance to seeking medical treatment.

"You're bleeding," Tanya pointed out.

She swiped at her cheek. "It's just a little cut. I can't go to the hospital. I don't have health insurance. I can't afford it."

"I can. Which way?"

"No. Just take me to"—she hesitated—"the food pantry. Sometimes Myra leaves the back door unlocked. I can sleep there tonight."

Tanya looked at her more carefully this time. She'd met this woman at the food pantry yesterday. Lois had brought her in, given her bags of food and a bandage for her arm. Tanya had wowed her with her star presence, but neither of them had been able to erase the haunted look from her eyes. "You're Bonnie, right? You can stay with me tonight."

"Yes, how did—" Bonnie looked at her closely. "Oh, my gosh. Ohmygosh." She pressed her hands to her chest. "You're Tanya. You gave me your autograph. And now you saved my life. Oh, my gosh, I can't believe this. Meeting you was the best thing that ever happened to me."

"Getting away from your psycho husband should be the best thing that ever happened to you."

"I left him because of what you wrote on your autograph."

Make your own life. Tanya had been writing the phrase for years, but she'd never followed it. She'd been too busy following the course others mapped out for her.

"I'll have to go back to him in the morning. He won't be so mad then. He probably won't have the knife anymore."

Probably. Bonnie would bet her life on it. "Why go back?"

"I can't stay with you forever. 'Make your own life' is a nice saying, but I don't have any skills or money to make it happen.

I need Hank."

Yeah, like she needed a knife slice on the cheek. Bonnie needed a second chance, and Tanya wanted one too. To not be known for her big boobs and sexpot mouth. For the word *viper* not to be the first word people thought of when they thought of her. To not be known for her drug-dealing hard-rocking husband. All her life she'd been the bad sister, the sexy sister, the selfish sister, the party sister. She'd still be bad and selfish compared to Annie. Tanya would never be a saint.

But what if she was the sister who made a difference? The sister who took a stand? The sister who used her big mouth and love affair with the camera to stand up for the helpless? For Bonnie and all the other bruised women who thought their best alternative was to stay with the men who abused them.

She pulled up to a stop sign and watched as a red Hummer crossed the intersection ahead of her. The familiar fear flooded her. Luck wasn't on her side.

Make your own life. Now was the time to take her own advice.

The shower was running, and her mattress felt like she was sleeping on concrete. Annie stretched and groaned as her muscles protested. If the shower was on, someone must be in her house. Sleep made searching her mind like combing through fog for a missing contact lens. Tanya? No, Tanya had bailed on her. Annie listened again. No sound from the shower. She shook her head. Obviously, she'd been dreaming.

She sat up and realized she was on a hardwood floor with her rolled-up blazer as a makeshift pillow. Her aching joints weren't a dream. She looked around, finally establishing herself in Jason's apartment, as the bar scene and helping him home returned to her.

She had no idea what time it was except it was too dark to see her watch. What she needed was a hot washcloth to massage her neck. Maybe she'd sneak out to the couch and sleep there. Even a carpeted floor would be an improvement.

The light was on under the bathroom door. She'd probably left it on, in case Jason needed to stumble there in the night. She reached for the handle, but it turned and opened before she could grasp it.

She was dreaming. It was the only possible explanation for the perfect male body in front of her. Nick McAllister. She couldn't look away. She didn't make the attempt. This was a dream, her fantasy. "You look delicious," she heard a much bolder version of herself say.

He cleared his throat. She had to be dreaming if she thought that sounded sexy. "Annie, do you know what you're doing?"

She didn't, but she knew what she wanted. "Do you want me?" Reverend Annie would never dare ask such a brazen question. But she wasn't anyone's pastor or role model anymore. She was unemployed, fallen, and she had needs. During her twenties, while other women tried on men for size, she'd worn a chastity belt with God holding the key. God left her side today, and He took the belt with Him.

Nick shifted and discovered a female pressed against him. Delicious memories assailed him. He snuggled closer and wandered his hands over Annie.

"You're awake," she murmured.

"Oh, yeah."

"Do we need to have one of those awkward morning-after chats?"

"Not yet." This perfection of body and spirit couldn't last. They hadn't resolved anything. He wanted to see sex as a pleasant distraction, but Annie would focus on the giant complication.

"Nick, I know you didn't like me before last night. I'm feeling pretty well liked now, but hearing you say it will help a lot when the physical pleasure wears off."

"Wears off? It's only beginning."

She squirmed away. "What time is it? I promised to be back at the hospital with Myra at ten."

Nick sighed. He didn't have to sit through a painful morning-after chat. Annie was going to run out on him first. She flipped her wrist to look at her watch. Whatever the time now, she'd use it as an excuse to leave. She had an obligation to her parish to remind them to follow her words, not her example.

He rolled away and found himself on the cold, unforgiving floor, courtesy of the single-bed-width sleeping bag and cushion. "You'll come back tonight, right?" It was a long shot, but he couldn't stop himself from asking and hoping.

She looked at him. No smiles. No emotion at all. "I enjoyed our night. I won't deny it or belittle it. But my life belongs to God's service. Unless you're willing to give a portion of your life to that same service, our physical relationship can't continue."

"You'll only sleep with me again if I become a minister?" Surely, he'd misunderstood. He would never succumb to following his father's footsteps.

"No. I'll sleep with you again if and when you marry me."

He scooted backwards in an undignified crabwalk. He wasn't opposed to marriage. Commitment was honorable, a preferred way of life. If anyone had asked him during his twenties, he'd have said he'd be married by the time he turned thirty. Maybe with a family. He wanted the chance to be a better father than his own father had been.

But women found the real Nick McAllister unacceptable. They didn't want a handyman. They wanted someone successful and prestigious—someone they could be proud of. He'd tried to become that man. The women who connected with the right image never saw the man behind the mask. Nick knew that man would emerge sooner or later and make their marriage miserable.

"I'm not so desperate I'll marry for sex."

"I never thought you were." Annie hugged her arms around herself, looking young and vulnerable. "But I have principles."

"I can see how highly you value them." Disgusted with her hypocritical babble and the need for her that he couldn't control, he grabbed his duffle bag and headed for the bathroom. Her body had nothing more to offer him. The rest of her never had anything he was interested in.

If he kept repeating that mantra, by the time he died a ninety-year-old bachelor he might start to believe it.

"Don't act surprised to see me," Egan said as Heather opened the front door. "You knew I'd come."

"That doesn't mean I'm happy to see you," she lied. Her pulse did a funny dance, and her nervousness promised to outlast her deodorant. She led Egan to the kitchen. "You could have blown this off. I can make excuses to Dad."

He slapped his backpack on the table. "I don't need anyone making excuses for me, and you don't get an excuse for your algebra grade either."

"Why do you care?"

He stared at her for so long Heather was afraid something green and disgusting was hanging from her nose. She swiped her hand across her face.

"You're worth caring about," Egan said finally. He busied himself unzipping his backpack.

She stared at him as stupid tears made his image blurry. She'd never be as good a person as he, but a long time ago she'd held some of the same innocent hopes and dreams. Of getting good grades and going to college. Of making her parents proud.

But then she'd turned herself into the easiest lay in Jo Daviess County, all with the faint hope of getting a hug. Getting pregnant had seemed cool, a guaranteed hug a minute. But then Tanya gave her that horrible little book. Thinking about it scared her to death, literally. She couldn't count on her own life anymore, let alone someone to share it with. Nice guys like Egan should wear latex to look at her.

She pressed her fists to her eyes, trying to wipe them without ruining her mascara. She'd worn makeup to impress him. And now she looked like a sick raccoon. "You're wasting your time. Algebra's at the bottom of my priority list."

"Yeah, divorce sucks," Egan said, as if that was what was keeping her awake at night.

"My parents aren't getting a divorce."

He looked at her like she was a naïve moron. "I hope you're right."

She opened her mouth to argue but remembered he was the brain who was never wrong, so she shut up.

"Do you want to talk about it, or do you want to talk math?" His hazel eyes were filled with such compassion she almost confessed everything—how her dad ignored her, how she looked for attention with other guys, how the void widened and how she desperately tried to fill it, and how afraid she was of dying.

But she didn't have the guts to risk it. Egan kind of liked her. That innocent affection was too precious to jeopardize. "Let's go wild and crazy and talk math. Maybe we could even do math together." She wiggled her eyebrows at him. The tips of his ears turned pink, and she lost a little bit of her heart.

"Where is she?"

Annie jumped, caught in the guilty process of sneaking out of

Nick's apartment in yesterday's wrinkled clothes. She didn't recognize the bearded, unkempt man who approached her. Her first impulse was relief that he wasn't part of her congregation and likely not from Maplefield. "Who are you looking for?"

"Your sister."

Tanya, of course. Annie was standing next to her sister's car with the key in her hand. This man wasn't the noncommittal Officer Jacobs, she was sure of that. Recognition hit, and her relief evaporated. Tanya's bruises hadn't entirely faded yet. Annie didn't believe it was a coincidence Tanya had run out of town at the same time Zeke showed up. "I haven't seen her. Excuse me. I'm running late."

Zeke's hand wrenched her chin. "Where is she, Annie?"

His fingers brought stars of pain to her eyes. "You would know better than me."

His hand tightened until she was sure her jaw would shatter. "Tanya was right. You are high and mighty. Tell her how wrong it is to make millions and leave her husband without access to a penny. She has until three o'clock to get seven million to me, or I put a video of her and me having sex on the internet."

"I hope you rot in jail," Annie spat back.

He clicked his tongue. "Such un-Christian behavior."

"Get your hands off her." Nick barreled down the sidewalk. Annie wanted to weep with relief.

"Three o'clock or Tanya's on the internet." Zeke saluted her and took off in his Hummer.

Annie closed her eyes, unaware she was leaning against Nick until her head rested against his shoulder. "Thank you."

"Did he hurt you?" His fingers slid gently over her chin.

"No." She kept her eyes closed to absorb his tenderness. It was better than dwelling on Zeke's awful threats.

"Don't look now, but I just discovered how you made the front page of the paper."

Her eyes snapped open and were greeted by a blinding flash. "I'm with *CelebScoop*," a skinny, oily man yelled across the parking lot, clutching a camera that looked like it was on steroids. "On the scale of one to ten, how do you rate your threesome with your sister's husband and this man? Would you give a ten to your three-way with Tanya and her lesbian lover?"

Annie choked. "The police will want your film for evidence."

"They can buy a copy of the magazine. I'll say you were moved beyond words." He sauntered to a tan sedan and followed Zeke out of the lot.

Annie's knees buckled, but Nick's arm around her waist prevented her from falling to the sidewalk. "Who's going to hire a minister who makes those headlines?"

"Who would believe those headlines?" Nick countered.

"Only the people who matter."

"The wrong people matter to you." He disentangled himself and walked away.

He should be right. God knew the truth. God's opinion should be the only one she cared about. Compared to the people who judged her life, God's assessment seemed inconsequential.

Chapter 16

"Lois," Stewart shouted as he walked into his house. No one answered, confirming what he suspected when he pulled in the driveway and discovered her car gone. Not so long ago, she planned her day around him and hovered solicitously when he came through the door. Now she knew he was coming, and she took off.

Low voices came from the kitchen, so he headed there. Heather sat at the table next to the kid from Subway—Evan or Ethan or something. "Where's your mom?"

"At the food pantry." Heather barely spared him a glance.

"Did she eat all our food and go looking for more?" The mean and spiteful words poured from his lips despite his better judgment. The one perk of having a fat wife was she was pretty much immobile. She was guaranteed to be here. Stewart missed the guarantees in life.

Heather glared at him. "No wonder Mom kicked you out. You're such a butthead."

The boy twisted in his chair, his shoulders angled in front of Heather, like he'd protect her if her dad tried to hit her.

What kind of father was he? He belittled his wife, his daughter called him names, and her boyfriend thought Stewart had violent tendencies. He took a step back. "You're right. I'm sorry. What's Mom doing at the food pantry?"

"Handing out food, I guess." Heather shrugged, exposing a slim shoulder through the oversized neckline of her sweater.

The boy looked once, his Adam's apple bobbing, and quickly averted his gaze.

Stewart started to clench his fists before Heather's words registered. "She works at the food pantry?"

"She's in charge."

In charge? Lois hadn't been in charge of anything in years. Myra Turnaggle was going to have a cow when she found out someone else was calling the shots at her precious food pantry. No, no one would run the pantry without Myra's blessing. The irony hit him hard. The enemy in Stewart's budget war to rein in excess spending had more faith in his wife than he did.

"She has help," Heather continued. "Jason Somebody."

"Jason?" The flash of jealousy was as irrational as it was undeniable.

"Yeah. He's some sort of manager, so he's teaching her how to manage the food pantry. If you don't mind, we're kind of busy here. Egan's teaching me the FOIL method, and I have a quiz Tuesday."

"A quiz, right." He backed into the hall, feeling like an intruder in his own home. In the last two days, his family had turned into strangers. "Well, good luck. If you need anything, I'll be down the hall."

"Packing your stuff," Heather confirmed. "We're fine without you."

Everyone was, it seemed. If anyone had asked, he'd have said he was fine without them, too. He couldn't remember ever feeling so lost.

"Where are you going?" Tanya stood in Annie's bedroom, daring to question her plans as if she hadn't gone missing and then returned with no explanation.

If Annie had any energy to spare, she would have taken issue with her sister's effrontery. Instead she shrugged into her blazer and worried whether she should tell Tanya about Zeke's threats or save her the worry and go straight to the authorities. "I'm on my way to the hospital."

"Oh, my God." Tanya rushed to her side. "Is it Nick? I'll kill him."

Annie blinked. Tanya had never bothered to pretend an ounce of sympathy for Myra or even a polite question on Myra's condition. "Nick has nothing to do with me going to the hospital."

"You're in denial. I underst—"

Annie didn't understand at all. Myra's family needed her, and Tanya thought she could take over Annie's home and her possessions. "Did you return my car? I didn't appreciate your little swap."

Tanya's hands moved fussily around her without actually touching her. "Don't change the subject. Whether he was violent or it was date rape—"

"Rape?" That jarred Annie's full attention. "I'm going to the hospital to visit a parishioner who had a stroke. Everything between Nick and I was fully consensual." Her energy returned with the arousing memories of last night. She preferred to keep their passion a secret treasure, but she wouldn't let anyone believe Nick capable of anything other than exquisite attention to her desires.

Tanya's hands dropped to her sides. "But you took a long shower and immediately took your clothes to the laundry room."

"My clothes smelled like bar smoke." And in the shower she relived all the secret special things Nick had done to her.

"I see from the look on your face it was good," Tanya said, taking a step back. "I'm sorry I jumped to conclusions and even more sorry he didn't take me up on my offer."

Thinking of Tanya and Nick in bed together made Annie's stomach turn over. "So about my car?"

Tanya waved her off. "We've got more important things to

talk about."

She couldn't handle Tanya going back on her word and setting her sights on Nick, not with her own body still tingling. "I'm leaving for Minnesota tomorrow after church. Your tank is too unreliable for the trip. You're a movie star. Why are you driving a car that's worth less than your shoes?"

"You can't leave," Tanya insisted.

"I have an interview for an associate pastor position with another church."

"The people here need you. How can you turn your back on them?"

The people of Maplefield had turned their backs on her, and now she was at fault for respecting their wishes by leaving. "They don't need me anymore. Since when do you care about what anyone other than yourself needs?"

"You are so self-centered." Tanya grabbed her arm and pulled her down the hall. "I thought you were a person of God."

"I am." She hated when people used those words to force her to defend her behavior. She wasn't perfect, but she'd given her life to God. What more did He want?

Tanya threw open the door to the closet housing the water heater and furnace. Huddled between them was the waitress Annie had looked for last night. From the cut on her face, she could only assume someone else had been more successful in finding her.

"This is Bonnie, whose husband considered it his marital right to come after her with a knife because she got a job where someone paid her to serve beer and wouldn't give her a black eye if the beer was warm."

Annie winced. She should have recognized that Hank wasn't going to be reasoned out of his threats. If she hadn't stopped looking, Annie might have found her first and taken her to safety. She knelt to make her position as nonthreatening as possible.

"Hi, Bonnie. I'm Annie. We met at the grocery store and last night. I'm the pastor of Good Shepherd Church." For twenty-four more hours, assuming the paparazzi photographer waited that long to publish his new pictures and threesome fiction.

"I'm glad you decided to come see me," Annie continued. She didn't know what she was supposed to do with this woman. Myra's family was waiting for her at the hospital. "Did Tanya offer you any food?"

Bonnie gave a small nod.

"We, uh, polished off your brownies together last night," Tanya said sheepishly. "I gained five pounds, and I look it, too."

Annie rolled her eyes. "Go borrow one of my blazers and get over it." She returned her gaze to Bonnie. "I'll cook you a normal breakfast, and then you can use my shower to freshen up."

"Actually, if I could shower first, I'll make the breakfast," Bonnie said, slowly rising to her feet.

"Even better."

"She's terrified her husband's going to burst in and find her," Tanya said after Bonnie was closed in the bathroom.

"Your husband's out there looking for you, too." Annie changed her mind and decided to warn Tanya about Zeke's threats.

"I know. That's why I understand the importance of bringing a safe house for battered women to Maplefield. A place they can run to when their husband or boyfriend flips out because the soup's cold and the beer's warm. A place where women can stay while they build up an income and the skills to live on their own and support their children."

It was a noble goal, but Annie had dreamed plenty of her own and she hadn't made a positive difference to anyone. "The town also needs a fire truck, a new sewer system, handicap access in the city hall, and a teen center. Are you going to solve all of Maplefield's problems?"

"No. But you and I together can combat domestic violence. I'll front the money—"

"And I'll do all the work." Tiredness settled over her again. "No, Tanya. God has a plan for my life."

"What if this is God's plan for you?"

"It's not." She was a minister. She belonged inside a church.

"If you were open to God's plan, you would see the possibilities of what I'm asking and take a couple days to pray about it. But you're too busy making God's decisions for Him." Tanya stormed down the hall.

Annie sank to the floor. She'd prayed plenty in the past few days. Begging God to get her out of the mess she was in. If He didn't, she'd explained to Him, she'd be unable to do His will. Tanya was right. She'd never asked and certainly never listened to His will.

But that didn't mean ministry wasn't her calling. She'd spent hours and days in prayer, listening for direction, before she entered the seminary. If God was making her second-guess her decision now, He was angry with her for setting Him aside for personal pleasures with Nick. She wouldn't lapse again. She'd taken vows to her God and her church. Nothing would separate her from them.

"Some guys just pulled up. They're looking for me." Bonnie pulled the bedroom curtains over the window, bunching them together in her fist so there was no gap in the middle.

Tanya was sure Annie would know what to say to calm Bonnie's chattering teeth, but God apparently had bigger plans for her sister. Like sitting at the bedside of a comatose woman who wouldn't know she was there.

Tanya pried the curtains from Bonnie so she could glance out and then moved back before the paparazzi could snap her picture. She was quick enough to thwart a photographer, but not Jake. She turned to Bonnie. "These people are on our side." She hoped. "I'm going down to talk to them. You want to come with me?"

Bonnie's eyes widened, and she shook her head negatively.

"All right. Then stay here." Tanya cast about for something to keep the woman occupied. "Read Annie's Bible or something." She turned to the mirror, grabbed a comb and performed a quick fix on her hair, then used Annie's reddest lipstick to flesh out her lips. She could improve her appearance more but not without Jake thinking she was blowing him off or primping for him. Sucking in her bloated stomach, she sauntered to the front door.

She ignored the stutter in her pulse and sneered. "Hardball, my knight in shining armor. Arriving, once again, after I saved myself."

"I didn't come to save you."

"To break my heart then." She pouted at him, which every man knew was pure sex wrapped around a heart of steel.

"I need your help with Zeke."

"You're out of your mind." She'd paid her dues. She couldn't afford more. She slammed the door.

Jake caught it with his shoulder and wedged his foot between the door and the frame. "Zeke's looking for you. If we set it up so he finds you, we get him."

"I'm not bait, and I'm not an expendable casualty."

"You'll die a hero. The media will make sure of that." He didn't try to contradict his low value on her life. Obviously, he wouldn't spend a second mourning her.

"I don't want to die. I'm selfish. I'd rather have myself alive than save your greater good."

Jake just looked at her.

"All right, I want a body double." She was caving because a man looked at her, and not even a nice look. She was turning pathetically soft. No wonder her husband and every other man thought they could take advantage of her.

Jake gave her a long once-over. "If your body could be duplicated, men would buy clones instead of *Playboy*."

"A compliment? My heart's going thumpity-thump. Wanna hear?" Regaining her footing, Tanya pulled his hand over her breast. He was noticing her body. She had the advantage, and she had to capitalize on it.

Jake's look turned to one of derision. "You dropped out of school too soon. That's a plastic enhancement, not your heart."

Embarrassed and determined not to show it, she pushed his hand away. "Your loss."

Jake sighed. "Tanya, I don't want your body."

She stared, unable to believe what he was telling her. If he didn't want her body, she had nothing to keep him interested. And she wanted Jake's interest. "Are you gay?"

He laughed roughly. "No. I need you to help me close the case on Zeke. Then I want you for your mind."

Now she laughed, although the disappointment that slammed through her didn't feel the least bit funny. "Couldn't you have picked something believable? You almost fooled me."

Nick ground his teeth. Anyone with a brain could see how much Tanya needed him. Her stubbornness was destroying both their careers. "You need a lawyer who will show you how to deal with your husband troubles without doing all the work for the police. It's their job to figure out how to bring him in."

"I'm not asking for your two-fifty-an-hour advice," Tanya shot him down. "I'm asking you to stay with Bonnie while I do something just because it's the right thing to do."

"I'll stay with her," Jason said.

"Thanks." Tanya beamed her supermodel smile at him. "She'd be more comfortable with a woman, but Annie ran off to preach the Gospel to dying old ladies."

"They take less work to save, and she gets instant Heaven bonus points," Nick said, scorning his first reflex to defend Annie. Anyone less good would have refused to minister to the very people who strung her up for a public flogging. She had every right to spend the day catching up on sleep. She certainly hadn't done much of it last night.

Tanya turned her gaze on him but no smile. "Annie's honest about her God fixation. If you can't deal with it, walk away. And leave her heart in one piece when you go."

Her words whacked at Nick's chest like a sledgehammer. He'd tried to walk away from Annie since the first moment he saw her. Now he was afraid his heart would splinter when he finally succeeded. She touched him without restraint, yet with a dewy-eyed wonder. When he looked into her eyes in those moments he believed she possessed a true purity of soul.

Springing the marriage ultimatum on him freaked him out. But when he forgot she was a preacher looking for the sanctioned approval of her congregation, he saw it as her way of stressing the deep connection they shared. The devil tempted him to give her what she wanted, for the lifetime promise of being allowed to sink his body into hers.

"Another reason you'll never be my lawyer, Nick." Tanya interrupted his thoughts, wilting his growing arousal. "Nobody daydreams about another woman when they're supposed to have their minds one hundred percent on me."

"The business and personal parts of my life are separate." And he was at Annie's house courting business right now.

"Dream about me naked, not my sister, when you're standing in front of me."

"You and Annie are really hung up on making sure I'm thinking about the person I'm with." But only Tanya's concerns had a basis.

Tanya grabbed his arm, her fingernails digging painfully into his flesh. "If you sleep with my sister and pretend it's me, I'll do everything in my power to make sure you never practice law on this planet again."

Nick yanked his arm free, furious that Tanya considered Annie's appeal so low her suggestion could be possible. "I have too much respect and lust for Annie for that to ever happen."

Tanya hesitated, then smiled. "I don't want to sleep with you, and I don't want you as my legal counsel. But crazy as this sounds, I actually like you, Nick."

He was too confused to figure out how he scored that point. All he knew was this conversation hadn't made him like her more. In fact, his good sense screamed for him to reconsider offering Tanya his legal services. Unfortunately, she was the only celebrity he had a chance of breaking in with.

Tanya drove around town for an hour and a half in her junker station wagon. First thing tomorrow she'd trade it in for something sporty and sinfully expensive. She waved at everyone, gave autographs at stop signs, flipped the bird to the paparazzi photographer who popped up every fifteen minutes, and ignored Jake, who was her constant tail. And she hated every minute of it. She wasn't in top viper form, but this nicer version wasn't her true self either.

A teenaged boy ran across the intersection toward her. "Can I kiss you?"

She so needed a different life where she made a real difference. "Lift your shirt."

"I beg your pardon." His face turned bright red.

"You heard me." She waited while he complied and then

scrawled in pen across his navel, *'Tanya was here.'* "Sweet dreams. I'm off to scoping out a location."

She blew him a kiss and drove onto a gravel road a mile out of town. She parked the car, propped up the hood, patted her stomach to make sure it was flat, unbuttoned her Gucci blouse two more notches, and hoped like heck Jake knew what he was doing.

Her mind returned to his comment about wanting her for her mind. No one wanted her for that. Her body would always be her best selling point. But there was no reason she couldn't use the attention her body drew to point attention to whatever she put her mind to.

Perhaps, like Annie, Tanya had a calling in life, too. She leaned against the front bumper and considered accepting while she waited for Zeke to show up and show his undying love for his wife.

***

Myra wasn't getting better. The doctors held slim hope for her. Her children, although grieving, seemed to be taking the situation well. Annie slipped out of the room to give the family time alone together, promising to return for an evening visit. Hopefully, as she took some free time, God would inspire her with a final sermon for her congregation.

She unlocked her car and slid into the driver's seat. Tanya had added over five hundred miles to the odometer and had left the gas gauge on empty. Annie would have to fill up the tank to make the twenty-mile trip home from Dubuque. A minor inconvenience compared to the problem of moving her belongings from the manse.

She turned out of the parking lot onto the road. A red Hummer came from nowhere to fill her rearview mirror. The church didn't have a replacement pastor for her, and she didn't know where she was going yet. Surely, no one would expect her to move out immediately. On second thought, that thinking banked on Stewart Fitzsimmons turning charitable. She ought to consider alternative arrangements.

She braked for a stop sign, but the car didn't obey. She slammed down the pedal. What was wrong with her car? She just blew a stop sign. She glanced in the rearview mirror expecting to see red-and-blue flashing lights and saw only a truck grill. The Hummer had pushed her through the intersection.

Annie pressed both feet on the brake pedal and put all her muscle into turning the steering wheel toward the gas station entrance. The other vehicle nudged her none-too-gently over the curb and back onto the road. Sweat and paralyzing fear poured over her. Think, Annie, think.

A red Hummer. Zeke Britman had been driving one this morning. Her gaze dropped to the dash clock: 3:07. The internet video may or may not be true, but Zeke obviously had no intention of stopping there. And Annie was his target this time.

Fear didn't obliterate all her common sense. Keeping one hand clenched on the steering wheel and her eyes on the too-deserted road, she fumbled through her purse for her cell phone. She managed to punch the buttons for nine-one-one, but as she began to speak, she was jarred from behind. The phone fell to her feet. She reached for it as Zeke gave her a shove. Her chin slammed into the steering wheel, and the phone slid under her seat and out of reach.

The Hummer grew more insistent, pushing her onto a less-traveled road out of town. Annie shouted the location with the faint hope the nine-one-one operator could hear her and send help. She floored the gas pedal to get away, but the car didn't respond. Tanya not filling up the gas tank was now more than a minor inconvenience.

Annie had to go on her guts. And faith, she reminded herself. She still had her faith.

It was time to stop kidding herself. God wasn't looking out for her. She'd failed Him. He was busy preparing a welcome to His Kingdom for His faithful servant Myra.

Annie still had her wits. They suffered a hard blow as she looked in her side mirror and saw Zeke out of his car and marching toward her. She slammed down the power lock button and groped frantically under the seat for her missing phone.

With a loud bam, glass shattered over her back. "I'm going to ask you one more time." Zeke grabbed her shoulder through the broken window, piercing her skin with either his fingernails or a shard of glass.

Annie rose slowly, trying to focus through the pain in her shoulder. She hadn't located the phone.

"Where is Tanya? And don't lie to me again about switching cars. You've wasted enough of my time."

"I—I think she went back to L.A." Annie might not see eye-to-eye with her sister, but she'd never sensed evil and violence in her. Tanya had endured enough of it as a child for the *betterment* of her family. Annie had no intention of offering herself as a sacrificial lamb, but her turn to help the family cause had come.

"Where's the seven million?" Zeke asked.

"If she's carrying it around, I wish she'd used it to put gas in my car." Annie tried to pull off a breezy reply.

Zeke ripped open the door and yanked her out of the car. "This is your lucky day. I have a full tank. I've changed my plans so we can go to Mexico. Consider it a religious experience."

Annie tried to pull away, but there was no escape.

Nick helped Bonnie through the process of filing a restraining order. In the midst of all the legal explanations and possibilities of Hank retaliating, Jason and Bonnie established a shy, almost painfully sweet camaraderie. Gone was the jubilation and triumph she had brimmed with yesterday, when she celebrated after escaping from her abusive home. Gone was Jason's easy charm and flirtatiousness, which he bestowed on females without regard to age or beauty.

In all the times Jason had convinced Nick to join him in the bar scene he detested, Nick had never felt more uncomfortable and out of place than he did watching Jason and Bonnie take the first tentative steps toward holding hands. When his work was done, he left them alone in the living room and wandered into Annie's kitchen. The coffeepot was on and full, so he rummaged through her cabinets for a mug, taking absurd pleasure in handling her things, knowing her hands had touched them last.

Strains of Jason's and Bonnie's quiet conversation leaked back to Nick as he tipped the pot to fill his mug.

"I'm going home after church tomorrow," Jason said.

Going home? He'd never breathed a word of this to Nick.

"I don't want you to take this the wrong way, but I'd like for you to come with me."

Nick sloshed coffee over the edge of his mug, scalding his fingers. He shook the droplets off his hand and hurried to the living room to stop Jason from making plans he wasn't capable of following through.

"You must be in a hurry to get back to the status quo of securing your inheritance through the auction house." Nick was relieved. Jason had come to his senses. Life was returning to normal. Soon Nick would once again feel moderately content as a successful lawyer with ordinary clients.

"Actually," Jason looked in him in the eye. "I'm quitting the auction house."

The mug slipped from Nick's hand, bouncing as it hit the carpet. Coffee sprayed in a brown stream, toning the beige carpet with dark blotches. "Does Mom know?"

"I called and told her I was coming home. I want to tell her the rest in person."

The cup didn't break, but the rug was messed enough to add some personality to the house. "How do you intend to pay the rent? Or are you counting on me to attend to those pesky details for you?"

Jason straightened. "I have to follow my dreams. I majored in journalism. I can scrape together enough to pay the bills by freelancing."

Nick could have argued that point. Independent journalists without credentials made about as much as starting handymen. Instead, he said, "This woman is married and is filing a restraining order against her husband. No offense, Bonnie, but that's a lot of trouble to take on when you've got plenty of your own, Jason."

"That would stop someone who's selfish and self-absorbed, which you think describes me perfectly. But it wouldn't make Reverend Annie think twice before helping a person in need, and that's the kind of person I want to be." Jason gave Bonnie's hand a small squeeze.

"You want to be a writer or a minister?" Nick kicked the mug in disgust. It hit the wall and shattered.

"Why can't I use my writing to inspire greater good? When Dad wrote the will, he did it with the intention of making me grow up. I know this wasn't the way he envisioned, but I hope someday I'll become a person he would have been proud of."

Nick stared at him, feeling small and selfish. He thought of his career and missed opportunities only in terms of what it meant for himself and his mother, not of strangers who might need a helping hand to make it through a rough patch. "Do you need to borrow my truck to get home?"

"I appreciate the offer and the vote of confidence. If Zeke

leaves Tanya's station wagon in one piece, I figure she'll be happy to unload it on the first taker. I plan to be him."

"Would someone please explain to me," Bonnie said in her quiet, shy voice, "why Zeke is looking for Tanya in a green station wagon when she was last seen driving a white sedan?"

"Annie's Cavalier." Nick felt the blood drain from his face. Tanya and her half-baked police force had left Annie vulnerable and unsuspecting. He hoped with every fiber of his being she was sitting in the hospital preaching the Gospel to harmless old ladies. The ways Zeke Britman could abuse the hope and generosity she offered were too terrifying to imagine.

"The drugs don't live up to their promise, do they?" Annie asked.

Zeke shoved her against her car. "What are you talking about?"

She didn't know. All she knew was that she had to say something while she figured out what to do. Her best chance to come out of this unhurt—or even just alive—was to escape before he tossed her in the Hummer and pointed it toward Mexico. Or a cliff. Or the river. But a deserted roadside offered few options for a woman who lived by her dwindling faith. "The high," she stuttered. "It used to be the best thing in your life. Now it's not enough, and everything else in your life is crumbling, too."

"Nice analysis. What else did Tanya tell you?" He grabbed her arm again and jerked her toward his vehicle.

She tried to plant her feet, but weight and strength were on his side. "You and I are alike," she said desperately. "You depend on drugs. I depend on God. Drugs and God have both abandoned us, and we're trying to throw something together to make our lives worth living again."

"Exactly. We'll have a nice little life with you turning tricks to buy my coke in Mexico, or Tanya will pay a ten-million-dollar ransom to get you back. Then you'll be home, and I'll have my drug money."

Upping the dollar amount by three mil couldn't be a good sign. Somehow she managed to laugh. "Tanya? She doesn't give a rip about me. She only wants the things I have. My grandparents' love, my boyfriends." She laughed again. "If I go with you, she'll decide she wants you back."

He stopped walking. "She betrayed me. I'll never take her back."

So far, so good. But Annie still couldn't draw a full lung of air. "What did she do?"

"She made a tape of me talking about my empire to hand over to the DEA."

"Empire?"

"Sixty-two percent of the cocaine in Orange County is supplied through me." He puffed with pride.

"You must have given a lot of people amazing highs. Why aren't they tripping over themselves to help you out?"

"Everyone's so scared of getting busted no one will give me a hit. I intercepted the tape and taught Tanya a lesson, but I went too easy on her."

Annie shuddered. She'd seen the bruises that passed for *too easy*.

"Tanya found my list of bank accounts and supplier names. I can't pay anyone now. The people who aren't trying to squeeze money out of me want me dead for exposing their identities and territories to the authorities."

A car drove by. Zeke glanced at it, but when it didn't stop, he turned his attention back to her. "To my truck. We're too exposed out here."

Out of the corner of her eye, Annie saw the car back up. She kept her gaze on Zeke. It didn't look like a police car, but she wasn't picky. "Why would Tanya turn on you?"

"Her career. Everything is about her career and overblown reputation. She wants to be a wet dream with an attitude, but not one on drugs and not one who'll give anything to her husband in the bedroom."

"So you slapped her around?" Surely, he could see he'd acted irrationally and show some remorse.

"She was messing with my drugs—the only good thing in my life. She deserves what she got."

Annie suppressed a shudder. She had to get away from this madman. "What about your career? Your songs have been hits, and you have a big recording contract."

"My hits have only made it because of her, and my label's dumping me because of the drugs."

And his drug supply had been cut off. Zeke sounded like a man with nothing to lose. Annie had nothing lose either.

Another car slowed, and Zeke looked back. Annie wrenched her arm free and ran for the first car that had parked twenty feet up the road.

"Hey." Zeke lunged for her, shoving his hand into her back.

She stumbled against the open door of her car and grabbed a handful of broken glass on the driver's seat. Zeke spun her to face him. The shards dug into her palm, and she remembered the horrible things this man had done to her sister. Abandoning her turn-the-other-cheek philosophy, Annie threw the glass at his face and ran.

Chapter 17

"Hey, Tanya, pack it up."

She blinked as Jake approached. "What are you doing? You're going to blow my cover."

"Too late for that. Zeke was looking for you in a white Cavalier."

For a moment she blanked on why. White car. Annie. The one she'd *borrowed* and just as carelessly returned. "Oh, my gosh. Why are you here talking to me? Go protect her. Now."

Jake grinned. He was as sexy as any movie star she'd ever met. "She doesn't need protecting. Annie did it herself. Zeke is in custody of the locals. As soon as the docs repair his cornea, we'll grill him."

"Cornea?"

"His eye, in case you skipped that part of anatomy class." Jake made a tsking sound. "Your sister really upstaged you."

Tanya turned away. Of course, she was glad Annie was all right. She was even more relieved she didn't have to bait Zeke into a face-to-face encounter.

Jealousy stung. Annie had managed to impress Jake, something Tanya hadn't been able to accomplish. Tanya was supposed to make the headlines, but every time she was poised to move into the limelight, Annie sucked the publicity away from her.

"You did good, Tanya." Jake's voice almost sounded tender. "I'm glad he didn't come after you. I'm having fits, knowing I put you in his path again."

She faced him. "Have you ever dated a supermodel, Hardball?"

He slammed down the hood of her car. "Never considered it."

"Think about it now."

He met her gaze, steady and unaffected. "You ever going to call me 'Jake'?"

"Only in bed." She sashayed to her car and slid behind the wheel. But she had to wipe her sweaty palms on her jeans before she could drive away.

By the time Nick located Annie's car by the side of the road, the only people in sight were cops and a tow truck driver. The cop blocking traffic on the road motioned for him to turn around and take another route. "Crime scene, buddy."

"That's my girlfriend's car."

"She's not in it. The victims were taken to the local hospital."

Victims, plural. Nick's hands began to shake. If Britman was hurt, Annie must be in worse shape. He swung in a clumsy U-turn, pointed his truck in the direction of the hospital, and floored the gas pedal. Once there, he ran through the emergency room doors and toward the automatic inside doors leading to the room units.

"Stop. Sir. You can't go in there without permission."

He almost didn't pause but then changed his mind. The woman behind the reception desk could save him time by telling him what room Annie was in. "I need to see Annie Lane."

"You're not family. Have a seat over there." She pointed to two rows of yellow vinyl chairs.

"I'm the person who cares about her more than anyone else."

The receptionist gave him a look of pure scorn. "Ruining her life is not caring about her. My sister lives in Maplefield and goes to her church. I know who you are. You step through those doors or anywhere else you haven't been invited and security will be on you so fast you won't see an eyelash of Reverend Annie."

"I care about her," Nick repeated. The words sounded weak and unbelievable. He stomped to the coffee vending machine and fed quarters to it for the next hour while the receptionist's words whirled in his head.

He'd tried not to care about Annie. He tried to disdain her, but when he first realized she was in danger his whole world stopped. He couldn't deny he cared. The fear and nausea building in him made each of these grueling minutes revolve around her.

Tanya sauntered through the front doors and headed for the reception desk. "I'm next of kin for Annie Lane. Page her doctor for me."

The receptionist's mouth dropped open. "Of course, of course." She scurried to do Tanya's bidding.

Nick squeezed his hand, the paper cup crumpling under the pressure. Hot coffee squirted onto his fist. Oww. Twice in one day. He wiped his hand on his jeans and marched to Tanya's side, ready to insist he be part of any conversation pertaining to Annie's welfare.

Instead of the doctor, the next person to walk through the automatic doors was Annie. She smiled at the aide at her side and wore her own clothes as if she'd just been visiting little old ladies instead of being treated herself. He'd worried about her for this?

"What happened?" Nick said, his voice in a low growl.

Her smile disappeared.

Tanya whipped on him. "Don't yell at her." She walked to Annie and hugged her. "I'm sorry."

Annie winced at the touch. Her hands came around Tanya,

and Nick focused on the bandages covering them. "Don't touch her. You're hurting her," Nick ordered Tanya.

Annie backed away from both of them. "Just a couple cuts on my hands and back. Surface wounds."

"From what?" Nick still didn't have a clue what had happened, and his frustration refused to stay locked inside.

"Glass." She didn't look at him, only at Tanya. "Zeke is—I'm sorry. I didn't know what else to do."

"Don't you dare apologize. Don't you know you're a hero? Hardball is ordering your statue bronzed right now."

Annie laughed weakly. "I don't know who Hardball is, but I'm not a hero. And Tanya, if you ever take my car again, you leave me with a full tank of gas." She walked away.

Nick sprinted to catch up to her. He lifted his hand to touch her shoulder but was afraid of hurting her so he let it drop. "Where are you going?"

"To see Myra."

Saint Annie. He stepped in her path. "Thwarting hardened criminals is all part of a day's work, huh? Take a break. Let me buy you dinner."

"I don't need—" Her stomach growled.

He carefully took her hand. Her body was receptive, even if her mind resisted. He angled his body to protect her from stares or anyone who might try to hurt her again and led her to the outside doors.

"I'd rather not go to a restaurant with an audience," she said as they wound through the parking lot to his truck.

Nick's temper began rising. She was still worried about what being seen in public with him would do to her precious reputation. He pushed the thought aside. His common sense still hadn't returned. Annie had been assaulted and endured the indignities of the emergency room. She deserved some private pampering. "I'll arrange everything."

Annie had no idea what Nick's idea of *arranging* entailed, but for the first time in years she was more than ready to hand over the control of her life. She trusted him, which scared her almost as much as it comforted her. She sat in his truck in a Dubuque parking garage and closed her eyes, waiting for him to return from his *arrangement errands*.

She tried to prepare herself for the interview questions her new parish would ask on Monday. But she couldn't clear her mind. Tanya, Zeke, and Nick paraded through. Mostly Nick and the awakening he'd delivered to her body and soul last night.

The sound of the door handle lifting shot her with memories of Zeke smashing in her window. Her eyes flew open. It was only Nick, smiling at her through the window. She pulled up the lock. He opened the door before she could reach for the handle.

"Dinner for two." He offered her his hand. "We won't have an audience."

"Good." She brushed her lips across his cheek as he helped her down from the truck. He was acting so nice, like her injuries were more than insignificant scratches. Like caring for her was the center of his life. Like he actually cared about her.

"All I intended was privacy. Don't take it the wrong way."

"Where are we going?" She didn't know how she could take it the wrong way when she had no clue what he was talking about.

He led her into a lobby and then into an elevator before she could form an impression of anything beyond him. They emerged from the elevator, and he slid a key card into a door. She stepped inside and stared at the king-size bed. How could she not take this the wrong way? There was no other way to take it. "You said you were taking me to dinner."

"Room service. Filet mignon. Should be ready in ten minutes."

She requested privacy, and he'd certainly arranged it. She should have mentioned she'd be happy to eat carryout food in his truck. She walked to the window, nearly flattening herself against the wall to avoid touching the bed as she passed by. The thing was massive. How could she not think about sex with that thing here? A bed. A real bed. She looked back at Nick. The bed filled the space between them like a massive white elephant.

"We can eat at the table," Nick said. "Dim the lights and—" He glanced at the bed and cleared his throat. "You won't know it's here."

If he dimmed the lights, she might slide into a dreamy romantic state and jump him like she had last night. She needed a level head and absolutely no excuses. "The lights stay on. All of them."

A knock sounded on the door.

Nerves fluttered to Annie's throat. She was a minister with an unraveling reputation alone in a hotel room with a man. And she was fairly sure at least one of her parishioners worked in the Dubuque hotel industry. "I have to go the bathroom." She escaped, but not before Nick's grim features etched themselves in her mind as he went to deal with the intrusion. She locked the door, hating herself for not thanking Nick for the trouble he'd gone to on her behalf.

By the time she finished fiddling with the towels and reading the labels on the soap packages, Nick was alone in the room. Their meal was set up on the table as formally as any restaurant dinner. She left the light on in the bathroom, hoping the extra fluorescent light would squash the mood she felt forming.

As punishment for her earlier cowardice, she had to walk by The Bed again. The devil was tempting her. Jesus had withstood him, and so would she. Of course, Jesus hadn't given in the first time, so He didn't know what He was missing.

Nick looked at her, and his jaw tightened.

She sat down. Nick pulled the silver cover off her meal with an exaggerated flourish, revealing the grilled meat, seasoned squash, and rice pilaf. Her stomach rumbled in response to the delicious smells, and she reached for her knife and fork.

Nick quirked a brow. "You've given up saying grace? Or is that just a show you put on when you're courting lost souls for God?"

She winced and looked down at her food, trying to formulate a quick prayer. The words of thanks stuck in her throat. She had only Nick to thank for this food. If it were up to God, she'd be filling her tummy on vending machine coffee and candy bars as she sat with Myra.

"I'm saving my conversations with God for the important stuff. He might listen better if I don't yammer in His ear all the time," she tried to joke.

"I'm not important?"

She paused to stare at him. He sounded hurt, but he looked impassive. Her heart begged to assure him he was the most important person in her life, that no one had meant so much to her since the time her life had revolved around Danny in college. But her life was supposed to revolve around God. To let him know how much he meant to her was to destroy the foundation of her life.

"Of course, you're important. I wouldn't have slept with you otherwise." She said the words as flippantly as her stiff tongue would allow. "I was under the impression you preferred not to be prayed over. Sex with me must have been more of a religious experience than you're willing to admit."

"I hadn't thought of it like that. I need a repeat to make that determination."

Annie gulped. She meant to put him in his place, not challenge him to put that trampoline to use. "You said we were here for the room service."

"We are." He cut into his steak.

Annie took another peek at the six-pillow-wonder behind her, and then stabbed her filet. The meat was tender and cut easily. Unfortunately, the worst of her injuries was a glass cut on her right thumb that required three stitches. The steak knife bit into the most tender area. She adjusted positions and tried again.

"I'll do it." Nick scowled at her. He pulled her plate toward him and sliced her food with quick, bold strokes.

She expected him to push her plate back when he was done. Instead, he held up a pink square of filet on his fork and offered it to her.

She stared at the morsel and then shifted her gaze to his face. He didn't smile, but he wasn't mocking her either. She leaned forward and slowly took his offering into her mouth, savoring the tender bite. "Delicious."

He raised his fork again, and she opened for him, closing her eyes to experience the taste more deeply. Warm, moist heat settled against her lips. Nick's tongue slipped inside and touched the tip of her tongue. She shivered and reached for his shoulders. His solid presence offered her an anchor in the tide of sensation.

She moaned—no, that low throaty sound came from Nick. After one kiss, she couldn't tell where he ended and she began. Oh, it wasn't just a kiss. He was making love to her mouth. Knowing he was enjoying the experience as much as she made it—impossibly—more exquisite.

"I didn't plan this, Annie. I swore to myself if you agreed to come up here, I wouldn't take advantage of you or the situation. But I need you."

If she hadn't already melted, she would have now. She pressed her palms to his cheeks. "Yes."

Nick had been handed the keys to heaven, and he couldn't use them. The gauze on Annie's hands pressed against his face. That simple gesture could be causing her pain. He pulled away. Physical pain from the separation lanced through him. "I'm sorry. I have no right to ask this of you. You're hurt. I don't want to hurt you more."

"I only hurt when you turn your back on me."

He wanted her too much to pretend he could walk away. Her needs and desires were his own. He leaned into her until his lips met hers. He kept the pressure light, thinking of the trauma she'd endured today. She deserved to know he had worried, that her fate mattered to him. He tried for words, but they wouldn't come. He could only feel and show. Yes, he would show her. Until she forgot about God and thought only of Nick.

"Today is for you." He leaned over her and touched his tongue to the hollow of her throat. Her head fell back on the pillow. Her low moan reverberated through his body. He'd make her forget her pain. He'd make her forget the other Man she pledged her life to.

He poured his heart into the unspoken promises. Her cries of pleasure became a balm on his soul. He drank from her mouth as she screamed his name. Her cries were only for him. Not even God was allowed to overhear and interfere.

"I love you," she whispered. The words were spoken so softly he wouldn't have heard had he not been in tune with every fiber of her being.

And Nick went straight to heaven.

Annie's final night as Maplefield's moral beacon was spent in an anonymous hotel room in the arms of a man she'd known less than two weeks. In good conscience she'd have to recom-

Lane to Heaven

mend it to anyone facing a similar situation.

Nick had taken her to see Myra in the evening. Afterward, she made the deliberate choice to return to the room with him. He'd accompanied her on a visit to Myra and her family again this morning. Myra's bright, observant children didn't question or condemn, but Annie didn't doubt they understood the nature of her and Nick's relationship.

Annie watched out the car window as Nick drove them the final miles back to Maplefield. Sunday morning and all its accompanying obligations had arrived. He pulled to a stop in front of the church.

"Will you stay?" She was used to offering the no-pressure question, and it slid casually off her tongue. But as soon as the words were out, his answer took on monumental importance. This was her life. She needed him to at least show a token willingness to share it.

His eyes cast up toward the steeple. "No."

"You're not obligated, of course, but it would mean a lot to me to see you there."

Nick's jaw clenched. "I told you about my father. I haven't been to a service since his funeral."

"Now's a good time to come back." She tried to keep her reasoning breezy. "It's a one-time deal. I won't be back at this church to push you into multiple commitments." She swallowed the commitment she wanted to ask of him. She'd sworn she wouldn't sleep with him again until she got it. Then she discarded her resolve as soon as her desire peaked.

"If I do it for you once, you'll expect me to make church part of my life. Next Sunday you'll say, 'See, that wasn't so bad. Give it another try.' "

Subconsciously, he already realized a church service wouldn't kill him and might add something meaningful to his life. But Annie needed to focus on a more pressing issue. "Will I see you next Sunday?"

"I don't know." He stared out the truck window before turning to her. "You're the one who keeps talking about leaving."

She knew better than to bank on hope, but it filled her anyway. Hope for a commitment that assured her love wasn't a wasted emotion. A gold ring would sanction every action between them and give her a career a badly needed conservative swing. "Will you consider coming with me?"

The look on his face told her better than words that he hadn't considered it and his instinctive reaction was anything but favorable. "I'm a lawyer. My practice is in Chicago."

"Is that location important to the movie stars you hope to represent?"

"I'll set up an office in L.A. as well."

She opened the truck door. She had her answer. If she didn't like it—well, that was her problem. Nick hadn't kept his priorities a secret. "Ask my sister to loan you a wing of her home."

"My interest in your sister is purely professional." That he could speak such an outrageous lie with pompous indignation told her volumes about his courtroom acting skills.

"Right. When you get settled, have your secretary send me a thank-you note for my 'professional' help with your career."

"Annie—"

Her heart had been ripped from her chest. She wouldn't let him see how much she ached for him while he was still hung up on his celebrity conquest. She stepped out of the truck. "Thanks for the ride, Nick." She slammed the door and walked into the church, realigning the center of her life.

Tanya's direction in life now involved more than hawking cosmetics and sex. It had crystallized as soon as she'd taken a stand for Bonnie. Even without Annie's support, she was going to pull it off. She sauntered into Maplefield's diner and slid into a booth across the table from Jason. "I need a human interest story. Do you want to write it or not?"

He looked at her. The awe and blind lust that had once greeted her were replaced with wary interest. "Not."

Tanya sat back. She recognized he wasn't putty, but she hadn't expected a refusal. "I'm handing you your dream. Are you up to the task, or are you too scared to go after what you really want?"

"Are you asking me to write the big biography of your life or a little human interest story to exploit Bonnie's plight? The former I'll do. The latter, no."

Now he'd turned into a mind reader. "I have no intention of exploiting Bonnie. But her situation is too common. I want to create options for women like her. Options don't do any good if women don't know they exist."

"Did you ask Bonnie how she feels about using her situation?"

Tanya thought of the way Bonnie gripped the curtains as fear dictated her every action. "Fine. You want to exploit someone, write the sorry details of the abuse I've gone through. We'll use the book proceeds to bankroll domestic abuse shelters around the country."

One part of her couldn't believe she had suggested this. But the part of her who grew up in a marketing environment knew the book would not just sell but be a smash success. She also knew with deep certainty it was the right thing to do and would ultimately lead to her finding peace with her life.

Jason smiled slowly. "Now I'm on board. Since we're partners of a sort, could I borrow your '87 ugly-as-sin Oldsmobile to drive back to Chicago and tie up my loose ends?"

"Can't. I already traded it in." At last, her words triggered an emotion. Tanya felt her power returning with Jason's disappointment. "But I owe you a Mercedes. It was because of me that you trashed yours." She pulled the keys out of her bra and pressed the warm metal against his palm. "If you drive this one into the river, I won't buy you another."

Jason tossed the keys from hand to hand as he stood. "Bonnie's coming with me. My mother offered her a room until you get your shelter up and running."

Tanya appraised him. If she thought he would so much as raise his voice at Bonnie, she would have called Jake to haul him in on any charge they could make stick. But Jason was growing up, and he had been very, very gentle with her. She smiled slowly as she rose to her feet. She approved the match, but she preferred to bestow her blessing another way. Grabbing his shirt collar in her fists, she hauled him toward her and slid her lips open-mouthed over his.

He stood stock still for several beats and then pulled back. "You want to give me a thank-you gift, invite my mother to your next party." With a jaunty salute, he walked away.

Tanya could scarcely believe it. A malleable frat boy walked away from the World's Sexiest Viper without looking back.

"You're losing your touch, Tanya." Nick walked into the diner and slid into the spot Jason had vacated.

She inwardly shuddered, as she lowered herself back into her seat. She couldn't let Nick be right without messing with his mind first. Even if she stopped being the World's Sexiest Viper, she would always be Tanya. "Naa, you're brother's growing up. Maybe I'll let him write that biography, or maybe I'll sleep with him until he's so goofed up he doesn't remember how to write his name."

Nick paused in the motion of signaling the waitress for coffee. "That's not something to joke about."

"You're right." She accepted the waitress's offer of coffee for herself and waited until they were alone again. She leaned forward, thrusting her cleavage up over the plastic tabletop.

"Come to L.A. with me."

He blew steam over the rim of his cup, apparently more interested in hot caffeine than hot sex. "Any special reason?"

"I need a lawyer." She pitched her voice to its sultriest. "And I need him bad."

Chapter 18

Stewart lowered himself slowly onto the hard pew. A few years ago the congregation battled over cushions. Stewart won. Unfortunately, his hemorrhoids had given him fits ever since.

Mother sat down next to him, giving him a chance to position himself more comfortably. She also forced him to slide next to Kathy Patterson. Kathy's expression was pure gloat. Her husband John, by contrast, sat rigidly.

"She's finally going," Kathy whispered. "We did it, Stu." Lois had called him Stu when they were dating, and he turned all mushy inside. When Kathy said it, he just got annoyed. "Your wife has some nerve," she yammered on. "It just shows how deeply Reverend Annie influenced her."

Stewart didn't know what Kathy was talking about until he saw his wife saunter up the aisle. Her fingers were curled around the elbow of a young man that Stewart might have considered clean cut and handsome if Heather had brought him home to introduce to the family. They settled into the pew five rows in front of him.

"She certainly moves fast," Mother huffed. "You're better off without these loose women in your life."

This was better off? Sitting between two matrons he could barely tolerate on a rear end so sore his temples were throbbing? "Who is that guy?"

The man put his arm around the back of the pew, his hand cupping Lois's far shoulder. Stewart clenched his fists. She was his wife. He was the only one with the right to touch her like that.

"Jason Vonkall. He's her mentor or some such nonsense." Kathy patted his hand. "A very recent development. She's just trying to make you jealous."

Jason's hair didn't have a strand of gray and wasn't thinning. His skin didn't wrinkle or hang on his face. He wore jeans to church and acted like he owned the place. At one time Stewart had looked like that. Back then, Lois looked at him like he'd hung the moon.

Now Stewart tugged on his tie and straightened his suit coat. He kept his lips firmly pressed together to minimize his jowls, and he picked up the hymnal to keep his hands away from Kathy's dry, scaly touch.

The organ music switched from the prelude to the opening hymn. Reverend Annie walked up the aisle. The service began as it had hundreds of times before, with song, scripture, prayer, and announcements. The sermon was appropriately titled "Moving On." Annie mostly recounted good things, telling the congregation to keep up its giving spirit, identify needs in the community and fill them, and be open to what the Lord would bring into their lives next.

Stewart mostly tuned her out. Good things had been few and far between in the past five years. Before Reverend Annie, his wife still kissed him before he left for work in the morning and his daughter asked him to help her with her math homework. The last time Heather had asked, he'd had a long day at work and was running late for the first interview with Annie. Yes, it had all started that day. And today it would end.

"This is not an easy time for me," Annie said from the pulpit. "I leave with regrets. I leave with work undone. And I leave with the knowledge that I have not lived up to the standards my congregation and my God expect of me."

Run out the violins. No one was going to wring an ounce of sympathy out of him. She'd created her own problems—and everyone else's.

"Thank goodness. She's really resigning," Mother whispered. "I had a contingency plan in case she used this time to assert her innocence and line up the gullible people in this congregation—like your wife—behind her. I'll volunteer to head the pastor selection committee. You and Kathy will be on it with me. We'll find someone with moral convictions to head this church."

His hemorrhoids acted up, making the urge to squirm unbearable. He didn't want to be his mother's yes-man. He wanted to go home and sleep in his own bed, where he could roll over and feel his wife next to him. He wanted to sit in his recliner while his daughter crawled on his lap and tucked her head under his chin.

The service had concluded without him noticing. Five rows up, Jason handed Lois a hankie and stood by solicitously while she wiped her eyes. The loss of Reverend Annie was hardly something to get broken up about. Stewart took a quick survey of the congregation. His wife wasn't the only one blowing her nose and looking like someone had died. In fact, the only people smirking stood on either side of him.

The aisle was jammed as Stewart made his way out of the pew. Annie hadn't run out after saying her public "goodbye." She was receiving people in the back of the church as she always did. Everyone felt compelled to give her a tearful hug and tell her how much they'd miss her. It was nauseating.

Mother shared his sentiments. She parted the sea of people like she was Moses. Like an obedient slave, he followed in her wake.

"I assume you've called to shut off the utilities in the manse," Mother said as she approached Annie. She didn't offer a handshake or a hug.

Annie's smile slipped. "No. I've been a bit rushed in my preparations. Aren't you just as rushed to find a replacement?"

"This congregation certainly needs moral direction." Mother was in vitriolic form this morning.

"No one more so than our family," Lois said from the other side of his mother. Stewart hadn't realized she was so close. The sound of her voice stole his breath. "Perhaps if we take a long time finding a replacement, we'll be forced to take responsibility for our own failings instead of blaming them on Reverend Annie or whoever is unfortunate enough to follow her."

"You could start taking responsibility by not strutting around with your teenaged boyfriend, taking your husband back, and locking your daughter in the house at night," Mother shot at Lois.

Stewart cringed and expected his wife to do the same. Instead, she laughed—the deep throaty kind that used to cause crazy stirrings in his body. "I would not presume to provide Stewart with a stronger moral base than you." She didn't glance at him as she addressed his mother. "So I'll leave him to your ministrations. It's what you've wanted for the past twenty years anyway. Reverend Annie, I will miss your moral beacon." She hugged the minister and sailed out of the church with the preppy frat boy trailing her.

Annie offered her hand to Stewart. "You got what you asked for. I hope you don't regret it."

He took her hand for appearances' sake only. He regretted everything about these past five years, but nothing more than thinking it wouldn't hurt to give this female minister a chance.

"What"—Nick had to swallow the grit in his throat—"do you need a lawyer for?"

Tanya pursed her sexpot lips. "Are you going to be picky?"

"Yeah, I am picky," he answered. A few days ago he wouldn't

have been. Since then, Annie had ruined him for all other women. His body wasn't even giving Tanya a token interest.

"I've got some contracts," Tanya said. "I need to find out which ones I can get out of without being sued up the wazoo."

"Have your agent fax them to me. I don't need to go to L.A. to look at them." This was his lucky break. Where was his excitement, triumph, and satisfaction?

Tanya smiled, the first one he'd seen where she didn't look like she was plotting his sexual demise. "You're really hung up on Annie, aren't you?"

She loved him. He hadn't walked away before that miracle occurred. He knew he should have, but it was too late now. If he told her he was moving to L.A. with her sister, she'd believe professional dealings were only a side benefit. "I have a business in Chicago, and I'm not making any sudden moves."

Tanya rose from the table. "Your first official duty as my lawyer is to cover my coffee tab."

"I didn't sign on to be your personal assistant." But she'd already walked out of earshot.

He took a sip of his own coffee, now cold sludge. He could bill her for this conversation as well as the forty-nine-cent drink. He'd reached his goal. He was a lawyer with a high-profile client. Tanya's name would open doors in Hollywood and grant his mother the access she'd been denied for years. In the eyes of every woman he'd dated, he had finally made it. His father would role over in his grave at what he'd turned his prestigious career into.

Capitalizing on his success only required he bury his true dream and with it his one shot for happiness.

"Reverend Annie."

She preferred privacy for her last few minutes in the church office, but her preferences no longer held weight in this building. She folded her sermon notes in her Bible and looked up. "Hi, Heather."

The girl shifted in the doorway, her pink winter coat open to an oversized sweatshirt. "Do you have a minute to talk?"

She'd dreamed of Heather coming to her with this simple request, but she never imagined it would happen after she had nothing left to offer. "Always, but you know I'm leaving. I won't be around for long-term counseling."

"Yeah, that's cool," she said as if she preferred it that way. "I, um, need to tell my mom and dad something, and I don't know how to bring it up."

Heather was pregnant. She'd driven a collision course with the inevitable for the past two years. "You want to try it out by telling me first?"

Heather laughed nervously as she closed the office door. "A week ago you would have been the last person I'd tell, but then you slept with Nick and totally trashed your reputation, and I started thinking maybe you could understand."

The silver lining of being a preacher-slut: she could finally reach the promiscuous teenage crowd. This was not a strength she intended to highlight in tomorrow's interview. "I've always made an effort to reach out to you, Heather."

"Yeah, but you've never had sex before, so you never had a clue."

Annie decided it was better not to respond to that statement.

Heather shifted her weight. "I've slept around. I guess that's common knowledge. And I always figured condoms were optional."

"And now you're pregnant," Annie said, wanting to make her confession easier.

Heather laughed harshly. "I wish. I mean, I thought getting pregnant could be cool. All that attention. A baby who worships you for no reason except you're her mom."

Annie crossed to the front of the desk and sat down in one of the two leather chairs, hoping Heather would follow her lead and sit next to her. "And now?"

Heather flopped in a chair. "I'm going to die before I ever get pregnant." She covered her face with her hands and started to cry.

Tanya would appreciate the dramatic flair. Annie knelt on the floor in front of the girl, rubbing her arms gently. "Now, Heather, you're young. You have your whole life ahead of you. You have lots of time to make babies—with the right guy."

She cried harder. "That's just it. I've finally met the right guy, and I can't let him touch me because I think I have AIDS."

Annie's instinct was to jerk her hands away, but she kept rubbing, keeping the supportive touch she was sure Heather needed. "Did someone you had sex with test HIV positive?"

"I don't know. I don't think any of them have ever been tested."

"Then how—"

"Tanya gave me a book about STDs. I read it and realized how stupid I was."

"Do you have symptoms of AIDS?"

"I have symptoms of everything. I had a fever and felt achy a couple weeks ago. I thought it was the flu, but—"

Annie forced herself to keep a level head and not get sucked into Heather's terror. "You need to see a doctor and get a blood test to find out exactly what you have and don't have. Then you'll know what to worry about and what's just panic talking. The doctor will treat any illnesses."

Heather lifted her wet, spiky lashes. "There's no cure for AIDS. I'm going to die."

"New treatments come out every day, helping people live longer and better with the disease, and many other STDs are completely curable. Let's find out if there's anything worth worrying about first."

"There is," Heather said darkly, "but you're going to leave before you find out."

"I can stay long enough to help you tell your parents." Stewart was going to burn her at the stake for this. But at least for the moment, someone needed her again.

"Just Mom. I'll wait until I know how much longer I have to live before I tell Dad. He'll be less likely to kill me then."

Heather was so relieved to tell somebody. For the past three days a brick of fear had pressed so tightly against her chest she couldn't breathe. But Reverend Annie hadn't run from her like she was a leper. Of course, Annie wasn't Jesus. She hadn't given her a miracle cure.

Annie was going to help her tell her mom, and soon they'd deal with concrete facts instead of this mushrooming fear of the unknown.

She walked out of the office and came face-to-face with her dad. "Heather, I didn't see you in church. You could have sat by me."

If Dad wanted to think she'd actually sat through the boring service, she wouldn't disillusion him. That would come soon enough.

"Heather Gertrude, you haven't been talking to that tramp, have you?" Grandma Trudy demanded. She was everywhere with Dad. It was amazing she didn't make him hold her hand to cross the street.

"I like to talk to myself."

"I was referring to—"

Heather rolled her eyes. "Any normal person has sex more than once a century. Reverend Annie proved she's normal. What's not normal is our family, you treating Dad like a five-year-old and me doing the town."

"If you want to come to my house for Thanksgiving, miss, you're going to have to clean up your attitude and give me an apology."

Heather looked at her dad. "Are you going to break it to her that I'm spending Thanksgiving with Mom, or should I?"

"Mother, excuse us for a minute." Dad took Heather's arm and pulled her into the office.

Annie was stacking papers on her desk. She looked at Heather. "Do you want me to stay?"

This wasn't the plan. They weren't going to tell Dad anything.

"You have no right to be in this office." Dad looked rabid. How could he hate Annie for one little lapse in judgment and not care as Heather made bad choice after bad choice and continually disobeyed him? "You're trespassing. Get out, or I'll call the police."

Annie looked at Heather. "Your call. Do you want me to go?"

The brick fell back on her chest. She wasn't ready to tell Dad. "You can't desert me now. I need you."

"Then I'll stay." Annie smiled at her, one of those reassuring, you-can-count-on-me grins. Heather wanted desperately to believe her. Annie turned to Grandma marching through the doorway. "Mrs. Fitzsimmons, you'll have to step outside. Stewart wants some time with his daughter."

"This is my family and my church. You have no right to tell me what to do." The chances of Grandma relenting were as likely as her taking her granddaughter in her arms and telling her she loved her no matter what. It wouldn't happen in Heather's lifetime.

"Grandma goes or I do," Heather said to Dad and waited for him to turn his back on her.

"Mother, can you give us some space, please?" Dad asked, at least giving Heather a token of priority.

"I'm family. I can help. Unlike that woman," Grandma spat at Annie.

"You haven't done a thing to help me in the last decade." Heather's anger momentarily overrode her fear. "All you do is tell me everything I do wrong. Believe me, I know I'm wrong. I started doing it on purpose so you'd know I exist."

"We know you exist," Dad said in a pat-you-on-the-head patronizing tone.

"Annoys the heck out of you, doesn't it?"

"No, honey," he insisted.

"Oh, for goodness sake, Stewart." Grandma stomped her foot. "She's pushing your buttons. Just ignore her and she'll beg you to let her move into my house with you."

"Mother." The vein on Dad's neck bulged. "Leave. Us. Now."

"I'm not going to allow you to stay in my house if this is the thanks I get," she harrumphed and stomped out of the office.

"Can she leave, too?" Dad tilted his head to Annie.

He was asking Heather's permission, but she couldn't give up Annie's presence. Once Annie took off for a better church, Heather would have to break her news alone. "I want her to stay. She'll help you not to freak out."

"About what?"

Geez, what was she saying? She was ready to tell Mom, not Dad. "Anything. I mean, if it has to do with me, it can't be good, right?"

"Heather, I know this isn't how you planned, but it's a good lead in," Annie prompted.

"Tell me what, Heather?" Dad asked, looking serious and concerned.

She shook her head. "It's better I don't spend any time with Grandma. I'm a complete failure to her. I can't shut up and take it when she makes nasty comments about me and Mom." When Heather died, Grandma would be sorry she hadn't been nicer to her only grandchild.

Dad sighed. "I'm sorry about Grandma. She's always been opinionated."

"In a stick-up-your-butt way."

Dad cleared his throat, but she could tell he was trying not to smile. "Yes, well, I'll talk to her, and I'll see what I can do about cutting that leash she has on me."

Stupid tears started leaking around her eyes, lodging the brick from her chest to her throat. "Will you notice me then?"

"Baby, I've always—" He stopped, probably realizing he was wrong. "What do you want from me, Heather?"

So many things, but really it all boiled down to one. She wanted to be Daddy's girl again. "I want you to love me."

"I do."

"No. Listen." She looked to Annie for an approving nod. She got it. Annie even looked proud of her. She savored it for a second before speaking. "I want you to still love me when you find out I'm dying."

"Don't be silly. You're not dying."

"Shut up and listen. You don't know a thing about my life. My boyfriends aren't imaginary, but I would have dumped them all if my dad would have just given me a hug."

"I'll hug you." Dad reached for her now. "All you had to do was ask."

Her instincts screamed at her to give in to what she really wanted and let him hold her. But she had to find out how far he was willing to go to give her what she needed. She stepped out of his reach. "Listen to the rest. Then you can decide if you want to hug me."

"The rest?"

Heather hugged her coat across her chest and took another step back. Annie placed a hand on her shoulder. At least someone knew the truth and was still willing to touch her. "I didn't just hug those boys."

Dad winced. "Your mother needs to put tougher limits on you."

"Mom, right. Good one. Blame it on her." She tried to laugh. Arguing about blame was easy. Anything to put off saying the awful words she had to say.

Annie squeezed her shoulder. A solid reminder of her support.

Heather took a deep breath. "I've been having unprotected sex. I need to be tested for AIDS."

Dad's face turned white. His arms hung limply at his sides. "AIDS?"

"All the sexually transmitted diseases actually." There was no going back now. "Gonorrhea, herpes."

"Herpes?" Dad parroted in a leaden voice.

"Guess you don't want to hug me anymore, huh?"

He just stared at her.

Her throat closed up. She wanted him to hold her. She'd done all of this because he wouldn't. And now—especially now—he wouldn't get close to her.

Annie's arms closed around her, offering comfort from behind. She didn't want Annie's hug. She wanted her dad's. But it would never happen. He'd be relieved when she died. He could completely forget her and the embarrassment she was to his name.

She ripped herself from Annie's arms and ran for the door. She wouldn't cry in front of them. She wouldn't let their last memories of her be one big blubbering mess.

"Heather."

She didn't know whether Dad or Annie had called her name. Maybe they both did. She ran out the door and bumped into Grandma. She didn't stop, even when Grandma started sputtering her customary crabbiness.

"Heather." This female voice belonged to Mom.

"No. Leave me alone." She spun out of the hands reaching for her and into the door of a bathroom. She pushed it open and rushed inside.

"Heather." She recognized that voice. Egan.

Through her tears she made out the urinal and Egan hurriedly fixing his pants. Oh, this was the perfect end to her miserable life. She'd run in on Egan in the men's restroom.

Nick wrote the numbers from the measuring tape in a notebook as his cell phone played its ring tone for the third time. He whipped the tape back into its metal container and fastened it on his belt before taking the call. "Yep."

"Rural living is turning your manners casual, Dominick."

"Hi, Mom." He tucked the phone against his shoulder and surveyed the front porch. The house would be his in less than twenty-four hours.

"Whatever you're doing, you're not giving me your full attention," Mom said.

She was good. He turned from the porch and glanced at the unmowed yard. "I'm checking out the house I'm closing on tomorrow."

"You're swamped with clients as it is. Why are you picking up more work out in the middle of nowhere?"

He shouldn't be irritated that she would assume that. Being a lawyer was his career. Even without the big-name clients, he was successful in terms of money and prestige. Only now for the first time was he looking forward to reading legal contracts when he signed the multitude of closing papers tomorrow. "This one's for me."

"You're buying a house? Out there?"

"Yes, I am."

"But why?" Mom sounded truly baffled. He'd never given

her a hint of how unhappy he was sitting behind a desk surrounded by papers. But she'd been more impressed with his law school grades than his ability to rewire a basement. "Your business is in Chicago. Your life is in Chicago."

But his heart wasn't. "My business is now partially in California. Tanya Lane Britman is my newest client."

"Congratulations, I think. So why aren't you buying a house out there, instead of—where are you again?"

"Maplefield, Illinois." Nick pulled out his tape measure again and strung it across the bottom step. "I know it doesn't make sense. But I need to do it." Annie was part of the draw, but she was pulling up her roots and moving out. He needed to do this for his own enjoyment, not because of the career advancement or the women who would be dazzled.

"Well, okay." Mom sounded as if she thought he'd left his mental faculties in Chicago. "When you're done with your closing, you need to come home. Jason's resigning. Our clients need reassurance we'll continue to serve them with the same sterling commitment to quality. I can't give them that certainty until we see how this plays out legally. I want to buy the auction house and continue running it."

"You?" Nick asked. The measuring tape whipped back, stinging his thumb. "Are you sure you're qualified?"

"You think I didn't learn anything about this business by being married to the owner for twenty-five years?"

Nick winced as he sucked his injured digit. "I didn't mean it as criticism, Mom."

"You boys aren't the only ones who can follow your dreams, Dominick. I've been a loving wife and mother. Now I'm looking forward to becoming a successful career woman."

"But your dream is to go back to Hollywood and rekindle your lost friendships and family ties."

"I would like to visit, but I'm talking about a life goal."

"Life goals are what you settle for when you can't have your dreams. You don't have to settle. I'm giving you your dream." And he was settling.

"You're working hard and overdue for a vacation," Mom soothed. "But we need you home now. Save your vacation time for the important stuff, like Christmas."

He loved his mother. He loved his half brother. They were his family, yes. But spending half a day together celebrating the holiday was more than enough for all of them. If he had a family—the kind a thirty-four-year-old man was expected to have—then saving vacation time for Christmas made sense. Right now, the thought of having a week off at the holidays just sounded lonely.

"The realtor's waiting for me to finish up, Mom. It's not a good time for a discussion."

"Then buy your house and come home. The future of Vonkall Auction House can't wait. We have a reputation to uphold and so do you."

Stewart's life crashed and lost all meaning. His little girl had a sexually transmitted disease. And he'd stood with his hands over his eyes and let it happen. He always believed his sweet, innocent child would return to him as soon as she had some decent moral guidance. But her innocence never had a chance.

He stared at the woman in front of him. Reverend Annie. She didn't deserve any title that put her closer to God. She was the devil who was ruining his life. Even worse, she'd ruined his daughter's life. She couldn't have done worse if she'd put a gun to Heather's head.

"Reverend Annie." Lois stood in the doorway Heather had left open with her abrupt exit.

Annie pinched the bridge of her nose. "Yes, Lois. Come in and close the door."

Lois paused when she saw him but then squared her shoulders and ignored him. "I—I don't know how to say this. Myra's son called. Myra's gone, Annie."

"Gone?"

"She died about half an hour ago." Lois's voice trembled. "I never imagined she wouldn't recover."

Annie looked devastated. An old woman's end of life affected her more than a young girl facing incurable diseases.

"They're asking for you."

"I'm not the minister here anymore," Annie said.

"What difference does that make?" Lois's cheeks gained color as she became increasingly agitated. "You were Myra's friend. Her family needs you. The whole community needs both of you, and now we're going to lose you both at once."

Stewart couldn't stand it anymore. "What about Heather? Doesn't anyone care if she dies?"

Lois blanched. For the first time today, she really looked at him. "What did you say?"

"Eighty-year-olds are supposed to have strokes and die. Seventeen-year-olds are not supposed to die of AIDS. What's the matter with you? Don't you care what's happening to your own daughter?"

"Heather has AIDS?" Lois clutched Annie's arm as she lowered herself into a chair.

"Heather has engaged in unsafe practices that put her at risk for contracting a sexually transmitted disease," Annie said.

"Don't sugarcoat it," Stewart snapped. "She's been sleeping with every boy in sight, and we've been standing with our thumbs up our butts letting her do it."

"Heather realizes she was wrong," Annie said, all cool and emotionless. "Now is the time to support her and show her your love. Condemning her and ostracizing her won't help her get through this."

Lois started to cry. She'd never been able to cry attractively, and now was no exception. She snorted, and her nose ran, and her face turned blotchy. She wrapped her arms around their traitorous minister, pulling her down to a semi-kneeling position. Stewart hoped his wife suffocated the dirtbag. "Annie, I can't do this all by myself. You have to stay. You have to help me."

"I know you're upset. What you need is to get Heather a blood test to find out exactly what's wrong. Then you need a knowledgeable, sympathetic doctor to treat her."

"I will. First thing tomorrow, I'll take her wherever we have to go."

"I'm going, too," Stewart said. His baby was going through a crisis. She needed him. She wanted him to hug her, not her mother. And he hadn't done it, he realized. He'd frozen, unable to touch her.

"Jason just left for Chicago," Lois cried. "I don't have anyone to run the food pantry."

"So close it down," Stewart snapped. "You've got more important things to think about."

"Starving people are counting on me to provide their Thanksgiving meal. Annie, please help us out. Stay for a couple days. I promised Myra I'd continue the food pantry for her if anything happened to her. And for the first time in years, Heather needs me. I have to be there for her."

"Heather's needed us for years," Stewart said, sickened with guilt. "We were just too stupid to notice."

"I can reschedule my interview to next week," Annie said. "Stewart, is it possible for me to continue using the manse for a few more days?"

After all the destruction she'd caused, she was asking a favor from him. She had unpardonable nerve. "No. You were fired for a reason. We have no obligation to offer you free lodging. From the beginning, you've tried to bilk the church out of every extra cent. I'm putting an end to it right now."

"If you don't mind the couch, you could stay with Heather and me," Lois said.

"It's my house." He'd change the locks and keep out his own wife before he let that woman inside. "As long as I'm paying the bills, she doesn't step foot in there. She destroyed our family."

"We destroyed our own family," Lois countered quietly.

A shiver tingled through him with the statement's truth. But Annie had contributed, too. She'd pushed Heather over the edge, and he was going to make Annie pay. "You still have the church's cell phone. Hand it over now."

Chapter 19

Heather couldn't stop crying. Egan washed his hands and sat on the floor of the stall next to her. His arms wrapped around her just the way she imagined her dad's would. But it only made her cry harder. "I'm so messed up."

"Hey, I'm the one you walked in on with my pants down. I may need therapy to get over it."

He was trying to make a joke. She recognized it, but she could only cry through it. "You're the sweetest guy I ever met."

"That's not much of a compliment. I've met the competition."

"I wish I'd waited for you."

Egan didn't say anything, just pressed his lips to her forehead in the sweetest kiss she'd ever felt.

She didn't know how long they sat like that. She'd almost stopped crying by the time the door opened. She would have stayed there forever, but Egan pulled his arms away and scrambled to his feet.

Dad walked in. "You lowlife jerk. Get your hands off my daughter."

"It's not what you think." Heather wiped her eyes so she could see both men clearly.

Dad slammed his fist against Egan face. "Stay away from her."

"No." Heather jumped between them, desperate to keep the

only guy who'd ever treated her with respect from getting hurt. "Egan."

He cradled one side of his face as he lay on the floor. "Does he hit you like that?"

"Heather, get out of the way." Dad's voice was deadly, but even now he wouldn't touch her to make her move.

"I'm going to press assault charges," Egan said, "and get you away from him."

"He doesn't hit," Heather said, crouching next to him. Already his face was turning red and puffy. She had to do something to fix it.

Egan touched his cheek. "Sure feels like it."

"I've never touched Heather," Dad said. "Which is more than I can say for you."

"He gave me a hug, Dad. That's all. That's all I asked of you." She sucked in a lungful of air. She couldn't start crying again. Egan needed her.

"But if you're not you-know—" Dad waved his hand vaguely. "What are you doing with him in the men's bathroom?"

"Getting away from everyone. Look, if you're done beating up on the best friend I ever had, I need to get Egan some ice for his face."

Dad reached down and offered Egan his hand. "I'm not going to apologize, you understand, just in case you have more going on with my daughter than she's telling me."

Egan accepted the hand up. "That's fine. And you understand I'm still going to file charges, just in case you hit her more than she's telling me."

Heather couldn't see and couldn't understand it, but she could feel the bond forming between the two most important men in her life.

Officer Michelson left, followed by Egan Dowers and the

Fitzsimmons family. The rest of the congregation was already gone as Annie tested the locked door one more time and walked across the parking lot. A red Corvette pulled alongside her, the radio turned so loud the bass throbbed down to Annie's toes.

Tanya flipped off the radio and leaned out the window. "Like it?"

What she'd really like was to go home, take an aspirin, and crawl in bed for the rest of the day. But she had a funeral to plan and a grieving family to console and—oh yeah—she had to have all of her belongings out of her house by tonight.

Even if she got everything down to the sidewalk, she had no idea what she'd do after that. Without a car, she'd be lucky to carry a single suitcase to the nearest hotel before her arm wimped out. And she'd yet to make contact with anyone at the repair shop who could tell her when her car would be ready to drive again. "What's not to like?"

Tanya grinned. "Exactly. Climb in."

She started to walk to the passenger side, too exhausted to consider declining. As wonderful as last night had been, she hadn't gotten enough sleep to give her the energy to walk two blocks, let alone accomplish everything she needed to do this afternoon.

Tanya stepped out of the driver's seat. "Uh-uh. This side."

"You want me to drive your car?"

"Not my car. Your car."

"My car's a white Chevy with—"

"Seeing as you helped apprehend my worthless husband, I can't make you drive a car that's going to give you glass splinters in your butt every time you sit down."

Annie's head was spinning. A flashy red sports car for a conservative minister trying to settle her reputation into a modicum of respectability? She couldn't think of a worse choice. "I can't afford—"

"I can, and I bought it for you. I wanted to get you a Porsche, but there isn't a dealership in this galaxy, so this'll have to do. A limo's coming to pick me up in about ten minutes. I can't take a Corvette on the plane to L.A."

"Right. So you're going back?" The domestic shelter idea had been spouted off in the exhilaration of the moment. Tanya hadn't meant any of it. She'd cleared her head and realized what it would mean to her career and viper reputation.

"I have to clear up some loose ends, get my divorce finalized. Nick's going to help me out."

Nick. He'd gotten what he wanted, after all. Searing images of last night flitted through her mind. His hard work paid off. "Are you going to marry him, or just sleep with him?" She couldn't go to the wedding. She didn't think she could keep in contact with Tanya at all if she knew Nick was lying on the next pillow in Tanya's bed.

"Marry him? Are you insane? He won't even come to L.A. I'd consider phone sex, but I don't particularly want to have any kind of sex with Nick. Even if I did, he won't so much as look down my cleavage. I asked him to be my lawyer. I need to cut some things out of my old life so I have the time to set up these domestic shelters. I'm serious about them, Annie. And I'm serious about needing people like you who can talk to the women. I'll make the options available, but I need someone else to be understanding and compassionate."

"You're not going to sleep with Nick?" Annie couldn't move beyond that point.

"I think he's a good guy. He's a fine specimen who probably would be pretty good in bed. The thought of sleeping with him leaves me cold. Coming on to every guy I see to get what I want is a hard habit to break. It's the only way I know how to do business. But I'm going to try to change. And I'm going to start by remembering there's only one guy I want. He's not Nick, and he's not Jason. When I get him, I want him for keeps."

The thought of sleeping with Nick left Tanya cold. Annie couldn't imagine it. Tanya was so wrong. The thought of Nick's lips pressed against her heated her until she had to squirm. But Tanya didn't need to know what she was throwing away. Annie would gladly keep this one for herself.

"Here's my ride," Tanya said as a limousine circled the parking lot. "Remember what I said about the shelter. You never have to be out of a job if you don't want to. I don't care if videos of you and Nick making love start circling the internet. You're in love with him, and he'll treat you the way a husband should. You'd be a fine example for women to see what a healthy, loving relationship should be." Tanya waved and walked away.

A healthy, loving relationship. What a joke. Nick slept with her to make his career. He got what he wanted. She got her desires filled, as well. Except her need for him continued to grow. And she was left wanting.

"How's your cheek, Egan?" Annie surveyed the garish blue, purple, and green bruise covering the left side of his face as she placed her order at the Subway counter.

"Feels almost as bad as it looks, but nothing's broken. You want cheese on this?"

"Yes." Annie watched him competently make her sandwich. It looked delicious. By now the floor tiles looked appetizing. A granola bar and several gallons of coffee had fueled her through her nerves at church, Heather's bombshell announcement, her police statement over Egan's eye, hours at the funeral home, and then more emotional reminiscing at Myra's home with Myra's family.

She was exhausted, but caffeine and nervous energy continued to pump through her. From one minute to the next, the direction of her life shifted. As if she needed proof, the door jingled, ushering in Nick McAllister. He arched a brow at her. "Is this dinner-on-the-go before you hit the road for your God-given destiny?"

"God hasn't revealed His intention for the next stage of my life." No wonder he had an aversion to religion, considering her righteous and high-strung tone, but she couldn't relax enough to speak naturally. "But apparently He wants me to stay in Maplefield for a couple more days."

"Good. Then I don't have to feel offended you didn't say goodbye after all we've shared."

"Lettuce, tomato, olives, vinegar, and oil," Annie instructed Egan as a way to avoid responding to Nick.

Nick turned to Egan as well. "That's a nasty hit you took on your face."

"If you'd attended church this morning, you could have entered the fray yourself," Annie said. No matter how much they'd shared, he didn't want to share her life. "Egan filed assault charges against Stewart Fitzsimmons. Egan, this is Nick McAllister. He's a lawyer." The single word left a bitter taste in her mouth. "He might be able to help you with your case."

"I appreciate it," Egan murmured. "But I can't afford a lawyer on part-time Subway wages." He fingered his cheek. "And this will go away. I'll probably drop the charges. I just want Heather to be safe."

Nick held a card across the counter. "Call me if you need anything? Don't worry about the bill."

Egan looked stunned. "Are you—why—"

"I've met Heather. She needs more friends like you."

If Annie needed another reason to feel it was impossible not to love this man, she only had to spend another minute in his company. She paid for her food, filled her soft drink, and settled into a booth with her back to Nick. She rewrapped half of her foot-long club sandwich and bit into tonight's half.

"Can I sit here?" Nick slid into the other side of the booth without waiting for an affirmation.

Annie's skin tingled. Her thighs ached. She averted her gaze so he couldn't read her thoughts. He scorned everything important to her. He ridiculed her principles. He hadn't given an ounce of consideration to her marriage proposal. But he'd slept with a supermodel's sister. Surely, he'd enjoyed chiseling that notch in his bedpost.

"I've spent all day wishing you were lying next to me again." His voice was husky and inviting.

Her gaze shot to his. She jerked back to see if anyone was listening, but Egan had gone into the back room. The restaurant was deserted. She returned her gaze to his forceful one. "Occupying your mind with your many lawyerly petitions and court motions would be a more wise use of your time."

He shrugged. "Not nearly as much fun. I believe it's your turn to organize the night's sleeping arrangements."

The absolute gall. She was not conducting an affair with him. "I'm having enough trouble finding a place to sleep. I don't need a second person to worry about." For the first time in her life, she was homeless.

"The church would rather have the manse sit empty than give you a roof over your head? That's Christian charity for you." Nick took a bite of his sandwich, mayonnaise squishing out the corners.

Mayo had never looked so appetizing. Although his sentiments echoed her thoughts, she couldn't stop herself from defending the church's actions. "I failed them. A leader has to hold to higher standards than her followers. I didn't."

Nick licked the mayonnaise from his upper lip. "Maybe that's your God-given destiny."

"To be a fallen leader?" Anyone who had an inkling of what

she wanted to do with a mayo squeeze-bottle and her tongue wouldn't dispute she was fallen.

He shrugged. "If you're last on earth, you'll be first in heaven. That's what you want, isn't it?"

He made her think. In a dozen words he encapsulated the sermon she'd delivered last month. But heaven wasn't her goal. She didn't give it more than a passing thought. Her service and her life were dedicated to the people of earth. Her joy was in bringing God's love into their lives. In those moments, she too was surrounded by that love. But His love was shining elsewhere now, and she was in the dark.

"If you want heaven, I'll give you heaven." Nick set down his sandwich and leaned across the table. "Jason went home. I have the apartment to myself. You can stay with me. I'll give you the bed, me, and heaven. What do you say?"

Tempting. Deliciously tempting. Nick McAllister was the devil incarnate. "I'm not sleeping with you again."

"Your loss."

Yes, it definitely was. Her carnal side whimpered for her to change her mind and take him up on the offer. "If Jason went home, why are you still here?"

"I'm closing on a house tomorrow." He leaned back and split open his bag of chips.

The reminder of how easily he'd duped her into thinking he was an impoverished painter embarrassed and angered her. Now he was raking in money from the townspeople as their lawyer while she was unemployed and homeless. "Don't you feel any guilt for taking the money and free housing I threw at you?"

"Not at all. I already offered to return the favor."

And she wanted so badly to take him up on it. "When a woman sleeps with a man in exchange for money, it's called something else."

His face hardened in anger, and she knew she'd gone too far. "I wouldn't force you, Annie. You know better. But I won't promise to keep my hands off you if you stay at my place. I don't have that kind of control. I want you. Too much."

Annie blinked. The last two words were gritted out as if in pain. Her stomach danced with anticipation, but her heart remained broken. He didn't want her enough to marry her. He didn't even want her enough to step into a church sanctuary. "You don't want me, not in any way that matters."

The chip bag crumpled inside his fist. "You're not your sister. Bringing a man to his knees doesn't become you."

"No, I'm not my sister." But they couldn't have a conversation without discussing her. "When you come to me, you get the leftovers. If you wanted the real thing, you should have gone for her. I don't want you on your knees, Nick. I don't want you at all unless it's me and only me that you want. Want isn't even good enough. I need you to love me."

She didn't wait for him to tell her it would never happen. She jumped up and stormed out of the booth before her shattered heart fell beneath his feet. He'd trampled on it enough for one day, enough for a lifetime of heartache.

It wasn't until she reached her car that she realized she'd left tomorrow's meal on the table inside. Ignoring her protesting stomach, she got in her shiny red sports car and drove away from Nick McAllister and the love he could never return.

Nick was ruled by his lower anatomy. It was the only explanation for why he'd jumped to suggest Annie sleep with him last night. He could have invited her to his house, making it clear he was just a nice guy with platonic intentions, then hope she took one look at the bed and got instantly horny like two nights ago in Dubuque.

But he didn't want to use the excuse of a convenient bed or

accidental sex. He wanted honesty. The absolute truth was he wanted her in his bed and couldn't depend on his control to keep his hands to himself.

So he'd slept alone last night after cruising the parking lots for over an hour looking for her white Cavalier, so he could apologize and give her a roof over her head. And now this morning, when he wasn't looking for her, she was in plain sight. He walked into the bank lobby where his closing was being held, and there she was at the pay phone with her back to him. Her shoulders slumped as she hung up the phone. The contents of the call hadn't been good news.

"Is Myra's family having a tough time coping?" he asked. The passing of one of Maplefield's most prominent members had been noted and discussed by everyone in town over the past twenty-four hours.

She shook her head. Starch infused her posture as she turned to face him. "The church I postponed my interview with is pulling me from consideration."

"Impatient, huh?"

"No. The newspaper report of our food pantry tryst changed their minds."

He lifted a brow. "That's a pretty wide circulation for a local paper."

"Someone wanted to make sure my reputation preceded me."

Her gaze held just enough accusation to tick him off. "If you wanted a third round in your quest to sully your pristine reputation, you knew where to find me last night. I don't need to resort to blackmail to make it happen."

Annie didn't return his anger. In fact, she looked more emotionless than he'd ever seen her. "In case I leave without seeing you again or vice versa, goodbye, Nick."

He told himself not to touch her at the risk of his tenuous hold on his control, then promptly ignored his advice by placing his hand on her tense shoulder. "Your supper's in my refrigerator. You're welcome to it."

"If I wanted it, I would have stayed and finished it last night."

He didn't try to argue as he pressed his apartment key into her palm. "Go get your food and take a shower. If I walk in on you in your towel, I'll try to have more control than an oversexed minister."

She flinched. He was glad to pull a reaction out of her, even though it made him more of a heel.

He was taking his bad mood out on her. With Jason home and his mother's summons, Nick could feel the ticking time bomb. The administrative work for the auction house and the Vonkall estate was going to bury him. Instead of hammering, sanding, and varnishing, he was going to file pages upon pages of paperwork. There'd be no chance of running into Annie, let alone continuing a physical relationship.

"Actually, that's reassuring. I'll take the shower." Annie spoke stiffly and formally. "I appreciate your friendship and support."

Nick watched her walk away. He'd managed to remain friends with all his ex-girlfriends. He'd rather fight than endure this forced friendship with Annie. He wanted her passion at the surface, but she was burying it just as he'd buried his dreams.

The tension in the car was reaching toxic levels. According to Mom, Dad hadn't attended one of Heather's doctor visits since she was two months old. He'd picked a doozy to jump back into the parenting game. Mom didn't trust him to do it right, so although she let him drive, she made it clear she was the parent in charge.

Never mind that a parent hadn't been in charge of Heather for nearly five years. They were too sucked into their own power struggle to ask who she wanted to join her. In truth, she wanted to spend the day with both her parents together before she died. But it'd be nice if they could at least pretend to get along for the day.

"Parading your baby-faced boyfriend before the entire church takes the cake," Dad said as he pumped the cruise control up another notch. Right now they were fighting over who was the worst example for her. They'd already gone through Mom's eating habits and Dad's workaholic tendencies. It didn't occur to them that she hadn't inherited either.

"You don't know what you're talking about, Stewart, so stop making a fool of yourself."

"I'm not buying that mentor smokescreen. What could that kid possibly teach a mature woman like you?"

"Public relations, to start with," Mom shot back.

"Oh, is that what they call it now?"

"You've got some nerve. You've been flaunting your mistress in my face for years." Mom didn't just sound angry. She sounded close to tears.

"I've been faithful," Dad said, puffing up with disgusting self-righteousness.

"Yeah, right." Heather meant to keep silent, but the outright lies were too much.

Dad met her gaze in the rearview mirror, somehow managing to look surprised and hurt. "Who am I sleeping with?"

"Kathy Patterson." She and Mom said the name together. There was no doubt.

"Kathy?" The car rumbled through some gravel on the shoulder before Dad straightened the wheel. "Give me a break. She'd freeze off a man's privates if he got too close to her. John's employees say she hasn't let him in her bed since nineteen-ninety-seven."

"It'd be crowded with both of you," Mom said.

"No, Kathy and I never—"

"You talk to her on the phone every night," Mom said, talking over him. "You're out late, at least once a week, with no explanation. I'm fat, Stewart, not stupid."

Dad pulled off the road into a gas station and parked the car. He turned in his seat to look directly at Mom, his expression grim. "Right after Reverend Annie joined our church, I noticed problems cropping up in our family life that hadn't been there before. Heather started mouthing off. You retreated into a bag of chips instead of telling me what was bothering you. I tried to talk to you, but you liked the new pastor and ridiculed my concerns. But Kathy worked in the church office, and she saw. Teresa Butterfield came to her for marriage counseling. After two sessions, she filed for divorce."

"Her ex-husband went on to beat a series of girlfriends and sliced his current wife's face with a butcher knife," Mom said. "Divorce is not always morally wrong."

"Kathy's own daughter came to Annie looking for her advice about her career," Dad continued. "The next day she announced she was moving to Florida. She hasn't come back to visit her mother once."

"She was thirty-five and still lived with her parents. She needed to get a life," Mom pointed out.

Dad smacked the steering wheel with his hand. "Annie encouraged Kathy's daughter to abandon her mother. She wrecked every family who came her way. We had to stop her. Kathy calls to keep me updated on the latest destruction, and we discuss it in more detail at weekly meetings. It took longer than we both thought for Annie to make a wrong move we could capitalize on. But it finally happened. I should be getting my family back now, not losing you."

"You're an idiot, Stewart," Mom said.

"How much sex went on in these meetings?" Heather wasn't going to let him off the hook by chalking his behavior up to simple idiocy.

"None. We met at Mother's house. You can ask her. She wasn't just at every meeting. She ran them."

No surprise there. If Grandma Trudy was involved in something, she was either in charge of it or vocally opposed to it.

"Your secret phone calls and meetings erected the walls and destroyed our marriage, Stewart, not Reverend Annie," Mom said.

"You could have been at home helping me with my math," Heather whispered, "and tucking me in bed." It sounded so childish, but it would have meant the world to her. Instead, she cried herself to sleep—she didn't want to think about the things she did before she cried herself to sleep—while her mother ate herself into oblivion. They were all idiots.

Annie stared at Myra's face, molded into a pleasant smile, the animation and wrinkles of life completely smoothed out. Her children had been pleased with the mortician's efforts. Annie hated this vacuum-sealed, perfectly coiffured version. Myra would have, too. Myra hated stuffy false appearances, and now she was permanently stuck with one.

"I miss you already," Annie whispered.

No response from the shell of her old friend.

"Your prayers were answered. I guess, since you're in heaven you already know. You prayed for me to get a sex life, and, boy, did I ever. You remember Nick McAllister—sweaty, unsuitable?" She imagined Myra was hooting with laughter, probably giving Saint Peter a knowing elbow in the ribs.

Annie leaned against the casket of the one friend who would have stood up against the self-righteous, self-important members of the congregation. Myra would have given her unconditional blessing when Annie lay down with Nick. Not even God would bless what she had done. "It's all over now, of course. Nick got what he wanted from me, and I—I have to start rebuilding my life and my reputation."

The thought depressed her. This was what God wanted for her life. He would find a way to make it possible. But that same life didn't hold the same appeal. She didn't want to give lip service to God's love when she didn't always feel it. She couldn't imagine preaching moral values when she wanted to dump them for another tumble in Nick's brand of heaven.

Nick was right. She was a hypocrite.

Just like his father. No wonder he hated her.

Chapter 20

Nick clenched his fist around the key. His key. His house. His dream.

He looked down just to see the piece of metal in his palm. The house was his. Yet the dream seemed more out of reach than ever.

He stepped out of the bank and watched a red Corvette zip into a parking space across the street in front of the food pantry. A scenario where a Corvette owner needed food pantry services didn't fit. He shook his head and walked to his truck. He'd spend a few minutes alone in his house before he headed back to the drudgery of his real life.

He glanced in his rearview mirror as he prepared to back into the street and nearly plowed his truck through the glass entrance of the bank. Annie stepped out of the Corvette and into the food pantry. He killed the ignition and jumped out of the truck. The house could wait. He needed to see Annie.

She was alone in the building when he stepped inside. She hadn't turned on the lights yet. The dimness combined with his memory of the last time they'd been in here alone. He shoved his hands in his pockets and took a step back. Regardless of the cruel comment he'd thrown at her earlier, his physical desire for her ran rampant. "Where's Lois?"

Annie swung around. He wanted to read instant pleasure in her gaze, but it was replaced so quickly by wariness, he was most likely projecting his own needs onto her. "She had some personal business to attend to today."

"Oh." He wasn't used to feeling awkward and didn't care for the feeling. "How's the roof holding up?"

"So far, so good. I don't expect any problems. You knew what you were doing, and you did it well."

A compliment on his handyman abilities shouldn't bring a rush of pleasure, especially when she knew he was a lawyer. "Did I really see you drive up in a Corvette, or are my eyes playing tricks?"

She laughed, really truly laughed, and he found himself smiling simply because she was so amused. If he didn't watch out, he was going to find himself smitten. The thought should have sobered him a lot more than it did.

"Tanya gave it to me. I'm surprised she didn't have you handle the transaction as her lawyer." She was back to thinking of him as a lawyer and, worse, in conjunction with her sister, which was pretty sure sign a fight or a freeze-out was coming.

A fight had the potential to land her in his arms, which was tempting, but their time together was down to minutes. He didn't want to spend it on hurtful words he would regret when all he had of her to surround himself with were memories. "I'm in the dark," he said about the car Tanya had given.

She flipped the light switch, filling the building with fluorescent light. "Better?"

"Uh—" He didn't know how to respond. She was teasing him, not angry. Apparently, she was still pushing for friendship. He had to admit it sounded better than regrets.

"Sorry, bad joke." She left the lights on and moved behind the counter. "Tanya gave me the car. Not exactly the style I would have chosen. I was going to trade it in for something more practical, but it's growing on me." Her smile was almost shy. "Being rich, famous, and spoiled, she apparently thought a broken window equaled a total loss."

The only sign of her ordeal was a flesh-colored Band-Aid around her thumb, but Nick still felt guilty about not making the connection in time to spare her a moment of terror. "She probably felt guilty about siccing her husband on you."

"That, too," Annie acknowledged.

"Take me for a ride," he said on impulse.

Her steady gaze met his. "We've been down that road. It's a dead end lane."

Heaven in her arms was hardly a dead end. But thinking about it made him ache. "I meant in your car."

"Oh." She blushed. "Right. There's not room in there for—" Her cheeks turned crimson. "Let's go." She hurried out to the car before he could fold her in his arms and kiss away that endearing embarrassment.

She drove. For the first few minutes Nick sat back and enjoyed the close proximity to her. Then he directed her where to turn, until they ended up at his house. The car idled in the driveway.

Pride washed over him as he stared at his house. He owned this plot of earth. Even the gravel that would crunch beneath his feet when he stepped out of the car was his. He turned to gauge Annie's reaction. "What do you think?"

"Of?" She looked at him.

"Of the house." What else?

She studied it through the windshield. "It's kind of ramshackle."

Ramshackle. That single word poked a needle through his excitement. "Okay, it needs work. But can't you see the potential?"

"Potential for what? This was Bonnie's house. Her husband isn't going to be thrilled to see us."

"Bonnie and Hank were renting. They hadn't paid in six months. The owner wanted to cut his losses and unload it."

"This is the house you closed on, isn't it? Did you represent the buyer or seller?"

"Buyer." He opened the car door. "Come on, I'll show you inside."

She met him in front of her car. "Representing the buyer doesn't give you permission to go in."

He couldn't wait any longer for her to figure it out on her own. "It does when I'm the buyer."

"You bought this house?" She looked stunned. "Do you know how much work it's going to take to make it presentable?"

He smiled. "I'm looking forward to it."

She studied him for so long he had to fight the urge to squirm. "So this is permanent? You're not going back to Chicago?"

"I'm leaving for Chicago this afternoon."

"Oh." She looked between him and the house as if he were mentally deficient. But then instead of railing about his stupidity or how he was leaving her, she smiled. "I'd love to see more. Will you show me the inside?"

Nick obliged. He wanted nothing more than to show her his dream.

He didn't know what he said in the next hour. All he remembered was that here was the woman he loved, in the house he wanted to raise her children in, and he was going to walk away from it all.

"You want to drive?" Annie held out her car keys to Nick. The house behind them no longer looked like it needed a wrecking ball. Thanks to Nick's vision, she knew the hardwood floors would gleam. The porch would wrap around the house like a cozy shawl. The kitchen would have granite countertops and top-of-the-line appliances.

And when Nick finished his day of work, he would soak in

the giant whirlpool in the bathroom and lay in the master bedroom in front of the fireplace. She hoped she'd asked practical questions, without allowing him to see her longing to be the woman sharing his hot bath and cuddling next to him among the flickering flames.

Nick didn't need any urging to take the keys of the sports car. Annie relaxed as he drove. "Thanks for showing me the house through your eyes. It's going to look beautiful when you're done." She wanted to ask to see the finished product, but she didn't think she could bear to walk through as a polite visitor. Not after she'd imagined herself integral to turning it into a home.

She'd believed she was an integral part of the Maplefield community and Good Shepherd Church, too. That illusion shattered when they kicked her out on her butt.

"I'm going to drive out on weekends to work on the house," Nick said.

"A vacation home?" It capsulized their relationship rather well—a vacation from real life. Even if she stayed and they saw each other on weekends, it wouldn't be real life. Even if she stayed. She'd never considered the possibility before, even in passing. There was no place for her in Maplefield. What would she stay for? To see Nick for a couple hours a week? She was beyond pathetic.

"A dream home," Nick corrected.

She couldn't keep her gaze on him. She was too afraid he would see her dreams reflected there. To cover herself, she fiddled with the glove box and popped it open. There in front of her was a jewelry box. Her gaze swung back to Nick. He'd read her mind. He felt the same way. The box in front of her was too big for a ring, but they hadn't known each other long enough for that, anyway.

"What's wrong?" Nick asked.

"Wrong?" Annie shook her head and smiled at him, knowing the love she felt was shining from her eyes. She didn't have to hide it any longer. "It couldn't be more right."

She reached for the box. There was no ribbon, no frills to wade through. Her love didn't require any trappings. She lifted the lid. Even if he'd bought the jewelry for a quarter from a gumball machine, it would dazzle her. A token of affection was still a token to treasure.

Annie stared at the contents. Necklace, earrings, bracelet. None of them were from Nick.

"What is it?" he asked.

"Tanya returned my grandmother's jewelry." She'd waited for this day, cried over it for half her life. And now that it was here she felt overwhelming disappointment and vaguely nauseated. Tanya needed this family connection more than Annie did. Annie had always known her grandparents' love. Tanya hadn't been close to them. Instead, she'd had their parents. And she'd had to earn their approval in a way that left no room for love and affection.

The sickness Annie felt was from her callous disregard for Tanya's feelings.

But the disappointment was from her own foolish expectations. If Nick wanted to give her a gift, he wouldn't leave it in her glove box on the off chance she'd check there. He'd set it in plain sight or hand it to her. Nick had never made promises or given any indication he cared for her in a way that would compel him to shower her with gifts. Until she'd seen the box from Tanya, she hadn't expected him to.

"You're not happy," Nick concluded. "Did Tanya mangle it? Keep part for herself?"

"No, it's all here. I'm happy to get it back." At least she was trying to be. "I just think maybe she deserves to keep some of it."

"That's easily fixed," Nick said.

Yes, it would be. She stared at the pendant and debated how much of herself to lay out for Nick. How much did she dare risk? If she did, what would she lose? Her heart was gone. Her reputation was in tatters. She couldn't possibly bungle her life anymore.

Carefully, she placed the cover back on the box and stashed it in the glove compartment. "I love you, Nick."

He glanced at her briefly and then back at the road. "You told me Saturday night."

That was it? She declared her feelings, and he responded with all the emotion of a block of wood. "I never told you." Already she wished she could take back the words.

"Yes, you did. While we made love." His gaze connected with hers this time and held. Now she could see the emotion—hot, steamy desire.

He didn't love her back. Even more, he didn't find her declaration particularly earthshaking. His new house might pull him in a new direction from his lawyer career. But clearly, she didn't have enough pull to throw him off track. She'd screeched to a halt at the barricade at the end of the dead end. She could either go around it and plunge off the cliff, or turn around and make a new life for herself. Neither option was palatable, but she was too strong to stop living because a man didn't return her love.

She would survive. After all, she'd walked this road before.

Heather had to pee in a cup, watch a needle poke in her arm, and bleed enough to fill four vials. Finally, she had an embarrassing pelvic exam where she lay under an oversized piece of tissue paper and recited how to make every sandwich on the Subway menu.

Her feet plodded on the tile floor as she returned to the

doctor's office to hear the fatal results. Her stomach churned, and she focused on the garbage can three feet away in case she had to suddenly hurl. She wished she'd died a week ago, before she'd known anything was wrong. But then she would have died without knowing how good she could feel about herself from working a real job and how nicely the right guy could treat her.

She didn't want her parents to bear the shame of what she had done. She was too chicken to let them wait for her while she talked to the doctor alone. If they didn't come with her, she'd have to tell them herself. And this time she didn't have Reverend Annie to prop her up.

Mom squeezed her hand as she sat down next to her. The doctor shook hands with them all and smiled—actually smiled—before she handed down her death sentence. It seemed beyond cruel.

"Mr. Fitzsimmons, please have a seat." The doctor nodded to the open seat next to Heather.

Dad shook his head and folded his arms over his chest as he stood across the room. "I prefer to stand."

"He doesn't want to get too close, in case breathing the same air as me will give him what I've got." Heather tried to joke, but it was so true and hurt so much, she had to wipe away tears as she said it.

The doctor leaned closer, full of Reverend Annie's brand of compassion and understanding. Heather closed her eyes and imagined it was Reverend Annie breaking the news. Somehow it seemed easier coming from someone who tried to look out for her while she'd gone astray. "We're not dealing with a virus passed through the air or by exchanging germs while you give a friendly hug."

A friendly hug. Yeah, she got lots of those. *Egan.* She squeezed her eyes tighter, feeling the tears leaking around the edges. It wasn't fair to bring him into this and burden him with something that wasn't his fault, but she couldn't let him go. He was the only one other than her mom who would give her a hug and let it be just comfort.

"Most of your tests came back negative," the doctor/Reverend Annie said. "You're not pregnant."

"Thank goodness," Dad muttered.

"You're HIV negative."

Heather opened her eyes. "I don't have AIDS?"

"No. You will need to be retested in six months because it sometimes doesn't show up right away, but I don't expect it to be a factor. What you do have, Heather, is chlamydia."

"What's that?" She blanked, not sure if she should feel intense relief or get scared again. She didn't have AIDS. She wasn't going to die. Or was she? She couldn't remember what she'd read about chlamydia in Tanya's book. Everything ran together so she only remembered the most dire symptoms and consequences.

"Chlamydia is a very common bacterial sexually transmitted disease. The longer it goes untreated, the more risk there is that it will damage a woman's reproductive organs and cause infertility."

The terrible irony punched her tender stomach. She'd been having sex to get pregnant, and because of it she might never be able to get pregnant and have that baby who was guaranteed to love her.

The doctor went on explaining. Somehow the flu symptoms she'd felt a couple weeks ago were connected. "Chlamydia is easily treated with antibiotics. You'll need to take them for a full ten days. Don't engage in intercourse during this time."

Yeah, as if she was going to have sex again this century. She'd never felt so icky, even when she'd been *doing* it. She didn't want any of them touching her ever again. The only boy she would consider wrapping her body around someday . . . he could do so much better than her. He was going to be a doctor. She wouldn't let him settle for a girl with a disease.

This doctor started talking about the importance of informing her past sex partners so they could be tested and treated. Oh, now that was certainly going to be fun. She could hardly wait to go back to school and broadcast her leprosy. "A condom is a must for any future sexual activity," the doctor said. "Don't depend on your partner to supply one. You have to take responsibility for your sexual health."

"She won't engage in any sexual activity as long as she lives in my house," Dad said.

Yeah, that was a good one. "How are you going to stop me when you don't live there anymore?"

Dad was ready to kill her. She could see it in his eyes. Probably by strangling. Which meant he was going to have to touch her, actually put his hands on her.

"What do you get from having sex with those boys that makes you go back for more?" Mom asked, freezing Dad's forward motion before he could touch her.

"Nothing." She felt the sobs coming but couldn't stop them. The words blubbered out, and she couldn't stop them either. "I wanted to feel important to someone, part of a family. I thought if they would hold me, if I could make a baby with someone—anyone—but it didn't work. I have nothing, and I've made you and dad more miserable. If I died, you'd probably love me, at least a little after I was gone. But now that's not even going to happen."

"Heather, we do love you." Mom hugged her. She was crying, too. "We don't want you to die. I'm going to take care of you and help you get better. And we're going to be a real family, even if it's just you and me."

And then Dad was there, too, his arms wrapping around her from behind. "Don't. Not without me, please. I'm sorry I'm such a jerk. You wanted me on my knees and begging, Lois. I'm here. Please. Let's all be a family again. I don't deserve you, either of you. But I love you both so much. You're my life. I need you both in my life."

And right there on an uncomfortable folding chair with her dad's tears mixing with hers on her cheek, Heather knew everything was going to be okay. She didn't need to sleep with everyone she met to find her place in the world. Not when she had a friend like Egan and could be her daddy's girl again.

Nick should have been halfway to Chicago by now. Instead, he was standing in line to pay his respects to Myra's children. He'd barely met the woman, yet he felt like he'd known her. Certainly he wished he'd known her better. Myra would have liked him better as a handyman than a lawyer. Maybe that was the reason he couldn't leave without saying goodbye. It was like saying a final goodbye to his handyman dream.

He said the proper words to her family and walked past the casket. Food donations were piled around in lieu of flowers. Myra would appreciate that. Rather than fight his way through the crowd of people, most of whom he didn't know but who were either curious about him or were sending hostile vibes for his role in Annie's downfall, he walked out the side door.

Annie stood on the sidewalk next to a suited man smoking a cigarette. "Tomorrow morning. I'll have everything ready by nine," the man said. Nick assumed he was the funeral director. "We could move it to the church if Myra's children prefer."

She shook her head. "I've spoken with them several times. They want me to officiate. The church refuses to allow me behind its pulpit, no exceptions."

"Nine o'clock then," the man said, stubbing out his cigarette and walking back inside.

Annie turned her gaze on Nick. She loved him. The memory

of her words warmed him. He'd been stunned that she wanted him to know. Why she would hand him such power he couldn't understand. And he'd had no idea how to respond.

"I thought you were leaving," she said.

"I am. Right now." He didn't move. He wanted to hear her say it one more time. He was a greedy son-of-a-gun. He couldn't say it back, but he wanted—bad—to watch the words roll off her tongue and straight into his heart.

"You were right about me," she said instead.

"About what?"

"About me not practicing what I preach. I'm not worthy to call myself a servant of God. I know I'm a fraud, but I can't walk away from the ministry."

"Myra would have wanted you to say her eulogy."

She shook her head. "That's not what I meant."

"You're the most genuine person I know." He meant it. Her love for him was genuine. He believed that. Whatever her faults, she wasn't the same person as his father. He'd taken too long to come to that obvious realization.

"That's a lovely compliment." She didn't smile or give any facial indication of pleasure. Instead, she held out her hand to him. "Thank you for being part of my life, even if it was a short time."

Nick stared at her hand. She was saying goodbye. Not the kind people said when leaving town for a few days. The kind where lives never crossed again. He'd bought a house. He'd be back. Maybe not frequently, maybe not on a permanent basis until he retired. He wanted to think of Maplefield as his home. He didn't yet, but someday . . .

She knew he was coming back. She wouldn't be here when he did. He took the key for his house and pressed it into her palm as he took her outstretched hand in his. He couldn't shake her hand. If she were saying a final goodbye to anyone else, her arms would be wrapped around him in an affectionate hug. He lifted her hand to his lips and pressed a kiss to her knuckles. "Stay at my house tonight. Stay as long as you're in town. It doesn't offer much, but it gives you a roof over your head."

"I appreciate the thought, but Myra's children have been generous with her living space. And I don't have to worry about returning your key."

"I don't need it returned." He clung to her hand as he felt her beginning to withdraw. "I have two copies. Keep it in case you change your mind."

She pulled her hand free. "Thank you."

His cell phone rang. His mother or brother or Holly, no doubt, demanding why he wasn't home yet. He wasn't home because he didn't know how to make a home out of the places he lived in. No matter how much he sanded and sawed, he wasn't sure he would succeed on this one unless Annie repeatedly used that key he gave her.

"You should answer that," Annie said. "It could be another celebrity client. That's certainly more important than talking to me." She walked into the funeral parlor without sparing him another look.

Nick stared after her, unable to think of anything more worthy of his time than sharing it with her.

It seemed fitting that her last ministering duty would be in the form of a funeral. The service was moving. Myra had been too full of life and left too big a hole in the hearts of everyone who knew her for it not to be. Praying over Myra's body next to the freshly dug hole in the cold ground choked Annie with sobs. Where was God in all this misery?

The luncheon following the funeral was in the parish center of Good Shepherd Church. For the sake of the mourners, Annie declined attending to avoid stirring up trouble. The decision isolated her and her grief.

God, where is my direction? What is Your purpose for my life?

She stopped at a pay phone again and dialed the pastor placement center at her main church office. In the past few days, she'd become a familiar voice to them, and the lady on the other end recognized her immediately. "Reverend Lane, I've been trying to reach you. Do you have a new mailing address?"

What a ridiculous question. Of course not. How could she when she didn't know where her next pastor position would take her? "Not yet. I was hoping you could help me find out which parishes are actively looking for a new leader."

The woman on the other end tittered. "Um, well, you see, we've run into a little problem."

"Problem?"

"Yes, I'm mailing papers that explain it all."

"Explain what?" A pit was forming in her stomach. The woman had never given her the run-around before. In every other conversation, she'd been as helpful as possible.

"The church is conducting an investigation into your conduct. Should they find your activity to be outside the realm of morally acceptable behavior espoused by our Church, the administration will take the necessary steps to revoke your license. Until then, you are placed under probation where you are not allowed to hold a ministering position in our Church."

Annie replaced the receiver. Her ministry was over. The newspaper photos, the tabloid pictures that would soon hit the newsstands, and the interview with Stewart Fitzsimmons and John Patterson—all would show her morals to be below an alley cat, let alone those of a conservative, pure servant of God.

God's direction for her life suddenly crystallized. He didn't have a purpose for her. He had no use for her at all. He didn't love her enough to forgive what she had done to her reputation and to His pristine name.

Nick didn't love her enough to forgive her for believing God's love was the answer to every problem. He'd certainly laugh to learn God had stopped loving her now. Nick had seen through her from the beginning. She'd been living a lie just so she could get a little loving.

God didn't care what she did with the rest of her life.

Nick didn't care either.

And Annie didn't have a clue.

Egan held Heather's hand, his fingers laced with hers. His touch infused her with confidence, and right now she needed it. She'd told him last night about the chlamydia. He'd sat with his arm around her and listened. He didn't stiffen up or pull away. Afterward, he held her for an extra-long time and told her what happened before didn't matter, only the choices she made now.

But right now the choice she wanted to make was run. If not for Egan's steady strength, she probably would have. "Troy," she yelled, just as he and Veronica reached the door to the school parking lot. "I need to talk to you."

He looked over his shoulder. She thought he was going to blow her off, and she'd have to chase him down in the cold parking lot. But Veronica stopped and waited for them to catch up. "Still haven't pushed Egan past the hand-holding stage?" She laughed. "You're losing your touch."

Heather squeezed Egan's hand. Veronica had waited only to ridicule them. "Hand-holding is as far as Egan and I are going for a long while," she said. She looked directly at Troy. "I have chlamydia. It's a sexually transmitted disease."

They both drew back like she was a leper, but Veronica managed to snicker while she did it.

Heather kept her eyes on Troy. "All of my past sex partners need to be tested. You especially, because we engaged in sex without a condom."

"I ain't got no disease," he shot back. "You got it from someone else."

"Maybe." She surprised herself by not only sounding calm but feeling it, too. "But I might have passed it on to you. Which means all of your sex partners should be tested, too."

Veronica turned white. She pulled her hand free of Troy's. "I'm not a slut. I've only slept with two people. I can't have a disease."

Troy pushed Veronica's shoulders. "You said I was your first."

"You said nothing bad would happen if we didn't use a condom." She shoved back.

Idiots, just like her. Well, Heather was starting to use her brain. She'd even eked out a B minus on today's algebra quiz. "You don't need to be a slut for it to happen to you. You just need to make one bad decision. I've made enough of them. Get tested, Veronica, for your own sake."

"You sleazebag, you're ruining my life."

"No, I'm finally taking responsibility for my life. I won't be a slut anymore." She smiled, knowing it was true, no matter how long the stain on her reputation lasted. Egan knew the truth and believed in her and so did her parents. She was loved. And she would never again mistake something cheap and ugly for the true, pure love in a simple hug.

Giving Annie the key had been an act of selfishness. Nick supposed he'd find comfort knowing she was in his house, even though he couldn't be there. Minutes turned into hours, and the legal paperwork buried him deeper. In a secret part of his mind, he'd held the fantasy he would straighten everything out at the auction house by noon, give his law partners a jaunty wave, and be back in Maplefield by evening.

As the hands on the clocks marched toward midnight, he finally acknowledged it wasn't going to happen. He'd ignored his obligations for too long, and now he was a slave to them. He plowed through the papers and the jargon, finally falling asleep at his desk as the morning light streamed through the blinds.

"Dominick."

"Huh?" He struggled to raise his head and orient himself. It sure hadn't taken long to fall back into the habit of sleeping at his desk. He thought of waking up in bed spooned against Annie and groaned. The ergonomic office chair didn't come close to easing his discomfort.

"You didn't go home last night, did you?"

He looked up and rubbed his eyes. He was dreaming about Annie while his mother stood in front of him. "Hi, Mom."

"You need to find a wife who will make sure you're home in bed every night."

It sounded more like a curfew threat than a temptation. "Trying to catch up."

Mom walked behind him and began to massage his shoulders. "I admire your dedication, but you have to take care of yourself."

"My dedication." He laughed without humor. "I'm chained to a job I hate."

Her hands stilled. "You like being a lawyer. You're good at it. It's who you are."

He swiveled in his chair, his pent-up frustration spewing out. "I might be good at it, but I hate it. It's not who I want to be. That's why I never married Holly. I don't hate myself this way. How could I love someone who wants to keep me here?"

Mom stared at him, looking aghast. "I had no idea you were unhappy. You were the one who chose this life."

Theoretically, he'd had a choice. But he'd never felt it. "It's what everyone else wanted. I wanted to be good enough for your love and Dad's and the prom queen's. This was the path that got everyone's nod."

"I love you. I would have regardless of your profession." Mom groped behind her until she came up against a chair and sank into it. "So you really wanted to be—wait, let me think for a minute. An actor? You were also fascinated with Gloria Glenbard movies."

"Because I could watch her and think 'that's my grandma.'"

"I wish you could have met her." Mom looked sad. "Now, your dream job. You were always tinkering with things. You were only five when you tried to fix my leaky faucet."

"And flooded the kitchen," Nick remembered. "An auspicious beginning to becoming Mr. Fix-it."

Mom steepled her fingers under her chin. "If that's really what you want, why are you killing yourself to grow your business with clients like Tanya?"

Wasn't it obvious? She should be jumping at the opportunity. "For her connections. You'll have a direct line to the 'in' Hollywood crowd. Those people who turned their backs on you and sided with Grandma when you married Dad will welcome you back and give you the welcome of Grandma's spirit."

"That's where I was afraid this was leading. Jason gave me a very similar explanation."

He couldn't believe it. His brother and his foolish whim had beaten him to it. "It was my father who forced you to give up that life. I should be the one to make it up to you."

"He didn't force me. I made the choice. And I'm not going to let you boys force me into any society that I'm not ready for. I'm corresponding by mail with a couple people."

Mom had built her own bridges. She hadn't wallowed in regrets as Nick had always assumed. Or maybe she'd realized what Jason and Nick were trying to do and felt obligated to do her own legwork. "When did this start?"

"We've been communicating for a couple years. Maybe we'll patch things up. Maybe we'll agree to keep our separate lives. But that's my prerogative. Tanya has nothing in common with my mother or my old friends."

For years Nick had been so sure he was working toward giving his mother what she needed. But he'd never asked her about her feelings. He'd never taken the time to get to know the real person behind the self-sacrificing mother. The realization was humbling.

"The people I'm writing to have told me Mom regretted the complete cut she gave me," Mom continued. "If she'd lived, I think we would have found our way back to each other. That's enough. I don't need big parties and the cover of *People* magazine to claim my acceptance. I'm happy with my life now. It's time for you to do what you need to be happy."

He wasn't happy, not as a lawyer, not chasing celebrities, not trying to prove he was good enough for his father. Only one person loved him in spite of what he tried to become. He'd been too much of an idiot to snatch the gift with both hands while he had the chance. He didn't know if he'd get another chance, but he had to find out.

Chapter 21

"You told your mother about me?" Tanya couldn't believe it. She and Jake had agreed to keep a low profile on their tentative relationship. She wanted a few days to savor it for herself before the press ran with it and turned it into something it wasn't. And then Jake did something stupid to ruin it.

"I told her about you as soon as your involvement in the investigation became public. This was just a courtesy update." He dipped his fingers in the water pooling around the marble fountain sculpture in Tanya's front hall.

"You're pushing forty, and you give your mother play-by-plays of your sex life. No wonder you're still single."

Jake didn't take offense. Comments that would emasculate a lesser man rolled off him. "I wouldn't have mentioned you if I was talking sex."

Tanya swallowed and had to look away. She was in over her head precisely because they hadn't had sex yet. Sex was the instrument she used to initiate her male relationships. Without it, she was stripped of her power and everything familiar.

And yet she'd enjoyed her snatches of time with Jake more than with any other man. "What did you say about me, then?" she asked.

He smiled slyly, and she wished she could retract the question without him thinking her a coward. She really didn't want to know what he and his mother—good grief—thought of her. She wasn't the kind of girl men took home to meet their mothers, unless it was for shock value.

"How do you feel about the Catholic Church?" Jake asked.

"I haven't gotten around to seducing the pope yet. My schedule's always so booked when I'm in Rome."

"It would mean a lot to Mom for us to marry in the Church."

"Marry?" Tanya repeated. "Have you lost your mind? We haven't even slept together."

"Actually, I was thinking we could save that for marriage."

"I'm already married."

Jake didn't blink. "We'll wait until your divorce is finalized."

"I'm not a good bet in the relationship game for the long haul."

"Mom's saying a rosary for you."

She looked around for something handy to throw at the swine. He crossed the distance of the room and clasped her hands before she could locate anything. Then she could focus on nothing but him. "You don't know me," she said. "I'm not what the tabloids write about me."

"Then I don't know what I'm missing because I don't read them." His thumbs brushed once over the backs of her hands. "If you don't want me, Tanya, say so, but don't push me away because you're scared."

"I'm not scared," she denied reflexively. Scared of a man and what he could make her feel? Not Tanya. *Never.*

The truth was she was scared of Jake in a way she'd never been scared of Zeke. Not that Jake would hurt her physically. But that he had the power to capture her heart. And to break it.

"Then marry me. I'm asking you."

"Really? It sounded more like an order." He was serious. He, who'd seen her at her least sexiest, who'd seen the vulnerable woman behind the mask of sex and glamour. And he wanted the real part of her.

Jake released her hands. "Have your lawyers draw up a prenuptial. I don't want your money. I don't want to make money off you or our marriage." He slid a single finger down her cheek. "My mom wants us to spend Christmas with her, but she's offered her blessing for me to go to your sister's for Thanksgiving with you."

"You've got it all worked out, don't you, Jake?"

They both froze. She'd said his name. She hadn't made him wait for sex. She'd let the intimacy slip, and she felt more exposed than if she'd declared her love for him. In that situation, they both could have discounted her words as meaningless, just another trick in her bag. But she'd called him Jake.

His smile this time was heart-stoppingly tender. "What do you think of June?"

A June wedding. Tanya couldn't think of anything she'd like more. "I'll wear white. If I'm going to wait that long for sex, I might as well be a virgin."

Today was Thanksgiving, and Annie had nothing to be thankful for. She stood in the food pantry helping Heather and Egan assemble the food packages they would soon deliver to families in need around the county. Lois and Stewart were at the grocery store picking up the turkeys to complete the meals.

Heather was lovely, cordial, and had never looked happier. Egan's heart was in his eyes whenever he looked at her. Watching them, Annie believed even the most broken reputations could be repaired.

"Holy flying pigs. You didn't tell me your sister was coming to help deliver the meals," Heather said from the window.

"My sister? She's not. She's doing the movie-star thing in L.A."

The words were no sooner out of Annie's mouth than Tanya sailed through the door of the food pantry. The man behind her was the cop who'd questioned Annie after her encounter with

Zeke. Tanya had probably decided to hire him as her bodyguard. His eyes scanned the room like a man on duty.

"This is a surprise," Annie said, stepping forward as the teenagers stood with their mouths gaping open.

"That was the plan." Tanya looked pleased with herself. "How can I help?"

"Help?"

"Of course. Why do you think I'd come to a food pantry on Thanksgiving?"

"I doubt people want autographs with their meals." Less than a minute in her sister's company, and Annie's tone was already acerbic. It wasn't fair. Tanya looked younger, freer, and happier than when Annie had last seen her. Everyone was. And Annie hated herself for pouting and begrudging others their happiness.

"No autographs." Tanya didn't take offense. "I'd love to deliver meals in person though."

Annie thought of the domestic shelters Tanya was laying the groundwork on. So many women needed every bit of light they could scavenge out of life. A surprise visit from Tanya would surely give them a boost. She might not stay for the day-to-day drudgery, but maybe she didn't have to in order to make a difference.

Annie, on the other hand, preferred the day-to-day. To watch people progress from fear and cynicism to hope. It was her favorite part of ministering, and something she could continue with or without the cleric's collar. The realization should have come days ago, but she'd been so stubborn in seeing only her own narrow vision of God's plan.

Annie touched the necklace at her throat. "I've been meaning to call you. To thank you."

"You can say it in person." Tanya's gaze fixed on the jewelry.

"I'd like to say it in private." She nodded to the back room. A "thank you" shouldn't be so difficult, but nothing seemed to come easily when her sister was involved. "Please."

"This is Officer Jacobs," Tanya told Heather and Egan. "You can call him Hardball."

"Call me Jake," the man insisted.

"He's all bark and no bite, I promise." Tanya laughed as she followed Annie to the back room. "You found the jewelry." Her voice sobered.

"Yes." Annie tugged on the blue sweater she'd traded in her blazers for. "You offered me a brand-new car cheerful as you please and never mentioned a set of fifty-dollar jewelry. I would have chosen the jewelry over the car."

"The jewelry was harder for me to give up." Tanya rubbed her hand over her bare wrist. "But it means more to you. For you it's a symbol of love."

"Grandma loved you, too, but she spent more time with me and knew me better. She thought you were secure in our parents' love. They never pretended to love me."

"I'd have traded their brand of love for Grandma's real thing."

"I understand that now. I didn't back then." Annie unclipped the bracelet from her wrist. "I want you to keep this as a reminder that Grandma and Grandpa loved you. That I love you."

"You're going to make my mascara run." Tanya wrapped her arms around her.

Annie was unprepared for how tightly Tanya clung to her. Her speech hadn't been that emotional, just honest and way overdue.

"Do you think we could try to be sisters again? Like we used to turn to each other first when our elementary school lives hit a snag?"

"I'd like that." Now Annie was the one who had to brush tears from her eyes. "I've missed my big sister."

"Stop, stop." Tanya waved a hand frantically in front of her face. "I'm going to bawl like a baby, and I've got a man out there I'm trying to convince that I'm not an emotional wreck."

Annie laughed. "Okay, I've got something to dry your eyes and make you smile."

"You and Nick are an item."

Tanya's way-off guess sobered her quickly. Daggers pierced her chest without warning. "No. He's, no—" Now she was the one who had to take a moment to compose herself. Why did it have to hurt so much?

"I'm sorry." Tanya looked bewildered. "It was so obvious he was hot for you, and you're in love with him."

He was hot for her, while she was in love with him. Tanya summarized their relationship with dead-eye accuracy. Being hot for someone was fun while it lasted, but it didn't cause alterations to anyone's life plans. "He cooled off," Annie said. "Diddling a minister isn't quite so exciting when the person you're diddling is no longer a minister."

"I'm going to kill him," Tanya vowed.

"No, you're not." Having him know the depth of her pain would only humiliate her more. She wasn't jumping off the cliff. She was turning her life around. "You're not going to say a word to him about me. I'm getting on with my life."

"You have a new church?"

"No, I want to work for you. Your shelters," Annie clarified. "I want to help. I want to make a difference to people who need me."

"You're sure? You're not just saying that because no one else will hire you?" Tanya looked skeptical.

Annie didn't blame her. "No. Although you should know that Jesus could return to earth and demand the church reinstate me, and they still wouldn't do it. I've misstepped that badly."

Tanya snorted. "You became human. I'm not going to burn

you at the stake for that."

In the past two weeks Tanya had become human for Annie, too, not just a face on a tabloid magazine or an icon to be resented for the bad in Annie's life. "The things I loved about being a pastor are the same things I'd still have working in a shelter. I'd be a vital part of a community. I'd be able to help people and watch them grow in confidence and faith, whether that faith is in themselves or God."

"I don't want religion forced down anyone's throat," Tanya said.

No problem there. Annie couldn't stomach it herself. "I've stopped believing God is a panacea."

"God didn't do this to you."

"Yeah, well, He didn't make an effort to stop it either." She hated this bitter shell that hardened with each passing hour. How long would she have to wait for joy to return?

"Maybe He wanted you to find your way to my shelter."

"Are you preaching religion to me?"

Tanya gave her a sheepish smile. "I'm thinking of going to church again. Hardball's mother is saying the rosary for me twice a day. She's putting so much effort into it I figure I should give her some payoff."

In a detached way, Annie saw the humor in a guy named Hardball having a sweet church-going mother, but she didn't feel any amusement.

A commotion stirred in the front of the building, indicating the entrance of more people. Tanya touched the bracelet on her wrist. "Thank you." She walked to the front.

"Tanya? Oh, my gosh, you came back," Lois shouted.

Annie followed in time to see the two women embrace like old friends. "This must be the lucky man who enjoyed the pleasure of begging for you." Tanya winked at Stewart.

He blushed to the roots of his graying hair.

"Looks like it worked," Tanya surmised.

"Worth every penny," Lois said.

"I'm making a hefty yearly donation to the food pantry in your honor as my thanks," Stewart said.

"You're my parents. I can't listen to this," Heather cried, holding her hands over her ears.

"Our car's filled with turkeys to unload," Lois said.

Heather grabbed Egan's hand and dashed outside.

As the laughter subsided, Tanya introduced everyone to her cop-bodyguard-boyfriend. Stewart touched Annie's arm and backed her up a step, separating them from the crowd. "While we're on the subject of my wife making me beg, Lois says I have to apologize to you or she won't sleep with me tonight."

"Oh?" A more sophisticated response was beyond her. She'd been prepared for Stewart to give her the cold shoulder or ignore her if he was feeling generous. In keeping with his previous actions, she expected him to cut her down and order her out of his town. But apologize? Not in her lifetime.

"So I'm sorry," Stewart said. "I wasn't excited about a female minister to begin with. When you came to town, things went downhill with my family. Blaming an outsider was easier than shouldering my responsibility and changing myself." He crossed his arms over his chest. "I'm not saying you were always right, you understand? You'd have spent the church out of every penny if I hadn't fought you on every suggestion."

Annie felt her lips curve into a smile before she could stifle it. "I understand."

"And I'd still rather have a sixty-year-old married man behind the pulpit than some upstart woman telling me how to live my life."

But women in a domestic shelter just might prefer one of their peers. Annie thought of Lois making Stewart beg and let her smile grow a little wider.

"I can't do much to get you reinstated, even if I was willing to stick my neck out."

"Which you're not going to do unless Lois threatens not to sleep with you," Annie finished, surprised to find that the bitterness was gone. She didn't have to fight Stewart over budget restrictions or lecture from a pulpit. She could provide personal counseling to meet individual needs without worrying that tossing back a beer at Al's Bar would destroy her reputation.

"Yeah, she's really something." Stewart's gaze rested on his wife.

"Your daughter's a special kid, too," Annie said.

"Yes, she is. Thank you for being there for her when she finally came around."

Annie watched the teens reenter the building. "Hey Egan." She tossed him her car keys. "You and Heather take the Corvette to make your deliveries."

Stewart grinned at their delirious expressions. "If they crash it, you've got nothing to blame but your own bad judgment, Annie."

"That's why I'm unemployed and alone." It was time to stop blaming Nick and God and take responsibility for her life. "My own bad judgment."

Nick tried his house, Myra's house, the manse, the church, and his old apartment. No Annie, no red Corvette. The inside of his house didn't hold her toothbrush or any other sign to show she'd been there at all. He pulled in front of the food pantry, not feeling hopeful. The place looked dark, and there wasn't a car parked anywhere on the block.

If he'd listened to his mother, he would be warm and comfortable right now, eating turkey and stuffing. No, if he were back in Chicago, he wouldn't be comfortable, no matter how plush the surroundings and how much food filled his stomach.

Nick tested the knob on the front door, and it surprised him by turning. He let himself inside and looked around the food pantry. Empty. Someone had forgotten to lock the door. He felt as empty as the quiet building. Where did he go from here? If he gave up on Annie—

He shook his head, his life stretching bleary and unbearable.

He'd call Tanya and convince her to tell him what she knew. He reached for his cell phone and came up empty on his belt loop. He'd locked it in his trunk so he could honestly claim he didn't hear it when his family called to cajole him into joining them for dinner. He turned for the door to retrieve his phone. Action was good. Anything was better than standing and contemplating what Annie would say when he finally tracked her down.

"That was fast. I didn't expect you back so soon."

He froze. He dreamed of her voice too often not to recognize it. He turned around.

Halfway across the room she froze. Whoever she was expecting, it certainly wasn't him.

Nick found his voice first. "I was looking for you."

"Guess it's your lucky day."

"I hope so." God, he hoped. "I'm praying it is."

She snorted. "Yeah, you and God are real tight. Say a prayer for me, too, will you? God and I aren't on speaking terms right now."

The sarcasm and derision of a God she'd devoted her life to threw him. "What happened to you, Annie?"

"You were right. I'm a hypocrite. I always tell people to throw themselves on God when the going gets tough. Then the going got tough for me, and I realized God wasn't going to help me out of this mess."

"What mess?"

She just looked at him like he of all people should know. "I'm done preaching. I still believe He's there. Maybe He'll even be there for me someday, but I'm not banking on it."

"So what are you going to do?"

She laughed, but it sounded sad. "Not wait around for you to come to your senses and take up the position as the new center of my world."

I love you. Echoes of her words continued to bounce off the emptiness of his heart. He didn't want the echoes. He wanted the real thing. Hearing her say it again would fill his heart. But she was already turning away. She wasn't going to make the first move this time. He'd pushed her away. If he wanted another chance, he was going to have to make himself vulnerable, maybe even beg.

He watched her move further away and knew he had nothing to lose. But he could gain a full life of happiness. The love he'd looked for all his life and never found was finally within reach. If only he could convince Annie he was worth taking a chance on.

"You're the center of my world."

Annie froze as Nick's words flowed over her. Fantasy words, too good to be true. "I don't have anything to offer you."

"That's not true." He placed himself in front of her. His hands hovered at her shoulders before he dropped them to his sides.

She ached for his touch. A gentle caress, a hard shake. Anything.

"Your faith made me start to believe again."

"That must have been God's plan then." The bitterness she thought she'd conquered welled again. "Take all Annie's faith and give it to Nick. Take Nick's cynicism and give it to Annie.

He's probably laughing at the hilarious switch he pulled."

"Your faith is shaken. It's okay." His green eyes, which she'd thought were so cold when she first met him, were warm as melted butter. "God knows what He's doing. Sure, give Annie Nick's cynicism. She'll overcome in a couple months what it took Nick thirty years to do. Give Nick Annie's faith, because he needs all he can get, and she's so strong and so solid she'll find more and build her faith even stronger out of nothing."

The tears built in an aching mass behind her eyes. Nick believed in her, truly believed. She didn't deserve this kind of faith.

He brushed a finger down her cheek. "Looking at you is my inspiration. You look at people, and you see the good." His fingernail skimmed her neck. "You have such a big heart." His finger glided lower, pausing on her chest. "Your sister steals your boyfriend and your family's love and all the attention and ignores you for a decade. Then she needs help, and you welcome her home with no questions."

He made her sound selfless. Nothing could be further from the truth. "I only cared about protecting my reputation."

Impossibly, his eyes warmed even more. "Your reputation is that you put everyone else above yourself. You see a need in the community and do what you can to fill it. You see a person hurting and figure out a way to help them help themselves. You follow your heart, even when it turns the world against you."

"I'm never going to be a minister again."

Her announcement didn't cause him to miss a beat. "But you're still going to do all those things I just mentioned. That's why you're at a food pantry on Thanksgiving Day and not dining with celebrities in L.A."

Quite possibly Nick understood her better than she understood herself. It scared the heck out of her. She shook her head, splattering tears across her cheeks.

"Okay, enough about you." Nick cracked his knuckles and shifted from foot to foot. "I'm not as selfless. I want to talk about me."

Annie worked to bring her tears under control.

"I quit my law firm in Chicago."

She was surprised but not shocked. Law could never compete with the comfortable fit of a screwdriver in his hand.

"My partners are buying me out so that'll give us a nice nest egg. I don't expect to quit law altogether, at least not until I can support myself—and you and our children—as a handyman. And I want a lot of kids, so that might never happen."

Annie jerked back. "What are you talking about?"

He placed his hands on her shoulders, holding her in place. "I want to make my life in Maplefield with you. If you don't want my house, we'll buy another. If you don't want Maplefield, we'll go somewhere else. Bottom line, I want to make my life with you."

"But you don't need me anymore. You've got Tanya. You got what you wanted."

His hands slid down her arms, clasping her hands. "Okay, I do get a little thrill out of having your sister as a client. She wants me to head her team of lawyers for her domestic shelters. If my working for her bothers you, I'll give it up. You are more important to me than any client, than any celebrity."

He'd give up Tanya to be with her. Annie covered her face with her hands, no longer able to contain her sobs. His hands were still holding hers and got caught in the messy tears.

"That's not enough?" He misunderstood. "Tell me what else I can do. Tell me what you need. I know I'm a real jerk and a total loser and you can do better. But, oh, Annie, I need you."

"You could start by telling me you love me," she choked out.

"Isn't it obvious? I love you." He wrapped his arms around her, nearly choking all the air out of her with his tight hold. "I love you so much."

She rubbed her face against his shirt, trying desperately to dry her eyes so she could see him when he spoke those words. She pulled back to look at him. His image was only a little blurry. "Say it again."

"I love you, Annie Lane. Take me to heaven and let me make you Annie McAllister."

This time the air did leave her body. "You want to marry me?"

"Oh, yes. I want to spend my life with you."

"Okay."

"Okay? Yes? Yes, you will?" He lifted her off her feet.

"Yes." She wrapped her arms around his neck and hung on for the ride. There was no place she'd rather be than in his arms. "I love you, but then you already knew that."

"You can say it again. I don't mind."

"Good, because you're going to hear it for the next fifty years."

"Sixty," he corrected. "We're starting heaven, right now, on earth."

ABOUT THE AUTHOR

Sara Daniel grew up in small-town Illinois, where she began writing romance in junior high. She now lives in the Chicago suburbs with her husband and three children, where she continues to fulfill her dream of writing romance. She loves to hear from her readers. Visit her website at SaraDaniel.com or send snail mail to P.O. Box 957082, Hoffman Estates, IL 60195.